Mr. Shipley's Governess

By

Joanne Troppello

Mr. Shipley's Governess
By Joanne Troppello
Published by Mustard Seed Marketing Group,
LLC
www.mustardseedmarketinggroup.com
This is a work of fiction. Names, places,
characters and events are fictitious. Any similarities
to persons, living or dead, are completely
coincidental. If a trademark, service or product was
named, all are assumed property of the respective
owners. If these terms were used in this work, there is
no implied endorsement. Please note that except for
review purposes, reproduction of this book in whole
or in part, electronically or mechanically is
considered a copyright violation.

This book is dedicated to:
My wonderful husband, John who has endured
my long hours at the computer and has continually
supported my dream to write the stories created from
my imagination. He is my best friend and holds the
key to my heart. I love you!

I would also like to dedicate this book to my
nieces and nephews:
Natalie, Autumn, Adele, Wilhelm, Sofia,
Michelle, Gabriel, Grayson, Elijah, Emerson,
Summer, Luciano, Lorenzo and Arianna
May you all continue to dream big dreams.
God is big and He has wonderful plans for all of your
lives. You all have a special place in my heart!
It Only Takes a Mustard Seed to Make a
Dream Grow!

Chapter One

Sophie Baird put one foot in front of the other on the path, crunching brown leaves as she walked. Her hands warmed by her coat pockets. The wind softly caressed her face—a face whose eyes held a pain which dug deeply into her broken heart. At twenty-five years old, she'd known the passion of faith in God, but now simply existed as a wayward traveler with no expectations. The faint flicker of her fiery spirit kept her going, but in recent days it was no match for her defeated hope. Her Irish roots ran deep within her soul and dueled with the defeat threatening to overpower her life.

She had grown up in a home with devoted parents who'd come straight from the Emerald Isle after they'd married. Sophie recalled tales of generations past. Her father had told her that she possessed the same fire which burned in his people. Remembering her parents brought a smile to her lips. They had died three months ago in a terrible car accident. How could God take them when they still had so much of their lives left to live? *I needed them in my life.* The saddest part of all—they'd never made it back to visit family in their beloved Ireland.

The cobblestone path led her home to a place no longer alive with joy. It sat quiet, as if the lonely old cottage in the woods waited for something or someone to come and make things right again. She wiped back a tear as she neared the faded oak door. This place meant the world to her. Sophie's father had built it stone by stone when he and her dear mother first came to America. Her parents had lived in the humble cottage for a few years until their income had increased. Then they'd moved into a more spacious ranch house in the suburbs.

Sophie enjoyed the picturesque cottage, considering it her haven. After the accident, she had stayed in the family home as a means of connecting with her parents. She could sense their heart and soul throughout the entire stone structure. The rusty old lock opened more easily than she thought it would. She pushed the heavy wooden door open and entered the kitchen to hang her coat on the peg by the doorway. Taking in a deep breath, she resignedly stared at the pile of bills and paperwork stacking the table which needed attention. For a while now she'd procrastinated on settling her parents' meager estate. In order to find closure and try to move on, she must settle everything.

"First, a cup of tea." She spoke to the empty room. "Nothing soothes the soul like a hot cup of tea. At least that's what mom used to say." She started flipping through the mail, separating the junk from the bills. A few minutes later, the kettle whistled shrilly on the stove. She poured the hot liquid—over the stainless steel infuser filled with chamomile tea leaves—into the dainty white-flowered china cup. The set had been given as a wedding present for her parents from Sophie's aunt in Ireland. Her Irish heritage held a special place in her heart, especially considering the tales told by her parents. Unfortunately she'd never had the chance to visit Ireland, but she planned to someday. Remembering the conversation with her mother, brought tears to her eyes

"My darling girl, your father and I want you to go to Ireland. It is our gift to you."

"Mom, you and dad were supposed to go. Your savings, does this mean you can't go?"

"Oh, silly child, I insist that you take the ticket. If your father hears you refuse…"

"Refuse what?" Sean Baird had questioned as he'd entered the room. "My jewel, I will hear none of this. You will take this trip and finally see the land that flows through your blood." Sophie recalled embracing her parents in one of their final times together before the accident. As the memory faded, she sipped her half-finished, tepid tea and sighed. She dared not dream of traveling to Ireland now due to lack of finances. *Even if I had the money, I wouldn't want to go without mom and dad.*

* * *

"Papa..."Anastasia Shipley quietly spoke up from her enormous canopy bed. "Do you think she'll be coming soon?"

"Ana, what are you talking about?" Sebastian questioned and then smiled indulgently at his nine-year-old daughter.

Anastasia struggled to sit up in the big bed that threatened to swallow her tiny frame. "You know... the governess."

Sebastian roared with laughter and slapped his leg. He put his e-reader down and stood up from his oversized *papa bear chair*, as Ana had fondly christened it. He came to sit on the edge of his daughter's bed. "We don't call them governesses these days. We're not living in a Jane Austen novel. She'll be your tutor."

"Why not?" She pouted. "I so much prefer governess, don't you?"

Her high-pitched voice bordered on petulant, but still sounded endearing to him. How could he not love her vivacious personality? Although, the little angel-on-his-shoulder reminded him not to let her behavior go too long without reprimand. "You *prefer*? When did you become such a proper little lady?"

"Since the day I was born." Her head tilted and she gave him a lop-sided, yet ladylike grin. *Boy, am I going to have trouble with her when she starts dating. She'll have all the boys wrapped around her finger just like she did to me from the moment she came into this world!*

He chuckled. In his heart, he knew Anastasia yearned to see him cheerful again—he'd barely laughed since his beloved wife passed away. That day, something inside him died, but he struggled to stay emotionally available for his precious and precocious daughter. "Who told you that?"

"Mrs. Andrews told me. She said you wouldn't have it any other way."

"Did she?" He shook his head and kissed Anastasia on the cheek.

She held out her hands. "Well, Papa? When is my tutor coming?"

"I don't know. We have to wait now. I've only just placed the advertisement online."

Sighing dramatically, she continued. "She has to come soon. Mrs. Andrews does her best, but—" *Here she goes again...old beyond her years.* With everything that had happened in her short life— sickness, loss—Sebastian's heart hoped for some normalcy to return to their home.

Mrs. Andrews bustled into the room with her

usual cheerful flurry and set the tea and cookies on the table. "Is she after you, sir, about that tutor? When I try to help her with the lessons, she will have none of me. I don't have much education, but I do the best that I can, filling in right now until…"

He waved away her concerns. "Don't worry, Mrs. Andrews, you're doing an excellent job as housekeeper *and* my daughter's teacher."

"I pray this tutor comes soon, before your proper daughter drives me crazy." Mrs. Andrews mumbled good-naturedly as she exited into the hall.

"Papa, you know I love Mrs. Andrews, don't you?" The way she tilted her head and grinned from ear to ear, made his heart constrict with love. *If only I could be a better father for her…have more of myself to give.*

"Yes, dear, and she knows it, too. Now let's have some tea."

Anastasia sank back into the mountain of satiny flowered pillows and Sebastian watched as she beamed contentedly. Obviously, she eagerly anticipated the arrival of this tutor. Sebastian knew she desperately needed someone to talk to, especially a young woman figure. Two lonely years had passed since her mother died. For the first time in months, he noticed hope resurfacing in her eyes. His wife used to remind him of the saying *hope springs eternal*, and he desperately yearned for that to ring true.

Sophie shook the raindrops off her black and white polka-dot umbrella and unlocked, then opened the door. Carrying the bags into the cottage, she began the task of putting all the groceries away. When finished, she turned on her tablet and went online to search the classifieds. She'd taken some time off from her job as a teacher at the elementary school. Desperately wanting a change, she needed to make a decision about the future. Still enjoying teaching, she loved the children in her class, her pride and joy. She perused the job listings and sat back with a frustrated sigh.

Maybe there's nothing here for me right now. She had money put away in savings and could take more time between jobs, but the mere thought of living in limbo made her want to scream. More time was not the answer—something to distract her numb heart and take her away from this place—was the only thing she longed for at the moment.

Standing up to get a soda, she saw it, right at the bottom of the list. She'd missed it the first time around. This seemed perfect even if not exactly what she'd planned for. The position certainly fit her current circumstances—offering a chance to get away from this town and put distance between her and the beloved cottage with all of its precious memories. Never one to make impulsive decisions, Sophie sensed an inclination to jump at this opportunity. Led by whom, she wondered…certainly not God. She imagined He filled His time with more important things than her future. Lately, her Christian walk lacked its past fervor. Shoving all intense thoughts to the back burner, she reached for her cell phone. She needed to get this job.

* * *

Sebastian strolled through the courtyard garden with head bent low and deep in thought. He hoped for a successful meeting with the prospective tutor this morning. His main goal—to find a good match for his daughter's personality and restrictive health needs. Sitting down on a stone bench, he turned his gaze toward the mansion. A movement near one of the balconies caught his eye. Mrs. Andrews settled Anastasia outside her bedroom into a big comfortable chair, tucked snugly in with blankets to keep out the chilly air.

Sebastian observed his daughter staring down into the courtyard. From his vantage point, he noticed her eyes drinking in the beautiful sights of the autumn garden. The bright red roses from the spring time were her favorite. Even for a young child, Anastasia appreciated the natural world. Sebastian's wife had cultivated that gift in their daughter. She'd taught her to revel in the beauty of God's creation. To know He created flowers, trees, and birds of the air, and that He made her. The Father of the Heavens loved all His children and wanted them to take hold of his salvation.

Anastasia had accepted this teaching as a young child before her mother passed away. Little Ana knew her creator. Sebastian overheard her talking to God all the time. Of course, she experienced her moments of tantrums and the usual childish chicanery, but sometimes he believed she paid too much attention to the heavens and not enough on earth. Sebastian smiled as he remembered her consistent response. "Oh, Papa, if only mama were still here…she'd understand. I know God doesn't get tired of hearing me speak. You should try it Papa, I know it would help." *From the mouths of babes…maybe I should take her advice.*

* * *

Tremors swept through Sophie's body as she drove up to the expansive home of her possible future employer. She tried to get a grip on her anxiety. The last time she'd experienced such nervous energy happened when she interviewed for the position at the elementary school. Slowly exiting her car, she willed herself to walk up to the wide double doors. Telling herself not to worry only caused her mind to continue spinning. "Tutoring a young girl can't be any more difficult than handling twenty-five ten year olds," she muttered.

Sophie timidly approached the front steps. Out of habit, she almost whispered a prayer, but stopped herself. God didn't care about her anymore. She took hold of the solid brass, lion head knocker and pounded the thick cherry wood. A butler opened the door, which surprised her at first. Then she remembered where she stood—in front of an estate with a long tree-lined private driveway. In her muddled state of mind, Sophie hoped she got through this interview with dignity.

The butler politely ushered her into an elegant room with antique furnishings. Surprisingly her distracted mind noticed that the room looked like a study and parlor put together. Sophie stood still, waiting patiently, until the man—whom she presumed was Mr. Shipley—turned around from his position of gazing out the French doors. The butler announced Sophie's entry and shut the doors behind him. "Ms. Baird, please have a seat. I trust you had no problems finding my home."

Sophie wondered why his use of the word *home* and not *house* seemed endearing. It almost brought him down to an approachable level in her mind. She kept imagining various scenes from her favorite Jane Austen novels—*Emma, Pride & Prejudice, Persuasion*—and pictured this man as the Lord of a manor house.

"Ms. Baird?"

"Oh, I'm sorry. No, I had no trouble."

Mr. Shipley moved to sit in the leather chair behind the large mahogany desk. Sophie thought he looked so approachable one moment and then distant the next. "I received your resume. All of your references checked out fine. I spoke with Mrs. Edmonds. She praised you and your teaching abilities."

Sophie clasped her hands in her lap, trying to stop them from shaking. "She's a great administrator. I enjoyed working with her." She glanced at Mr. Shipley's hands—he seemed preoccupied with his pen, twisting it between his slender, well-manicured fingers.

"Ms. Baird...uh, may I call you Sophie?"

She heard a tone of vulnerability in his voice. "Yes." She kept her answers short, not wanting to say anything foolish because at this point she barely trusted herself. For some reason this man had an effect of rattling her senses and she'd only just met him. Maybe it was his obvious wealth or his handsome good looks or his piercing brown eyes.

"Sophie, would it be impertinent for me to inquire why you left your teaching position and are seeking employment with me?" Mr. Shipley cleared his throat. "I only ask because this involves my daughter."

She shifted in her chair trying to figure out

how to respond to the one question she did not want to answer. "Mr. Shipley, I..."

"Please, call me Sebastian. If you'll be working with my daughter, I expect us to be able to speak freely as much as possible."

Sophie nodded and took a deep breath. What should she say? Tell him the entire truth? She focused on hiding the nervousness threatening to overtake her. *Slow and steady...relax.* Her gentle reminder to herself failed to ease the tension. He broke the silence. "Let's take a walk outside. It's a beautiful day." He ushered Sophie through the French doors behind his desk onto the terraced courtyard.

"Sebastian...I," she hesitated at the awkwardness of saying his first name. "It's complicated. My reasons are personal. I needed time to reevaluate." What a lame response, but she grasped at straws. She had not expected such a probing question in this job interview.

"Is there a man involved?"

Sophie stared, aghast. "Excuse me?"

Sebastian held up his hand. "Please don't be offended, Sophie." He spoke with an air of authority. "This sounds like a case of trouble in paradise."

Maybe he's the one reading too many romance novels. Some nerve he has. "Mr. Shipley, I resent any delving into my personal affairs. I am here for employment, nothing more. Excuse me, but I don't need this." She spun on her heels, hastily searching for the nearest exit.

Sebastian touched her arm and even that light touch sent shivers down her spine. His eyes implored her and embarrassment colored his clean-shaven cheeks. "I'm sorry, Sophie…may I still call you that?"

Reluctantly, Sophie nodded her permission and followed him further into the garden. *What am I doing? I should leave now.* She noticed the vibrant red and gold colored flowers and shrubs. The bright rays of the sun accentuated the colors of the autumn garden. "I was wrong for being so forward." Sebastian began to apologize. From hearing the hesitation in his voice, she knew that apologies came with difficulty for him. He stopped walking and faced her. "I'll make no excuses for the fact that I love my daughter very much and will only accept the highest quality for her. Are you the best person for the job, Sophie?"

His direct question caught her off guard. Nervy, but honest—at least he loves his daughter very much. She definitely could respect that quality in him. Sophie stuck out her chin and replied as calmly as her shaky nerves would allow. "Yes, sir, I believe I am." Would those six words of affirmation be enough to win over the confidence of this dignified man?

"Would you care to have lunch with me…and my daughter? It will give you a chance to break the ice with my Ana." His abrupt change of subject and the plaintive note in his voice strangely affected Sophie. One minute this man appeared confident and overpowering, and the next, timid and almost child-like—and very appealing.

"I'd love to have lunch with both of you. It would be a great opportunity to get to know…um, does she like to be called Ana or is that a name you call her?"

When he smiled, she couldn't help but smile back. He looked even more dashing when he was happy. Obviously, his daughter brought great joy to his life. "I've been calling my daughter Ana since the day she was born. It seemed to fit her. My wife wanted a very formal name, thus Anastasia. She became Ana right from the start for me."

"You're the only one who calls her Ana." Sophie stated, starting to understand their family dynamic. She was Daddy's little girl. Sophie immediately connected with that especially because of her close relationship with her own father. For a fleeting moment, she hoped she was not getting involved with a spoiled child, but she just as quickly silenced the thought. Sophie made it a practice not to prejudge anyone and she didn't want to start now.

"Yes." Sebastian led the rest of the way back to the house in silence. Sophie's mind raced with questions and she still hesitated accepting this job. Her connection with God severed—she felt no peace, only a sense of unease kept her company.

* * *

Bright sunlight streaming through the windows warmed all three occupants in the dining room. Sebastian sat at the head of the table. He watched with great interest as his daughter bubbled over with chatter like a rushing mountain creek. Anastasia spoke excitedly to Sophie, and Sebastian felt a sense of peace wash over his being. *Maybe she's the right one.* After having interviewed several fully qualified, yet incompatible candidates, he'd begun to think he would never find a suitable prospect—until now. Laughter interrupted his thoughts. He looked questioningly at his daughter and Sophie.

"Your daughter is hilarious, Sebastian."

"That's something I know very well. She keeps me going."

"Papa!" Anastasia whined.

Sebastian reached over and lovingly touched his daughter's cheek as she pouted. "That's the truth now, and you know it."

She rewarded her father with a wide smile, lightly poked his nose and grabbed another muffin off the serving plate.

The door to the dining room opened slowly, and the butler entered, "Sir…"

"Yes, Nigel, what is it?"

"You have a phone call. It's urgent."

"I see. Thank you." Nigel handed him one of the cordless phones and then silently left the room. "Excuse me, ladies." Sebastian stepped out, intently listening to the voice speaking on the telephone.

When Sebastian came back into the room he was met with his daughter's sad face. "No, Papa, not again. You said you wouldn't have to go. Not for a long time. You promised."

Now would probably not be the best time for a tantrum. As he came back to sit next to Anastasia, he distractedly wondered what Sophie thought of his daughter's behavior. He hoped she didn't head for the hills after this episode. "I never said I was leaving, did I?"

"No, but I thought...?"

Sebastian heard relief in his little girl's voice. He hugged her and promised not to leave her alone anymore.

Sebastian turned to Sophie. He figured questions would be swarming her mind as she wondered why Anastasia became so upset with him getting a phone call and assuming he was leaving. Did he need to explain anything to her about his business trips? Ever since his wife died, he'd buried himself in his work and his daughter had suffered from his absence. He was ready to make the necessary changes. "Miss Baird, can you start tomorrow morning?" Sophie hesitated in answering and doubts began assailing Sebastian. "Is that too soon? Maybe later on in the week to get your affairs in order?" Part of the job description called for the tutor to live on the premises. He hoped she would be able to start work soon.

"I think I can manage and if I forget to bring anything, I only live forty-five minutes away."

"So that's a yes?"

"It is." He noticed her nervous smile, but figured a little bit of nervousness was good— hopefully that would keep Sophie on her A-game with his most precious treasure. "I'll be here tomorrow morning at nine. Is that okay?" He nodded. "Great." Sophie started to walk out of the dining room. She stopped when Sebastian called her name. "Yes?"

"I'm glad you accepted the position. You can see Mrs. Andrews on your way out. She'll make arrangements for your personal belongings to be brought to the house and show you your room before you leave."

"Thank you."

* * *

Sebastian sat upstairs with Anastasia in her bedroom. She lay back in bed with pillows propped up behind her. She'd grown ill after a bad fever had struck at the age of five and she nearly died. Since then she'd suffered from poor health. He made certain Ana received the best possible medical care. A physician came by the house once a week for a house call, but still he worried. Any loving father would be concerned about his child, but especially when the child was ill. Even with more money at his disposal than he knew what to do with, he still couldn't make that money heal his daughter. Nothing seemed to work, but he had to keep hoping for the best. As he watched Ana nod off to sleep, he hoped his impressions of Sophie were right—that she and Ana would make a good match of teacher and pupil. In his heart, he knew he needed to entrust his daughter's education and care to God's providence.

Chapter Two

"Papa, I'm glad you don't have to go on another trip."

"Me, too, but if I have to go again, I'm taking you with me." Sebastian planted a kiss on his daughter's cheek. "Your new tutor will be here soon. Are you excited?"

"Will Miss Sophie go with us?"

He peered at her curiously. "Go where?"

"On your next trip…you said you would take me with you."

"Hmm, well I hadn't thought about that one." Would he bring Sophie on the next business trip? Since he was taking Ana along, she'd need her tutor, right? He could cross that bridge when the time came. For now, he wanted to make sure both teacher and student worked well together.

"I am excited that she's coming." Sebastian marveled at how quickly her mind raced as she jumped back to his original question. Indeed Sophie was going to have her hands full in the classroom, but he knew she'd be able to handle Ana well. Tap. Tap. A knock sounded on Anastasia's bedroom door. Sebastian answered. "Come in."

Nigel entered. "Sir, Miss Baird has arrived. Mrs. Andrews is assisting her with unpacking. Would you like to see her when she is settled in?"

At the mention of the tutor's arrival, a slight case of nervousness settled upon him. This is it. *At least I hope so.* "Yes, please ask her to join us in the dining room." Nigel exited the room and Sebastian turned his attention back to his daughter. He observed her playing a puzzle game on her tablet and noticed an absolute calm about her. *Guess I'm the only one nervous about the situation.* After a few minutes, he beckoned for Anastasia to follow him downstairs to the dining room.

* * *

Sophie took a deep breath and quietly entered the room, hoping not to intrude. Accepting the role of live-in tutor would likely take maneuvering on her part—adjusting to life in a mansion, yet not completely being part of their family. The warm welcome she received as she joined them helped to ease the nervous tension in her body. "Good morning, Sophie. I trust you've found our accommodations to your liking." Sebastian smiled.

"Yes, Mr. Shipley, everything is perfect."

Almost too perfect—she definitely was not used to living in such opulence. When Mrs. Andrews had brought her to the bedroom assigned to her, she hoped her mouth wasn't gaping to the floor. The bed was a four poster king-size with an elegant canopy. She hadn't been able to stop staring at the luxurious bedding and burgundy draperies. Mrs. Andrews had rescued Sophie from her kid-in-a-candy-store moment to assist with settling in and unpacking.

"Not exactly." He stood up and pulled out a paisley upholstered chair for her at the table.

"What do you mean?" She wasn't sure if she should worry or not.

"The morning will not be absolutely perfect until you call me Sebastian."

*Oh, that's all…*what a relief. Sophie relaxed. "I'm sorry. Things are fine, Sebastian." Would she ever get used to calling this dignified man by his first name? She glanced over at Anastasia seated across from her. "How are you feeling this morning?"

"Happy. I'm glad you're finally here."

"Finally? You only met me yesterday."

Sebastian grinned. "My Ana has been waiting a long time for a good tutor who would stay on for the long haul. She's had a few, but none to establish a consistent relationship with."

Sophie's shoulders tensed and her insides quivered. Suddenly it seemed as if she had a lot to live up to. "So, you're going to trust me?"

"Shouldn't I?" Clearly, Sebastian was teasing her.

"We barely know each other, and this is a big responsibility." Sophie made a face and mouthed *Oops*. "Did I actually say that?"

His boisterous laugh filled the room. Despite the heat of embarrassment rising up her cheeks, she took a keen liking to the masculine rumble of her employer's laughter. It was a sound she could truly grow to enjoy.

"Sophie, I'm glad you feel that this is a big responsibility."

"You are?"

"Yes."

"Why?"

"Because," Sebastian gestured with his hands, "it shows that you care. You'll do a great job. A small amount of fear is good, you know. It gets the adrenaline flowing."

"Papa trusts you because God sent you." Anastasia chimed in to the conversation and Sophie welcomed her moxie. Although, the direction the conversation headed made her uncomfortable—she was not on good terms with God.

"God?" *Please let's change the subject.*

"You believe in God, don't you?" Sophie heard the optimism in the child's voice.

"Yes, of course." What else was she supposed to say? She couldn't explain the rise and fall of her

Christian faith to the little girl. Sophie allowed Anastasia to occupy her attention with animated ideas of future learning activities until Sebastian stood up and interrupted his daughter's chatter.

"I'm going to leave you two ladies alone to get more acquainted. I'll be in my office if you need me."

"Papa, may I go outside for a bit?"

"You must use your wheelchair, darling. You'll have to wait until Nigel is ready to help."

"Oh, I can take her, myself, Sebastian. We'll be all right. I'll make sure Anastasia doesn't wear herself out."

Sebastian consented and started to leave. "I'll send Nigel in with her chair."

Sophie watched Anastasia finish eating her bowl of fruit. She hoped to dig deeper to find the hidden treasure of her young heart and mind. She wanted to teach and bring her out to experience life. Sophie fleetingly thought to ask about Anastasia's illness, but she steered clear of that topic for now— not exactly the best ice breaker for teacher and pupil. She eagerly wanted to help her student.

Sensing another presence in the room, Sophie nearly jumped out of her seat when Nigel spoke. "I brought the wheelchair, Miss Baird."

"Oh, hello, I didn't hear you come in." *I need to get used to the seen-but-not-heard butler.* Please, call me Sophie."

Nigel cleared his throat. "Mr. Shipley would not be pleased with that." Sophie's smile vanished. Had she offended Nigel? "Miss Baird, it's not that your suggestion does not please me…I hope you understand."

She reached a hand to touch his arm. "I think I do." *Note to self—remember that Nigel abided by standards of proper etiquette*. No doubt about it, she'd receive her own education while residing at the Shipley mansion.

Anastasia stood up to hug Nigel. The older man barely cracked a smile, but Sophie observed the warmth mirrored in both of their eyes. "Nigel, if you can't call her Sophie, and she doesn't want you to call her Miss Baird, why not say, Miss Sophie?" Her brilliant smile charmed both teacher and butler.

Nigel bent low and tapped her softly on the nose. "I might give that a try, Miss Anastasia, but I must check with your father first."

"Of course," she replied, obviously trying to stifle the giggles. Nigel turned to leave, and the young heiress peered expectantly at her new teacher. "May we go now? I don't take trips outside very often. I'm excited about this one. I'll show you our garden."

"Yes, yes we'll go. Let's get you ready."

Sophie enjoyed an interesting afternoon in the garden with her new student. The trip outside proved to be an excellent ice breaker in Sophie getting to know Anastasia. Of course, Sophie had erected walls around her own heart and didn't plan on allowing them to crumble any time soon. After an hour of pleasant conversation, Sophie noticed Anastasia seemed fatigued—definitely a sign to bring her back inside. Nigel appeared at the right moment and Sophie followed him as he carried the sleeping child to her room. Sophie muttered, "One of these days I'm going to get that man to smile. He'll come out of his shell."

Sophie moved to open the door for Nigel, and he gently placed Anastasia on the bed. He swiveled to face her. "Miss, I could get Mrs. Andrews to assist you."

She waved away his concerns. "Oh, no, that's not necessary, Nigel. I'll see to Anastasia myself. I want to help wherever I can." Nigel started to leave, but Sophie stopped him. "She won't be insulted will she? I don't want to intrude with something she's been doing…" She let her words trail off.

Never missing a beat in maintaining proper decorum, he responded. "It is fine, Miss. You are right. Mr. Shipley would want you to be there for Miss Anastasia, as long as you are comfortable with such tasks beyond your teaching, of course."

"Yes, I would love to help Anastasia, any way I can."

Nigel gave a slight nod and left the room. Sophie pulled the covers back, maneuvered Anastasia under them and fluffed the pillows. She sat back on the bed and smiled, her work completed. Now she must brace herself to go downstairs to interrupt Sebastian.

* * *

Sophie tried to steady her rapidly beating heart as she knocked on the dark wooden door. She felt like Queen Esther trying to gain an audience with King Ahasuerus. A moment later, she heard Sebastian respond for her to enter. He glanced up from the mound of paperwork spread across his desk. She thought she detected an expression of surprise on his face. *He did say he'd be in his office if I needed anything.*

"Is everything all right?" he asked.

"Yes, I was hoping I could speak with you, but if now's not a good time, I can come back."

"Please forgive my manners." Sebastian stood up and offered her a seat on the leather chair in front of the desk. "How did your morning go?"

"It went well. I guess I wanted to know what you'll be expecting from me while I'm here." There, she'd said it, but didn't feel any relief from her nerves. She hoped he'd understood what she meant.

Sebastian's eyebrows rose. "Well, to teach my daughter. I thought we established that."

Sophie inched forward on the chair and hurried to assure him. "Of course, I understand that part of my job description. I was curious what your involvement would be in regard to supervision of my teaching."

He leaned back and stretched his arms over his head. This time, he was not wearing his black suit jacket and she got a better glimpse of his broad shoulders and solid form in his white buttoned shirt. She had to refocus her attention onto his words and not his muscular body. "I see. I suppose you can think of me as an interested observer. I did check out your references, and I trust your experience with children. In no way will I hinder your method of operation unless, of course, you decide to suggest a field trip on an African Safari." Sophie chuckled and Sebastian rested his arms on the desk. "You find that amusing?"

"A little. You don't have to worry about the safari right now. That's part of the curriculum for next semester." It felt good to banter back. She saw him barely begin to smile, and spoke without thinking, "You're very serious, Sebastian, aren't you?"

She immediately experienced regret, but Sebastian's response alleviated repercussions from her slip of the tongue. "Actually, yes, I am, but I do have some sense of humor. I think you'll be good for Ana, and I'm glad you're here."

Sophie took his words as her exit cue. "Thank you for speaking with me."

"I hope I've cleared up any uncertainties in

your mind."

She nodded and started to leave.

"Mrs. Andrews usually serves dinner around six o'clock. I hope you don't mind, but I think it would be good for Ana if you eat with us, unless you have any objections."

"Oh, that would be fine. I'll see you later." As she closed the dark cherry wood door behind her, she wondered if eating with the family would be a good idea. So much for doing her job and remaining emotionally isolated. *I can still keep things from getting personal…I hope.*

* * *

"*The girl walked through the woods and searched for her missing cat. She had to walk all day before she found little Emma, hiding under the briar patch.*"

"Excellent. Good job, Anastasia. You're a very good reader."

"Thank you, Miss Sophie. I love to read. Papa reads me stories when I go to bed. He told me I'm a good reader." Sophie heard a hint of pride in her words and held back her smile. The more time she spent with Anastasia, the more she grew to like her and even enjoy her company.

"A love for reading is an important ingredient to being a good reader."

"What can we do next?"

"You actually want to do more work? I'm surprised and pleased. I like a willing student." So far, so good with regard to the studies—however, was this child too good to be true? Sophie recalled the many different personalities of the children in her class at the elementary school. Sally Beckett came to mind. She was a student similar in make-up to Anastasia. Both shared such a love for learning…it was refreshing. Sophie figured so much of Anastasia's good manners and unlikely decorum for one so young, was due to her upbringing.

She smiled shyly. "I love to study. I want you and Papa to be happy with my work."

Sophie sat back and marveled at the maturity and willingness to work, in this nine-year-old child. She anticipated further developing their teacher student relationship. She enjoyed teaching without force feeding information or pulling teeth. Many of her students disliked anything work-related at all. *I'm sure I'll see some signs of attitude one of these days.*

"I'd like to give you an exam. It will allow me to find out your learning level and where we'll go from here. Are you okay with that?"

"Yes. When do I take it?"

"Let's get started now. When you're finished, I'll give you the rest of the afternoon off."

"I'm ready."

Earlier, Sophie had located the perfect place

for the makeshift classroom. She planned to meet with her student in the sunroom at the far end of the mansion. The sunlight which illuminated the space created a warm and relaxing environment—*should be the ideal spot to cultivate further learning*. Sophie handed her student the examination and got her settled with a good pencil. Then she strode to the other end of the room. "Will you be able to concentrate, Anastasia, if I open these doors? I'd like to let a little fresh air inside."

"Okay." She barely lifted her blonde head from the exam paper she huddled over.

Sophie turned the doorknob and opened the glass doors. She called behind her as she walked. "I'm going to sit outside for a bit. A little incentive for you." She chuckled. "You can join me when you're finished."

Sophie stepped onto the manicured lawn and breathed in the crisp air. She spied a stone bench surrounded by green shrubs and sat down. The peaceful atmosphere of this place slowly began chipping away at her hardened soul. She turned her head at the sound behind her. A sparrow perched on a branch of an evergreen tree. It pecked at the needles and hopped deeper into the tree, then onto the ground, in search of food. *His eye is on the sparrow*...the familiar words came unbidden to Sophie's mind. She shook her head, needing to clear the words, not yet ready to accept them. Standing abruptly, she walked the few feet toward the sunroom. She entered the room and shut the doors. Anastasia glanced up curiously from her workspace but then focused again on finishing the exam. *Good, no questions. That's all I'd need right now.* Turning to face the glass doors, Sophie closed her eyes as a tear slowly slid down her cheek.

Chapter Three

"Are you awake?" Sophie called softly as she quietly knocked, and then entered her young charge's room. Anastasia had given Sophie free reign to come in her room whenever she'd pleased—something Sophie had avoided until now. She hoped Anastasia found the news as exciting as she did.

"Yes." Anastasia answered from the comfort of her warm bed. "I was thinking about my mama playing the piano. I still remember her sitting on the bench. The music was so beautiful. She even let me sit next to her, but most times I liked to sit underneath the piano and listen to her play."

"What a beautiful memory. Do you know how to play?"

"No. Mama died before I ever learned. I was too busy listening to the music." Her sudden outburst of tears startled Sophie.

"It's okay, honey. Let it out." Sophie sat on the bed, reaching to hold Anastasia. At first, the moment felt awkward—Sophie was a teacher, not a mother and not even an aunt. She wasn't used to comforting children when they cried. That had never been part of her job description as a teacher. She clumsily smoothed blonde curls from Anastasia's eyes and smiled. With her thumbs, she wiped away the tears from her cheeks. "We must eat lunch. Your father will be waiting for us."

"Waiting for what?" Anastasia quickly pulled away from Sophie's embrace.

"Doesn't that beat all!" Sophie exclaimed. "I rushed in here to tell you before, but it slipped my mind when...I'm sorry."

"It's okay. I haven't cried about my Mama in a long time." Sophie noticed her imploring expression. "Would you brush my hair like my Mama used to? You can do it while you tell me about Papa."

How could she refuse that face? Standing on shaky emotional ground, Sophie inhaled deeply. She hated to interfere with Anastasia and the memory of her mother. By no means did she harbor any inclinations to try to replace Mrs. Shipley in the little girl's heart. However, the plaintive look on her face tugged on Sophie's emotions. She patted the pink velvet cushion of the vanity chair. "All right, little Miss, come down out of this big bed and sit here. We need to get you prim and proper for your father. He's such a dashing gentleman, you know." *Dashing gentleman? At least Anastasia won't take too much notice of those words. He is dashing, though.*

~ 33 ~

Sophie began brushing the long, curly locks of golden hair when Anastasia interrupted her. "I like it when you call me *little Miss.* Can that be your nickname for me?"

"You want a nickname?"

"Papa said he started calling me *Ana* first and then my grandpapa and Uncle David did too. I think you should have your own nickname for me." Touched by this admission, a tear rolled down Sophie's cheek. She quickly wiped it away, not wanting Anastasia to see her cry and think she'd upset her. Quite the contrary—her wish honored Sophie.

She took a deep breath and plunged ahead, enjoying their new-found camaraderie. "If you want little Miss, then little Miss it is." They shared more laughter and Sophie hugged Anastasia from behind.

The young girl quickly turned around in the chair. "Wait, Miss Sophie, you still didn't tell me what the surprise is. What is Papa waiting for?"

A refined, deep voice in the doorway answered the question. "I am waiting for you two ladies to get moving. Haven't you told her yet?" His question was directed to Sophie. She shook her head. *He must think me flighty!* "You flew up those stairs so fast I thought you couldn't wait to tell her."

"We got busy with girl talk." She didn't want to say too much about their conversation.

"So, I guess that means you didn't eat lunch yet." He stated rather than asked.

Sophie glanced at the clock on Anastasia's night stand. "We've been up here that long?"

"Long enough."

"Oh, I'm sorry." *Way to go,* she chided herself.

He flicked his hand nonchalantly, as if waving aside a pesky mosquito. "That's fine. Mrs. Andrews was kind enough to pack a picnic lunch for us."

"We're going on a picnic?" Anastasia squealed in surprise.

"Even better." Sophie heard the excitement filling his voice. "I'm taking you two ladies boating on the lake."

The young girl hurried across the room into her father's outstretched arms. "We'll have so much fun."

Sophie watched as he gently squeezed her shoulders. The tenderness between father and daughter threatened to bring up her melancholy over missing her own father. *Keep it together. Not in front of Sebastian.*

"I hope so. Are you two ready?"

"Well, I've never been sailing before, but I guess I should change," Sophie half-stated, half-asked, motioning to her mid-length denim skirt.

"Good idea. A sturdy pair of slacks and a windbreaker will do better. My little Ana, you must also find something suitable to wear. I'll help Nigel get the boat ready and will be back in fifteen minutes to pick you up."

"You don't give much time."

"I run a tight ship." Sebastian patted her arm and smiled as he left the room.

Would she feel such sparks each time he touched her? Focusing back on the task at hand, Sophie quickly moved toward Anastasia's closet. She found a warm pair of cotton slacks and a fleece shirt. "Don't forget to wear your jacket. I know we're in the middle of Indian summer, but we'll be on the water, and the breeze can be cool."

"You worry too much, like Papa," she retorted with a pout.

"Would you like my help or not, honey?" Sophie laid the clothes on the bed. She never wanted to treat her little Miss as helpless. In her opinion, she thought Sebastian coddled his daughter a bit too much. The result—was a potentially spoiled child.

"I can do it." Ana sounded determined.

Sophie decided to leave the child alone for a moment. "Okay. I'll be back in a few minutes." She then walked out of the bedroom to go change her clothes as well.

A few minutes later, Sophie came back and knocked on the door. Anastasia answered. "Come in."

Sophie smiled when she saw her all dressed and ready to go. She had even tied a blue ribbon around her hair at the nape of her neck. Sophie knew the task took determination on Anastasia's part and she was proud of her. "Good job." She wanted to say more, but held back, to keep from embarrassing the child. "After you, my little Miss." Sophie made sure she grabbed Anastasia's jacket on her way out.

* * *

Peace I leave with you, my peace I give to you; not as the world gives do I give to you. Let not your heart be troubled, neither let it be afraid. Although verses from the Bible usually remained in the far recesses of her mind, they came unbidden to her now. Not understanding this sudden resurgence of God's voice, she tried hard to shove it back. The shifting of the small form sleeping near her side interrupted these quiet musings. Sophie looked at Anastasia and smiled. She cared for this child and continued fighting off the motherly feelings bubbling in her heart. *Teacher and student...remember the boundary lines.* She'd been prepared for a close student-teacher bond, especially working one on one. Yet these new emotions in the last few weeks at the Shipley mansion threw her out of her comfort zone.

Emptiness filled her heart with a longing to communicate with God, but in her present spiritual state, that void remained unmet. In the deepest depths of her spirit, she knew where to turn, but stubbornness—and more importantly—a deep sorrow halted any progress in her relationship with the

Father. Somehow, she sensed that these walls with God needed to come down before she could ever truly let others into her heart.

"You're deep in thought."

That statement brought Sophie back into the moment. "Um…yes, I guess so."

Discussing God was not a subject she wanted to share with either one of the Shipleys. Much to her relief, Sebastian courteously let the subject go. He glanced at Anastasia sleeping next to her. "She's out like a light, almost right after lunch. I didn't expect her to get so winded. We've only been out on the lake for a little over an hour."

"I think she needs some time. She's not used to such an active day, but I know she enjoyed it." Sophie gazed tenderly at her young charge. "She's precious."

"Yes, she is. My father decided to remain in England for now because he heard such glowing reports of his granddaughter's new tutor."

"Oh, so he was coming to check up on me?"

"I guess so. He dotes on Ana more than me."

"No, that's not possible." She teased him.

"Sophie Baird, I must say you are indeed most refreshingly down to earth. You're much different than most of the high society ladies I associate with here and in England."

Wow, more refreshing than the high society ladies! *More brownie points with me for this charmer*—after the initial levity of the moment, she remembered that *this charmer* was her employer. Maybe she shouldn't be worried about brownie points! "Thank you," she responded quietly. "That's the nicest compliment I've had in a while, and I don't think you give them out easily."

"You're right, I don't."

Sophie locked his kind words in the bank of her heart and savored them. She remained silent for a while and stared out at the serene lake. Basking in the warmth of the sun, she ventured to ask, "Where does your property line run along the lake?"

"All around." Sophie glanced back in surprise. "I own the lake." She hoped her face didn't show her astonishment. Of course he owned the lake. After seeing his estate, should she have expected any less? Every minute she spent with him, he reminded her more and more of a modern day Mr. Darcy. *Time to get your head out of the clouds,* she reminded herself.

"Oh. That's nice." What a lame reply. Couldn't she think of something better to say than that? If her mother was looking down from Heaven now, she'd be disappointed in her daughter's lack of social etiquette. Anastasia woke up suddenly. Sophie shifted to help her sit up. "I'm sorry. Did I wake you?"

Wiping the sleepiness from her eyes, Anastasia shook her head. "No, I just woke up." She peered over the rim of the boat. "Are we at the house yet?"

"Almost, my dear." Sebastian patted her shoulder. "Sit back and relax. We'll be there soon."

"No." Her firm voice startled Sophie and she wondered if Sebastian was shocked at his daughter's response. He looked like he'd seen this tone from her before. Sophie leaned forward and waited for Anastasia's next move. "I'm sorry. I didn't mean to say it so loudly." She paused and Sophie instinctively knew the child needed to share something important. Anastasia definitely appeared to be more complex than any other child she'd dealt with in her teaching career—but she was up for the challenge. "I want to tell you both something. I know I am getting better. I prayed about it. God healed me." She stopped, almost as if waiting for an argument. When no debate came, Anastasia moved over to settle into the crook of her father's arm. He and Sophie both acknowledged their support. The rest of the boat ride continued in an unspoken, agreed upon silence.

* * *

Sophie's hands moved flawlessly over the ivory keys as a sweet melody filled the air. Her heart relished the emotional therapy of playing music. Making an effort to play quietly, she hoped no one woke up from the noise. She continued with the song, when she suddenly became aware of another presence in the room. Rubbing sleepy eyes, Anastasia stood in the arched doorway. "Mama." One word, spoken in a sleep-muddled state, which made Sophie cease playing immediately. "No, please don't stop." With slow steps, Anastasia came closer to the piano. She stopped, staring at Sophie in seeming recognition.

Exactly what I didn't want to happen. Sophie beckoned. "Come sit here beside me." Rewarded with a big smile from the little girl, Sophie continued playing.

"That's the same song Mama used to play." At least she was fully conscious now and aware of whom Sophie was. The last thing she needed right then was to cause any confusion in the young girl.

"Do you want me to teach you?"

Anastasia hesitated for only a moment, and Sophie guessed she remembered her mother playing at this same piano bench. "Yes, Miss Sophie, I would like that." Sophie nodded and started from the beginning again. She began explaining to her young student where to place her fingers and what the notes were. As the lesson continued, Sophie's excitement grew as she noticed how much Anastasia enjoyed the moment.

***

Completely engrossed in the piano lesson, Sophie failed to notice Sebastian standing by the doorway. Like a mouse following the Pied Piper, the melody had drawn him away from reading and downstairs to appease his curiosity. For the longest time, lack of music had left his house lonely and wanting for happier times. Sebastian still never understood why he had kept Katherine's piano. No one ever played it since she passed away. When she died, so did the music from their lives. Even the cleaning staff nervously dusted the beautiful black instrument, careful not to press any keys. Two years after his wife's death, everyone in the household still thought of the drawing room as *Katherine's room*.

Conflicted in his emotions, Sebastian remained quiet, uncertain how he felt about Sophie intruding in Katherine's space. At this point, he was not emotionally ready to welcome anyone to take Katherine's place in their lives—even if only at the piano. However, he peered more closely into the darkened room and saw the pure joy on Anastasia's face. He decided to go back upstairs to his Agatha Christie novel, glad for this bonding experience between Sophie and his daughter.

Chapter Four

"Can you tell me a story, Miss Sophie?"

"You'd like to hear a story, hmm…?"

"Yes, we're finished with our lessons for today. Please…"

"Okay, but it's a long one."

Anastasia excitedly clapped her hands together. "Let's move our blanket over on the grass by the lake. We can relax while you tell the story."

Sophie acquiesced. How could she say no to such excitement? They settled in by the lake and she began.

A long time ago in a land far away, there lived a little princess. She was the only daughter to her father, the King. Every day the King would take his daughter out to the courtyard garden, and they would speak about many things. They talked about the birds that came to drink from the marble fountains. They spoke about the myriad of colors and scents of the flowers that bloomed in the garden. But the most important thing they spoke about was his kingdom.

The King did his best to train his daughter up in the ways of wisdom. He knew that one day his daughter would grow up and take over the rule of the kingdom. The little princess greatly enjoyed sitting at the feet of her father. She enjoyed his stories and always paid close attention. She knew that her father would want her to dig deeper to find the "nugget of truth," as he always said.

On one such day, the King was regaling the little princess with funny tales, when suddenly, he grew serious. He said that he had a tale of great importance to tell her and she must listen very carefully.

The King began his story. A baby blue bird was perched on a branch, trying to decide if he was ready to fly. He was very scared and not quite ready when his stronger, older brother came along and started to make fun of him. The jesting got out of hand and the older brother pushed him off the branch. The baby blue bird cried out in fear and kept falling down. He tried to flap his wings, but they weren't working and he couldn't do it. He was headed toward a crash landing, but the Wise Old Owl came to his rescue and caught him just as he neared the ground. His brother was laughing at the little blue bird's failure and soon, his friends all came out to see the commotion and joined in the jeering.

The little blue bird was not hurt, the King said, he had only bruised his pride. So he struggled out of the Wise Old Owl's wing and hopped away as fast as his little legs could carry him. By the time he got to the deep woods, he was so tired that he hid in the bushes and closed his eyes. He did not know that the Wise Old Owl had been quietly following him the entire time, making sure that no danger came to him. When the owl got closer to the bush, he could hear the tiny sobs from the little bird.

The Owl approached the bird and lightly touched him, trying to wake him up. "Little Blue Bird, what's the matter?"

The bird sat up and replied in surprise, "You saw me fall. You caught me. Everyone…they all laughed at me. I'm never gonna fly."

The Wise Old Owl smiled and replied, "Yes, you will. I can help you." The little blue bird shook his head and couldn't believe that this feat would be accomplished. The Owl waited patiently, his wing outstretched. Finally, the little bird seemed to decide, and hope shone from his eyes.

The King continued with his tale. He said that the Wise Old Owl and little bird walked down the path together. They came to the end of the path at the cliff. The Wise Old Owl said, "This is where you will learn to fly."

"…here?" The little bird choked out.

The Wise Old Owl leaned down and looked right into the eyes of the little bird. "Will you trust me?"

"Yes." The little bird answered, without hesitating.

"We will go together. I will hold you in my wing and then you will start to fly when you're ready." They got to the edge and jumped. The little bird was held safely in the Owl's wing. The Owl was giving instructions and then opened his wing. He told the little bird to start flapping his wings. As they were half-way down, the little blue bird stood up tall and jumped. He faltered at first, but then flapped his wings and soon he was flying next to the Wise Old Owl.

The little princess clapped her hands and said that was such a wonderful tale. The King smiled and asked her what she learned. She thought for a moment and then replied. She said that the Wise Old Owl must be like God, always walking with us and protecting us. She said that he held the little bird in his wings until he was ready to jump out. The little princess thought some more and said that the Wise Old Owl—like God—waited patiently while the little bird decided if he would accept his help. The King smiled and hugged his little princess. She pulled away and said that she forgot one more thing. He looked curiously. She said that all things are possible with God. The King nodded and took the little princess by the hand, as they walked out of the garden.

"Are you sleeping, Anastasia?" Sophie asked.

"Yes." She kept her eyes closed, but Sophie

saw her mouth twitch as if trying to hold in her laughter.

Chuckling, Sophie reached over to tickle the young girl. "I hope you heard my entire story."

Cute giggles were her only response. She finally opened her eyes. "Yes, I did. It was wonderful."

"I'm glad you liked it."

"Do you believe in God?" The question came out of nowhere and Sophie wanted to avoid discussing it in depth. Where she stood in her relationship with God certainly fascinated Anastasia. Clamming up and ignoring the question wouldn't do anything to further their own tender relationship—she opted to move forward with caution.

"Why do you ask?" Sophie questioned, with uncertainty.

"Because I never hear you talk about God, but your story was about Him."

Out of the mouth of babes… The child made a good point, but that still wasn't enough for Sophie to completely bare her soul. "I believe in God. I just…"

Anastasia's hand reached out reassuringly and touched her arm. "It's okay." The little child's calming eyes soothed Sophie's nervousness on the subject.

Tears threatened to spill over so Sophie stood up abruptly. "Maybe we should get you inside to rest. I don't think your father would be happy if he knew how long I'd kept you outside."

"Do we have to go in now?"

"Yes, little Miss. No pouting on me now." Before she even had a chance to turn around, Nigel approached them. *Always at the right time*, Sophie thought. She wondered how he appeared exactly at the moment anyone needed assistance. He helped Anastasia into her wheelchair. "Hello, Nigel. Thank you."

A few minutes later with Anastasia resting comfortably in her room, Sophie strolled out toward the garden. She sat on one of the marble benches. Soaking in the fresh air and sunshine, she relaxed in silence. Anastasia's direct question about God plagued her mind. Extremely glad she'd dropped the issue, Sophie marveled at her student's observation skills. "I guess I haven't said anything about God. That actually was the first time."

"The first time for what, may I ask?"

Startled, Sophie quickly turned around. "Sebastian, do you enjoy sneaking up on me?"

"No." With a roguish grin, he sat down next to her. "Work bored me. I was already outside walking in the garden when I saw you sitting here. You looked like you could use company."

Her silence spoke volumes—at least she hoped it did. Though, did she truly want to discuss the conversation with him? No. Yet, to remain closed off might offend him. She glanced around. Apparently, this garden lacked the privacy she desired. Distractedly, she wondered where the vantage point from his office stopped. For future reference, of course, in case she might want to escape for much needed solitude. Sebastian interrupted her musings. "Perhaps I was wrong to disturb you. I can leave."

When she faced him again, his nearness unnerved her. His piercing brown eyes and thick, wavy chestnut-colored hair caught her attention. *Don't stare now.* "No, maybe talking is good."

"So, what was the first time?"

She smiled shyly. "If I didn't like you, Mr. Shipley, I'd say you were being a bit impertinent."

"You do like me because I'm so charming." He flashed his roguish grin again. "I know you are dying to talk."

Their deepening camaraderie amazed Sophie. Not ready yet to let all of her walls fall down, she relaxed to a small degree with him. She admitted to herself the loneliness in her heart of late. The ache from missing her parents continued to overwhelm her. Now removed from her comfort zone—home, work and friends—she acknowledged that she missed not having any adult conversation while spending her days with Anastasia. "I was thinking about this story I told your daughter."

"Would you care to share it?"

"It's a bit long, but the moral is that God always protects us and waits patiently as we decide whether or not we want to accept His help. All things are possible with God."

"You sound as if you have trouble believing those words."

Surprisingly his frankness encouraged her to continue sharing. "I used to believe those words, but not now. My parents died…and…I don't know if I can talk about this. I, uh, thought I could." She abruptly stood up and nearly bolted out of the garden, but Sebastian grabbed her hand.

"Please, don't go." Sophie stared at him, speechless. Did he need someone to talk to as much as she did? She probably shouldn't stay, but the wistful expression on his face beckoned her to remain with him. "We can talk about something else."

Slowly, she sat down again. A sudden shyness came over her but she forged ahead. "Anastasia's doing really well. She's so observant."

He only then let go of her hand, and her skin still sensed the warmth of his touch. She tried hard to focus on what he said next. "Do you want to take a walk?"

"Sure." Sophie desperately wanted to run away. She felt drawn to this man and that attraction scared her. It wasn't right. There were boundaries between them—professionally and socially. Yet, she couldn't make herself leave.

Sebastian motioned for her to follow him. "Do you ride horses?"

"No, well, I went horseback riding on a class trip. Does that count?" She laughed and the tension in her shoulders began to loosen.

He chuckled. "Not exactly what I was thinking, but it's a start."

As they continued walking, Sophie figured out their destination. "I didn't know you had horses here."

"There's a lot about me that you don't know."

"Are you flirting with me, Mr. Shipley? Because I don't think that's appropriate behavior coming from my employer."

"Touché," he fired back.

This playful side to Sebastian appealed to Sophie. However, she reminded herself to tread lightly—her heart was in a fragile state and she needed to protect it all costs. *The flirting means nothing. It can't lead to any future relationship.*

He led her to the stables. "I don't remember a time when I've not ridden a horse. Fortunately for me, my father noticed my love for them early on and cultivated it." She listened with interest as he continued animatedly to share the story he'd heard many times from his father. "My mother was a bit nervous about her three-year-old son on a horse, but my father had been compelled to insist on this. He appeased her fears by having me ride on the same horse together with him. That was until he gave me my first horse when I turned six."

Sophie nodded her head. "I can understand your mother's fears. Did you help care for your horse?"

"Actually, I tried, but my efforts probably frustrated the groomsmen more than helped them."

Sophie chuckled and watched as Sebastian's expression became serious. "I never got a chance to pass on my love for horses to Ana." He gripped the railing of the fence surrounding the stables. "She got sick early on, and then my wife died."

The levity between them dissipated into thin air and a somber atmosphere took its place. She wanted to encourage him, but grasped for the right words. What could she say to help him when she had no solution for her own grief? "When Anastasia gets better, you can teach her how to ride."

Sebastian turned to face her. His sad eyes broke her heart. For a vulnerable moment, he appeared defeated. "We can only hope and pray for a miracle." Did he believe his own words? She wasn't certain. He then resumed his stance, staring into the stables.

Taking a risk, she stepped closer and gently squeezed his hand—hoping he perceived her gesture as friendly and not flirtatious. "I haven't talked to God in a long time so I may have no right to say this, but I have peace that she'll be healed."

"Thank you." Two words then he remained silent for an uncomfortable minute. Sophie didn't know where to look. Certainly not at him, so she stared at the horses in the stable. "My wife, Katherine, was a concert pianist. She had a special talent. She would have appreciated your performance for my daughter. You play very well."

His praise stunned her, but intrigued her all the same. Was he angry with her for playing Katherine's piano? She worried she'd overstepped the boundaries in his home. "I'm sorry. I don't know what came over me. I simply had to touch the keys. Then I kept playing. I was hoping not to wake anyone up, but Anastasia came downstairs."

He held up his hand and smiled. "It's okay, Sophie."

"You're not upset with me?" She couldn't handle it if he was disappointed with her.

"No." He slowly spun around and leaned his elbows back on the fence. "I was slightly annoyed you disturbed Katherine's room. Then when I saw how happy Ana looked, I walked away and let it go. Now I see there was no harm done. It could be good for both of you."

Sophie took a deep breath. "Thank you for understanding, and I do apologize for intruding. Please forgive me."

"There's nothing to forgive. I see the same passion in your eyes for music that Katherine had." The sadness she saw written all over his face at the mention of his wife tore at her heart. Like her, he was no stranger to grief.

His direct gaze flustered her. She backed up a step. "I should check on Anastasia."

As he moved closer, her heart skipped a beat. "I have to get back to my office and do some work. I'll walk you there."

They journeyed back to the house in silence. Sophie wanted to fill the stillness with conversation because not talking made her nervous. However, she feared saying the wrong thing, so she kept her thoughts to herself. The situation grew more uncomfortable with every step. She wondered if he found the dead air as awkward as she did. One sideways glance at his face and she found her answer. He appeared uncomfortable too. Much to her relief, they quickly approached the entrance. She promptly excused herself. As she hurried up the marble stairwell in the main hallway, she felt Sebastian's eyes boring holes into her back.

***

Sebastian watched Sophie race up the stairwell. Everything inside him ached to follow after her to continue their conversation—they shared the pain of loss—but decorum and professional boundaries held him back. Running his hand through his hair, he sighed in frustration and returned to his office. He decided to bury himself in work, the one thing proven to maintain his focus. More than he cared to admit, he'd thought about Sophie often. He'd created excuses to interrupt the lessons simply to catch a glimpse of his daughter's teacher. Chiding himself on his foolish romantic notions, he tried to get into work mode again to accomplish something before dinner.

He sifted through contracts on the desk, but couldn't concentrate so decided to check his emails instead. When Sebastian had told his brother he committed to spend more time with Ana, David had stepped up. Thankfully, his brother, continued competently to manage their overseas accounts— negating another trip to England for Sebastian. If their business demanded a trip, Sebastian had promised Anastasia to take her with him. He hoped Sophie shared his excitement in coming along.

Leaning back in the chair, his mind wandered again. He counted the weeks Sophie had spent with them. "Only four and already she's getting into my head." When he had decided to hire a tutor for his daughter, he'd never imagined developing feelings for this person. *If you can even call them that. I barely know the woman. How can I have feelings for her?* Sebastian believed in God and knew his success came from trusting in divine intervention and inspiration. One of his favorite scripture verses came to mind. *Commit your way to the Lord, trust also in Him, and He shall bring it to pass.* He committed all of his plans to the Lord. Past experience taught him to ask God first about His plans and not to maneuver things his own way. When God controlled the situation, He worked everything out for the good of His children. Now came the hard part, trusting his budding attraction to Sophie—to God's direction.

* * *

Sophie tried to read in the sitting area, adjacent to her bedroom, but her mind raced with possible explanations of Sebastian's absence at the dinner table. Jane Austen's *Emma* had no answers for her tonight. Tossing aside her e-reader to the other side of the divan, she stood up in frustration and paced the room. She wondered if he'd felt embarrassed by his vulnerability at the stables earlier. He'd only appeared briefly right as Sophie and Anastasia had finished eating. He told them he'd planned a field trip to the museum for tomorrow. Sophie stared out the window and recalled Anastasia's excitement with her father's plans. After overanalyzing her absentee host, she attempted to push aside any thoughts of tension and confusion and decided to get ready for bed—eagerly anticipating the field trip and another chance to talk to Sebastian. As her mother used to continually remind her, there was no use in borrowing trouble.

Chapter Five

"Isn't that a beautiful painting?" Anastasia stared at it with childlike wonder.

"Yes, it is." Sophie moved forward for a closer inspection. She noticed the deep blue sky and calm seawater. People strolled along the beach. Some sat on towels and blankets. Seagulls flew overhead and scavenged the sand in search of food. The artist had portrayed a brilliant sun, its rays reflected off the gently chopping waves. A bright white boat sailed in the distance toward the horizon. Dolphins splashed and flipped in the water, performing a show for intrigued spectators.

Studying the painting evoked childhood memories for Sophie. Five years old and energetic, she had run across the sand, following her dad as he'd flown a bright red ladybug kite. She loved ladybugs and remembered trying to catch and speak to them as if they actually heard her voice. On that particular day, her mom had sat near their beach house, in front of an easel, painting a picture. Soon tired of running around after the giant ladybug in the sky, little Sophie had pranced over to her mom. She'd leaned her head on her shoulder as she'd watched the painting come to life before her amazed eyes.

"Mom," she had whispered, "That's me and dad and the giant ladybug. You painted us."

"Yes, my darling. I want you to remember this moment forever...how beautiful it is here. God made this wonderful ocean. Remember how much I love you."

"Miss Sophie...Miss Sophie." She felt a slight tug on the sleeve of her white Cable-Knit sweater. "Papa is calling for us to go over there."

"Oh, yes...let's go." She blinked and took a deep breath as she wheeled Anastasia over toward where Sebastian stood in front of some other paintings.

"What do you think of that painting, Miss Sophie?"

"It's quite lovely. The colors are very vivid."

"I agree." Sebastian edged into the conversation. "It makes me feel as if I could jump right in and be part of the painting."

"Oh, wouldn't that be fun?" Anastasia giggled. "I'm glad you brought us to the museum, Papa. I love it here."

Sophie observed Sebastian bend low to kiss his daughter on the cheek. The affection between father and daughter nearly brought tears to her eyes as a reminder of her own father. The fact that Sebastian had decided to take Anastasia to the museum surprised Sophie. Glancing at Anastasia, she could tell that the young girl appeared fine and extremely happy to be out of the house. She knew that Anastasia needed to experience the world and not stay confined to the old mansion. She respected the limitations of the young girl's ailment. However, she thought Sebastian coddled her too much.

"Papa, shouldn't we go to the next painting?" Anastasia's question to her father interrupted Sophie's thoughts.

"Oh, yes, dear."

Sophie noticed how the next painting captivated Anastasia's attention even more. What a great idea to take Anastasia on a field trip! She playfully nudged Sebastian's arm. "A penny for your thoughts."

"I'm sorry for being so forward yesterday. That's not like me."

She wasn't expecting such a forthright response from him. "I wasn't offended. When you didn't come down to dinner last night, I thought you were upset over our conversation."

"I got caught up in my work." He stared down at his feet and she tried to figure out if that was the real reason. "Also, I was embarrassed by my behavior."

This time, Anastasia shook both of their

hands, vying for their combined attention. "Papa, Miss Sophie, are you both okay?"

Sebastian hurried to explain. "Everything's fine. I'm about ready for a lunch break now. Are you hungry?"

"Famished." Anastasia clapped her hands in excitement.

Sebastian reached for her hand. "Where did you learn that word?"

"Miss Sophie explained it in one of our lessons."

Sebastian glanced over at Sophie, and she shrugged her shoulders. "I told you she was smart and yes, I'm famished, too." They laughed and made their way to the café on the third floor.

* * *

After returning home from the museum, Sophie stood next to Sebastian and they watched as Nigel carried Anastasia up the stairs to her bedroom. "I didn't think she would be so exhausted."

Sophie noticed the slight anxiety in his voice. "I'm sure she'll be fine." She touched his arm in understanding. "You should get back to that report you mentioned. I can tuck her in bed."

Relief shone on his face. "You don't mind? My brother texted me three times in the last hour. I guess I forgot to tell him about our field trip today."

She smiled in assurance and waved him on. "It's fine. Go ahead."

Sebastian walked to his office door and then stopped. "Sophie, I'll be at dinner tonight."

Words that made her want to dance with joy, but she contained her schoolgirl giddiness with nonchalance. "Oh, okay."

Sophie passed Nigel in the hallway. "Thank you." He nodded and she vowed again to make the butler crack a smile someday. She entered the bedroom and quietly closed the door behind her. As she carefully pulled the covers up and tucked in Anastasia, the girl rubbed her sleepy eyes and seemed to brighten a bit. "Miss Sophie, can you read to me before I go to sleep?"

"Yes. What would you like to hear?"

"Shakespeare."

"Shakespeare?" Sophie asked, incredulously. "When did you hear about him?"

"Mama used to read from the big brown book on the dresser. I didn't understand all the words, but I loved hearing her read them."

"Okay." Sophie stood up and retrieved the leather-bound book. "Any particular sonnet you'd like to hear?"

"You pick."

Sophie leafed through the book, amazed that her young student enjoyed the Bard of Avon as well. She had fallen in love with William Shakespeare during her senior year in high school and the Bard came in a close second to her favorite author, Jane Austen. "I'll read Sonnet 18. It's my favorite." Sophie finished reading and Anastasia had sat up in attention the entire time.

"Oh, please read one more."

"I think you should rest, little Miss."

"Please…"

"Okay, only one more. I'll read Sonnet 116."

Sophie loved the line: *Love is not love which alters when it alteration finds, or bends with the remover to remove…it is an ever fixed mark…and is never shaken.* Would she ever find that love with her own Mr. Darcy or Mr. Knightley? Maybe reading sonnets of love was not the best therapy for the moment. She needed to keep her mind clear and heart free of emotional attachments toward her employer. "That was lovely." Anastasia's words jarred her back to the present.

"Lovely? I think so too." Sophie reached out and brushed back the blonde curls from Anastasia's face. "Sometimes, I think, for a nine year old, you are very mature. You're a special girl."

She grinned shyly before blurting out, "Were you ever in love?"

"Where did that question come from?" *This little girl is full of curiosity, especially my own personal life!*

"Shakespeare."

"Really...hmm. I was in love, once, but that was a long time ago."

"Was it a really long time ago?"

"Are we playing twenty questions tonight?" Definitely time to start tucking her in again. Sophie was not prepared for a deeper conversation about her past. "I think it's time for you to sleep. You had a long day."

"Okay, but can you sit with me while I fall asleep? Mama used to do that."

"Yes. Now close your eyes."

Anastasia grabbed hold of Sophie's arm. "Wait, I didn't say my prayers yet."

"Oh, but don't you only say them at night before bed?"

"I pray before my afternoon naps, too." The guilt over Sophie's own lack of personal time with God gnawed at her conscience. Without warning, Anastasia closed her eyes. "Thank you, God that you brought me Miss Sophie. I love her very much. Thank you for my wonderful Papa and the trip we took to the museum today. Please keep Grandpapa and Uncle David safe wherever they are right now. Please forgive me for my sins today and keep us safe. Amen."

"Now, go to sleep." Sophie kissed Anastasia on the forehead. She turned off the lamp by the bed and closed the lavender striped drapes to keep out the afternoon sun.

As promised, she stayed until Anastasia drifted off to sleep. Sophie wished she could fall asleep that easily at night. However, her parents' death still weighed heavily on her mind—especially in the quiet night hours when she lay alone on her bed with only her thoughts to keep her company. She watched the young girl and hoped nightmares of her mother's death never haunted her dreams. A tear escaped Sophie's eyes as she thought about Anastasia saying she loved her. Afraid to let anyone else get close, anxiety began to consume her heart. The people she'd loved had died, and she'd built walls around her heart, not wanting to let anyone in. Ironically, her young student had begun to chip away at those walls, and Sophie permitted her free reign. That realization hit her hard like a ton of bricks.

Sophie gently rubbed the soft skin of Anastasia's small hand and watched her sleep. She tried to pray for healing, but a feeling of unworthiness before God hindered her. In quiet frustration, she stood up, turning to go. Anastasia's references to her mother made Sophie uncomfortable. She did not want to cross the boundary lines of comparisons in the young child's mind.

"I'm sure Sebastian would not be happy with that." The very thought of him caused her to smile. A reality check quickly set in and she contained her giddiness then walked into the hall. "He is my employer and nothing else." She had to remind herself to keep a level head. Going to the kitchen for an afternoon snack, she hoped to distract herself with some of Mrs. Andrews' delicious chocolate chip cookies and adult conversation while Anastasia napped.

* * *

Sebastian took a deep breath and picked up the phone to dial his father's number. He'd put off this conversation long enough. Their father-son relationship was decent, but in the last few years, his father's good intentions felt rather overwhelming. After Sebastian's wife had died, he'd pulled away emotionally from his only family—father and brother.

"Hello?" His father's welcoming voice reminded Sebastian of great family memories.

"Good afternoon, Father."

"Sebastian, how are you? I haven't heard from you in a while."

"I know. I should call more often."

"How's the new governess working out?"

Here we go...he did not want to start explaining anything to his father. "You mean, *tutor*? She's doing fine. Ana has bonded well with her."

"What's her name?"

"Sophie."

"So when are you coming for a visit?"

He started to regret making this call. Sebastian

sighed. "Not this subject again."

"I would like to see my granddaughter. She's never been to England."

"Father, you know how I feel about Ana traveling in her condition."

"I understand. Did you speak to David yet? He was trying to reach you before."

"Yes. I answered his text messages. We went to the museum this morning."

"You took the day off?" He heard the disbelief in his father's voice. "Highly unlike you."

Before he started speculating, Sebastian hurried to stave him off. "I wanted to spend time with my daughter."

"Ah, so you can understand why I want to see her, too."

Touché!—Still no way I'm taking my daughter to England right now. "My door is always open. You can come here."

Alexander chuckled. "We'll see. When you make your trip here, bring Sophie with you. I'd like to meet her."

My father is definitely like a dog with a bone over some issues. "I'll cross that bridge if and when I get there." From his peripheral vision, Sebastian noticed Sophie walking by his office. Her presence distracted him and he missed what his father had asked.

Alexander repeated the question. "How is

Ana's health?"

"She's doing fine. Although, she did get exhausted going on today's field trip.

"Is Dr. Macy continuing his home visits?"

"Yes. I should get going now. I'll call you later this week."

"Have a good night, son."

Sebastian hung up the phone and held himself in check. He wanted to find out where Sophie went, but figured stalking constituted grounds for her to resign. His fascination with her gave him pause. "She's not even my type." He pictured his wife, tall and slender with light blonde curls. Sophie's petite form and auburn hair contrasted with his wife's appearance. *Now, how to get back to concentrating on work?*

* * *

"Would you like milk with the cookies? Or I can make tea."

"Milk is fine." Sophie turned to Mrs. Andrews. "I can get it. No need to serve me."

"Oh, pish-posh. It's my job and I love it."

"I can tell. How long have you been with the Shipleys?"

"For a long time." She didn't elaborate but smiled and patted Sophie on the arm.

Sophie left the subject alone, not wanting to

pry. The boundary lines between her and Sebastian's household staff had already been drawn. She didn't want to rock the boat and challenge the status quo. Her own job was on the line and she enjoyed her budding relationship with Anastasia, not to mention her infatuation with Sebastian. "Is it okay for me to go read in the library?"

"Of course, dear. Mr. Shipley wouldn't mind. Go up to the top of the stairs and turn left."

"Yes, I've walked by and have been eager to investigate. I love old books and it appears he has a great collection."

"Mrs. Shipley was an avid reader, especially of the classics."

"I've heard. I read some Shakespeare to Anastasia earlier. She's a bright young girl."

"You're right about that." Mrs. Andrews picked up a tray with cookies and a tall glass of milk. "I'll walk with you to the library. I need the exercise."

Rather than argue, Sophie graciously accepted her hospitality and followed her out of the kitchen. As they passed by Sebastian's closed office door, she couldn't stop herself from staring. She imagined him working at his large mahogany desk. Mindlessly, she trailed after Mrs. Andrews as the older woman slowly started climbing the massive marble steps of the main stairwell. The genial housekeeper continued her conversation non-stop.

Mrs. Andrews set the tray down on a cherry

wood side table in the library. "If you need anything else Sophie, let me know. I'm very glad you're here. I can see how much Anastasia has connected with you." With her usual flurry, she exited the room.

"Thank you." With great anticipation, Sophie spun around and gazed up at the immense assortment of books lining the floor to ceiling bookshelves. With a world of possibilities at her fingertips, she slowly walked by the shelves, running her hand along the spines of the books. "This room is amazing." She enjoyed the new technology of e-books, but holding an actual book in her hands still remained her favorite of the two choices. In awe of her surroundings, she imagined herself as Elizabeth Bennet in Jane Austen's *Pride and Prejudice*. Randomly stopping at the far end of the shelves, she chose a leather-bound collection of 16th Century poetry and settled into a high-backed velvet cushioned chair. Reverently, she checked the index for Shakespeare's sonnets. As she flipped through the pages, a folded sheet of paper fell onto her lap.

Her curiosity piqued, she slowly picked the paper up and began to read it. *My dearest Katherine. You are my special treasure.* Hesitantly she read on, not wanting to intrude on Sebastian's privacy, but his stirring words intrigued her. She sensed the passion he'd had for his wife. Her respect for him grew as she read of his deep love for Katherine and how he desperately wanted to take away her pain and suffering. A tear ran down Sophie's cheek as she respectfully put the letter back in its resting place. She hugged the book to her heart and hoped to one day experience such an intimate love.

* * *

"Papa, thanks for taking us to the museum today."

"You already thanked me, Ana."

"I know, but I had so much fun."

"I'm glad."

"You liked it, too, Miss Sophie?"

Sophie put down her glass of water. "Yes. It was nice."

Mrs. Andrews bustled in at that moment and placed trays laden with roasted chicken, mashed potatoes and mixed vegetables on the marble sideboard. "Enjoy your dinner." Sophie nodded her thanks and turned to observe Sebastian's conversation with his daughter. His affection for Anastasia evidently shone through as he tenderly responded to her incessant chatter. Sophie admired his patience with his daughter—especially for a busy man like himself.

"Did you enjoy your time in the library, Sophie?" Sebastian's question jarred her back into reality. Memories of his words from the love letter to his wife still danced in her mind. "Mrs. Andrews mentioned that she took you there this afternoon."

"Yes. You have a beautiful collection of books. I love to read."

"Ana enjoys reading as well. I think she takes after her mother in that respect."

Wanting to change the subject, she nodded to Anastasia. "What was your favorite part of the museum?" Sophie imagined the wheels turning in the young girl's head.

"I liked the painting of the beach the best. You liked that one too, right?"

"I did. I enjoy going to the shore. It brought back happy memories."

"Can we go to the beach some time, Papa?"

"We'll see, but let's get started on our dinner before it gets cold." Sebastian led them in saying grace and Sophie's mind wandered helplessly back to his romantic letter. With each passing moment, she grew more intrigued by the man who wrote it.

Chapter Six

Sebastian's head bobbed forward as he started nodding off to sleep in the corner of the drawing room. A noise in the hall startled him. Squinting and rubbing his eyes, he heard Sophie enter the room and slide open the drapes on the French doors. She kept the lights off and as he became more alert, he understood why. The glow of the moonlight shone into the room. It was a breathtaking site, even for him. Remaining hidden, he wanted to determine what restlessness brought her downstairs at midnight. She shut the door to the room and then sat at the piano. Her fingers moved skillfully over the keys. Her melancholy song filled the room and it seemed to match the mood of the pale moonlight and surreal feel of the room. Sebastian felt guilty for intruding on Sophie's intense performance, yet her private agony intrigued him.

His heart constricted for a moment with memories of his wife, Katherine, and the sweet melodies she used to play. She had hardly ever played any melancholy songs. Sebastian listened to Sophie and the sad strains of music engulfed the room. He sensed her pain, as if she put her whole broken heart into the song. Leaning his head back, he closed his eyes and relaxed his body. As Sophie continued playing he started to drift off to sleep again. His arm slid down the side of the divan, knocking a book off the table to the right. The noise brought him out of his light sleep and obviously startled Sophie. She stopped playing.

"Who's there?"

He stood up. "Don't worry. It's me, Sebastian."

"Mr. Shipley?"

Sebastian heard the mixture of anxiety and surprise in her voice. He figured she feared his reaction to her intrusion on Katherine's piano. "I'm sorry. I didn't mean to startle you."

"How long were you in here?"

"Since before you came in."

"Why didn't you make yourself known?"

Sebastian hesitated answering. She made a good point. It was rude of him not to make his presence known to her. For selfish reasons, he'd remained quiet. "I don't know. I guess I wanted to stay and hear you play."

"I know we've already talked about this, but are you sure you're not angry with me for playing the piano?"

"No. I've missed hearing the music." He made his way across the room toward the piano. "Though, if I can be honest, your songs are very melancholic. Do you ever play happy songs?"

She tilted her head back. "I do. I've been teaching Anastasia happier songs. I…"

Sebastian touched her arm and grinned. "Lighten up, Sophie. I'm teasing."

"Understood." She quickly moved her arm away. He wished she wasn't so skittish around him. "Maybe we should go to bed now." As soon as the words escaped, Sophie's eyes opened wide and her hand covered her mouth. "I'm sorry. I didn't mean, you know, I meant separately. Okay, insert foot in mouth." Obviously embarrassed, she started walking away.

"Actually sounds like a good idea." Trying to keep a straight face, he watched her spin around with a stunned expression. He held her gaze a moment longer than necessary than burst into laughter. "I'm kidding and only trying to make you feel better."

"Oh. I honestly didn't mean anything by that comment."

"It's fine."

She bid him good night and hurried out of the room. Sebastian watched her flee in a flurry of silken robe and nightgown and couldn't keep himself from smiling. His mind flitted back to Sophie's reaction to his touch. The split second contact even affected him.

With a sigh, he turned back to the piano and ran his hands gently over the keys, glad to see the beautiful instrument in use again. Standing there for a few moments, he finally decided he should make his way upstairs to his room for some much needed sleep—although, after their midnight encounter, he didn't think he'd fall asleep anytime soon.

* * *

The next morning, Sophie came downstairs and entered the dining room. She overheard Sebastian speaking on the phone. Not one for eavesdropping, she tried not to listen, but caught his statement. "I worry about Ana." She thought about stepping out of the room to give him privacy, but he concluded his conversation and joined her at the table.

"That was my father."

"Oh."

"Is Ana still sleeping?"

She poured herself a cup of hot pomegranate tea. "Yes. She seemed exhausted last night, so I'm sure she'll sleep in for a while yet."

"I hope she didn't get too tired from our excursion yesterday. I wouldn't want to be the cause of a relapse for her health."

Sophie wanted to appease his fears. "I think she'll be fine. Getting out of the house is good for her."

"You're right. Why don't you take the day off? I'll stay with Ana today. You've been working hard."

His suggestion caught Sophie off guard. What would she do with an entire day to herself? "I'm fine. I don't need any time off." She reached for the honey and added a spoonful to her cup. Was he actually serious about taking the day off?

"Go and enjoy yourself. Do something fun that you haven't done for a while."

She took a sip of tea. "If you're sure. It's a nice day to take a walk." Oddly unsettled, she went to the serving board to choose her breakfast from Mrs. Andrews' wonderful buffet. All she could think about was how to keep busy the entire day since Anastasia had recently occupied the majority of her time. The remainder of the meal passed in quiet pleasantries.

After eating and then excusing herself, Sophie climbed the stairwell and walked toward Anastasia's room, peeking inside. "You're awake."

"Yes, I am, Miss Sophie."

"Your father is going to spend the day with you."

"He is?" The little girl clapped her hands in excitement.

"Yes." From what Sophie had deduced, Sebastian's work schedule kept him busy so this would be a welcome special day for both of them.

"Are you going to be with us again?" *At least*

she seems to want me to be with them too. The sentiment warmed Sophie's heart. She would feel lost without her little Miss today.

"No. I think you and your father should have time alone together." Sophie came into the room. "Let me help you get dressed."

Anastasia sat up in bed. "Remember, Miss Sophie, I want to get dressed myself."

"Fine, but I'll be right here if you need help."

* * *

Sophie breathed in the crisp autumn air as she strolled down toward the post office. The postman usually delivered the mail to the mansion in the morning and picked up any letters needing to go out. Sophie had finished writing a letter to her aunt and decided to walk the two miles to the post office. She loved the exercise and enjoyed the fresh air. Her aunt Grace lived in Ireland and she had told Sophie she enjoyed receiving her letters rather than emails, so Sophie kept her aunt up to date the way she liked. The last time they saw each other was many years ago when her aunt Grace and her cousins, Erin and Aidan, came to America for a family reunion.

Partial to autumn, Sophie delighted in the sound of leaves crunching beneath her feet as she walked. Childhood memories came to mind of how she and her friends played in the pile of leaves her dad had just raked up. Never once had he grown agitated, but simply joined the children in their fun and jumped in the leaves with them. Afterward, he'd continued making a game of it, convincing the children to get the leaves back into the pile. Thinking about her dad brought on the ever present sadness and she slowly brushed away the tear rolling down her cheek.

Sophie sighed and continued down the path. A rustling in the bushes to her right caught her attention. She laughed as two squirrels chased each other, making noises and running up the tree next to the bush. Fascinated by nature, she tried to impart that love for God's creation to Anastasia. The child exhibited the same eagerness to spend time outdoors as her teacher. Sophie felt a kindred spirit with her young student.

"Will you look at that?" The sight of the squirrels' antics brought some much needed levity to her morning. One of the squirrels laid flat on a horizontal tree branch. It looked like a position a cat might find himself in, but she never saw a squirrel lying like that before. She shook her head in wonder and kept walking.

Anastasia would have loved to see those squirrels. She imagined her gleeful giggles. Sophie wondered curiously what Sebastian planned for the day with his daughter. As she'd predicted to herself this morning, she missed Anastasia already and she'd only been tutoring her for two months now. They'd made a surprising connection in such a short time. Not to mention Sebastian—she pushed thoughts of her employer out of her head as she neared the entrance to the post office. She held the door open for an elderly woman. Then she followed her inside, heading to the counter to purchase postage for the letter to her aunt.

The postal clerk greeted her with a cheerful smile. "Miss Baird, would you like to take the mail too?"

"Sure." Sophie picked up the mail which he laid on the counter. With receipt in hand for postage paid, she thanked him and headed back outside. Sitting down on a bench near the entrance, she quickly glanced through the pile. She didn't like to search Sebastian's mail, but had been expecting a letter from her attorney. She found two letters addressed to her, one from a friend in California and the other piece from her lawyer.

Dreading to revisit painful memories of her parent's death, Sophie sat in silence for a few moments, holding the unopened envelope in her hands. She wiped away the tear rolling down her cheek.

"Are you all right, Miss?" The woman she'd held the door open for earlier, on her way into the post office, sat down on the bench beside her.

"I'm okay, thank you."

"I hope you haven't heard bad news."

"No, I'm fine." Not in the mood for pleasantries, she tried to respond as politely as possible without inviting further conversation.

The woman placed a hand on Sophie's shoulder. "Everything will be all right, dear. You'll see. God has His hand on your life."

Before Sophie thought of an intelligent response, the woman walked away. She stared at the crinkled envelope she'd unknowingly bent in her hand. Taking a steadying breath, she opened it and pulled out the familiar stationary. Quickly scanning the letter, her heart pounded as she neared the end.

"Sell the cottage? He's got to be kidding. I'll never sell." She read on. He advised that her parents' estate broke even, and if she wanted to sell the cottage he knew a respectable realtor.

Sophie smoothed out and folded the letter, then stuffed it back in the envelope. Grabbing the rest of the mail, she stood up. Tears blurred her vision, but somehow she managed to make it back to the mansion. Teardrops kept falling and she hastily wiped them away as she neared the driveway, not wanting anyone to ask questions.

* * *

Sebastian relaxed in the garden on a lawn chair and watched delightedly as his daughter painted his portrait. He pictured the canvas coming to life with each brush stroke as she tried to capture this moment with her father. "Are you finished, dear?"

"Papa, you must sit still. I'm not done yet."

"Fine, but can we talk?" He wanted to maximize each moment with her—no time like the present to have a meaningful conversation with his daughter.

"You can talk, but I'm painting." When her cheeky attitude came out, he recalled memories of his wife. Anastasia got her sassy, yet sweet personality from her mother.

"So, how do you like learning with Miss Sophie?"

"I like her."

"I didn't ask if you like her. I know you do. I asked if you like learning with her. Do you have fun?"

"Of course. Miss Sophie is a good teacher."

"What have you been learning about?"

"Why? Do you want to come to class, Papa?" Her teasing tone made him smile.

"No, Ana. I'm simply interested in everything which concerns you."

Anastasia furrowed her brow and gazed intently at the canvas for a moment, seemingly displeased with her progress. Sebastian's heart nearly burst with pride as he observed her. Making a few more brushstrokes, she stepped back, gauging her work. "I learn a lot, Papa. She teaches me about nature and God's creation. I learn all my science and math lessons, but I love English best of all. Miss Sophie's stories are great."

"I'm glad, dear." Sebastian wanted to get up and give his daughter a hug, but he anticipated her wrath if he moved from his position on the lawn chair. He closed his eyes for a moment and relaxed in the sunlight. Thinking about the past two months, he thanked the Lord for bringing Sophie into their lives at a time when Ana sorely needed guidance. Especially since his business kept him busy, he treasured any time he spent with his little girl.

Anastasia's laughter interrupted his thoughts. "Papa look...there's a blue bird on my easel. It's sitting there, staring at me. Like the one from Miss Sophie's story."

Sebastian recalled his conversation with Sophie about this specific tale and Anastasia's questions about God. "Did you like the story?"

"I did, but I don't think she believed it."

He found it interesting to now get her point of view on this issue. "She didn't believe her own words? Why do you say that?"

"The lesson was that God is always there for us and He helps us not be afraid. He waits for us to take His hand." She continued painting as she spoke. "Miss Sophie never talks about God, like you do or Grandpapa does. So I asked her."

Sebastian involuntarily moved forward. "You asked her what?"

"Papa, please don't move."

He obediently settled back into position and Anastasia told him about the conversation. Fatherly pride welled up in Sebastian's heart as he realized his innocent little daughter had matured into an intelligent young lady. Anastasia painted for a bit longer then announced, with delight, that she finished.

Sebastian strolled over to inspect the canvas. Apparently ignorant of her aptitude for painting, he stared at the portrait, trying not to let his surprise show. Her evident talent astounded him. Guilt assaulted him for having missed so much of her formative years. He promised himself to start prioritizing his time—lessening his hours at work and spending more time with family. In thinking about reprioritizing, his thoughts turned to Sophie. He wondered at how easily he included her with his family, after such a short time.

"Papa, let's go inside and try some of Mrs. Andrews' apple pie."

He nodded and agreed. Somehow, as if by magic, Nigel appeared and helped him settle Anastasia into the wheelchair. Then the butler picked up the canvas and easel, and followed Sebastian inside.

* * *

Sebastian leaned against the ivy covered stone wall when he noticed Sophie strolling aimlessly through the garden. A quickening in his spirit urged him to pray for her. He asked for her heart to soften to God's love and for the Lord to ease the heavy burden she carried. She walked intently toward the Italian style water fountain. Sitting down on the marble wall of the pool, she leaned precariously over the edge to touch the cool water. Sebastian remained hidden as he observed her leaning even closer to put her hand under the cascading water of the fountain. From his vantage point, he detected tears rolling down her cheeks. Decorum advocated that he leave her to this private moment, but his heart compelled him to stay.

"Sophie, are you okay?" Obviously startled, she tipped forward directly into the pool. *Oh no! I should've left her alone.* Sebastian reached out to grab her, but was too late. "Oh my goodness. Are you okay?" Sophie sat with her arms on bent knees, wet hair clinging to her face. For a long moment, she remained quiet and Sebastian stood still, waiting for her reaction. *Do something*—he urged his body to move forward to help her. Earnestly, he leaned over the pool wall and stared at her downturned face.

"That's the second time you asked if I was okay."

Delicately, Sebastian moved the hair from Sophie's face and then quickly pulled his hand away.

Would she even want his help? He'd caused her to fall in. She moved to stand up and he assisted her out of the pool. They both sat down on the marble wall. "I'm truly sorry, Sophie. I can't believe I startled you and made you fall in. That's a first for me."

"There's a first for everything."

"So, what have you been up to today?"

"Just came back from the post office. I've been trying to relax. Actually, I'm beside myself with boredom. I don't know what to do without Anastasia."

Those words made Sebastian smile. "We should get you inside. There's a chill in the air. I don't want you to get sick." He aided Sophie to her feet and solicitously offered his arm as he escorted her toward the house.

"What did you and Anastasia do?"

Sebastian realized she wanted to avoid any serious conversation about herself right then, so he respected her privacy. "We went to the park and got ice cream. We watched a movie back at home. Oh, and Ana painted my portrait."

"Sounds like a fun day and I can't wait to see her portrayal of you."

"Just beware that she'll probably try to get you to sit for your own, as well."

"I have no problem with that."

He wished to extend the walk back to a leisurely stroll rather than an urgent mission, but he knew she needed to get into dry clothes. "Are you sure you're okay?" He shook his head as he asked for the third time.

"That's the—"

"Yes, but this one's a charm."

"Three strikes and you're out." Sophie chuckled. "Honestly, I'm fine. Why do you keep asking?"

"I thought I heard you sniffling before by the fountain."

Sophie glanced up abruptly and narrowed her eyes. "You had to be pretty close by to hear me."

"Guilty as charged. Again, I apologize for frightening you and making you fall into the fountain. I saw you sitting there and didn't know what to say and then I heard you and…"

She held up her hands. "Sebastian, it's fine. Don't worry." She flashed him a reassuring smile—a bit too reassuring for his overactive imagination. "Anastasia's out on the terrace."

He watched her hasten up the grassy hill toward his daughter and sighed. "Oh well, I can't push. *Besides that, old man, Sophie's business is her business and it shouldn't be anything more.*

Chapter Seven

Sebastian stood vigil by Anastasia's bedside. After tossing restlessly in a feverish state, she'd finally fallen asleep a few minutes ago. His paternal instincts to protect his daughter kicked into overdrive. He pulled the down comforter up near her chin and gently brushed back damp strands of blonde hair from her sweat-beaded brow. She moved slightly and rolled over on to her side. Sighing in frustration, he turned to look out the window. Storm clouds filled the ominous sky, mirroring his gloomy mood.

"Sebastian."

He swiveled at the sound of the familiar voice. "Dr. Macy."

"Should we talk out in the hall?"

Glancing at his daughter, he followed the doctor out of the bedroom. "How is she?"

"The fever is very high. We need to keep her cool and hope it breaks."

"It will break, Dr. Macy. We have to believe."

The doctor noncommittally patted Sebastian's

arm. "Come on and get an old man a cup of tea. She's resting now. I'll check on her later."

Leaving Anastasia, even if only for a short time, was the last thing he wanted to do in the moment. Resigning himself that he was powerless to help his daughter, he followed the old family friend down the hall toward the stairwell.

* * *

Sophie's fingers moved swiftly over the ivory keys, pounding out the harsh notes. She played the melody from memory, and the melancholic strains echoed her heart's heaviness. Anxiety over Anastasia's sickness created an emotional upheaval inside her heart. Her attorney had called last night, asking if she'd received his letter. He needed to ascertain her position on selling the cottage. She shared her desire to keep her parents' home. As she had expected, he strongly advised against that course of action due to the costs and financial stress which would become her responsibility. Sophie realized Mr. VanOrden simply wanted to protect her, but his insistence only added to her stress.

As she played, her thoughts wandered to Sebastian—another source of emotional turmoil. Not quite ready to admit her blossoming attachment, Sophie tried with great difficulty to curb any thoughts of him. That proved futile in only seconds. She pictured his warm and caring attitude toward his daughter, and she grinned as she remembered her own fall into the fountain. Living in Sebastian's home and getting to know him better, she'd begun to loosen some of the chains binding her heart. The Shipley Estate was a safe harbor in her mind. However, she realized she stood on dangerous ground if she allowed her feelings to grow stronger. Sophie had never entertained the idea that Sebastian possibly reciprocated these developing emotions. She exhaled a bit too audibly and continued to pound out the notes.

"Are you trying to break my piano?" His voice interrupted her thoughts and her playing.

Sophie glanced back toward the object of her daydreams. "No, only thinking too hard." Regrettably, the words left her mouth too quickly. She cursed her terrible compulsion to say whatever came to mind and divulging too much information. Maybe he'd walk away without asking what occupied her thoughts.

Surprisingly, he kept silent, reclined on the divan in the corner of the room and closed his eyes. Thankful for the mutual desire for silence, she turned back to the piano and continued playing. Part of her became slightly bothered that he so freely invaded her personal therapy sessions. Maybe he actually needed to hear her play. After several more minutes of playing, her eyes started watering. Sebastian walked up to the piano and put his hand on her shoulder. He sat down next to her and began playing a song. Sophie remembered the tune as an old Irish lullaby that her mom used to sing to her.

"You know that song, don't you?" She slowly nodded, and he smiled encouragingly. "Well…"

Taking her cue, she closed her eyes and quietly sang the cherished words. While singing, glimpses of her mother's smiling face came to Sophie's memory. During her early childhood, her mother had sung this song to her before she'd tucked her into bed each night. She sang the final words and opened her eyes as tears ran unbidden down her cheeks. "I'm sorry. You must think I'm an emotional wreck and cry over everything."

"No, I don't think so at all. My nanny sang that song to me and my brother, David, when we were little."

"She was Irish?"

"Yes."

"My mom sang it to me, too." Fear of complete vulnerability stopped her from direct eye contact. "My parents died three months before I came to work for you."

"I'm sorry for your loss."

"It was a car accident." What else was there to say about that awful day? It was the worst moment of her life. In an instant of frustration, she faced him directly. "When does the pain go away?"

She saw empathy mirrored in his eyes. "I don't think it ever completely leaves, but in time the pain will lessen." He gently squeezed her hand. "I understand."

"I know you do."

Sophie heard footsteps coming down the hall and quickly pulled her hand away.

Mrs. Andrews hastily entered the room. "Excuse me, Mr. Shipley...the fever broke. Little Anastasia is awake."

Sebastian jumped to his feet and hurried out the door, but stopped in the hall. "Sophie, please come with me."

She heard the desperate hope in his voice and followed him upstairs.

* * *

Sebastian intently observed Dr. Macy examining Anastasia in her room. After the doctor completed the exam, Sebastian rushed to his daughter's bedside and motioned to Dr. Macy that he'd be out in the hall in a moment. He gently hugged his sleepy eyed child. "I love you, and I'm so happy you're feeling better. Sophie is going to stay with you while I see Dr. Macy."

"Okay, Papa."

Sebastian followed Dr. Macy into the hall and closed the bedroom door behind him. "This is good news, right? The fever broke."

"Yes, it is good, but Sebastian, the increased episodes of fevers and fatigue are troubling me. Maybe we should take her in for more tests."

"You know they couldn't find anything the last time. I don't want to put her through the trauma again, if I don't have to."

"Fine." He held up his wrinkled hand. "I want you to promise me if things continue to get worse, you'll have Anastasia see my colleague at the hospital."

"Very well." Sebastian patted him on the shoulder. "Thank you for coming to the house. I'll call you if anything changes." He watched Dr. Macy leave and hoped he took no offense at the lack of an escort out. Wasting no more time, he returned to his daughter.

For over an hour, Sebastian had remained in the room with Anastasia. He sat in the big armchair near the bed, with his little Ana snug under the plush floral covers and mounds of silk pillows behind her. "I heard mama playing the piano before."

Her statement caught him off guard. "You heard mama playing?"

"I heard the piano." She sounded confused.

"It was Sophie, honey. Remember, she plays."

"Oh, right. I forgot." She giggled, like the sound of music to his ears. When his little girl suffered, he was beside himself with worry and frustration. "Let's have some cookies."

"Mrs. Andrews is not here right now, so we may have to make them ourselves."

She clapped her hands in excitement. Sebastian stood up to pull back the bed covers. "Let me find your clothes so you can change out of your nightgown." Opening the armoire, he picked out tan slacks and a white sweater. Pivoting back to help his daughter, she'd surprised him by managing to climb out of bed by herself. With no help from him, she pulled her nightgown off.

"Ana…"

"Papa, I'm okay. I can dress myself."

Hesitating a moment, he sighed. Especially due to her sickness, he knew she chased after a sense of independence. Her health was so out of her control. *Maybe she needs to feel in charge of something.* "I'll be right back." When he returned a few minutes later, she sat on the bed, dressed and waiting for him. "Let's go, my little Princess."

Downstairs in the kitchen, Sebastian helped Anastasia get onto a stool by the granite island countertop.

"This is going to be so much fun."

"What's *going to be so much fun*?" Sophie asked as she entered the room.

"We're making sugar cookies." Anastasia grinned at her announcement.

"Oh, my favorite. My mom taught me the best

recipe. Do you need help?"

Sebastian closed one of the cherry wood cabinet doors and smiled. "I think we need all the assistance we can get." Sophie joined the fun and started to help gather ingredients. Sebastian paused in turning on the oven. "I don't know where Mrs. Andrews keeps her recipes."

Sophie pointed to her head. "Don't worry. I have it all up here."

"Let's get started already," Anastasia mumbled, while playing with the cookie cutter shapes.

"Aren't we impatient today?" Sophie chuckled.

Sebastian stepped back and observed as Sophie started delegating the operation and Anastasia helped out as best she could. Watching his two girls work so well together warmed his heart. Mentally categorizing Sophie as one of his girls startled him. The special way she interacted with his daughter made him realize how well she fit in the picture. Somehow, she'd flown under the radar and into the heart of his family. Two years had passed since his wife died. In all that time, he'd never once allowed romantic thoughts of another woman to occupy his attention until now. The idea of thinking of Sophie in such a way frightened him because he feared losing the memory of his wife to making new memories with her.

If he became emotionally involved in a relationship with Sophie, he'd run the risk of vulnerability and getting hurt—a peril in all romantic journeys of the heart. He also shied away from testing the waters with Sophie because he was uncertain of her relationship with the Lord. Had she actually accepted the gift of salvation? As a Christian, he respected God's admonition regarding same-faith marriages and not being unequally yoked to an unbeliever. Having had a godly marriage with a fellow believer, he knew the importance of such a union. Suddenly a puff of flour flew into his face. Sebastian coughed and held up his hands in surrender. "Hey what's that all about?"

Sophie chided him. "You're too busy daydreaming and missing our entire baking experience." He watched Sophie and his daughter place the variety of shapes—stars and hearts—on the baking pan.

"What do you say, little Miss, should we sprinkle on some cinnamon? I sometimes like to dip the warm cookies in powdered sugar after I take them out of the oven. Then they're really sugary. I'm sure Dr. Macy would love that." The way she smiled at his daughter warmed Sebastian's heart. He accepted the possibility of Sophie's romantic involvement with someone else. She might not even feel the same way about him—not exactly the drama he was interested in at the moment. Though, deep down, he knew his heart thought otherwise. "We have about nine minutes to wait until the cookies are done."

Sebastian nodded toward his daughter. "Ana, why don't we go into the parlor and I can read you a story while we wait."

"Maybe I should read you a story, Papa. Miss Sophie is helping me with some harder stories and chapter books."

"Sure. Lead the way." He swept his daughter off the stool and mouthed a "thank you" to Sophie as he entered the parlor.

* * *

Sophie hung back as Sebastian exited the room. She enjoyed watching him interact with his daughter. Her eyes clouded with tears as she remembered her father and how he had held her hand. How he'd helped her climb over the rocks that made walking the forest path hard to maneuver for a five year old. They'd often taken walks into the woods and picked berries while he'd sung old Irish tunes and told folk tales of his childhood. In her eyes, he'd been her hero—nothing could stand in his way and she'd felt safe in his arms. "Dad, I miss you so much."

Sebastian called from the other room and she wiped a tear from her face as she hurried to compose herself. The timer rang. "The cookies are done. We can dip them in the powdered sugar in a few minutes." She pulled out the hot baking sheets. The fresh baked aroma brought the inseparable pair back into the kitchen.

A short while later, story time neared its end. Sophie had closed her eyes and lounged on the divan. Anastasia snuggled with her father on the sofa. Sophie listened as Sebastian's deep voice animatedly finished reading the story of *Sleeping Beauty*. "The Prince kissed Aurora, and she woke up from her sleep. The whole kingdom also awakened from the spell. The Prince and Princess got married and lived happily ever after. The end."

"Papa, I love that story. I wish I could be the Princess."

"You are my little Princess."

"No, I mean, when I get all grown up, I want to find a Prince like hers."

"I know God has someone special in mind for you."

"Yes, a Prince like you." She giggled.

Sophie silently agreed with Anastasia's sentiments about Sebastian's prince-like qualities. She wanted to believe she'd met her Prince Charming in him, but dared not hope for the happily ever after story book ending.

Chapter Eight

Sophie stepped up to Sebastian's closed office door and hesitated a moment before knocking. Finally mustering the courage, she tapped the solid wood with her knuckles. She heard his voice beckoning her to come in. Slowly entering the room, she clasped her hands in front of her. "Would you like to come with Anastasia and me on our picnic? I wouldn't bother you, but she was insistent I ask."

"Of course, I'll come. Give me ten minutes."

Surprised yet pleased, she watched as he started tidying up his desk. The mere idea of spending more time with this man warmed her heart. *Keep your voice calm. Don't give yourself away*—remain professional at all costs. "Okay, we'll be waiting outside."

Several minutes later, Sebastian came out the front door of the mansion and Anastasia ran into his arms. "Papa, I'm so glad you're coming."

He kissed her cheek. "I wouldn't miss it, darling. Now let's get in our carriage."

"We're going in the carriage?"

"Yes, Ana. I thought you'd like that surprise." The young girl clapped her hands and watched eagerly as the carriage pulled up.

Sophie leaned close to Sebastian. "How on earth did you manage to get Nigel to pull all this together in a matter of a few minutes? I only just asked you to come along."

"Magic." He grinned.

Oh, how she loved his mischievous grin. Would wonders never cease? She gave him another brownie point for romantic gentleman-like behavior. *Now I can check off riding in a carriage from my bucket list!*

"Where are we going?" Anastasia turned back to ask her father after he assisted her into the carriage.

Sophie accepted Sebastian's hand as he helped her and then he sat down across from his daughter. "Now that we have a carriage ride and don't have to walk, we have a change of plans and can journey farther." Sophie could tell he enjoyed surprising them. "You'll see when we get there. Sit back and enjoy the ride."

Sophie followed his advice and relaxed. Sitting back against the black velvet cushion, she stared out the window. The horses began their slow trot and soon the scene outside exploded in a myriad of colors passing by her view. Blessed with a warm, sunny day, she wished the Indian summer lasted longer. Surprised at Sebastian's willingness to allow her free reign in bringing his daughter outside to enjoy the fresh air as much as possible, she knew her student cherished every minute of it. Sophie loved nature. She saw Anastasia light up with each moment they'd spent outdoors. She'd surmised that Sebastian's fear prevented his daughter from experiencing life, but she saw his perspective changing.

After a fifteen minute drive, the carriage pulled to a slow stop. Anticipation bubbled up inside Sophie's heart. What a wonderful day to spend outside with her two favorite people. Sebastian broke the silence. "We're here. I hope everyone's hungry. We have Mrs. Andrews to thank for this delicious lunch." He picked up the wicker picnic basket and stepped down first. "This is going to be a good day." He assisted both of them to exit the carriage.

"It's so beautiful out here, Papa. I wish I could live outside."

"Sure you do, darling. You love your big comfortable bed too much to sleep outside."

She placed her hands on her hips. "I could do it. It's God's creation, and I love flowers and trees."

He playfully wagged his finger at her. "Flowers don't stick around all year."

"I know, but there's so much to love."

"You've been spending far too much time out here." He joked.

"Not enough time." Sophie smiled and tilted her head.

Sebastian gave an exaggerated sigh. "I don't know about either of you, but I'm starving and ready to eat." Quick to act, he set the picnic basket down and laid out the blanket. "Are you ladies coming or not?"

"Oh, we were enjoying watching you work." Sophie teased him.

"Yes, Papa, you're doing such a great job, we didn't think you needed any help." Sophie chuckled as the young girl followed suit with more teasing.

"All right you two." He raced over to pick up his daughter and carried her to the blanket. He then turned toward Sophie and held out his hands. "Shall I carry you too?"

"No, I'm fine." Warmth crept up her neck and cheeks as she wondered what it would feel like to be embraced by his strong arms. For one second, she yearned to respond affirmatively, but remembered her role as tutor. Reluctantly holding her thoughts at bay, she joined Sebastian and Anastasia for the picnic lunch.

* * *

Sophie pulled her car up to the driveway entrance of the Shipley estate and punched in the security code by the iron gate. When the gate swung open, she drove down the long, tree-lined path which looked more like a road than a driveway. Driving around the side of the mansion, she parked in the garage. As she exited, she shook her head in amazement that she lived in this grand house and had permission to keep her car with the other family vehicles.

Opening the door to the kitchen, she craved a piece of Mrs. Andrews' special meatloaf pie. "I hope she made some. I'm hungry."

"Made some what?"

Not again! Sophie jumped and bumped her head on the refrigerator door. "Why do you always sneak up on me?" She rolled her eyes at him.

Sebastian calmly strode in the room, took cookies from the pantry and bid her good night. "Only picking up my midnight snack. You're the one who's sneaking around. I'll see you in the morning."

How infuriating! Sophie wanted to smack him. As she watched him leave, she wondered how he charmed her at times yet also drove her crazy. Taking a deep breath and rubbing the bump forming on her head, she relaxed and chuckled over the situation. Then she heated up dinner in the microwave and carried it and her bag upstairs to her room. She had just returned from her parents' cottage on an expedition to find her mother's journals and other special belongings. Those journals held valuable lessons and treasures from her mom—she needed to keep those memories in her mind.

* * *

The next day, Sebastian found concentrating on work extremely difficult. His attention kept wandering outside to where Sophie and Anastasia read in the garden. He leaned back in the chair and folded his hands behind his head. "Why can't I stop thinking about her?"

Trying to focus, he shuffled papers around on the desk. Over an hour ago, David had faxed him a contract for his review. *I'm sure he'll be calling soon.* Perusing his brother's additions, Sebastian checked the ones he wanted to keep and scribbled his own changes. David had tried to get him updated with technology, but Sebastian was old school. Much to his brother's chagrin, Sebastian still preferred faxing over email. *One of these days*, David would always say, *you'll start to see things my way.* His thoughts wandered back to their picnic yesterday and he recalled how Sophie laughed and listened so intently to his daughter. Her care and concern for Anastasia was evident in her every action. The best part— Anastasia fully reciprocated the attachment. However, his feelings for Sophie more than complicated the situation.

* * *

"I'm so glad you're my teacher, Miss Sophie."

"I'm happy to teach you. You're a very bright student. It's a pleasure to help you learn."

"Are you going to leave someday?"

More deep questions out of left field which she was not prepared to answer. "Of course not." The moment the words left her mouth, she realized she'd made a promise in haste. Her future in the Shipley household was uncertain. At any moment, Sebastian could decide to enroll his daughter into school. The young girl's ill health was the only reason holding him back. Sophie hoped daily for Anastasia's healing even though that would mean she'd be out of a job. She knew the pain of broken promises and hoped her path enabled her to keep that one to Anastasia.

The young girl stared blankly at the book in her hand. "Mama left me."

Amazed at the fragility of Anastasia's maturity, Sophie reached over and hugged the young girl. One moment wisdom beyond her years flowed from her mouth. The next, her insecurities jumped out and tugged at Sophie's heartstrings. She realized she needed to open up and talk about her own parents' death in order to help Anastasia.

Sophie brushed the stray curls from Anastasia's face. "My mom and dad died in a car accident not too long ago. I can understand the pain you're going through. I know you lost your mother at a younger age than I did, but no time is ever a good time." How horrible not to possess any uplifting words for encouragement. Bringing God into the conversation was not an option—although deep down she knew the young girl needed to hear about His love. All she could offer in the moment was the simple truth that she shared her pain. Her feeble attempt worked because the little child reached up to touch Sophie's cheek.

"Thank you." Seemingly satisfied, Anastasia sniffled and turned back to her book.

* * *

Later on, Sophie offered to help Mrs. Andrews prepare lunch, but the housekeeper shooed her away. Obediently exiting the kitchen, located in the western wing of the mansion, she directed her little charge into the adjoining sunroom. They went in to relax before lunch. Sophie loved this room. The glass panels on the twelve-foot high ceiling opened to allow access for fresh air. She'd never seen a sunroom this big, excerpt for the Ruppert Gardens House she'd visited last spring with her parents.

"This is someone's home." She shook her head in disbelief. "I can't belief I get to live here."

"Did you say something, Miss Sophie?"

"Oh, nothing. I'm simply admiring this sunroom. I love it in here." She took Anastasia's hand. "Did you ever hear your family history?"

Anastasia shook her head, no.

"Follow the story teller into the flower forest and I'll let you in on some secrets I learned from your grandfather's journal." Anastasia eagerly followed her teacher.

In one of her excursions into Sebastian's library, Sophie had found a family history journal, which piqued her interest. She'd learned of the home's origin in the early 1920's and that a fire ruined a major portion of the structure in 1939. Sebastian's paternal grandparents, Edward and Eva Shipley moved to this home from England in 1936, one year before Eva gave birth to their son, Alexander. Sophie remembered reading the words of Sebastian's father in his journal. They'd touched her and reminded her of an old movie.

Edward Shipley came to America to open a second office for their printing business, but still made frequent trips back to England where his brother, Roland, managed the fort. Alexander went to boarding school in England and moved back to the family estate in Stratford to live with his uncle. Roland's wife, Alissa, bore no children so Alexander willingly fell into the family business. Alexander married in 1967 and his father died later that year. Alexander then decided to keep house in America and England. His wife, Cecily, loved flowers and since she spent the majority of the year in America, they built an enormous greenhouse onto the mansion.

* * *

Sebastian chose that moment to come into the sunroom. He stood quietly back while he observed Sophie. He knew his daughter's learning had improved dramatically since Sophie came on board to handle her education. He tried to get a handle on his feelings for Sophie and he pictured his father telling him to go after the young lady and tell her how he felt. "And how do I feel, anyway?" Sebastian asked aloud. "It's not like I can be in love with her." *Leave it alone buddy.*

He heard footsteps behind him. "Mr. Shipley, are you joining the ladies for lunch today or will you be eating in your study?"

"I think I'll join the ladies. Thank you, Mrs. Andrews." She nodded and left to complete the meal preparations.

Sebastian sat down on the divan and finished his coffee, waiting for the history lesson to end. Uncertain about the road ahead for himself and Sophie, he prayed and asked God to take this burden from him and reveal His will. He wanted to walk the path that God directed him along and not move one step ahead or behind. Placing the coffee cup down on the doily on the end table, he leaned his head back. In only a few moments, he dozed off and dreamed he trekked across a grassy field. As he climbed the hill, he needed to shield his eyes from the harsh glare of the mid-day sun. Climbing even higher, he hiked more slowly to keep from tripping over jutting rocks. Finally he arrived at the summit. A lone dogwood stood at the other end of the plateau and he noticed someone resting under the shade of the tree. His legs, like lead chains anchoring him to the ground, made each step labored. The sun blinded his eyes, slowing down his progress.

He finally reached his destination and, even with the sun behind him, the aura around this person hurt his eyes. Though he perceived her form as that of a woman, her identity remained a mystery to him. As he moved closer, the light grew more intense. Seeming to sense his presence, the woman faced him. Sebastian recognized his wife, but she appeared different. When she spoke, he immediately knew her voice. Trying to run to her, the leadenness of his legs held him back.

"Sebastian, you need to let go. Don't be afraid to love again." Then she focused her attention once more on making the daisy flower ring, not saying another word. He swiveled and began hiking down where he'd come from.

Anastasia pounced onto the divan like a cat stalking its prey and embraced her father, startling him from his daydreaming. "Papa, wake up. It's lunch time." He sat up and rubbed his eyes, astonished he'd fallen asleep so easily.

"I'm sorry, Sebastian. I told her not to wake you."

"It's fine. I shouldn't be napping anyway. After lunch I have a lot of catching up to do with my paperwork pile which never goes down." He gave her a crooked grin and stood up. "Ladies, let's eat. I'm joining you today. Hope you don't mind."

"Not at all." He thought he'd detected a pleased smile on Sophie's face.

"That's won-der-ful," Anastasia replied in a singsong voice. "Miss Sophie told me all about our family stories. It was great."

Sebastian glanced at her. "I don't mean to interrupt you, dear, but let's pray first. Then we'll eat and you can tell me everything."

"You think I talk too much, Papa, don't you?" He couldn't help but smile when she gave him a big toothy grin.

He lightly tapped her pixie-like nose. "I wouldn't have it any other way." Mrs. Andrews arrived with their lunch. Sebastian nodded in her direction. "This looks delicious as usual." The housekeeper smiled and went on her way to bring in the rest of the dishes. Sebastian prayed for the meal then turned to his daughter. "So, what did you learn on your journey into the flower forest?" Sophie raised her eyebrows. He'd been caught having eavesdropped on her history lesson. Leaning closer, he tried to redeem himself. "I wasn't listening long. Honest. You saw me. I was sleeping."

"Hmm, exactly what you'd like me to believe."

"Excuse me." Anastasia interjected into their conversation.

"Oh, I'm sorry dear, I got distracted." Anastasia finished sharing what she'd learned on her adventure, and they enjoyed their meal.

* * *

After lunch, Sophie had started reading to Anastasia until the child grew tired and began nodding off. Slowly standing up from the divan, she gently guided the young child's sleeping head onto the flowered cushions. She glanced back at Sebastian and whispered. "I thought you had a stack of paperwork to attend to."

He lowered the newspaper and his piercing brown eyes stared back at her. "I'm taking a break."

"Some coffee break…it's more like a day off."

"You think so? Well, I challenge you to a game of rummy, if you know how to play."

Accepting the challenge with pleasure, Sophie snatched the newspaper away. Boldly taking hold of his hand, she led him over to the game table in the corner of the sunroom. "Bring it on, Mister." She relished teasing him. "My da enjoyed playing cards." She realized she'd slipped up and called her father *da* instead of *dad*. Since she'd been working for Sebastian, she hadn't yet shared much about her heritage. She sat down across from her opponent.

"Your *da*. I see. I thought you had Irish roots. You were born in America, right?"

"Yes."

"Ever been to Ireland?" Shaking her head no, she efficiently shuffled the deck. "You're pretty good at that."

"I told you. My dad loved to play cards. He was a great teacher." The well of sad emotions started to bubble over so she changed the subject. "I presume you were born in jolly ol' England."

"How'd you guess?"

"The accent kind of gave you away."

"Really? I'd hoped no one would notice." He flashed his debonair smile.

Sophie dealt out seven cards each, placed the pile down, and turned over one card. She looked up expectantly at Sebastian and waited for him to make his move. He nodded, checking out his cards. "You can talk and play at the same time, right?"

"Sure."

He picked up a card. "So, do you want to talk about it?" Then he placed the card down on the table.

"That's a little bold. I thought the English people had more manners." She grinned and threw down three aces.

"See, I knew you were hiding something."

"So, what do you mean by *it*?" Sophie hedged. The mood had been light and enjoyable and she hated to spoil it by rehashing her depressing life.

"Why you were crying the day you fell into the fountain?"

"You mean, when you *caused* me to fall in? I don't know. It's your turn."

Sebastian drew a card. Raising his eyebrows, he added it to his hand.

"Didn't you ever learn not to make facial expressions when playing cards?"

"No. I guess I need to learn from you."

"Me?"

"You have the poker face." He placed a card on the table.

The game continued for a time in silence. Should she open up? Did he even want to know about her personal life? Would sharing her story scare him away? Sophie finally offered more information. "That day I got a letter from my attorney and it brought all the overwhelming emotions back. His letter mentioned the issue of selling their cottage, and I am *not* selling."

"Is everything okay now?" The concern she observed in his warm brown eyes nearly was her undoing. *Keep it together. Don't fall apart on the guy...he is your employer after all.*

She nodded in affirmation and laid down a jack, queen and king of diamonds.

"Your parents were born in Ireland?"

"Yes. They came over after getting married. My dad was a carpenter by trade. He built a tiny cottage where they lived until they had saved up enough money and their business expanded. Then they moved to the suburbs." She watched as Sebastian picked up another card. "I truly miss them. I don't know why I can't let go."

"Do you believe in God?"

"Why?" She immediately regretted her defensive tone.

"He's been known to help people in similar situations. I can vouch for that."

"I did, once. I'm not sure how I feel now." Sophie picked up a card. Inspecting her hand, she put more point cards on the table. She sniffled. "I know I'll be okay. They say time heals all wounds, right?" She smiled hesitantly.

"I think I can understand what you're going through. I was angry at God when my wife died." He placed down a ten of diamonds, to her three diamond cards. "I had a dream about my wife just before."

His honest admission touched her heart, but scared her all the same. She hadn't expected their conversation today to become this serious. "Is that an odd thing? Have you had dreams about her before?"

"For a month after she died, I kept dreaming

about her. Then the dreams suddenly stopped. Time does have a way of healing those wounds. I know now I couldn't have made it through without God's help." He held up his hand. "I know you don't need a sermon right now. I'm simply sharing. For some reason, I feel I can be open with you. I hope that doesn't make you uncomfortable."

"No, I'm fine." Thinking about her next move, Sophie drew another card from the pile. Keeping her eyes on the cards in her hand, she hoped her question about him dreaming of his wife, had not pushed the limits of their fragile intimacy.

"She said I *need to let go* and not to *be afraid to love again*." *Apparently, he wants to continue sharing with me.* However, how could she respond to such a comment? He momentarily laid his cards face down on the table and rubbed his eyes. "I thought I had let go. Enough time has passed."

Their conversation had reached the limit of her emotional vulnerability and she needed to stop talking. In her gut, she knew the truth—fear pushed her away from this caring man seated across from her. *Distract yourself with the game.* Sophie picked up the fourth ace from the pile and placed it down with her three ace point cards. She then put her remaining card face down on the pile of discarded cards and won the game. "I told you my dad was good." The somber mood prevented her from gloating too much so she only gave him a slight nod. "I need to take a quick break before I wake Anastasia up for her afternoon lessons."

Sophie stood up and held out her hand. "Great game. We'll have to play again so I can repeat my victory." *What a lame thing to say*, she chided herself. Inside, her common sense berated her silly senseless side. Could she make any more of a fool of herself? *This poor man has bared his soul and I'm still talking about beating him at a stupid game.* She began walking toward the kitchen, but swiveled around. "Thanks for the company and conversation. It was nice." She needed to get away from his piercing eyes before they delved deeper into the depths of her broken heart and realized her budding feelings for him. As far as she was concerned, she couldn't escape fast enough from his presence.

Chapter Nine

Sebastian sat in his office daydreaming again about a certain petite brunette. She ruled his every thought and ran havoc in his daily routine—of course this only happened by his own fault. Sophie had done nothing but simply be the wonderful person who she was and he had fallen for her. However, could he truly trust his emotions? Ever since his wife had passed, his heart had hardened. Sophie had brought the sunlight to begin melting the ice inside him. He recalled her parting comment after they'd played cards the other day. *Thanks for the company and conversation. It was nice.*

"Nice?" Her statement had given him pause for concern. Did she reciprocate his budding feelings? He brought his fist down in frustration on the piles of documents on his desk. Wondering and wishing did nothing for his situation. *Get back to work, buddy.* He tried to focus on the many emails clogging up his inbox.

Over an hour later, he scrolled through the

favorites on his cell phone to find David's number then pressed *call*. When his brother answered, Sebastian heard an unusually noisy commotion in the background.

"Hello?"

"David, it's me. I've changed my mind. I'm taking a flight in the morning, so tell Hilde to prepare my old room."

"Why the sudden change of heart?"

Now was not the time to bare his soul. "I want to be there to support my little brother." Sebastian hedged.

"Sure. I know when you're lying. Are you running from something?"

"No." He deliberately kept his answers short.

"Running from *someone*?" His brother's teasing tone grated on his last nerve.

"No, David. I have to go, but I'll see you tomorrow." Sebastian abruptly ended the call and swiveled in the chair. Immediately he regretted his irritation. *Just because I'm confused doesn't mean I have to take it out on my brother.*

His stomach tightened in a knot. He could only imagine Ana's protests when she found out. His desire to flee from the emotional web he'd entangled himself in—superseded the need to stay with his daughter and negated his promise not to leave her behind. If she traveled with him, Sophie must come too. However, he wanted space and time to clear his head. Desperation to figure out the meaning behind his dream about Katherine—and where his heart wanted to lead—motivated him to move forward. He surprised himself that leaving his daughter came so easily for him. Rationalization took the lead and he ignored the guilt over going on this two-week business trip. "It will pass quickly and Sophie is quite capable of caring for Ana in my absence. Now for the hard part." Taking a deep breath, he left his office in search of his daughter.

* * *

Sophie finished grading Anastasia's history exam while her young student worked studiously on math word problems. As Sophie reached the end of the paper, she sensed a presence in the doorway of the library. Without glancing up, she teased. "You're stalking us again. Shouldn't you be getting your work done?"

"You'd be surprised what an hour of focused energy can accomplish." His deep chuckle filled the room. "I guess I have been dilly-dallying and not getting much accomplished all week."

Anastasia ran over to her father and gave him a big hug. "Hi, Papa, how are you?"

"Hello, sweetheart, I'm fine, but I needed to speak to my two favorite people."

Not too excited about his statement and the

serious tone to his voice, Sophie's shoulders slumped. Anastasia verbalized Sophie's racing thoughts. "Is something wrong?"

He caressed his daughter's cheek. "No, dear. Everything's okay. Uncle David needs me to come see him and help with work."

Sophie watched with a heavy heart as the young girl clung to Sebastian's arm. "Papa, please don't go."

"It's my business, too, young lady. I have to go this time." He poked her lightly on the nose. "I'll treat you ladies to dinner tonight. I need to go into town, and then I'll be back to pick you up later. We can go to Lucia's."

"We get to dress up?" So quickly the young girl went from sad to giddy.

"Yes, you do."

Sophie tilted her head in his direction. "How dressed up are we talking?"

Sebastian gave his charming smile. "It's dressy. Is that all right?"

"I think I can manage." As she said those words, her mind started rummaging through her closet. Did she even have something fancy enough to wear out to dinner?

"Great. I'll see you ladies at seven." Like a man on a mission, he left the room.

Sophie gulped in a breath of air and turned toward Anastasia. "Please finish your last problem and then we'll play dress up." She leaned back in the chair and muttered, "I'll try to get presentable if that's at all possible." *Wouldn't now be a great time for Sebastian to take me on a shopping spree like Richard Gere did for Julia Roberts in Pretty Woman!*

* * *

Sophie had been frantically searching through her closet, not finding anything suitable to wear to dinner, when Mrs. Andrews had come to the rescue. At the exact moment of Sophie's ultimate frustration, the housekeeper happened to pass by in the hall. "Are you all right, dear?"

Holding several dresses haphazardly in her arms, she helplessly gawked at Mrs. Andrews. "No. Actually, I'm trying to find something to wear to dinner tonight."

"Where is Mr. Shipley taking you?"

Sophie responded without questioning her assumption. "To Lucia's."

Mrs. Andrews nodded her head and put down the basket of folded laundry she'd been carrying. "Ah. I see. I'll be right back." In no time flat, she reappeared with an exquisite blue velvet gown in hand. Sophie looked at her quizzically as the housekeeper held the dress out to her. "Try this gown. I think you're the same size."

Realization dawned on Sophie and panic set

in. "I can't wear her dress, especially not to dinner with *him*."

"It was a gift to Katherine from her father-in-law, but she never got a chance to wear it."

"What about Sebastian? He'll recognize the dress."

"I doubt he'll remember it." The eager older woman took the other dresses out of Sophie's arms and pressed the velvet gown in their place. "He was on an emergency business trip one year during his wife's birthday."

Sophie shrugged, still uncertain if she should wear Katherine's dress. "If you're sure."

"I am. Katherine was taller than you, but this isn't a floor length dress. It should fit fine. If you need help getting ready, let me know. I'll be cleaning the guest rooms on this floor."

"Thank you so much."

"No problem. Glad to help." She gently patted Sophie's arm then started humming as she picked up the laundry basket and left the bedroom.

This generous act of kindness by Mrs. Andrews made Sophie think again about *Pretty Woman*. Sophie stood in front of the long oval mirror and held the dress up against her body. *Maybe I can start to believe in fairy tales after all.* She couldn't think of a time when she'd worn a gown this elegant. Butterflies fluttered in her stomach. Was she getting too dressed up for dinner? *Well, he did say wear something dressy and Mrs. Andrews heard where we're going.* Thinking about Sebastian's possible reaction to this gown brought goose bumps up and down her arms. Time to get ready—she couldn't wait!

***

Trying to occupy his mind as he waited for the ladies to come downstairs, Sebastian sat on a bench in the foyer reading the newspaper. Due to his nerves, it was a futile attempt, but he needed to do something to keep busy while waiting. *This emotional turmoil is precisely why I need to leave for England.* Hearing soft footsteps on the stairwell, he tilted his head up. As he tried to control his gaping mouth, he figured his eyes must be wide as saucers. The sight of Sophie wearing a royal blue velvet gown nearly took his breath away. *No, don't focus there!* Staring a bit too long at her neckline, decorum forced him to rein in his wandering eyes and focus on her beautiful face. He appreciated how she had pinned her hair up on top of her head—leaving little ringlets hanging down. The way the curls gently wisped at the nape of her neck made him want to kiss her delicate skin.

Sophie and Anastasia continued down the stairwell and Sebastian tried to regain his composure. He held both of his girls' coats over his arm, but didn't think he could move to help either Sophie of Anastasia slip into them.

"See, Miss Sophie, our fashion show was a good idea."

"You had a fashion show?" He realized his question sounded lame, but nothing intelligent came to mind. Thankfully, Sophie stepped into action, took her coat and helped Anastasia get bundled into her own.

"Yes. It was fun." Sophie grinned mischievously and boldly took Sebastian's arm, leading him toward the front door. "You owe me dinner."

"Owe you?" Somehow he managed to squeak out.

"Yes, since I beat you at rummy."

Distractedly, he reached for Anastasia's hand. "Well then, let me escort you ladies to your carriage."

"Papa, we can't ride in the carriage to Lucia's. It's too far."

He chuckled and gently nudged her chin. "I know, my princess. I was trying to be funny." Glad his answer satisfied his inquisitive daughter, he led them out to the waiting car.

Anastasia chattered the majority of the drive to the restaurant, which pleased Sebastian. Still preoccupied by the beautiful and intelligent woman in the passenger seat, he hoped to recover his wits and engage in clever conversation during dinner. As he listened to Sophie speak with his daughter, he realized with certainty that his two-week trip came at the perfect time. Anastasia would be in good hands, and especially with how he'd reacted to Sophie's appearance tonight—a short separation would do them all some good.

* * *

"Did you want to order a drink?"

"Oh, I'll have an amaretto sour and could I also have a glass of water with lemon?"

The waiter left and Sebastian peered at her. "Are you okay?"

"Yes, I'm fine." Nerves still raged inside Sophie. She had noticed Sebastian's guarded appreciation of her appearance tonight. His reaction pleased yet frightened her at the same time. *Stop overanalyzing every detail in life. Be thankful and enjoy the moment.*

"Papa, can I get the spaghetti and meatballs?"

"Sure, honey. You can have whatever you want."

Sophie glanced at the menu again. "So, what's good here?"

"I love everything on the menu!" Anastasia excitedly gestured with her hands.

Sebastian nodded toward Sophie. "This has been her favorite restaurant ever since we came here to celebrate her fifth birthday."

To be included in their special place touched

her heart. "Thank you for inviting me along to dinner tonight."

"My pleasure."

Anastasia then vied for Sebastian's attention as she began chatting about her schoolwork. Sophie took the chance to once again peruse the menu selections and finally decided on the chicken cacciatore. Shortly after, the waiter returned to take their orders. When he left, Sophie noticed the serious expression on Sebastian's face. "Ana, I know you aren't happy I have to leave again."

She pouted, hitting her small fist against the table and nearly knocked over her glass of water. "Do you really have to go?"

He gave her a stern, warning look. "Yes. Uncle David needs my help, honey." Sophie tried to read his hesitation, but remained silent and let him continue. He turned toward her. "I'll be gone for two weeks. You'll be fine. Mrs. Andrews and Nigel will be there, and they can run the household with their eyes closed."

She nodded. "I'm not worried."

"Thank you." He leaned forward, placing his elbows on the table. "I had not expected to have to leave again for a while."

"Can we go with you?" Anastasia asked.

Sophie saw his eye twitch. She'd never seen him this high-strung before. Obviously bothered about something, he'd chosen not to divulge any further details other than the necessary ones. He reached out to hold his daughter's hand. "Not this time, Ana. I know I promised you could come, but I'll be back before you know I'm gone."

She brought her other hand to cover his. "Okay, but I'll miss you very much, Papa."

The waiter innocently interrupted the sentimental moment and brought the salads to the table. Bowing their heads, Sebastian then said grace. When Sophie opened her eyes, she noticed a tear running down Anastasia's cheek, which the little girl quickly wiped away. A sense of relief mixed with a twinge of sadness overwhelmed Sophie over Sebastian's announcement of his trip. She hoped his absence would give her breathing room—to figure out her own feelings and try to focus on her job.

Chapter Ten

Sebastian had been in England for over a week now and he called home every day at five o'clock in the evening. Sophie knew Anastasia eagerly anticipated those calls. When she honestly admitted her true feelings, she earnestly longed to hear his voice as well. Last night Anastasia's health had taken a turn for the worse again. Sophie had decided to sleep on a cot in the young girl's bedroom in case her condition worsened even further. If she saw no improvement soon, she'd need to call Sebastian and she dreaded that call.

Sophie pulled the covers closer to her chin and tossed restlessly on the narrow cot near Anastasia's bed. Her dreams whisked her away in unfairytale-like fashion to a funeral for an unknown person. Hesitantly, she sat down in one of the seats toward the back of the crowded room. The minister started the eulogy—speaking flowery words about the deceased. Focusing in, she tried to decipher the identity of the person. However, as she listened more closely, she realized the minister neglected to mention the deceased's name. Growing more curious by the minute, Sophie quickly scanned the crowd for familiar faces. Not seeing anyone she knew, she wondered why she even attended this funeral.

One by one, several people took turns standing up to share memories about their friend and family member. Uncomfortable, Sophie desperately wanted to leave, but instinct compelled her to look into the coffin. The moment came for the processional to begin and people said their final good-byes to the deceased—then gave condolences to those left to grieve. She waited in line for a while and glanced over at the family. Blinking in astonishment, she saw Anastasia standing next to an older gentleman and a woman with long blonde hair. Sophie's heart started beating rapidly as she approached the coffin. With slow hesitant steps, she finally peered inside. Gaping in shock, she saw Sebastian's lifeless body. Unable to think clearly, she could only stare at him. Her uncertainty held up the line of mourners. Anastasia walked closer to the coffin. "He's my father."

"I know, dear."

"What's your name?"

She blinked and stared incredulously. "You don't know who I am? It's me, Sophie." *How could she not know me?*

"I don't know who you are, ma'am. I must get back to my family."

Those words knocked the wind out of her and she gasped in shock. What was happening? She gripped the cold, metal edge of the coffin. "Sebastian, what's going on?" Her leaden feet prohibited her from moving away. Finally, she found the strength to leave.

A cold, clammy hand reached up to grab her hand. Startled, she whirled back toward the coffin. Sebastian whispered, "Help me." He's dead…how is he talking? She screamed and then suddenly woke up.

Sitting on the cot, she sighed and rubbed her face.

"What an awful dream!" Pushing back the covers, she stood up to turn on the lamp on the end table. She kept the light dim so she could check her young patient without waking her. The feverish burning of Anastasia's forehead alarmed Sophie. Then she noticed the young girl's swollen neck. When she gently moved her head, Anastasia moaned. "Honey, wake up. Tell me where it hurts."

"My neck and my mouth," she whimpered. "I'm so hot, Miss Sophie. My teeth hurt." Closing her eyes tightly, she rolled onto her side.

Dread exploded inside Sophie's heart. How would she tell Sebastian? *This news and the separation from his little Ana will crush him.* "I'll be right back." With a fire in her belly, she raced downstairs to call Dr. Macy.

Sebastian arrived home at two in the morning from a party held at the home of one of his clients. Not particularly fond of social events, he understood their necessity toward achieving success in his business. In his haste to get out the door earlier, he'd forgotten to bring his cell phone with him. Now, he needed to check for any messages, but he longed for a good night's sleep as soon as possible. *Who would've thought being the social butterfly could exhaust a person so much?* Making a quick stop in the kitchen first, he filled a glass with water. When he reached the top of the stairs, he walked passed David's room and his brother practically tackled him in the hallway. Water sloshed from the glass onto his hand.

"Are you trying to give me a heart attack? What are you doing?"

The serious expression on his brother's face immediately caught Sebastian's attention. *Something's wrong.* His heart began beating rapidly and he forced himself to pay attention to what David was saying. "Ana's tutor called."

"What happened?"

"She's taking her to the hospital."

The simple statement propelled him into action. "Oh, no." Sebastian rushed down the hall to his room and placed the glass of water onto the dresser near the door. He heard his brother hobbling after him. David had broken his leg the past week in a skiing accident while vacationing in Switzerland— hence, the reason for his absence from the party tonight.

David huffed in exasperation and leaned on his crutches in the doorway. "Aren't you even interested to hear the message?"

Sebastian stopped in his tracks and blinked. "I guess that would be helpful, huh?"

"She has a fever. Her neck is swelling. Her mouth hurts and she's in pain."

My Ana…why did I leave you? Feelings of helplessness and guilt settled upon him like a vice grip on his gut. How could he have so selfishly left his little girl? Sebastian furrowed his brow. "Neck swelling…have you heard of it before?"

"No, but that's why she's going to the emergency room. Sophie called Dr. Macy and he'll try to make it to the hospital."

"I have to get there." Snapping back into action, he frantically threw clothing onto the bed. *I know I'm forgetting something.* He rummaged through the dresser drawer. *Where is my passport?*

"Sebastian, relax. I booked you a flight. You leave at four this morning. So you'd better hurry up and get to the airport. I took the liberty of having Daniel pack your bags." Sebastian stared at his younger brother in astonishment and then noticed his suitcase and carry-on bag to the right of the door. *Will wonders never cease?* "I know. I don't often show it, but there's a brain working up here." David grinned boyishly, pointing to his forehead.

"Are you going to be okay? I can't leave you, either." He nodded toward David's cast.

"I'll be fine." He waved Sebastian's concerns away. "I'll probably move down to the guestroom for now, to be closer to the office. Daniel can assist me with the stairs. Or," he smiled mischievously, "I can use the dumbwaiter, like we did when we were kids."

The shared memory made Sebastian smile and he shook his head. He walked over to his brother and placed a hand on his shoulder. "Thank you."

* * *

Sophie had been playing the waiting game with the doctors at the hospital for over two hours now. The EMTs had rushed Anastasia to the emergency room at eleven-thirty in the evening. Sophie had tried to call Sebastian's cell phone as soon as she realized she needed to get his daughter some medical attention. When she got his voice mail, she'd scrolled through her contact list for the emergency contacts he'd given her. She'd dialed his home number in England, hoping not to aggravate whoever answered the phone this early in the morning.

Dr. Macy approached, interrupting her rambling thoughts. "Hello, Sophie. I got here as fast as I could. My wife and I were visiting her relatives in Lancaster."

She eagerly welcomed him. Waiting by herself had been lonely. "Thank you so much for coming. I appreciate it. I hope she'll be all right." The weight of the world rested on her shoulders. She desperately missed Sebastian in that moment.

He clasped her hands between both of his. "She's in good hands right now. We have to trust in God." She noncommittally nodded in agreement— yet, her spirit rejected his simple faith. The barriers erected around her heart still stood strong and kept her hope caged tightly inside.

* * *

"What is taking the doctor so long?" Sophie complained as she stood up to stretch her arms over her head. Pacing back and forth, she then slumped again into the hard plastic chair.

"Hence, one of the reasons why they call this the waiting room, dear," Dr. Macy chuckled and patted her arm.

"I know, but I'm worried. She didn't look good, she was in a lot of pain, and her fever was so high."

"There's no use worrying until we know all the facts."

His words failed to comfort Sophie. How

could he be so matter of fact? Then she remembered whom she was speaking to—a doctor. Of course he responded in such a way. Wishing Sebastian there with her wouldn't make him appear any more quickly, but that didn't stop her from hoping. The responsibility for his daughter fell into her lap, yet she was powerless to help. "I wish I could do something."

"You can take a walk. I'll stay here in case the doctor comes back with any news."

She weighed his suggestion, wondering if she should take a break. Her cramped muscles begged her to get moving. "Okay. Do you want coffee or anything to eat?"

"Coffee is fine, with two sugars." He reached into his wallet to give her money, but she held up her hands.

"It's on me. Thank you again for coming. I'll be back." Sophie left to head down the hallway. The cafeteria had closed for the night and wouldn't open again until the morning so she settled for the vending machines. Heading toward the vending area, she turned left around the corner but ended up near the chapel.

The sound of someone weeping inside caught her attention. Her feet frozen to the cold tile floor, she wanted to run away—but a calm voice in the room held her captive. "It's okay, mom. God will help us through this."

"I know." The woman's confident answer

tugged at Sophie's heart. "We should get back to your father. We don't know how much time he has left." Sophie quickly spun away from her eavesdropping as the mother and son exited into the hallway. In their absence, she entered the room and quietly sat down in one of the pews. Closing her eyes, she took a deep breath. After sitting in silence for a few seconds, approaching footsteps from behind startled her.

"I'm sorry for interrupting." Sophie recognized the woman's voice—the mother with the son. "I forgot my Bible. Could you reach it for me? It's on the floor." Sophie bent down to pick up the well-worn Bible and handed it to the woman. She noticed tears clouding her eyes. "Everything will be fine if you trust God again. He knows your pain."

Those words and the peaceful expression through her tears, made Sophie jealous. How could this woman have such peace and assurance in God while her husband fought for his life?

The young boy called for his mother and she turned to leave, but first nodded to Sophie. "Thank you."

Sophie watched her go and then stared up at the cross near the altar. The dam holding back her emotions broke and the tears flowed. She still couldn't wrap her head around the fact of seeing true peace emanating throughout a traumatizing experience. Would she ever find the same sense of calm through life's storms?

* * *

When Sophie came back to the waiting room, she noticed the attending physician walking away from Dr. Macy. Anxious to hear the news, she quickened her steps. She hoped for a ray of sunshine in this hopeless situation.

"I was about to send in the calvary."

I guess I have been gone for a while. Sophie nodded and handed him his coffee. No time to waste on further pleasantries, she needed to know if Anastasia would make it through this. "What's the diagnosis?"

"We were already aware Anastasia had a compromised immune system, hence her consistent weakened state and susceptibility to illness. Such a compromising immunodeficiency is a predisposing factor of Ludwig's angina."

She nearly zoned out as he explained in physician jargon. "Excuse me, what?"

"I'll explain." Dr. Macy responded to Sophie's outburst. "Sometimes this disease can occur without any precipitating factors, but with Anastasia, it did. Ludwig's angina is a disease where the submandibular and sublingual spaces are inflamed, most often occurring in children with dental infections. It's frequently life threatening."

"I did not understand one word, except for *life*

threatening." She rubbed her forehead and tried to focus as he continued.

"It's a bacterial disease that impedes the airway, swelling the neck, causing fever and a general malaise and dysphasia."

So much for focusing—Sophie reached her limit as the gracious listener. "Enough of this doctor mumbo jumbo." She raised her hands in frustration. "Is she going to be okay?" Dr. Macy cringed at her words. "I apologize for sounding rude. I'm simply very worried, and I can't sit still when I hear words like *life threatening.*"

"Sometimes this disease can be fatal, but it was diagnosed in time, and the doctor is starting an aggressive intravenous therapy of antibiotics. She'll have to go to the ICU tomorrow. The prognosis is good. The doctor thinks she'll make it through without any complications. In regard to her immunodeficiency, he thinks it's something she'll grow out of, but only time will tell."

The prognosis is good. Those words stood out and gave her hope. "Can we go see her?"

"Yes, but we can't stay in there long, since it's getting late and most of the patients down in the ER are sleeping. Since she's a child, though, they're going to allow one family member to remain."

"I guess I'll be staying then. Let's go in. Is she awake?"

"Yes, but very sleepy."

Somewhat disoriented with the myriad of issues weighing on her shoulders, Sophie remembered Sebastian and spun around. "Oh, wait. I need to pick Sebastian up from the airport soon. His flight is due in shortly. I can't stay."

"It's okay, she'll be fine, Sophie." Dr. Macy patted her arm reassuringly.

He led her back toward the nurses' station. Sophie thanked God for Anastasia's speedy recovery. Her thankful response surprised her, but she shook off any depth of thought about faith. The only thing which occupied her mind, in the moment—asking permission to see her little Miss.

* * *

The flight attendant stepped out into the aisle and asked everyone to pay attention as the captain needed to make an important announcement. *That doesn't sound so good, but maybe I'm being a bit melodramatic. I'm sure nothing's wrong...and I'm groggy from sleeping.* Sebastian shifted up in the seat and hoped for the best with this announcement. "Ladies and gentlemen, please remain seated and belted in. We are experiencing extreme turbulence. I urge you to stay calm. The flight attendants will be around to make sure everyone understands all safety instructions and is comfortable."

Okay, not so good! His first instincts led him

to pray. "Lord, protect us." Three whispered words which brought him peace only because of whom he spoke them to. In his heart, he knew God was able and had a plan even if the plan might not be what Sebastian wanted to hear.

A few harried minutes zipped by while the flight attendants bustled about, making sure the passengers remained calm. Suddenly a loud bang rang out from the back of the plane and the lights flashed off. In the darkness, the commotion started. Sebastian's only recourse was to close his eyes and pray God revealed His glory—showing favor and saving them. With urgency, thoughts of his daughter flashed before his eyes. He needed to get to her. *This can't be my final moment.* Desperately he longed to wrap his arms around his little Ana. His thoughts roamed to Sophie and he ached for a second chance in life to test the waters of love again.

Chapter Eleven

Thankfully, Dr. Macy waited down the hall to allow Sophie a few moments of privacy with Anastasia before she left to pick Sebastian up at the airport. As she observed the sleeping child, she found it hard to believe the doctor's prognosis of a full recovery. Her emotions played tug of war in her heart. The gentle tugging of the Holy Spirit urged her to place complete trust in the all-powerful heavenly Father who knew all and saw all. However, she held back from taking such a leap of faith. She still stood at the bottom of the ladder—too afraid to climb to the top and jump into her Father's waiting arms. Trying to hide the despair from showing on her face, she lightly squeezed Anastasia's hand and kissed her forehead. Sighing in frustration, she shook her head and exited the room to locate Dr. Macy in the waiting area. "Do you agree with Dr. Matthews' prognosis?"

"We can only hope for the best and need to give God—and the medicine—time to work. He has not forgotten this precious one, and we can believe for a miracle." In her mind, God failed to significantly figure into the equation. Medicine must be the answer to Anastasia's complete healing. She knew God existed and had once placed complete trust in Him, but she'd burnt the only connection she'd had to her faith. Listening to Dr. Macy ramble on about *God this* and *God that* only irritated her even more.

The tone of the conversation reminded her of the boat ride with Sebastian and Anastasia when the young girl had declared that God had healed her. A sudden heaviness on Sophie's chest threatened to overwhelm her. She needed to escape the confines of the hospital. "I should go." Speeding off, she got halfway down the hall before glancing back. "I'll leave my cell phone number with the nurses' station in case anything changes."

Dr. Macy nodded and saluted her with his aged hand. "I'll be staying, dear. I cleared it with the head nurse."

She had not been expecting that, but his decision to stay eased some of the pressure on her chest. "You need some sleep. Your wife must be worried."

"I called her with an update. I'll leave when you get back with Sebastian. What time was his flight?" *No use fighting him, he'd already made up his mind.*

"He had a four a.m. flight, and it's midnight here. So that means it's five a.m. in England.

Hopefully his flight left on time."

"When is he scheduled to land?"

"In Philadelphia at four a.m. So, I guess I don't have to leave yet."

"No, but you should go home and get some sleep. Have Mrs. Andrews wake you up, if you don't think you'll get up on time."

"Okay, but what about you?"

"I'll sleep in the lounge chair in Anastasia's room. Maybe by the time we all wake up, Ana will have woken up, too."

"Maybe." Despite her dismal perspective, it was difficult not to latch onto his optimism. "Thank you again for coming and staying. You're a good friend to this family."

"And now, a friend to you, as well." His contagious, lopsided grin warmed her heart. She smiled in return and hurried down the hall.

* * *

Back at the mansion, Sophie entered her bedroom and closed the door behind her. Following Dr. Macy's advice, she had requested that Mrs. Andrews wake her up in two hours. She hated disturbing the housekeeper while she slept. However, she knew she needed an extra push, aside from the alarm clock to wake up. The emotional and physical stress of the entire ordeal had begun to take its toll on her. As expected—though groggy—Mrs. Andrews had given her ever-cheerful smile and agreed to wake Sophie.

Slipping under the covers, a sudden urgency to pray for Sebastian overtook her need to sleep. Fighting the raw emotion of the moment, she wanted to completely disregard the impulse. Then she remembered the words of the woman at the chapel and spoke hesitantly into the darkened room. "I'm not sure my prayers matter anymore and I don't understand this urgency to pray, but please, God, keep Sebastian safe. Anastasia needs her father. I need him too." Tears spilled from her eyes and she closed her eyelids tightly as wet lashes brushed against her cheeks. She continued her silent prayers until moments later when sleep finally claimed her.

Exactly two hours later, Sophie heard a knocking sound in the distance and pulled the covers up, trying to drown out the tapping. *Ignore it...you need more sleep.* A light shake on her arm roused her and she groggily opened her eyes. Squinting, she made out Mrs. Andrews' form standing by her bedside. "Sophie, dear, it's time." *The dreaded words*—instead, she wanted to hear, *go back to sleep.*

Memories of childhood days complaining to mom rushed back to her and she grumbled. "Do I have to?"

"Yes, you do. I feel like I'm back forty years telling my little Jake to get up for school."

"Well, I don't want to disappoint you." Sophie rolled over again. "We gotta make this real, so I should ignore you and go back to sleep."

"Oh, that was never a good experience for Jake. I'd drag him out of bed."

Throwing the covers off, she slowly dragged her legs over the edge of the mattress. "I get the message."

"Do you want me to call a taxi?"

She waved her concern away. "No, I'll be fine."

"Are you sure?"

"Yes, I'll be okay after a quick, cold shower…and maybe a cup of green tea to go." She clasped her hands and fluttered her eyelashes at the housekeeper.

"You don't have to sweet talk me. I'll be happy to make some, especially if it'll keep you awake. We don't need you getting in any accident now." She turned to walk out of the room.

"I'll be fine, really." *I don't know what I'd do without that woman!* Her feet still dangling over the edge, she fell back onto the fluffy down comforter and sighed. *Don't stay down here too long*, she warned herself. The coziness of the warm bed beckoned to her. A minute later, and with great effort, she dragged herself from the bed into the bathroom. A cold shower would definitely do the trick.

Sophie parked her car and walked across the parking lot toward the terminal. She double-checked the paper with Sebastian's flight information and headed to the entrance for Gate A. As she continued down the long, wide corridor, she noticed how busy the airport was, even for this early in the morning. Glancing up at the ceiling, she observed missing tiles and dangling wires. *What a mess…I hope none of those tiles fall and hit me or anyone else in the head.* From behind, she heard hurried footsteps and a man caught up with her. "Gate A…this way?"

He only said a few words, but his thick accent—Indian, she guessed—made her pause for a moment, as she tried to understand him. "Oh, yes, that's where I'm headed."

He nodded, and then quietly fell into step with her as they strode down the hall. A moment later, curiosity got the best of her and Sophie surreptitiously glanced over at him. She detected a decisive determination in his eyes. *He's definitely a man on a mission.* He carried a bouquet of roses in one hand and a newspaper in the other. They came upon the elevator and as she suspected, the man followed her inside. Reaching for the second floor button at the same time, they shared an awkward moment with hesitant smiles and then she ended up pressing it. As soon as the doors slid open, the man motioned with his hand for her to exit. Sophie nodded and exited. He then quickly picked up his pace and brushed passed her, walking into the crowded waiting area.

Sophie scanned the room and saw no available seats. She then walked over to the terminal gate and leaned up against the wall separating those waiting, from the entrance to the gate. One or two flight attendants walked by and a few minutes later, a captain exited the gate. From a side-long glance, she noticed her Indian friend meandering through the crowd, like a bubbling brook, seeking direction. Most people politely answered his request for assistance. Although one man rudely cut him off before he had a chance to finish asking his question. *Poor guy*—she had enough on her plate to deal with, but if he received another harsh rejection, she planned to step in. Finally, a little old lady took pity on him and guided the man over to the flight schedule. Sophie smiled as the woman hooked her arm with his and tried to help him locate the flight he needed to find. *Exactly what I should be doing.* Sophie realized she needed to check on the status of Sebastian's flight.

Her cell phone rang as she walked over toward the screen showing the flights. "Hello?"

"Sophie, Sebastian—" She heard Dr. Macy's frantic voice then the call got disconnected.

"I hate cell phones." Shaking her head in frustration, she dialed his number then pressed the send button. He called her back simultaneously.

Fearing the worst, she hurried to answer the call. "Dr. Macy...what's wrong? Is there a change with Anastasia?"

"She's in the same condition. It's Sebastian." Two words which rattled her to the core and set her heart to pounding.

"What do you mean?"

"I was reading the Bible and talking to Anastasia, when I decided to check my cell phone messages. Remember I shut my phone off." He was rambling again and it nearly drove her mad to discover the point to this conversation.

"Yes."

"Well, Mrs. Andrews left a message. She said Sebastian called home when he was on the plane. Something happened."

Like a horrible action sequence in a movie, devastating images flooded her mind. "I don't understand. Did they crash?" Sophie blurted those words out then realized where she was and stepped away for more privacy. The woman, whom she had been standing next to, turned sharply, obviously very interested.

"Let's not get worried without cause."

Was this man insane! "Without cause?" She exclaimed, then took a deep breath. *I need to calm down. Getting frustrated will get me nowhere fast.* "Okay, what did she say?"

"She said he sounded calm, but something

happened. There was some loud bang in the rear of the plane, and he mentioned the pilot had explained they were experiencing extremely turbulent weather conditions. His message was all very choppy, which is understandable."

Pent up emotion from the events of the last twenty-four hours threatened to spill over in that moment. Helplessness suffocated her—she could do nothing to help either Anastasia or Sebastian. "What do we do now?"

"Can you check to see what the flight schedule says? Are you near a screen?"

"Yes, but you don't honestly think it's going to say flight 724 crashed, do you?"

"No, but please check."

Try turning down the sarcasm a notch, she reminded herself...*Dr. Macy only wants to help.* "Fine." Silently, she walked back toward the screen. Quickly scanning each line, she desperately searched for his flight number. Seconds later—which had actually seemed an eternity—she found it. "Flight 724...delayed."

"I figured as much." He spoke with such peace that she wanted to reach into the phone and shake him. Didn't he get it? Sebastian's plane could have crashed over the ocean. He could be dead and Dr. Macy acted like nothing had happened. "Since you're not a relative, I don't think you'll get very far discussing the status of the flight with airport personnel. I'm surprised David hasn't called yet to tell us he got a call." She heard him sigh. *Maybe he does realize the gravity of the situation.* "Give me some time, and I'll try to find out what's happened. Are you okay to drive?"

His question shocked her. "You want me to leave?" Panic nearly brought her to her knees. "What if he's coming?" She glanced at the terminal gate, but it was empty. *Please, Sebastian...please come back to us.*

"Stay if you want." His calm tone helped center her back to the present. "I'll call you when I know something."

"I'll be waiting." Sophie ended the call and wanted to slump to the floor in despair. Instead, she chose to sit in the empty seat she just spied and closed her eyes—trying to pray.

* * *

Every time a new flight landed and passengers exited the gate, Sophie's heart quickened. Expectantly, she longed to see Sebastian waltz down the hallway. Reality continued to dash her hopes. A masculine hand lightly touched her shoulder, and she almost jumped out of the seat. Her Indian friend quietly sat next to her. *Now is not the time for small talk or helping you find your flight number.*

"I'm sorry for startling you."

Okay, so he's actually going to start a conversation. "No problem." Before she thought to put the filter on, her helpful nature popped out. "Do you need help?" Immediately she regretted asking and silently berated herself for speaking without thinking.

"I think you do." His decisive tone gave her pause. It wasn't too long ago that this man appeared lost and unsure of himself as he asked people for help. She stared at him questioningly, then saw the same spark in his eyes which she'd seen earlier—he was still a man on a mission. "I heard what you said, *he's not coming.*"

His comment wasn't creepy enough to raise the hairs on the back of her neck, but still made her wonder about this guy. "Yes."

"Is he your husband?"

"Oh, no—"

"He will be fine. These are for you." With a genuine smile, he handed her the roses he'd been carrying this entire time.

Sophie's mouth dropped open. Complete confusion set in. What on earth was going on? "You were waiting for her."

"I just found *her*. God will watch over Sebastian."

If she could look at herself in a mirror right then, she knew she'd see a gaping mouth staring back at her. He knows his name? Impossible. Who was this guy? Chills shook her body and she closed her eyes in shock. Seconds later when she opened them, she watched as the man simply walked away. She couldn't let him leave without an explanation. He then headed toward the elevator rather quickly.

"Wait. Wait." She called, hurrying after him. "Who are you?"

"Just a friend, that's all."

Reaching out her hand, she tried to stop the door from closing.

"Trust in God." With those three words, the door slid closed and he was gone.

Sophie leaned up against the cold marble wall and this time she slumped to the ground in defeat. A few people passed by—no one saying a word. In her crouched position on the floor, she rested her head on her elbows for what felt like hours. When her cell phone rang, she glanced at the time and realized only thirty minutes had elapsed. The third ring jolted her back to some semblance of action. She recognized the number. "Dr. Macy!"

"Yes, dear, it's me. They found him."

"Oh, God—" *Please let him be alive.*

"He made it. They rushed him, along with half the other passengers to the hospital. There were some casualties."

"What happened?" Knowing he was alive gave her a second wind. She needed details now. Gone was the Sophie who had been fearful of hearing bad news—like someone half-hiding behind a pillow while watching a horror movie. *Thank you, God...he's alive.*

"The plane crashed over the Atlantic and the airline decided to take the passengers back to England."

"England!" She'd hoped to see him soon and to find out their reunion would have to wait made her want to pout like a child.

"Yes. They were on the British airways, so they went back. They had only been about two and a half hours into the flight when they began experiencing turbulent weather patterns. The captain thought they would have to reroute the flight and had advised the passengers of the situation. Shortly after that, I was told there was a malfunction and the plane crashed."

She started zoning out again with Dr. Macy's long-winded explanation and thought of her Indian visitor. "He said he'd be fine."

"Excuse me?"

He's never going to believe this. Sophie took a deep breath and explained her unusual visit. Even while sharing the details, she couldn't stop marveling at the odd encounter.

"Maybe he was an angel."

His suggestion threw her for a loop. "An angel...I don't think so."

"They do exist, you know."

"I don't know." She hoped he refrained from a

theology lesson.

"How else did he know Sebastian's name?"

"Well—" He had a point there, but she still wasn't ready to accept the theory of an angelic encounter.

"Come to the hospital and we'll figure out what's going on."

"Is Anastasia awake?"

"Not yet, but she will be." She latched onto the assurance she heard in his voice. For the moment, borrowing his faith would have to suffice.

"Dr. Macy?"

"Yes?"

"Don't you think we've had enough excitement lately?"

"I believe so, and I discussed that very thing with God this morning." His chuckle made Sophie laugh. "Come on back, dear. I'll be waiting."

"You're the real angel." Relief flooded her voice. Even though Dr. Macy had his eccentricities, she didn't know what she'd have done without his steady encouragement. "I'll see you soon."

Chapter Twelve

Sophie sat in the waiting room of the children's ICU—her new temporary home. *This certainly is a nicer waiting room than the one down in the ER*. Anastasia still had not woken up, but her fever had subsided. Resting on the arm of the sofa, Sophie curled her legs up on the cushions. Somehow, she had managed to convince Dr. Macy to go home to his wife. She welcomed his support, but could tell the time away from home had been wearing on him. Thankfully he left without argument. Soon she planned to call David to find out any updates on Sebastian's condition, but first sleep beckoned her name. Leaning her head back and stretching out her legs, she quickly drifted off to sleep.

In her dream, she entered an old Victorian style home and climbed the stairs toward the bedroom on the second floor. She slowly opened the door of the first room on the right. Stepping inside, she recognized it as her childhood bedroom, although situated in a different home. Drawn to the familiar floral print comforter, she fell back on the bed and stared up at the ceiling fan. The circular motion lulled her to sleep. Later on, someone tugging on her arm woke her. Quite disoriented, she groggily opened her eyes and saw her mother and father standing at the foot of the bed. Their peaceful expressions warmed her heart and they extended their arms for a hug.

Sophie sat up and dropped the teddy bear she'd been holding as she slept. Darting off the bed, she eagerly embraced her mom and dad. "We're safe with Jesus." *Was she saying goodbye? No, don't leave me again.* Her eyes watered and she could no longer hold back her emotional outburst. Her mom held her at arm's length, then leaned closer to wipe away the tears on her wet cheeks. As quickly as they'd appeared, they vanished from the bedroom.

"Ms. Baird, wake up." *Who is calling me? Where am I?* Sophie opened her eyes and saw someone standing over her. *Mom, is that you?* "Ms. Baird...Anastasia is awake."

Slowly sitting up, she tried processing this information through the haze. "Awake?"

"She's asking for you." When the truth finally dawned on her, she jolted into action and followed the nurse down the hallway toward the children's ICU.

Her heart began beating faster and she nervously smoothed her wrinkled blouse. The moment she'd been waiting for had arrived—all she wanted to do—wrap her arms around her little Miss and share this reunion with Sebastian. She wiped away a tear that started to fall. "Thank you, God." She recalled the Bible story of Peter's release from prison. The followers of Christ had prayed and believed for Peter's freedom, and when it happened, they stood in disbelief. Her reaction mimicked theirs. Opening the door with a flourish, Sophie smiled and greeted Anastasia. When she entered the room, the young girl responded with an even bigger smile. In her haste to hug her, Sophie nearly tackled the nurse standing near the bed, checking her patient's vital signs.

Ignoring the nurse's stern expression, Sophie reached over to gently caress her young student's face. "I am so happy you woke up. I've missed you."

"I've missed you and Papa, too." She glanced at the doorway. "Is he here?"

How on earth should she answer her? Sophie hesitated. She knew the question was coming, but now that Anastasia asked it, she feared divulging the whole truth. Anastasia only just woke up and to tell her now about her father—impossible in Sophie's eyes. "No, he's still in England." She hated hiding the facts from her, but it was the only option in the moment.

Another nurse poked her head into the room. "Ms. Baird, you have a phone call at the front desk."

"Thank you." She patted Anastasia's hand. "I'll be right back."

At the nurses' station, Sophie picked up the phone. "Hello?"

"Sophie, it's me, David. You weren't answering your cell phone."

"My battery is low and I turned the phone off. I forgot my charger at home. Have you heard any news?"

"Not yet. I haven't had any success getting straight answers. They said there's a lot of confusion right now with the number of passengers coming in from the emergency flight. I'm going down there."

Sophie remembered David had mentioned his broken leg. "Will you be going alone? It must be hard getting around on crutches."

"My father will be going with me. Is there any improvement with Ana?"

Sophie smiled when he said *Ana*…just like Sebastian did. "I was about to call you. She woke up a short while ago."

"Wonderful news." His concern and affection for his niece was evident in his voice. "Oh, Hilde is trying to get my attention. I think I have a phone call. Maybe it's the hospital. I'll call you later. Tell Ana I said hello and can't wait to see her."

He definitely is a fast talker! "And when is that going to be?"

"When you bring her to England."

Is he crazy? I can't take Anastasia out of the country right now. "I don't think that's happening any

~ 157 ~

time soon."

"We can talk later. I should take this call."

"One more thing," Sophie began.

"Yes?"

"What do I tell Anastasia? She asked if Sebastian was here."

"With limited details it's best not to say anything. I don't want to hinder her recovery."

"I was thinking the same thing but wanted to get your opinion."

"Give Ana my love. I'll call you."

Handing the phone back to the nurse, she thanked her and walked toward Anastasia's room. *Hopefully she doesn't ask any more questions about her father.* "Oh my, Mrs. Andrews!" Suddenly she remembered she'd forgotten to call her with an update. Turning her cell phone back on, she paused in the hallway. Leaning up against the wall, she dialed Mrs. Andrews' number.

"Hello?"

"Mrs. Andrews, it's me, Sophie."

"What's happening? No one tells me anything."

Sophie smiled as Mrs. Andrews complained. She'd noticed that the housekeeper tended to exaggerate at times. "I'm sorry. Anastasia woke up, and David is still trying to find out more on the status of Sebastian's condition. I promise I'll let you know anything that happens." Hopefully Mrs. Andrews accepted her apology. She hadn't purposefully neglected to call her.

"Thank you, dear. I know you're dealing with a heavy load right now."

She heard understanding in the older woman's voice. "I'll talk to you soon. I'm going back to see Anastasia." Her phone beeped—only five percent power left. *I guess I'm shutting it off again.*

* * *

"Does my Papa know I was sick?"

Great, another loaded question she was not prepared to answer. *Okay, here goes nothing.* Sophie took a deep breath. "He knows you're in the hospital." She hesitated and silently apologized to David for getting ready to deviate from his advice. *How do you tell a nine year old that her father was in a plane crash?* "He was coming here, and his plane had an accident."

"Like a crash?"

"Yes, like a crash."

Anastasia's eyes widened in shock and she leaned forward. "Is he okay?"

"Yes, but he was hurt, and is in the hospital too."

"He's here?"

"No, actually, he was closer to England, so he's in a hospital there."

"Is he hurt a lot?" The anxiety in her voice touched a chord in Sophie's heart.

"We don't know." She gently squeezed Anastasia's hand. "I spoke to your Uncle David, and he and your grandfather are going to the hospital to check on your father. I'm sure he'll be fine. We need to have faith."

She noted the tilt to Anastasia's head and quizzical expression on her face. "Believe, God, you mean?"

"Yes."

"You do believe, Miss Sophie."

She held up her hand to stem the young girl's enthusiasm. "Well, don't get too excited yet, but I'm coming around slowly."

A nurse came into the room interrupting their conversation. "Miss Baird, you have a phone call."

"Thank you." She turned to Anastasia. "Maybe it's your Uncle David again." Stepping out of the room she made the familiar trek down the hallway to the nurses' station.

She picked up the phone. "Hello?"

"Sophie, it's me, David."

What's the news?"

"He has head trauma, a sprained wrist, and a few bumps and bruises."

"That's all you know?"

"Yes. Don't worry. The doctor said Sebastian was one of the lucky ones. I'm going back in to check on him now. I'll call you in a bit."

"*Lucky ones.*" Sophie repeated those words quietly after she hung up. What would she have done if Sebastian hadn't been one of the *lucky ones*? *Get it together*, she chided herself. Anastasia needed someone strong and encouraging right then. Entering the room, she braced herself for more of the young girl's questions.

"Was it Uncle David? Is Papa all right?"

"Yes. He said that your Papa hurt his head and sprained his wrist."

"So, he's going to be fine." She visibly relaxed into the pillows and smiled. "I was afraid, Miss Sophie."

"I know, honey. You're being very brave right now. Your father would be proud of you. There's nothing to worry about now." She decided to change the subject. "How are you feeling?"

"Good, but tired."

"You have had a bit of excitement this last hour. I can step out for a while and let you take a nap."

"Can you wait here with me until I fall asleep?"

"Of course." Sophie moved the chair closer to the bed. She brushed back the blonde curls from Anastasia's face and watched as she closed her eyes. Her breathing became steadier and she slowly nodded off to sleep. Once certain Anastasia slept soundly,

Sophie quietly left the room and walked down to the nurse's station. "I'm going for a walk outside, but I'll have my cell phone on in case you need to reach me."

"We have your number."

"Thanks." Hopefully her battery lasted until she got home again to charge it. Entering the waiting room, she excited through the glass doors into the small greenhouse.

Strolling along the perimeter, her mind raced with thoughts of Sebastian and her relief that God spared him. Her heart empathized with a deep sadness for the families who lost loved ones in the crash. Only by God's grace was Sebastian spared. The pathway led her to a fish pond, and she sat down on the stone bench. Even with the evidence of God's grace, she still held back from completely surrendering her heart again to Him. However, the thawing had begun. Yet, she grew weary with the waiting game. She wanted to be reunited with Sebastian and have Anastasia healed. Many times, frustration got the better of her— patience was not one of her virtues. In the past she had *helped* some situations along, but now there was nothing she could do except to wait. Anastasia's assuring words from the other day that God had healed her came to mind.

"God did heal her. The antibiotics seemed to work." Then Sophie realized Anastasia had meant complete healing from her immune deficiency as well. She observed the fish swimming in the pond and wished for the freedom to trust God completely. Maybe one of these days she'd find true peace again.

* * *

Sebastian opened weary eyes to see David and his father enter the room. "Hello, David. Hello, Father." His throat ached and voice cracked when he spoke.

"Here, let me get you some water." David juggled his crutches, the plastic pitcher and cup—nearly giving Sebastian a bath—when Alexander came to the rescue.

"Thank you." Sebastian managed to say, holding back his laughter at the comical scene. He took a sip of the refreshing water and shifted gears to more serious ground. "I need to know about my daughter."

"I spoke to Sophie before coming here. Ana is awake and doing well. I don't know all the details yet. Do you want to talk to Sophie? She can fill you in on the specifics."

"Yes." When he tried to sit up in the bed, the quick movement made him dizzy. "Whoa, brother...you don't need to go anywhere." Thankfully, David guided him back to the pillows. "I can call her. Hold on." Sebastian watched as David dialed her phone number then he smiled. "We're a sorry bunch. You and Ana are in the hospital...me and my leg—and your governess—infecting you with lovesickness."

Not exactly amused with his reference to Sophie, Sebastian simply stared back at his brother. What could he say in retort? Not much, considering, his head still felt fuzzy and he had a pounding headache.

"Here you go." With a smirk, David handed him his cell phone. "We'll wait outside."

Sebastian nodded then put the phone to his ear. "Hello, Sophie."

"Sebastian?"

"You sound surprised."

"I am. It's nice to hear your voice."

He couldn't agree more with her words—her voice a healing tonic to his ailing body. "It's nice to hear you too. I wasn't sure I'd ever see you or Ana again." Rather than ruin their limited conversation time with depressing thoughts, he decided to change the subject. "How's my Ana?"

"I'm sure David told you she woke up?"

"Yes. Have you had any word from the doctor?"

"Not yet. He's due to make his rounds soon. Are you all right?"

Sebastian heard the concern in her voice, and it warmed his heart. "Yes, if you consider a splitting headache and a sprained wrist and some bruises fine. I'm one of the fortunate ones. I can't even imagine the grief of all those families who lost loved ones. Does Ana know what happened to me?"

"I'm sorry, Sebastian, but I told her about the crash." Her words came out in a jumbled rush and he needed to focus extra hard to understand her. "I did mention you're fine. I hope you're not mad. When I spoke with David, we agreed that I wouldn't tell her anything yet. Then she asked about you and wondered where you were."

When Sophie took a breath, Sebastian managed to jump back into the conversation, approving her actions. "You did the right thing. I would've done the same if I were in your shoes." Reluctantly, he needed to end the conversation. He couldn't leave his father and brother out in the hallway for hours. "David's waiting with my father to come back in the room, so I should probably hang up soon." With spur of the moment inclination, he plunged ahead. "Sophie, would you mind bringing Ana to England, as soon as she gets better? I need to stay here, and I'd very much like to see her and you, too." He waited for a tense moment, listening to the silence.

"If that's what you want, I'll bring her as soon as the doctor gives the approval for her to travel."

He breathed a sigh of relief. Simply knowing his daughter and Sophie would be in England shortly, made the entire situation more bearable. "Thank you, Sophie. You don't know how much that means to me." Suddenly timid, he hurried to end the call. "I'll talk to you later, okay?"

"Sure."

Sebastian called out. "I know you can hear me, little brother, so please feel free to come back in."

David smiled as he walked into the room with their father. "I'm not saying a word."

"Good, let's keep it that way." He handed the cell phone back to David. "I'm tired. Do you both mind if I rest for a while?"

"Go ahead, son." Alexander nodded to David. "Maybe we should leave."

"Do you want us to stay?" David asked.

"You can go. I'll let you know when they release me." After they left, Sebastian leaned back into the pillows and closed his eyes. He could still hear the screams from fellow passengers and feel the heat of the flames from the burning plane. *Will I ever forget those sounds and images?* Closing his eyes tighter, he whispered a prayer and attempted to exchange those horrible thoughts with images of Sophie and his little Ana strolling through the garden at home.

Chapter Thirteen

Anastasia's health had rapidly improved and the attending physician signed her release papers, recommending follow up care with the family physician. With her immunodeficiency disease in remission, the young girl's energy level had jumped through the roof. During the past week, Sophie barely kept up with her liveliness. The amazing transformation pleased Sophie beyond what words could express. Anastasia had resumed her studies with fervor. As a teacher, Sophie relished watching a student soak up knowledge like a dry sponge—with a fierce desire to learn more—validating all of her efforts.

Bundled up in her suede winter coat, Sophie set out for a walk. Spending time walking outdoors always brought her great pleasure and a relaxing time to think. Just as upside-down yoga poses offered a new perspective on life, that's how she viewed walking. A few months ago, brown leaves had covered the ground, but now she walked on a light dusting of snow.

Not yet prepared for the near arrival of Christmas, days had flown into weeks and she'd lost track of time. Sophie considered Christmas her favorite holiday. Memories flooded her mind of when she'd helped her mom bake and decorate cookies. The cookie making projects benefited their family and friends. Sophie's mom always shared the Christmas story while they made memories in the kitchen. Her most favorite Christmas tradition was when she and her father went to the local tree farm to pick a Christmas tree on the first Sunday in December.

Thankful she'd decided to wear her tan hiking boots for traction in the snow, she trekked carefully along the path. Curiosity over the Shipley family holiday traditions occupied her thoughts. Would she be included in those festivities? She certainly hoped for an invitation. Now that Anastasia felt better, Sophie feared losing her job. Of course, she wanted her student to excel and live a normal, healthy life— and to participate in the socialization of school. However, the thought of not seeing Sebastian or his daughter any more deeply saddened her and she did not want to get to that road any time soon.

* * *

Later on, Sophie lounged on the divan with Anastasia in the family room. They watched the movie, *Sabrina*, the original version with Audrey Hepburn. Sophie peeked down at Anastasia and noticed her rapt attention. The young girl soaked in every word and action. Originally, Anastasia had declined the offer to watch the movie, instead wanting to go outside. The snow then started falling more heavily in the last hour. Not willing to take any chances with a relapse in her health, Sophie wanted to avoid any outdoor excursions for the present moment.

Mrs. Andrews bustled into the room with her usual flurry. "Sophie, David would like to speak to you." She handed her the cordless phone.

Sophie nodded her thanks and lowered her voice as she answered, trying not to disturb Anastasia's movie watching. "Hello, David." She spoke cordially to him, but in her heart wished Sebastian had been the one calling.

"Hi. Why are you talking so quietly?"

"Anastasia and I are watching a movie."

"Oh. Anyway," he changed the subject faster than a jack rabbit in flight. "Sebastian is doing well. I've been holding him under lock and key. It's actually quite hilarious." When he laughed, she heard some of Sebastian's signature laughter in him. *They're definitely brothers.* "We're two invalids over here. How's Ana doing?"

"Great."

"So, when are you coming to visit Sebastian?"

"I'm not. Anastasia isn't ready yet." The

young girl looked up at the mention of her name. Sophie made a funny face, then gently turned Anastasia's head around with her hand so she faced the television again.

"I think Sebastian sorely misses his little girl."

"He hasn't said another word about us coming since we talked when he was in the hospital. I also spoke to him earlier today."

"Of course he's not going to tell you that, Sophie. I don't know if you've noticed, but he does not easily ask for help or let on when he needs something." She sensed the seriousness in David's voice.

"I have noticed."

"So, how are you doing?"

There he goes again with changing the subject. "Me? Why do you want to know?" She could feel herself getting defensive and didn't relish the sound of it, like chalk grating on a blackboard. She hated for David to think of her as a petulant child.

"My dear, Sebastian's too afraid to ask for himself."

"And he didn't ask you to find out either…you're meddling." It was amazing how freely she shared with David. *Must be that brother thing again.*

"I guess so. I have another call. I have to go. Please think about flying out here, soon, okay?"

"I will. I simply want to be certain Anastasia

is ready to make the trip." They said their good-byes and Sophie tried hard to focus her attention on the movie—much too difficult a task, of course. Her thoughts wandered to the object of their conversation. Did Sebastian truly miss her? Was David on target with his perspective on his brother? Only time would tell and she hoped the answer to both questions was the affirmative.

* * *

"Sophie, do you need anything? I'm headed out to get some groceries."

"No, I'm fine, thanks." She watched as Mrs. Andrews nodded and briskly left the front parlor.

Sophie turned back to the chair where she'd left her e-reader and the eBook of *Sense and Sensibility,* another one of her favorites by Jane Austen. Earlier, she'd brought down her crocheted blanket, a Christmas present from her mom. Snugly wrapping it around her, she settled comfortably into the oversized high-backed chair. When she'd first entered the parlor half an hour ago, Nigel had solicitously asked her if she wanted a fire lit in the fireplace. He'd barely waited for her response before getting a welcome roaring fire started. She hadn't yet gotten him to crack a smile, but she still kept trying.

Mrs. Andrews bustled back into the room carrying a tray of hot chocolate and cookies.

Sophie glanced up from her e-reader. She'd only read a few pages. "You *don't* have to fuss over me."

"Anastasia's sleeping so I have to take care of someone. I hope you like the cookies."

She bit into one. "Oh, they're good. What kind are they?"

"They're called Speculaas...Dutch almond, paste-filled gingerbread cookies. I learned some European cooking from my time spent in Holland, Germany and England back in my younger days."

"Wait a minute...I thought you were going to the store."

"I am, dear. Now read your book and relax."

"Thank you." Turning her attention back to the eBook, she eagerly entered the world of the Regency Era in England—their carriage rides, lords and ladies, governesses, soirees and life in the small towns. If she could time travel, she'd definitely visit their world. Ever since she'd picked up her first Jane Austen book her junior year in high school, everything from this time period had fascinated her imagination.

After reading for two hours about the exploits of Elinor and Marianne—the Dashwood sisters—Sophie closed the tablet cover with determination. Why not bring Anastasia to England to see her father? The young girl was feeling better and she could think of no reason not to take her. *Besides*, she thought, *I'll get to see Sebastian again!* Her mind began racing with plans. She wanted to surprise Sebastian, but needed David's help.

* * *

Sophie stared at her suitcase experiencing the dreaded fear that she'd forgotten to pack something. With no idea how long Sebastian planned to stay in England, she wondered how much to bring. Thankfully, Mrs. Andrews had offered to pack Anastasia's clothing. Her heart racing, she glanced at her watch. "Oh, great, we'd better hurry up." As she walked down the hall, she heard the housekeeper chatting with Anastasia.

"I'm excited to see my Papa soon."

"I'm sure you are child."

"I'll miss you, Mrs. Andrews."

"I will miss you, too."

Sophie walked in on the last comment. She observed the housekeeper wiping away a tear and the tender scene brought tears to Sophie's eyes too. "Are we almost ready?"

"Yes, Miss Sophie." Anastasia ran toward her, hugging her tightly. "Thank you for taking me to see my Papa."

"You're welcome, my little Miss." She turned to Mrs. Andrews. "I'll miss you, too, especially all of your wonderful cooking."

"Thank you, but you're in for a treat. I've heard that Hilde, the Shipley's housekeeper in London, can give me a run for my money in any cooking contest. Well, I'll go see if Nigel is ready to take your luggage to the car."

* * *

After a whirlwind of activity getting to the airport and finding their seats on the plane, Sophie breathed a sigh of relief as she sat down. *Maybe now I can relax.* "What time is it, Miss Sophie?"

"It's nine-thirty."

"That's the a.m., right, because it's the morning?"

"You are correct."

"What time will we get there?"

Sophie smiled indulgently at her curious young student and patted her knee. "We should arrive at the airport around four-thirty p.m."

"Will Papa be there?"

"No, your grandfather will meet us."

"Why won't Papa be coming?"

She gently nudged Anastasia's chin. "It's a surprise, remember? Your father doesn't know we're on our way to see him."

Sophie loved the sound of Anastasia's giggles. "Oh, that's right. I forgot. Papa's going to be so happy."

"I'm sure he will be." Even as she said those words, a sliver of doubt invaded her mind. True, Sebastian had asked her to bring his daughter to see him, but they hadn't discussed further details—and now here she was on a plane headed to England to surprise him. She leaned back in the seat and closed her eyes for a moment. The flight attendant came to review the emergency procedures and Sophie zoned out while listening.

"Don't forget to change your watch when we get there, Miss Sophie."

She nodded encouragingly. "I see you didn't forget about the time difference."

"No. You said England is five hours ahead of where we live in Philadelphia."

"Yes, I did."

"I'm so excited." She exclaimed and faced the window. "This is my first plane ride."

Sophie wondered in amazement how Anastasia's fearless attitude so seamlessly overcame any hesitation to fly—especially after her father's recent plane crash. Not about to open Pandora's Box and rock the boat, she kept quiet. Instead, she made certain Anastasia had fastened her seatbelt correctly. Then she helped her plug in the headphones the flight attendant had offered. *Now, if only the seven hour flight could pass by quickly.* After one final glance at Anastasia, Sophie closed her eyes to get some rest.

Thankfully, their flight arrived on time. *At least we're still on schedule.* Sophie did not want to deal with any unexpected changes to their plans. She grabbed her carry-on bag and tried to take Anastasia's as well. However, she met with resistance from her young charge. "I want to help, Miss Sophie." *Of course you do.* She mentally chastised herself and took a deep breath. Patience needed to rule the moment.

"Are you sure it's not too heavy?"

"I'm okay."

Sophie motioned for Anastasia to exit into the aisle first. Following the rest of the passengers off the plane, she listened as the flight attendant gave directions to the baggage claim area.

"I'll pull my suitcase."

"I'm going to have to disagree with that one. It's heavy and I can manage both our suitcases."

"Maybe Grandpapa should help."

"We won't see him until we get to the front of the airport." They walked for a few more minutes in silence and then reached their destination.

"Will this take long, Miss Sophie?"

"Hopefully it won't." She pointed toward an empty bench. "Why don't we sit down for a bit? The luggage should start coming out soon."

"Where does it come out?"

Sophie smiled at her inquisitive student. She directed her attention to the conveyor belt. "Right over there."

"You're my best friend, Miss Sophie. Is that okay, since you're a grown up?"

The way her upturned face grinned at her, touched a chord deep inside Sophie's heart. She thought for a second. "Well, I'm honored. Do you have any friends from church?"

"Some, but I don't get to see them during the week. Sometimes I wish I could go to school and play with the other kids."

The conveyor belt started moving, saving Sophie from having to respond. She was too tired to deal with the tough questions right then. "Can you stay here with the carry-on bags and I'll wait over there." When she noticed Anastasia's hesitation, she reassured her. "I'll make sure I keep you in view."

"Okay, I'll wait."

Sophie moved closer to the conveyor belt, making certain to keep her young student in her vantage point. She glanced at her watch. "Right on schedule." Soon more people congregated around the conveyor belt and she stepped back to check on Anastasia. A few minutes later, she spotted her suitcase. Quickly snatching it up, she placed it on the ground next to her. Anastasia's suitcase came shortly after and Sophie wheeled them both back to the bench. "We're all set."

"That didn't take long."

She patted Anastasia's shoulder. "Now it's time to find your grandfather."

Walking amidst the crowd, they weaved their way toward the front of the airport. Nervous energy consumed Sophie. She wondered how her first meeting with Alexander would play out. They'd never spoken before. From speaking with David on the phone a few times, she sensed his personality differed significantly from his brother's. A tug on her sleeve and Anastasia's excited words interrupted her thoughts. "There he is."

Sophie glanced ahead and noticed a distinguished looking older gentleman waving in their direction. Still holding onto Sophie's sleeve, Anastasia jumped up and down. "I see him. I see him." Alexander met them halfway, opening his arms to give his granddaughter a warm embrace. Anastasia nearly dropped the bag she carried in her enthusiasm to return his hug.

"Grandpapa, I've missed you."

"Oh, Ana, I've missed you too."

Sophie immediately observed the love shining in his eyes as he embraced his granddaughter. When he turned toward her, she sensed his welcome as well. "You must be Sophie. I've heard a lot about you."

"Hopefully, all good." She smiled hesitantly.

He chuckled. "Yes, my dear. You both must

be very tired. Please let me help you with the luggage." With the same determined spirit she'd witnessed in Sebastian, he took over—in a charming, gentlemanly fashion, of course. Left with no wieldy suitcases to handle, Sophie reached for the two small carry-on bags. Excitement written all over her face, Anastasia gave no complaints being left with empty hands. With a skip in her step, she eagerly kept up with her grandfather. Seconds later, Sophie caught up with them and Alexander glanced back. "Sebastian is going to be so surprised. Thank you for bringing our Ana." Her first impression of Alexander had matched her assumptions. His sincerity shone through and she liked him instantly.

* * *

The ride from the airport sped by and before Sophie knew it, they pulled into the driveway of the Shipley's London townhouse. As she glanced up at the looming three story brick home, her nerves got the best of her—making her afraid to see Sebastian again. She watched Anastasia bound excitedly out of the sedan. Seconds later, Alexander opened her door and peeked inside. "Are you coming?"

"Yes, I guess I should get out, shouldn't I?"

"Unless you plan on sleeping in the car…it's ten-thirty."

"It's that late already?" She scooted over on

the backseat. "Oh, yeah, the time-change."

He backed up and offered his hand as she exited. Taking a deep breath, she allowed him to usher her up the front steps. "Welcome to my home, dear."

The opulent surroundings reminded Sophie of a scene from a Danielle Steel novel. Excited voices down the hall captured her attention. Alexander hooked his arm through hers and led her toward the commotion. She halted at the door as she observed Sebastian's animated conversation with his daughter. Her sudden bout of shyness annoyed her immensely. Alexander gently nudged her into the room.

"Hello, Sophie. It's good to see you." The sound of Sebastian's voice unnerved her even further.

"Hi." No other intelligent words came to mind.

"Thank you for bringing Ana."

Alexander interrupted. "My little Ana, would you like to come with me to get some cookies and milk before you go to bed?"

"Okay, Grandpapa."

Oh great...now we're really alone. Stop staring and pull it together.

"How was your flight?"

Focus...he asked a question. "It was fine."

"Was Ana scared at all?"

"Surprisingly, she wasn't. I didn't bring up the subject with her."

She took a few steps further into the room and Sebastian pointed toward the divan. "Please sit.

"Are you feeling better?"

She watched as he rubbed his arm. "It's still sore, but other than that, I'm fine. I'm so thankful God spared me." He slid closer to her and his nearness sent tingles up her spine. "I don't even want to think about what Ana would do if I wasn't here."

Sophie silently agreed with his statement and wondered what she'd do if he'd perished in the flight.

"Are you hungry? Do you want something to drink?"

"We ate on the plane, but water would be nice."

He stood up and held out his hand. "I guess we should join the cookie monsters in the kitchen." She accepted his gentlemanly offer of assistance up from the divan and allowed him to lead her out of the room. "I know it's late now, but we'll have to talk tomorrow about Ana's condition and everything the doctor shared with you."

"Sure, no problem." She stifled a yawn, wanting nothing more right then but to go to sleep. Although, even in her tired state, she desired to soak up every possible minute with him. *Hopefully, I don't end up babbling, sharing something I'd regret.*

* * *

Sebastian sat on the edge of the grandiose four-poster canopy bed that engulfed his daughter. She rested snugly, nestled in among several pillows and blankets. Earlier, he had heard Anastasia beg Hilde to change the room arrangements and permit her to sleep in her great-grandmother's old bedroom. He grinned, as he recalled Anastasia begging her grandfather the minute she'd walked by the room. He knew the sweeping curtains with gold trim, the fluffy pillows and furry rug would catch her interest. The way she had entreated her grandfather—as only a proper young lady persuades, with great big saucer-like eyes and a winning smile—warmed his heart.

Witnessing Anastasia's childlike glee brimming over as she had raced into the grand bedroom and jumped on the bed when Hilde had turned away, made Sebastian chuckle. Whenever she got her way, it never surprised him. He realized Sophie remained the only one of the adults in his daughter's life not completely wrapped around her small fingers. *At least not yet*, he thought.

Shaking himself out of his contemplation, Sebastian leaned forward on the bed. He gently brushed back strands of unruly curls from Anastasia's face and brought his finger down to lightly poke her nose. "So, how has my princess been?"

"Great, I feel wonderful."

"That's good."

"How has my Papa been?"

"Great, I feel wonderful, too.

"I'm glad to hear it." He loved her propensity to banter with him. Her face grew serious and she stared into his eyes. "God was good to us, wasn't He?"

"Yes, He was. You're all better and He saved me."

"Were you scared?" He heard the hesitation in her voice. How should he answer that question?

"Not at all." Sebastian wanted to respond comfortingly. "I prayed and was a tiny bit frightened at first. Then I saw your face and knew I had to make it through to get back to you."

Anastasia sat up suddenly and hugged him tightly. "I would be so sad…" Understanding her unfinished sentiments, he hugged her back with the same intensity.

"Everything's going to be okay. God's watching over us." He planted a firm kiss on her soft cheek. "Now you should close your eyes. It's been a long day and I know you'll be talking our ears off tomorrow, so you'll need all the sleep you can get."

"Papa, I won't!"

"What're you hitting me for?" Laughing, he held up his hands to ward off further pillow attack. "It's the truth."

Making a funny face, she squirmed away and snuggled back into the pillows then pulled the covers up to her chin. Sebastian tucked her in and kissed her forehead. Then he left the room and walked downstairs to join his father, brother, and Sophie. Excitement brimmed in his heart when he thought about seeing Sophie again, even if only for a few minutes to say goodnight.

Chapter Fourteen

Sophie missed breakfast. When she'd woken up and glanced at the clock on the night table, she'd gasped. *Eleven o'clock...how could I have overslept?* She thought she'd set the alarm clock last night. Throwing back the covers, she hurried out of bed and into the bathroom. *I wonder if I've missed lunch too!* After a flurried few minutes of dressing and washing her face, she caught up with Sebastian in the hallway. "I'm sorry I slept in. Is Anastasia all right? I stopped by her room and didn't see her. I guess she's already been up for a while."

"Don't worry, Sophie." Even in her harried state, she noticed the serenity exuding from Sebastian—she took a deep breath, trying to mirror the calm attitude. "You're entitled to sleep in, especially after your day yesterday. Ana's in the dining room with my father. They spent the morning together catching up."

"What time did she wake up?"

"Oh, at seven-thirty."

She chuckled and shook her head. "I wish I had her energy."

They walked in comfortable silence down the hallway and then entered the dining room. "It's about time." Alexander joked. "A minute later and there would be no food left."

"Miss Sophie, come sit next to me." The young girl excitedly patted the seat beside her.

Answering with a smile, she sat down next to Anastasia and wanted to ask how her morning went. Sebastian spoke first. "Sophie, what do you think about holding off on starting Ana's school work until tomorrow? The three of us can go to the park this afternoon."

More time with Sebastian…a no brainer. She jumped at the chance—of course, outwardly she acted nonchalant. "That's fine. I'm sure someone will be happy about having no school work today." She directed her comment to the giggling child at her side.

Alexander cleared his throat. "I'm glad everyone has agreed to go to the park, but now it's time to pray and bless the food because I'm starving."

"Grandpapa, you can't be starving. You had a very big breakfast."

They all chuckled, except Alexander. "I have no answer to that comment except, let's pray." Sophie caught the conspiratorial wink he then directed to his granddaughter.

* * *

Sophie strolled alongside Sebastian, with Anastasia tucked in between them, since her young student wanted to hold both of their hands. "I'm glad we all bundled up." Sebastian shivered exaggeratedly. "It is cold out here."

"I'm not cold." Anastasia leaned her neck back and chimed in.

"That's because you're a little fireball." Sophie loved how he playfully teased his daughter and Anastasia enjoyed the bantering. "If you do start to get cold, let us know and we'll head back."

Sophie spotted a park bench a short distance ahead and pointed. "Let's sit down up there and rest for a bit."

"Good idea. This old man needs a break."

"You're not old, Papa, not like Grandpapa."

Sophie couldn't hold in her laughter. "It's a good thing your grandfather's not here to defend himself."

Sebastian wagged his finger at his daughter. "She's right, Ana. He'd definitely beat you in a tickle fight."

When they reached the bench and sat down, Anastasia grinned at her father. At least Sophie thought she saw her grin, but the scarf wrapped around the young girl's neck covered part of her face. "Can I walk around for a bit?" She mumbled. "I'll stay close by. You can still see me."

"All right, but don't go far."

Sophie watched Anastasia scamper off like a jackrabbit and for a moment, she wondered what to talk about. Sebastian broke the silence. "I truly appreciate you bringing my daughter all the way over here. You didn't have to. I don't recall that being part of your job description."

"It was the right thing to do." Suddenly shy, she glanced away. "I wanted to see you…to find out for myself that you were okay, of course."

"Yes, of course. I'm glad you're here, too."

Did he really just say that? Sebastian definitely surprised her by seemingly reciprocating her feelings. She subconsciously slid further away from him and turned her attention back to Anastasia. The young girl chased a chipmunk around a nearby tree. "Didn't you want to talk about Anastasia's health and what the doctor said?"

"That's right. We were all having so much fun I almost forgot this was a professional outing."

"Professional outing?" *I guess I shouldn't be surprised…this isn't a date.*

"I was trying to be funny." He gave her a serious look. "Are you okay?"

"I'm fine." Trying to focus, she began to explain the prognosis. "The immunodeficiency disease went into remission and her energy has been amazing."

He shook his head. "Exactly like she said that day on the lake, remember?"

"I remember." The memory vividly came to her mind. At the time, she hadn't put much stock in Anastasia's revelation, but now she'd come one step closer to believing.

"I feel like I was given a second chance with my daughter and life in general. I want to try to make up for missed time with Ana. Work has kept me too busy in the past. I missed so much time with Katherine. I was such a fool." Uncertain how to respond to his candor, she let him continue. "Life is so short, Sophie. I know you understand."

She thought about her parents and nodded. "I do."

"Can I ask you a personal question?"

She responded hesitantly. "Sure, although, I might plead the fifth."

Sebastian chuckled and dove right in. "You seem to be more serene since the last time we saw each other. Have you made peace with God?"

Wow, he definitely gets straight to the point! She took a deep breath. "Let's say I'm on the road to recovery." She held up her hand. "I'm only taking baby steps, so please don't preach at me."

He waved away her worries. "I wasn't planning to. I care, that's all."

"Thank you. Your concern is refreshing." She glanced over her shoulder. "Do you think we should bring Anastasia back?"

He turned toward his daughter. "Isn't she having a blast all by herself! A few more minutes of freedom won't hurt." He nodded in Sophie's direction. "You showed me that."

"What do you mean?"

"You took her outside to experience the beauty of God's creation—something I should have given more attention to. Especially after my wife died and no one was there to see to that." He ran his hands through his hair. Leaning his elbows on his knees, he tilted his head toward her. "I'm sorry for talking about Katherine. I hope that doesn't bother you."

"Why would it?" Before she could give his words further thought, he continued sharing.

"I don't know. I guess I haven't thought about her much until you came. In my grief, I buried even the happy memories."

"Happy memories are a luxury we need to afford ourselves."

He sat back and nodded. "You're right. I do feel better now that I'm remembering those good times."

"Do you think Anastasia is completely healed?"

"She's been sick for so long, part of me finds it hard to believe. Although, that's why Jesus called it faith, right?"

"I guess so." She hoped the conversation

changed gears. However, she couldn't fault him for bringing Jesus into the picture. After all, she asked the question about healing.

"You'll see. He'll prove Himself to you. He loves you that much."

Anastasia raced back over to her father, saving Sophie from responding. "Papa, can we go home now? I'm so cold." She trembled dramatically.

He hugged her. "I thought you weren't cold. We were freezing over here and couldn't wait for you to rescue us, right Sophie?"

"Yes, he's correct."

"You're joking, Papa."

He stood up. "No, we weren't too cold, but I was going to come and get you in a few minutes. We should take you inside." Sebastian took Anastasia by the hand and headed toward the car. Sophie stood still for a second, watching them walk away. She wondered if he was right. Would God truly prove Himself to her in the future? The question both frightened and excited her at the same time.

* * *

Since Sebastian had given Anastasia a reprieve from schoolwork, Sophie had the rest of the day to herself. They'd just returned from their excursion to the park and Sophie was glad to be nice and cozy inside. Earlier, she had heard Anastasia's giggles as she bantered with her grandfather. Apparently, they had been discussing which movie to settle in for that afternoon. She figured Sebastian and David had buried themselves under mounds of paperwork in the study. Left to her own devices, Sophie had taken a twenty-minute power nap. Now the restlessness set in and she decided to take a private tour of the London townhouse. Sebastian had given permission to explore to her heart's content. However, she still felt like Belle from *Beauty and the Beast* and hoped her wanderings remained free of any hidden discoveries—like the Beast's covered rose.

Sophie stepped out of her room and began roaming through the upstairs hallway. She found a narrow staircase at the end of the hall, which looked like the passageway to the servants' quarters of a bygone era. As she climbed her way to the top, she reached another doorway. Hoping it opened, she turned the knob. Cobwebs and dust met her senses and she coughed as she entered. Now she truly felt like Belle, ready for Sebastian to come up after her growling that she'd intruded on sacred family ground.

Realizing she stepped into the attic, she moved slowly, groping for a light switch. Noticing a string hanging from the ceiling, she pulled it. A single light bulb illuminated the room. She saw at once that she'd come upon a treasure trove of family heirlooms and memories. Sensory overload halted her progress and then a large, worn-looking brown leather book caught her eye. Gingerly stepping on the floor boards, she mentally thanked the person that had placed the wooden planks across the rafters.

Sophie reached for the book and opened the cover, as dust filled her nostrils, causing her to sneeze. One by one, she began slowly turning the faded pages and saw a younger version of Alexander and, she assumed, his wife. Continuing to peruse the book, she noticed their two young sons. As she reached the middle pages, she observed Sebastian on his wedding day. Sophie gasped—she already thought he was handsome—but in the photo, his happiness shone through. Suddenly overwhelmed and saddened for all that he and his daughter had lost when Katherine passed away, she started tearing up. Closing the book, she held it to her chest. She wanted to find love someday with someone, hopefully Sebastian—like he had shared with his wife.

* * *

Sophie enjoyed basking in the jovial atmosphere as the family bantered back and forth. Observing the interactions between Sebastian and Anastasia reminded her of the relationship she'd had with her own father.

"Sophie, can you please pass the butter?" Sebastian asked from across the table.

"Sure."

"How did your sleuthing go this afternoon?"

"It was fine."

"Did you find anything interesting?" Alexander interjected.

Sophie felt uncomfortable, disliking these questions. "I still feel weird, like I was snooping around." Flashes of the photographs of Sebastian's wedding day threw her off balance.

Alexander reassured her. "Nonsense, dear. This house is old and has a great history. My friends always cajole me into giving them tours."

"I need a tour, Grandpapa."

"Maybe, after dinner, we'll see."

Hilde brought out the roasted lamb, their second course and Sophie smiled as David's eyes grew big like saucers. He was so expressive compared to Sebastian's more reserved personality. "Looks delicious, Hilde."

"Thank you." The housekeeper nodded modestly and left the room.

Alexander stood up to dish out the meal and Anastasia volunteered to pass the plates to him. David then got up to assist his niece. Sophie watched the amiable commotion and nearly missed Sebastian's comment as he leaned across the table toward her. "So, where did your investigations take you?"

"To the attic," she responded vaguely, barely glancing at him. *Please don't ask any more questions.* The heat crept up her cheeks as she remembered how vulnerable she felt flipping through the family album. Would love ever truly be hers for keeps?

"Did you find anything that caught your interest?" He tilted his head and she couldn't help but smile at his boyish grin. "I'm simply curious. I haven't been up there for years."

"I found an old photo album."

"Now, I'm embarrassed. You must have seen all my baby pictures."

"You were a cute baby."

"*Were*, being the operative word."

"You're not too bad now, either."

"Am I interrupting?" David whispered conspiratorially.

Sebastian sat back abruptly. Sophie shook her head and hurried to respond. "Of course not." She handed David her plate.

With everyone served, Alexander sat down to say grace and then they began to eat. Sophie pushed the potatoes around on her plate with her fork, amazed that she even had the courage to comment to Sebastian on his looks. One of these days, she hoped to reign in her impulsive tongue. Glancing up, she found Sebastian staring at her. She smiled and concentrated again on her plate. Her heart kept racing. Something about that man stirred her senses and caused her to feel like a cheerleader with a crush on the star quarterback. She needed to get a grip on her emotions before they drove her into a tailspin of embarrassment.

* * *

Later on after dinner Sebastian reclined in the study, relaxing with a glass of brandy. He swirled the dark liquid and took a sip. The chaise lounge he relaxed in faced the French doors which opened onto a stone patio. The darkness hindered any view outside but his mind surged with other images. He pictured Sophie's sweet smile and tried to put the intoxication he felt around her in perspective. Approaching footsteps dampened his peaceful nightcap. "Hello, father."

"You know me that well, son?"

"It's your cologne which gives you away." He tried to keep his tone light. *Into the lion's den I go.* Turning around with a hesitant closed-mouth smile, he faced his father. "So what can I do for you?"

"Can't I visit with my eldest son for a bit? I haven't seen you for a while."

"I know when you're up to trouble so let me have the speech now then I can finish my brandy in peace." He disliked the tone he'd taken, but knew exactly where his father was going with this conversation.

Alexander sighed and rubbed his forehead. Then he sat down in the chair across from him. "What do you think about Sophie?"

"Well, I hired her didn't I?"

"You don't have to get defensive, son."

"I apologize. I guess I don't know how to answer your question. I'm still trying to figure it out myself." Sebastian gulped down his brandy in frustration and turned the tables on his father. "What about you? Do you like her?"

"She made a good first impression on me. Besides, I trust my son's judgment and I know he wouldn't allow anyone off the street to have such a strong impact on his daughter's life."

"There you have it...you've answered your own question."

Alexander chuckled. "I like her son, and it is okay for you to like her, too. Good night. I'll see you in the morning." Sebastian stared after his father's retreating form, wanting to believe his last statement—but not allowing himself the pleasure to dream. His wife's face flashed in his mind's eye and he guiltily tried to erase all images of Sophie from his thoughts.

Chapter Fifteen

Sebastian glanced down at his watch. *Five-forty five p.m.*

"Do you have a hot date?" David teased.

"We have a dinner party to host, you know." Enough to deflect his brother's questions…maybe, maybe not. He hated appearing so anxious like a teenager on his first date.

"Yes, and there's nothing for you to do. Exactly why Hilde is with us." David leaned back in the chair and stretched. "We only have to finish this final draft. I still need you for a few more corrections. I can then finish up if you must leave."

"It doesn't start until seven-thirty." Sebastian ran his hand through his hair and sat back down. "I guess you're right."

"Always am." He bantered with a wink. "Now let's get back to work."

* * *

Sophie had taken Anastasia on a field trip to the British Museum in Russell Square, London. Checking her watch for the time, she urged her dawdling student forward. "We need to head back soon."

"Oh, but isn't everything so lovely?"

"Yes, it's all *lovely*." Uncertain when the young girl had picked it up, Sophie had noticed she'd started speaking with a semi-British accent. Hoping it passed as a phase, she'd decided to neither discourage nor encourage this behavior. She knew Alexander found this performance cute and amusing. However, Sebastian's opinion remained undetectable to her.

"Papa has his dinner tonight, right?"

"Yes." She watched as Anastasia twirled in slow circles in the hallway.

"Is it going to be a *stuffy old meeting*, Miss Sophie?"

"Why would you ask that?"

"Uncle David was talking to Grandpapa." Sheepishly, she turned away.

Deciding not to get into a discussion on eavesdropping, Sophie dropped the subject. By the chagrined expression on the young girl's face, Sophie could tell she understood what she did wrong. She guided Anastasia toward the vestibule and the security guard greeted them. Holding the door open as they left, he wished them a good night. A light dusting of snow met them as they stepped outside.

Anastasia stuck her tongue out, trying to catch the falling snowflakes before they melted.

Sophie reached for her hand and led Anastasia to the car. She had decided to drive today, since their field trip took them all over London. The Shipley's butler, Daniel had offered to chauffeur them, but she'd declined—not wanting to monopolize his time. She had programmed the address of the Shipley's home into the GPS and waited for the signal to link up.

"Are you all right, Miss Sophie?" Anastasia cut into her thoughts.

"I'm fine." She turned toward the back seat. "Are you buckled in?"

"Of course I am."

"Look at the snow."

"I know. It's lovely."

"Are you ever going to get tired of saying that word?" Sophie marveled at the mind of a child—so impressionable, yet full of wonder. Lowering the heat, she slowly pulled out into traffic and headed home.

When they neared the townhouse fifteen minutes later, Anastasia perked up. "Can we have a snack before dinner?"

Sophie shook her head. "No. Remember you still have to take your spelling test."

"Do I have to? It's a field trip day."

"I know, but yes, you have to take the test.

You'll be done in no time."

"Is Ginny coming over? Grandpapa said Lord Stiles was attending the party and bringing Ginny too...so she could have dinner with me."

Sophie parked the car. "I believe you're right."

"Are you going to the dinner party?"

"No, I'm coming to your party."

"Yes!" Anastasia exclaimed. "I was hoping you would come."

"Then let's go inside so you can take your test and we can get ready for our party."

* * *

Sebastian glanced at the time—seven-fifteen—he was seriously running late. Botching the formation of his bow tie, he grumbled and raced out of the room, in search of David. In his haste, about halfway down the corridor, he collided with Sophie. Embarrassed, he reached out to steady her and rushed to apologize. "Sophie, I'm so sorry. Are you all right?"

Her rich laughter reminded him of a flowing stream. "Yes. I'm fine, but you look like you could use some help."

"I'm having trouble with my tie."

Her responding grin eased his sheepishness. *At least she's not laughing at me.* "Let me help you."

She stepped closer and as she expertly worked on his tie, he grew suddenly aware of her presence. The fragrance of lilacs pleasantly assailed his nostrils. Her delicate hands smoothed out his lapels and flicked away a piece of lint. "Oh that looks perfect."

Clearing his throat, he moved back and managed to respond. "Thank you." He started to walk toward his room and turned around. "Did you need me for something?"

When she smiled just then, his heart started beating faster. "No, I was going to my room when you nearly tackled me. My room is on the same floor, you know."

"Right...I'll see you later." He sighed then hurried into his room. Closing the door, he leaned against it. *Man, I feel like a schoolboy every time she's around.* Urging himself into action, he stood in front of the mirror, inspecting her handiwork. "Not bad. Now if only I can forget the way you make me feel, Sophie Baird." Slipping into his tuxedo jacket, he swiveled to answer the knock on the door.

"Who are you talking to?" David asked.

"Myself. When did you get back?" Sebastian smoothed out the black sleeves. "I didn't think you were going to make it in time."

"Five minutes ago. Your guests are waiting."

"How did you get ready so fast?"

"I keep a tux at the office. You know, in case I have to become 007 and save England."

"This is no time to joke around."

"Why are you so edgy?"

"I'm fine. Let's go." Irritated at his own agitation, he hoped David stopped pushing.

"I passed Sophie on my way in here. Did she help you with your tie?"

"Why?"

The way David cocked his head and the smirk on his face annoyed Sebastian even further. "Because I know that's not your specialty and the last time you asked me for help."

"Can we drop the subject and get downstairs?"

David pointed at him. "You know, you need a woman and you have a beautiful one right under your nose. If you don't go after her, maybe I will."

His comment set Sebastian's blood to boiling. He glared steadily at his brother. "Stay away from her David. She's not your type."

He held up his hands in surrender. "Ease up Sebastian. I'm only joshing you."

Regret hit him in the gut. *I've got to get a handle on myself before I erupt and do something I'll be sorry for.* "I apologize. Let's head downstairs and get this party over with, all right." He walked passed his brother and felt David's eyes boring holes in his back as he left the room.

Alexander came out into the hallway and Sebastian nodded in his direction. "Did Lord Stiles arrive? Is Anastasia with Ginny?"

"Yes, everything's fine. Sophie will be having dinner with the girls."

Sebastian thanked him and walked away—wishing his steps led him to Sophie and his daughter and not this dreaded affair.

* * *

Sebastian held a glass of red wine in one hand and a spinach quiche in the other. He'd grown weary of wearing his social mask and mingling with the guests. At the moment, he hid in the corner of the room, near a Corinthian column and statue. He took a sip of wine and bit into the quiche, mentally congratulating Hilde on a job well done. "You and Mrs. Andrews could go into a catering business and you'd become an overnight success."

Everywhere he glanced, he saw people laughing, all with drinks in their hands. Men flirted with beautiful women, wearing fancy dresses and showing off jeweled fingers and necks. His mind wandered to Anastasia's dinner party and he hoped she and Ginny enjoyed themselves. He planned to escape soon to check on them. A young woman passed him on the way out of the room. She smiled demurely and he responded reservedly, but quickly looked away, not wishing to engage in flirtatious conversation.

Sebastian infuriated himself because all his

thoughts kept focusing on a petite young woman, with intense blue eyes that read into his soul. A longing to be back home in America—sitting in the conservatory watching her teach his daughter or relaxing on the divan as he listened to the melancholy music her fingers made as they caressed the piano keys—consumed his soul. Sighing, he swiveled as he heard a woman's voice call out coyly.

"Sebastian, Sebastian Shipley."

Disappointed to be disturbed from daydreams of Sophie, he reluctantly turned around. A striking, leggy blonde approached his hideaway. She dressed to kill—of course he noticed, but still his thoughts returned to Sophie. He barely smiled, trying to think of a means to slip away without appearing rude.

"Sebastian, silly, don't you remember me? My father's one of your big clients."

"I'm sorry, Miss. I don't recall…"

Forever grateful for David choosing that moment to come to the rescue, Sebastian wondered how long his brother had watched him hiding. "Miss Delilah Scott, how are you?" David gallantly reached for her white-gloved hand and kissed it lightly.

She pouted. "I'm disappointed your brother does not remember me."

"Oh, he remembers you. He's simply tired from all the work we've been doing today for *your* father."

Sebastian's momentary brain hiccup left and

he painstakingly rose to the occasion. "I could never forget a beautiful face like yours. My brother and I are honored to be doing work for your father." He sensed Miss Scott wanted to prolong the conversation, but he needed to get away. "I would love to continue our discussion, but I must check on my daughter before we enter the dining room for dinner. David, please be so kind as to escort Miss Scott to her seat."

Sebastian breathed a sigh of relief as David winked surreptitiously at him and gracefully guided a disappointed lady toward the dining room. Thankful he had escaped so smoothly, Sebastian quickly exited the room.

* * *

Sophie ducked back into the alcove as quickly as possible, hoping she'd remained unnoticed as Sebastian walked by. Anastasia and Ginny had asked her to get the chocolate chip cookies Hilde had baked for their party tonight. She'd acquiesced to their request because she knew the housekeeper seemed preoccupied with the party downstairs. On the way out of the kitchen, she'd meandered toward the merriment and found a great hiding space with a vantage point of none other than Sebastian.

She noticed he'd tucked himself away from the guests and she wondered why he attended these parties if he disliked them so much. Then she'd seen the blonde woman with the seductive body language and a sugary voice approach Sebastian. Her hideout still within earshot, she'd heard the entire conversation and had gasped when he'd mentioned not forgetting the woman's beautiful face. Sophie wiped away a tear and closed her eyes. The glimmer of hope which had been brewing inside was wiped out in a heartbeat. She waited a few minutes, hoping Sebastian made it to the end of the hallway. Slowly peering out, she then raced up the stairs through the kitchen.

* * *

Sebastian knocked on the door to Anastasia's sitting room. "May I join your party?"

"Papa!" Anastasia ran over to give her father a hug. "We're almost done eating. It's too late, but Miss Sophie went downstairs to get our cookies. You can have some of those."

He chuckled, thankful for his daughter's giving heart. "I'm fine, sweetheart." He patted her cheek. "I only came up to check on you ladies. I have to go back down in a few minutes for our dinner."

"Okay."

"How are you, Ginny?"

"I'm fine, Mr. Shipley. We're having fun tonight."

"I'm glad you could come. I'd better go downstairs to say grace or your Uncle David will be coming up here to chase me down."

"We could hide you under my bed or in the closet."

As he mulled over Anastasia's appealing offer, he grinned. "That's all right. Good night, my dear. Good night, Ginny. I'll see you both tomorrow."

Sebastian blew Anastasia a kiss and stepped out into the hallway. This time, Sophie collided with him. She immediately backed away. "Oh, I'm sorry." He wondered at her odd behavior—why she avoided eye contact with him.

"Is everything okay?"

"I'm fine." Those words sucker punched his gut. He knew she avoided the truth.

He reached for her hand as she started to move aside into the room. Touching her silky skin sent shivers up his spine and this time he held on, not wanting to let go. She glanced up and he noticed her teary eyes. "Were you crying? Are you hurt?"

She pulled her hand away and sniffled. "No, my allergies have been acting up."

He nodded, knowing he was not going to get the entire truth from her. "Good night, Sophie." He locked his eyes on hers. "If you need to talk later, come and find me after the party. I can try to sneak out early." He watched her eyebrows rise cynically and he wondered why she clammed up. He sighed

~ 208 ~

and walked back downstairs to his guests, longing to stay to talk with Sophie.

* * *

Later on, Sophie tucked Ginny in. "Are you sure you don't want your own bed? There are plenty of bedrooms to go around."

"She wants to stay here." Anastasia excitedly bounced on the king-sized bed, answering for her friend. Sophie reached for her young charge mid-jump and pulled her back to the bed.

"Fine, but I don't want you two chatting all night. You need to get some sleep."

"Miss Sophie, can you wait while we say our prayers?"

She hesitated for a moment. "Sure." Delving into unfamiliar territory, she listened as both girls spoke freely with God about His forgiveness, love, and protection. The entire time, the emptiness in her heart grew—like a giant chasm splitting even farther apart. Sophie longed for a similar child-like faith. Taking baby steps toward such intimacy seemed too slow and she wished progress came more quickly.

When the girls finished, Sophie kissed them both on the forehead and then turned the light off and closed the door. She walked down the hall toward her room. Her mind urged her to wait for Sebastian to talk. Instead, she kept thinking about the beautiful blonde woman and realized she, herself, existed far outside of Sebastian's social circle. Back at the Shipley mansion in Philadelphia, Sophie never sensed the distinct difference in societal status. Sebastian always treated her as his social equal. Now, however, she felt inadequate and clearly saw the difference—it pained her deeply. Sophie pushed back the heavy draperies from the balcony doors in her bedroom and she stared outside at the full moon. She reminded herself of their professional relationship and reluctantly decided she needed to stop wishing for anything more from Sebastian. If only her heart agreed.

Chapter Sixteen

"You have an invitation from whom?"

Sophie stopped dead in her tracks when she overheard David's question and the incredulous tone to his voice. She waited quietly, hoping no one found her eavesdropping. Then she remembered the many times she'd spoken with Anastasia about why listening in to a conversation was rude. Even so, she couldn't leave just yet. She needed to find out whom they were talking about. Was it the beautiful blonde woman?

"Delilah Scott." Sebastian answered noncommittally. "These sandwiches look good. Do you want some?"

"You can't possibly be thinking of going?"

"We've got garden salad and pasta too. Besides, why shouldn't I go? Last night you were reminding me she was the daughter of one of our biggest clients."

"Yes, but what I did not get a chance to tell you, is our lovely Miss Scott is out shopping for a husband."

"You know this because—"

"I've heard it spoken of."

"I don't subscribe to the gossip mill. Lies hurt people."

"What if they're right?"

"I'd like to give Miss Scott a chance without judging her first."

"Give her a chance for what?" David exclaimed! "Are you forgetting about Sophie?"

"I'm answering the invitation from Miss Scott purely for business motives. If necessary, I will make that fact known to her. Besides, it's not a romantic rendezvous. It's a riding party—just a run of the mill social event."

"Then why wasn't I invited? I'm popular in all those same circles."

"Maybe you did something to offend her last night, as her escort to dinner." Sebastian chuckled.

"No, maybe she knows I'm privy to her little plan to hoodwink you and she does not want any complications."

"David, why don't you join me for lunch now? I think you're still in 007 mode."

From her hidden vantage point, Sophie saw David shake his head and walk to the serving board. "Don't say I didn't warn you. I'm waiting for the other shoe to drop here."

"And what was the first shoe dropping?"

Sebastian remarked dryly.

"Neglecting to talk to Sophie last night. You said she seemed upset. The two of you are destined for each other."

"I think we should drop this subject. Anastasia will be coming back soon and you know she'll have much to chatter about after her morning excursion with father."

"Fine." David sat down. "Let's eat so I can get back to work, while you go riding. Maybe I should make a grand entrance and crash this little shindig."

"Not a good idea, David."

He grumbled and they started eating their meal in silence.

Sophie took a moment to compose herself before entering the room. She felt the tension—thick enough to cut with a knife.

"Hello. How was your morning off?"

She sat down across from David, with Sebastian to her left. "It was fine, David, thanks for asking. I slept in and read for a while."

"Who's your favorite author?"

"Jane Austen is." Sebastian answered for her and continued eating.

"I wasn't asking you." David remarked.

Sophie glanced at Sebastian. "He's correct. I like Jane Austen's work."

David looked from his brother to Sophie. "Oh, I see."

Anastasia came bounding into the dining room with her grandfather a few steps behind. "Papa, we're back! We had so much fun."

"Yes, it appears your grandfather had a lot of fun." David smiled and teased his father.

Sophie hid her smile as she watched Alexander huff and plop down into the seat. *He even does that with decorum!* "Now I know how you feel, Sophie." He leaned closer and whispered. "She definitely is a bundle of energy."

"I hate to break up the fun, but I will be going away for a few days."

Sebastian's abrupt announcement brought tears to Anastasia's eyes. Sophie needed to move out of view so no one would notice her own watery eyes. She quickly stood up to get her food from the serving board. She listened as his daughter pleaded with him. "Please, Papa, may I come with you?"

"Not this time, honey. It's a riding party for grownups only."

"I can't wait to be a grown up!" Grumpily, she slumped into the seat.

"Ana, please don't slouch."

Sophie walked back to the table and sat down. She watched as Anastasia obediently sat up straight. "Yes, Papa."

Alexander nudged his granddaughter. "Let's go get some food." David joined them for seconds and Sophie stared at the meal on her plate. The news of Sebastian leaving had sucked the wind from her sails. *Not to mention the mysterious blonde woman in his life.*

"Are you all right?"

"I'm fine." What else could she say in that moment? Her assumptions tortured her emotions and she lost her focus.

"Are you sure?"

"Yes."

"So I guess this means you're not going to tell me what made you cry last night."

Sophie's heart yearned to share more, but her over-analytical mind prevented her from opening up to him. "Now's not a good time and you're leaving."

"We'll talk when I get back. I promise."

She nodded and Anastasia came back to the table, chattering and halting further discussion on the topic. Sophie finished her meal in silence, not in the mood for socializing. She wished she could run upstairs to her room and hide under the comfort of the covers and sleep the afternoon away. Even her favorite books couldn't entice her from her gloominess. *Hopefully Sebastian leaves well enough alone.*

* * *

After lunch, Sebastian had excused himself from the tearful goodbye of his daughter, and drove to the Scott family estate in East Anglia. He headed northeast from London toward Cambridge. As he drove and the minutes ticked by, he began doubting his decision to accept the invitation to Delilah's riding party. David's words kept echoing in his mind. *What if David is right? Am I unknowingly walking into the lion's den? I guess since I've been warned, I'm knowingly entering into this.* He shook his head, as if physically trying to clear his thoughts. *Maybe David's making a mountain out of a molehill.*

Sebastian strived to give a person the benefit of doubt to prove him or herself without prejudgment. He tried to behave like a gentleman, as his father had raised him. It was his life's creed as he modeled the proper etiquette and manners he'd learned from his father. "Well, Lord, if she digs in her claws, we'll figure something out." That's where he had to leave the situation—in the Lord's capable hands.

* * *

Shortly after Sebastian left, Alexander approached Sophie in the sunroom. "Sophie, do you have a minute?"

His serious expression gave her pause. "Sure. Is something wrong?"

He sat down across from her. "No. Before Sebastian left, I got permission from him to take Ana to visit my friend, Lord Jeremy Stiles."

"Ginny's grandfather, right?"

"Yes. He and his wife live in the West Country in Bath."

"Oh, Jane Austen's hometown, how exciting!"

"I guess that means you'll be joining us?" His grin was contagious.

She couldn't help but smile herself. "Me. You want me to come?"

He held out his hands imploringly. "Ana needs you, and I surely don't have the energy to chase her and Ginny around."

How could she deny his request? Besides, spending time with the girls would take her mind off of missing Sebastian—at least she hoped it would. "Yes, I'll come along. When are we leaving?"

"That's the spirit. We're leaving now."

"Are you serious?" She jumped up excitedly. "I'd better pack, and Anastasia will need help." As she practically skipped like a little girl out of the room, she heard Alexander's chuckles in her wake. Thankful for the diversion from thoughts of Sebastian, Sophie hurried upstairs to check on Anastasia.

Thirty minutes later, Sophie and Anastasia walked downstairs. Daniel carried the suitcases out to the trunk and Hilde waited by the door. Alexander came over to the housekeeper. "Thank you again for the wonderful seven-course meal last night. You outdid yourself once more."

Sophie watched the housekeeper graciously accept his compliment.

"I can drive, Sir, if you'd like."

"No, no, Daniel, I'm fine. I don't want to occupy all your time."

"Pardon my saying, so, Sir, but that's what you pay me for."

She noticed the gleam in Daniel's eye and his straight face. Alexander chuckled. "You have a point." He patted Daniel's shoulder. "All right, if you insist." He glanced at Sophie and Anastasia. "Then I'll ride in the back with you ladies."

"Now you can read me a story."

Alexander shook his head. "No, my dear, reading in the car makes me nauseous. Besides, you need the practice."

"I do not. I can read perfectly well." Anastasia defended her reading skills.

"Then I guess you need to get started on Shakespeare, right Sophie?"

"Miss Sophie already reads me Shakespeare. He's her favorite writer and Jane Austen. Oh, Grandpapa, can we go to Jane's house? She lived in Bath."

Sophie held up her hands, fending off any questions. "I did not put her up to that request, honest."

"We'll see. I'm not even sure if her house still exists. Let's get to Lord Stiles' house first." Anastasia agreed with a nod and Sophie followed Alexander and the young girl into the backseat.

Sophie made sure Anastasia buckled herself in. As Daniel pulled the sedan into traffic, she closed her eyes and tried to relax. Several minutes passed in silence as she recalled reading a description once from a tourist guidebook—about the *craggy coastlines, the countryside of ancient Arthurian times, castles and gardens and great cities of Bath and Bristol.* For the longest time she'd wanted to visit the United Kingdom. *Finally here and now I might even get to see where Jane Austen lived!*

Anastasia interrupted her thoughts. "Are you excited to see Jane Austen's house, Miss Sophie?"

"Remember what your grandfather said? We don't even know if it exists anymore."

"I know…but it's still exciting to see the town where she lived, right?"

"Yes it is." Sophie smiled at Anastasia.

"Are you excited, Grandpapa?"

"I'm happy to spend some time with Lord Stiles and his family."

"I miss Papa."

"We'll see him in a few days." Alexander reached out and gave her hand a gentle squeeze.

Sophie felt his eyes on her but she faced the window, hoping he excluded her from this topic of the conversation. She needed to put Sebastian out of her mind, not continue to think about him. Her eyes watered as she listened to Anastasia chatter amiably. Before the tears came and turned into a full-fledged pity party, she made the decision to enjoy this time with her young student and make the best of the situation.

* * *

Sebastian made the trip by mid-afternoon with no problems. Miss Scott scheduled the actual equestrian event for the next morning at nine, to be followed by a brunch. Now that he'd finally arrived at the Scott's Estate, he realized the thrill of the riding party attracted him—not Delilah Scott. The realization liberated him even more in cementing his feelings for Sophie. He had not succumbed to the wily charms of Miss Scott. All he could think about, he'd left back home in London. A butler came to open his car door before he even shut the engine down. Another butler offered to take his bags and then the grand entrance happened as his hostess came parading out of the 18th century manor, with her entourage of servants.

"Sebastian, dear, I'm delighted you could attend."

"Yes, I'm pleased to be here." Keeping his responses cordial, he heard David's warnings swim around his head. Wanting to nap before dinner, he hoped one of her attendants showed him to a room soon. He offered her his arm as an escort into her father's palatial home and listened cordially to her as she listed the roster of guests. Sebastian knew a few of them.

They strolled into the opulent foyer and Delilah stopped. Sebastian swore to himself that he saw her take a quick peek in the mirrors across the hall. "You must be exhausted from your drive. Ralston will show you to your room. Make yourself at home. Dinner will be served at six."

"Thank you." The two-hour reprieve to relax sounded wonderful.

She nodded and sauntered toward the front parlour. Sebastian followed the butler up the grand staircase to one of the many guestrooms. His eyes glanced at the family portraits which lined the wall. He remembered that he needed to get his family portrait updated to keep up with Anastasia's growth spurts. Unbidden, Sophie's face joined his family in his mind's eye. "Get a grip man," he mumbled as he continued down the stately hall.

* * *

Sebastian came downstairs expecting to see about twenty guests joining them for dinner but he was rudely mistaken. Delilah coyly tilted her head and tossed her blonde curls over her bare shoulder. He noticed her revealing black gown and fiery red lipstick on her parted lips. *What is going on? I should've listened to David.* "Am I early?"

"No, dear, you're right on time."

"Just out of curiosity, where is everyone else? Or is it fashionable in today's English society for guests to be late?"

"Oh, I thought you realized dinner would be served for you and me only. I'm sorry." She feigned distress and her ignorant behavior grated on his nerves. "Most of the guests are staying at their estates tonight. They decided to come tomorrow morning instead."

Sebastian's good breeding gave him the strength to hold his annoyance in check. He mentally gave David a point for predicting this behavior his hostess exhibited tonight. Uncertain of Delilah's true intentions, he gave in to his hunger and calmly joined her at the large mahogany table. His place setting was set to the right of Delilah's seat at the head of the table. *I guess it wouldn't be proper to move to the other end.* The thought brought a smile to his face and made this moment somewhat bearable—that and the knowledge he'd be home soon.

"I don't bite, Sebastian." Her seductive tone irritated him. "If you gave me a chance, you would find that out."

"You have a lovely home." Hoping to change her intimate focus, he asked about her father. "Will Lord Scott be joining us for dinner?"

"Not tonight. He's away." Reaching for his glass, she poured him some Pinot noir. "I hope you didn't come all the way out here to discuss business with my father." She ended her statement with a pouty expression.

He avoided direct eye contact as he took a sip of the rich red wine. "Actually, I came for the riding party. I'm an avid equestrian."

"Yes, I'm aware of that."

"You seem to know a lot about me."

"I make it my business to know about my interests."

Sounds like stalker behavior. The first course saved him from responding. He regretted his decision to come, wishing he'd stayed home with his daughter and Sophie. He silently prayed for strength to make it through this dinner without expressing his true thoughts about Delilah's actions.

* * *

"Pastries and desserts will be served in the parlour." After hearing Lord Stiles' announcement, Sophie, Anastasia and Alexander followed him and Ginny out of the dining room. They had finished a delightful dinner of poached eggs, vegetable beef soup, sirloin steak, potatoes, vegetables and the list went on. Ever since beginning her employment with the Shipley family, Sophie had been well fed—dining at the Stiles estate was no disappointment either.

"Jeremy, everything was delicious," Alexander complimented his host. "It's always a treat to come and visit."

"Yes, and it is a pleasure to see you again, my dear." Lord Stiles directed his words to Sophie.

"Likewise." She found herself still taking in the grandeur of the estate—even more spacious than the Shipley's mansion in the states. She'd thought Sebastian's home and the family townhome in London were opulent. They seemed understated compared to the palatial estate of Lord Stiles. The men sat down on the elegant high-backed chairs and Sophie and the giggling girls followed suit, sitting on divans. Seconds later, one of the household staff entered the room carrying silver trays filled with delectable desserts—which she placed on the surrounding marble side tables.

Lord Stiles patted his bulging belly and winked. "Everyone, partake until your hearts and stomachs are content."

Sophie watched as Ginny and Anastasia stood up and walked to one of the serving boards. They piled their plates high. Even though she could barely eat anymore, the sweet smelling delights made her taste buds water and she followed their lead. Lord Stiles' laughter rang out. "Are you ladies going to eat all that or are your eyes bigger than your stomachs?"

"We might surprise you, Grandfather."

"Oh, my Ginny." His uproarious laughter continued and Sophie thought if he had on a red velvet suit, he could pass for Santa Claus.

Sophie sat back down with her own plate piled high with sweets and she wondered how she planned on eating it all. She noticed Alexander smiling and watching his friend—she sensed a great camaraderie between the two men. On the drive to the estate he'd commented that he missed his friend's jovial antics and love of life. Sophie could certainly understand why. Lord Stiles exhibited such a refreshing zest for living. Alexander joined Sophie and whispered, "Are you enjoying yourself yet?"

She nodded affirmatively. He then called over his shoulder, asking his friend if he wanted desserts. Lord Stiles placed an order and Sophie watched Anastasia inch forward on the divan, hesitantly glancing up at their host. Sophie gently nudged Alexander to watch his granddaughter in action. The young girl's voice cracked with apparent nervousness. "Lord Stiles, do you know where Jane Austen's house is?"

"I know where it is, Miss, or rather was. It's been said that her house was on the property where Castle Inn now stands."

"Oh." The tone of her voice matched the dejection in Sophie's heart.

He wagged his stubby, bejeweled finger at her. "Don't you worry, young lady. Ginny and I will take you, your grandfather and Miss Sophie on a tour of our wonderful town of Bath."

"We will, Grandfather?" Ginny chimed in breathlessly. Sophie listened to the conversation and her excitement grew as well, but she tried to act nonchalant.

"Yes, my little Princess."

Sophie and Alexander then joined the discussion, and he handed a plate of desserts to Lord Stiles. She smiled when Alexander winked at his long-time friend and they watched the little ladies whisper and giggle over their new adventure awaiting them tomorrow.

Chapter Seventeen

The crisp air invigorated the eager equestrians, ready for the brisk ride on the Scott family estate. Sebastian surreptitiously glanced around him—he counted twenty-one riders. He knew a few of them socially. Already acquainted with his new friend, one of the Scott's racing horses, he inched near the front of the pack, anxious to race and fly like the wind.

Delilah had greeted Sebastian earlier in the morning with a brief hello. Nothing too flirtatious, although, she'd left her hand on his arm a bit too long for his liking. He had decided to let her behavior slide and instead focused his attention on a winning strategy. His hostess rode ahead and nodded in Sebastian's direction. Like a regal princess, she addressed her guests in a loud, but ladylike voice. "I'm so pleased to have everyone here today. Please enjoy yourselves and feel free to push your horses. They are my father's Thoroughbreds and as you all know, they have made a name for themselves. Please remember to be gentlemanly and step aside for all the ladies present." She flashed an attractive smile, raised her voice and declared the race to begin.

With a flourish, she urged her horse forward and took off galloping. None of the other riders appeared ready for her quick start, except Sebastian. "I knew she'd be able to handle a horse like that, but she most undoubtedly underestimated me." Their lead on the others kept increasing. He focused on the horse in front of him, but more on the path as they approached the wooded area. Delilah had explained the course to everyone before the competition started and had asked the guests to proceed with caution through the woods. However, her definition of caution defied good sense and Sebastian shook his head in disbelief at the way she carelessly flew over the terrain. He hoped her skills as a rider proved adequate and she kept herself from injury.

Trying to overtake the lead, Sebastian heard one or two riders catching up and he concentrated on maneuvering his way closer toward Delilah. A true champion racer, his horse moved very well. Sebastian deftly ducked his head as he rapidly approached a protruding tree branch. He lifted his head a bit and resumed his journey. Steadily gaining on his opponent, the thrill of victory seeped through him.

He inched nearer. "That's right, slow down, milady. You know I'm right behind you." Delilah obviously felt the creeping sensation of the chase run through her because she whipped her head back at his approach and then tried to speed up her horse's pace. Only a few steps away from Delilah, then one, two, three, he flew by her. His horse seemed to feel the same exhilaration that Sebastian felt and he raced on to win.

A few moments later, Delilah reached the finish line with a wry grin on her face. Slowly circling his unmoving form, she then came face to face. "Hmm, I wanted to test you out, but I didn't know you were that good."

"Neither did I," he remarked dryly. Just then, the third and fourth place riders came upon them. Soon everyone reached the finish line. Good-natured teasing and excited, adrenaline-pumped conversation flowed freely.

Delilah brazenly cornered Sebastian again. "So, what do you think of me?"

"Is this a trick question?"

"No, I'm simply curious if you find me attractive at all."

"Attractive?" Sebastian raised his eyebrows slightly and prayed for wisdom. *Here we go...David you were so right!* "Yes, if I'm not speaking out of line, you are an attractive woman." Mustering all his dignity, he tried to change the subject. "I think your guests are getting the look of hunger on their faces, Miss Scott." Although he really wanted to speak his mind and say, *please stop toying with me, give me my breakfast and aurevoir...I'm going home.*

A tad miffed, she retorted. "*Delilah*, you can call me *Delilah*." Like a proper socialite, she maintained her dignity and rode off to regale her guests with stories and laughter. Sebastian breathed a sigh of relief and watched her leave and suddenly missed Sophie more than he'd expected. He wanted to plan a picnic on a nice spring day and take her horseback riding through the woods *Looks like David was right. Now if only I can make a quick escape!*

Waiting in the background, Sebastian dismounted and stood near his borrowed horse. A few minutes later, the rest of the riders approached and dismounted in a flurry. "I guess they're all hungry." He marveled at how these people followed Miss Scott around like puppy dogs. "I know her father has one of the wealthiest estates in these parts, but come on."

"Would you care for some refreshment, Sir?"

"Thank you." Sebastian responded to the butler who offered him a glass of orange juice. He decided to get the mingling part over with and then head back to his room to prepare to go home. "I did my time already," he muttered, "and that dinner was an experience not to be repeated."

* * *

Sophie sat in the parlour reading, while Anastasia and Ginny played school. Anastasia chose the role of the teacher. She gave Ginny a lesson on grammar and the student did well until the exam. Glancing up from her e-reader, Sophie smiled as she listened to her student teach Ginny. "You must be listening to your lessons, my little Miss, because you're doing a good job teaching now."

"Thank you, Miss Sophie."

Lord Stiles and Alexander entered the room, saving Ginny from finishing the exam.

"So, who won?" Anastasia asked.

Lord Stiles appeared peeved. "Your grandfather."

Alexander patted his friend on the shoulder and playfully remarked. "Lord Stiles put up a good fight."

Ginny came over and hugged her grandfather. "I know he must have."

Lord Stiles' jovial mood returned as he beamed at her and abruptly changed the subject. With a quick flick of his wrist, he waved them off. "Now run along ladies and get ready. Our adventures are about to begin."

Alexander smiled at Lord Stiles interacting with the girls. Sophie turned to him. "What are you smiling about?"

"Oh, just a memory. When we were children, Lord Stiles and I made a wager against our respective equestrian abilities."

"Sounds like trouble to me."

"We made the wager in fun, but it turned ugly

when Lord Stiles grew upset because he'd lost in front of our friends. I made things worse when I laughed and commented that he was only trying to show off for the young Lady Christine."

"She was there?"

"Yes, she was one of the avid audience members. Lord Stiles rode away in a huff and he did not speak to me for a week."

The tale intrigued Sophie. "How did you stay friends?"

"Lady Christine shook us into reality and threatened that she would not accept Lord Stiles' future marriage proposal if he did not make amends with his best friend."

"Apparently, it all worked out then."

"Yes, fifteen years later, Lady Christine accepted his proposal and I was the best man at their wedding."

Lord Stiles came back with a flourish. "Are you two joining us or are you still gloating, Alexander?"

"No gloating, my friend. Those days are over." He grinned at Sophie and they followed their host out of the room.

* * *

Lord Stiles made a suggestion for their tour. "Let's begin our adventure in the *Gentleman's*

Carriage."

"What's that, Lord Stiles?" Anastasia tilted her head curiously.

"It's an antique carriage which belonged to my great-grandfather and I had it restored. I only use it for special occasions, such as today, or if I'm traveling a short distance to a party."

"Will Lady Christine be joining us?" Alexander asked solicitously.

"Yes, she returned from visiting her mother in York. She'll be out in a few moments."

They climbed into the roomy carriage and Sophie leaned back against the cushioned seat. She thought about Sebastian for an instant, but tried to push those thoughts away and focus on the day ahead. *I need to be here for the girls…not sulking in a corner all day.*

"Be aware this carriage is a slow and steady traveler so hopefully you young ladies won't chatter so much that my ears fall off."

Ginny laughed. "Oh, Grandfather, you're so silly."

* * *

After he ate breakfast, Sebastian made a quick and silent exit from the morning merrymakers. Walking the horse back the one hundred feet toward the stables, he hoped to remove any temptation from remounting and riding for hours. Also, he wanted to give the horse more time to cool down since he'd ridden hard this morning. Walking gave him a chance for quiet reflection—to pray, think and thank God for all of His provision and strength during these past few months. He fought the urge to stay with the groomsmen and the horse since he knew the other guests would reach the stables in a matter of minutes. He especially had no desire to see Miss Scott for fear she'd try to delay his escape.

Sebastian walked in the rear entrance to the manor house and made his way to the west wing and the guestrooms. Disrobing from his riding attire, he took a quick shower, and then began preparations to leave. He left a hastily written thank you note to Miss Scott with her housekeeper. *I'm sure she'll send her wrath my way once she reads it.* Dismissing the butler's offer to assist with the suitcase, he handled it himself then got into his car and started to drive home.

Later on, as Sebastian neared his London townhome, his body finally started to relax. He hoped to avoid any future contact with Miss Delilah Scott. However, he instinctively felt that his rejection of her advances might encourage her more in seeking his affections. He recognized her as a woman who went after what she wanted and usually got it. A few moments later, he pulled into the driveway. Parking the car, he tried to dismiss thoughts of Delilah and focused instead on Sophie's sweet face.

* * *

Lady Christine announced to the group. "I called ahead to have tickets waiting for us."

"Where are we going?" Sophie's curiosity got the best of her.

"We'll be visiting the Roman Baths at Abbey Church yard in Bath and then stopping by the Museum of Costume at the Assembly Room on Bennett Street, also in Bath."

Sophie nodded. "Sounds great and the weather seems nice for walking."

Seated next to Sophie, Lady Christine leaned closer to whisper. "We won't be walking from the baths to the museum. We need to take the carriage. My husband's leg hurts after long periods of walking." Not sure how to respond to her candid answer, Sophie remained quiet. "An old skiing accident from a vacation in the Alps years ago." Lady Christine explained, then sat back.

Sophie relaxed in the seat for the rest of the ride and listened to the other adults' conversation and the two young girls chattering and giggling about their coming adventure. Sooner than she expected, they arrived at Abbey Church Yard and received directions to the Reception Hall. Sophie made her way with Lady Christine to the front desk. The clerk advised them about the tour. "Touring the Baths will take about ninety minutes."

"Thank you."

Sophie watched the clerk hand over the tickets to Lady Christine. "Would you like the audio guide? It has an added feature which highlights through computerized imagery what the buildings had been like two thousand years ago, during the first and fourth centuries, A.D., as one-quarter of the baths are underground."

"Oh, but couldn't you come with us?" Lady Christine joked. "You sound like you know your stuff."

Sophie noticed the clerk appeared annoyed. "How many audio guides would you like?"

"Three, please."

When she completed the transaction, Sophie turned to her. "I like your sense of humor, Lady Christine."

"You don't have to be so formal with me, Sophie."

"I'll try not to be, but I honestly don't mind"

"I'm very pleased to have met you. I enjoy your company." Lady Christine continued sharing. "I hope my husband can walk the entire tour."

Sophie glanced at the map. "If not, it looks like there's a dining hall in the Pump Room, where he can rest."

"That's a wonderful idea." She gently patted

Sophie's hand. "I knew you were brilliant." They chuckled and hurried to join the men and little ladies.

"I thought you were never coming back." Lord Stiles teased Lady Christine and Sophie when they joined them again.

"We're back and ready to go, right Sophie? Can you lead the way? I'm terrible with maps."

She agreed and moved toward Anastasia and Ginny to show them the plan. "Our first stop is to the Terrace. That's on the upper level, looking down at the baths."

Lady Christine came up to Sophie and leaned close to her ear. "Don't worry about us when we lag behind. If my husband gets tired, we'll head over to the Pump Room and wait for you ladies."

Sophie nodded and both girls grabbed her hands, pulling her along. "All right, ladies, I'm coming."

They reached the Terrace and all three of them simultaneously gasped at the breathtaking view. "This is so neat." Anastasia smiled at her friend. "I'm glad your grandfather brought us here."

"I'm glad, too."

Sophie put on her teacher cap and explained about the tour—nothing like a great extracurricular learning experience. "We can walk around to get different views. Then we'll take a side trip through the Museum. The audio tour will give us an explanation about the religious history."

"Now I feel like I'm in school again." She heard the grumpy tone in her voice.

"No complaining, my little Miss. You need to keep up with your studies while we're here, too."

Ginny chimed in. "What's after that?"

Sophie glanced back to see if the others arrived at the Terrace yet. She saw them reach the top stair just then. "We'll head to the Pump Room to view some of the excavated remains of the Temple Courtyard and there will be hot dry rooms on either side of the bath."

Anastasia tugged on her sleeve. "What does *excavated* mean?"

"That means they dug out certain areas and found artifacts or pieces of past civilizations."

Ginny jumped up with a gleam in her eye. "Like hunting for treasure."

"Yes, something like that." Sophie enjoyed their enthusiasm. "Our final stop before heading over for refreshments at the Pump Room will be to see the King's Bath. That's the center of the hot springs and the inspiration for this Roman Temple." [1] Sophie ushered the girls along to the next stop and they waved at their grandparents as she called out. "We'll see you at the Pump Room."

* * *

They completed the tour in ninety minutes.

"We'd better head back to the Pump Room to find your grandparents." Sophie observed the girls as they strolled along and she smiled at their apparent amazement of this ancient structure. An avid history buff herself, she immensely enjoyed this field trip today. She only wished Sebastian had experienced it with them. Briefly, she wondered if the blonde woman had tried to kiss him yet.

Anastasia stepped in front of her. "Are you listening, Miss Sophie?"

Collecting her thoughts and depositing them in the recesses of her mind, she focused on her number one priority. "I'm sorry." She reached down to gently touch her cheek. "What were you saying?"

"I'm glad we're going to eat now. I'm hungry."

"Me, too. I hope Grandfather is not too tired from walking."

Sophie glanced around. "I don't see them anywhere. They probably went ahead to the dining room to wait for us."

"Miss Sophie, I like you better than my teachers. Anastasia is lucky she doesn't have to go to school."

Anastasia stomped her foot. "I want to go to school. I can't wait until Papa lets me go now that I'm better. Right, Miss Sophie, I'm better now."

"Yes, you are." They arrived at the Pump Room before Sophie needed to respond further.

Ginny pointed. "They're over there."

"Be sure you don't run, ladies."

"Yes, Miss Sophie." They replied in unison and made their way in lady-like fashion across the room.

Lord Stiles rose when they neared the table. "How was the tour?"

"Wonderful, Grandfather." Ginny exclaimed, giving him a big hug.

Anastasia stood in front of her host. "We loved it!"

Sophie absently listened to the girls' conversation and sat down at the table. Her love of architecture and design drew her eyes up to admire the big arched windows close by. She liked the secluded area where the maître d' had seated them. She took a quick survey of the surroundings and noticed the ceiling, at least thirty feet high. Massive arched and square windows lined the parallel walls. The chandeliers sparkled beautifully and the light combined with the sunshine made a glorious sight.

Alexander came over and interrupted her thoughts. "This was the hot spot since the eighteenth century. I bet you didn't know that."

"No, actually I didn't. Sorry you missed the tour. I could've stayed back to keep Lord Stiles and Lady Catherine company."

He waved his hand. "Nonsense, my dear. I've been here many times before. You haven't. I'm glad you enjoyed it."

The waiter came by to take their orders. After Sophie gave hers, she sat back in silence, watching the animated conversation and listening to the music of the solo pianist—which added to the festive atmosphere. However, her mind wandered again toward thoughts of Sebastian and she hoped she saw him again soon. The time away from him made her sad, but she still remained hopeless of any future together.

* * *

Sophie glanced at her watch, one-thirty p.m. They had finished their desserts of crumpets and English Cream Tea and Lord Stiles had abruptly made his way to the door. "I'm exhausted and if no one has any objections, I'd like to retire for a nap."

"Grandfather, we didn't finish the tour."

"Tomorrow, Ginny, dear…we'll finish our tour with a trip to Bristol and the West Country beaches." He directed his next comment to Alexander and Sophie. "Of course, that would mean extending your stay for one extra day."

Alexander nodded his assent, the girls giggled gleefully and Lady Christine delightedly clapped her hands. "We always enjoy company. We've missed your family, Alexander."

"My sentiments, exactly and I'll try to visit

more often."

Sophie smiled, but inside she grew suddenly sullen when she thought about another day away from Sebastian. *He might not even be home yet anyway.* She followed the group out to the carriage. When she climbed in, she sat near the window and stared outside.

Alexander's cell phone rang. "Hello. Oh, Sebastian, how was your trip?"

Sophie's ears immediately perked up and she wished she heard his response to Alexander. "We're just returning from a trip to town. We had a tour of the Roman Baths and dined at the Pump Room." Alexander listened to his son's reply. "Sounds like you had an interesting time. Better you than me." His last comment caught Sophie's interest, but she continued staring out the window. The girls chatted and their hosts spoke in quiet tones, but Sophie felt guilty for eavesdropping once again.

"So, he was right. Before you hang up, I wanted to let you know we'll be staying until tomorrow evening. I hope you don't mind. We're visiting Bristol and the beaches. Yes, she's right here. Hold on." Alexander passed his cell phone to Anastasia and she eagerly spoke with her father. Alexander turned to Sophie. "Sebastian said hello and he hopes you're having a nice time with us." She nodded, not wanting to speak and betray her feelings with a shaky voice. Taking a deep breath, she tried to focus on those around her and shake off her morose feelings.

* * *

After Sebastian ended the phone call with his father, he held up his hands and turned toward David. "Don't say a word. No, *I told you so*. Just give me a few minutes and I'll be ready for work."

"What are you talking about?"

"I know you heard my conversation with Father. You were right. End of story."

"Fine, let's get to work then."

He watched his brother leave the room and regretted not heeding his earlier warnings about Delilah Scott. Hopefully, he hadn't stirred up a hornet's nest and caused trouble to come his way—in the form of a scorned woman. He whispered a quick prayer for guidance and followed David into the office, trying to distract his mind with work.

* * *

When they arrived back at the Stiles' estate, Ginny and Anastasia ran inside, ignoring Lord Stiles' admonitions not to run. Sophie walked toward the main stairwell and stopped when Alexander called after her. "Sophie, may I speak to you for a minute?"

"Sure." She followed him into the parlour and

sat down.

He closed the door. "I'm sorry I agreed to remain without consulting you first. Is it all right for us to stay?"

"It's fine. I don't mind."

"Okay, but you were so quiet on the ride back. I wasn't sure."

Sophie sensed his serious demeanor and before he began delving deep into her feelings for his son—which she figured he intended to do—she stood up. "I think I'm going to head upstairs and read before dinner." She smiled and made her way to the door with as much dignity as she could muster. Glancing back, she managed to say, "Thank you for asking, though. I do appreciate it."

Chapter Eighteen

Happy to relax with no threat of interruptions, Sebastian lounged in a comfortable leather chair. His legs stretched out on an ottoman, and he tucked a fleece blanket around him. A few minutes earlier, Hilde had brought him a cup of hot chocolate. He opened his e-reader to Charles Dickens' *A Tale of Two Cities* and looked forward to reading the rest of the book. Anastasia worked on her studies with Sophie, Alexander had left earlier for a meeting at church, and David had gone out on an afternoon date.

Sebastian sensed another presence in the room, but kept his eyes focused on the screen as he read and ignored the intruder. David pounced mercilessly upon his prey. "I was at the London Zoo and my day was ruined by a visit from Miss Delilah Scott." Even though he heard the annoyance in his brother's voice, Sebastian continued reading. David pushed further. "Don't ignore me, brother. She put a damper on my date."

He broke his silence and laughed

uproariously. "You had a date at the zoo!" He stopped to think. "Oh, that's right, your new lady friend has a little boy."

David glared at him in irritation. "Yes, and that's not the point. I will not be stalked by Miss Scott at your expense."

"What? I'm not involved in this." He turned back to his eBook.

David deftly swiped the tablet from Sebastian's hands.

The Holy Spirit quenched Sebastian's initial reaction of putting on his older brother tone with David. Instead, he tried to see beneath his brother's annoyed veneer and listen. He acknowledged his part in this situation, hoping to appease his brother's agitation. "If I'd listened to your warnings in the first place we wouldn't be in this predicament now." David stared at him. "Calm down and tell me about your visit from Miss Scott. I'm sorry if she ruined your date."

"Susan, James and I did get on with our day. They weren't the least bit perturbed and walked ahead to see the elephant exhibit." David gave the tablet back to Sebastian. "I was the only one upset. It seems silly now, getting bothered over the antics of a woman."

Sebastian moved his legs to the floor. "Not just any woman, but a dangerous one like, Delilah Scott. I'm not going to be her Samson. What did she say, anyway?"

"She had the nerve to ask me if you were involved in a relationship at the moment. I tried to hedge and give her as little information as possible."

"What do you mean?" His heart started racing. "You told her about Sophie?"

"How could I tell her about Sophie, if there's nothing to tell? You still need to start something with her."

"I know, I've been thinking about her a great deal this past week, ever since I returned from the Scott Estate."

David spoke enticingly. "I have an idea."

Sebastian stood up and paced back and forth in front of the stone fireplace. "I can't wait to hear this."

"I've been thinking about this for a while now. You should simply ask Sophie out on a date. Where's the harm in that?"

"Oh, I could think of many reasons not to. Starting with, if it didn't work out, I don't think she'd want to stay on as Ana's tutor."

"Well, Ana's going to be enrolled in school when you get back, right? Her health's no longer an issue."

Sebastian sidestepped the topic, not wanting to think about Sophie leaving them. "Then she's going to know I'm interested."

David slapped his thigh. "Isn't that the idea?"

"Yes, but I don't want to seem too forward."

"There are ways around that. Start spending more time with her when she's with your daughter. Then she won't get suspicious of your true feelings until you're ready to share them. If she responds to your friendly overtures, you can respond, but not right away. Keep her waiting a little. You never know. You can develop your relationship into a deeper friendship through this." David grinned winsomely, with obvious faith in his plan.

"I don't know." Secretly, Sebastian hoped his brother's advice proved true again.

"Give it a try. It can't hurt."

"I guess not." Sebastian glanced down at the crackling fire. Then he looked up at David. "So, Mr. Romeo-matchmaker, what should I do about my stalker?"

His mischievous expression did not bode well for the object of their discussion. "How about we send Daniel over to her estate with a basket full of dead fish and hide them near the front door."

"Oh, real nice. Sorry, I don't think that's the Christian thing to do."

"Well, I'm not a Christian, so I don't have to worry about moral issues."

Sebastian experienced a momentary twinge of sadness over his brother's spiritual state and he prayed silently for his salvation.

David offered further advice. "Tomorrow is

Thanksgiving Day and even though that is not something we celebrate in England, I know you still wanted to enjoy the holiday. So I would wait until the end of the week and maybe pay her a visit or simply let it go and see if she strikes again. She might even forget about you."

"Thanks."

"I'd want to be forgettable to her." David retorted.

"Little brother, I'm actually going to heed your advice."

"I'm honored."

"I'm also going to spend some time with my daughter now. I feel like I haven't seen her in ages."

"You haven't. I've been keeping you busy with work." He pointed his finger at him. "Don't forget about this opportunity to spend some time with Sophie, too." He gave him a cheeky grin.

Sebastian patted his brother on the back and left the parlour in search of his daughter and Sophie. He found them in the library finishing up on the English lesson for the day. As soon as he knocked on the doorframe, Anastasia swiveled in her chair and waved excitedly. Leaving her schoolwork behind, she crossed the room and gave him a big hug. "Papa!"

Sebastian glanced at Sophie for permission to interrupt her class. "I guess that means I can come in." She graciously nodded. He returned his daughter's embrace. "How's my little Princess doing?

I've missed you."

She leaned her head against his chest. "I've missed you, too. Papa, are you done working?"

He brushed back wayward curls from her face. "For today I am. I was reading, but your Uncle David intruded on my peace and quiet. I thought it might be a good time to come bother my two favorite ladies." Anastasia giggled as Sebastian tickled her sides.

She pulled back and eagerly tilted her head up. "What should we do, Papa?"

"I don't know. I was thinking we could make some cookies. What do you say, Sophie?"

"Please, Miss Sophie, can you help us? We need you to tell us all the ingredients."

Sebastian watched Sophie slowly warm up to the idea. He hoped she remembered how much fun they all had last time they'd made cookies together. "I guess so. We did enjoy ourselves."

"Yes, we did." He recalled the puff of flour blown into his face and he couldn't help but grin at the memory.

"Let's go, Papa." Anastasia tugged at his hand and led him away.

He followed his daughter's lead, but purposefully lagged behind, deciding not to let Sophie get away so easily this time from talking to him. Anastasia let go of his hand and skipped off down the hall. "How are Ana's lessons going?"

"She's doing very well."

"How are you doing?"

"I'm fine."

Fine—the universal female word for *no, I'm not so fine!* When would she open up to him? He answered the dialogue going on in his head by realizing that he hadn't truly given her a solid reason to bare her soul. He tried again to chop down the barriers. "Are you going to tell me why you were crying the other day?"

"No." Her curt answers did not daunt him in the least. If there was one thing she may not have yet figured out about him—he was determined to a fault.

Apparently annoyed at the adults' dilly-dallying, Anastasia spun in circles and rolled her eyes. "Papa, Miss Sophie, come on."

Sebastian succumbed to her childish charms. "We're coming, dear." He realized his tactics had barely made a dent in the wall around Sophie's heart, but he would not give up easily. He'd thought they'd been making headway in their friendship and wondered why she'd acted so distant lately. Determination took control and he made it his mission to find out.

Sebastian stood back and watched Sophie put Anastasia to work searching for ingredients. Their strong bond still caused him to marvel and thank God that He had brought Sophie into their lives. *My ways are not your ways.* Those words from scripture definitely applied to this situation. When he'd hired

Sophie, he'd never in his wildest dreams expected to start falling for her.

Sophie's voice broke into his thoughts. "Hey, are you going to help or daydream?"

"Yes, Papa, come on. We need your help."

He lazily sauntered over to the marble counter and batted his eyes at Sophie. "I'm all yours. Put me to work."

Sophie's deer-in-the-headlights expression brought him back to square one. "Um…you can preheat the oven to three hundred-fifty degrees."

I don't think my match maker brother would approve of that behavior. Quickly, he toned down his flirtation meter before he scared her away. Preheating the oven, he touched his daughter's shoulder. "Ana would you mind going to the parlour to get my cell phone? I think I left it in there."

"Okay, Papa." Humming a tune, she began skipping out of the kitchen. As he watched her leave, he grew teary eyed thinking that not too long ago, she was barely able to walk.

Composing himself, he cornered Sophie. "So why were you crying?"

"Are we still on this subject?" She ignored him and continued searching through the cabinets for a baking sheet.

"Yes, we are. Please tell me." Sebastian reached for her hand, but she resisted. *She's not getting away that easily.* Inching forward, he took hold of her hand. He loved the feel of her soft skin.

"I…honestly, it's silly now."

"I'm sure it's not silly. Your feelings matter to me."

She raised her eyebrows. "You sure know how to get to a woman's heart."

"What do you mean?" He asked innocently.

"What is the one thing all women want?"

"I don't know…to be loved?"

"Yes, but to have their thoughts and feelings heard ranks pretty high up there, too."

"That's good. I'm waiting and you'd better hurry up because my daughter is sure to come back soon and report that she can't find my cell phone."

"You're bad."

He knew he'd sent Anastasia on a wild goose chase, but every extra second alone with Sophie mattered to him—especially when something serious had caused her pain. "I needed a chance to speak to you, alone."

"Can I have my hand back?" Her lips parted in a slight smile, encouraging him to continue.

"No, you can't." He grinned and held on.

"I don't want Anastasia to see us. She might get the wrong idea."

"What idea might that be?"

"Okay, this conversation is getting way too deep."

Slow and steady, he reminded himself…*this is*

a delicate situation. "I thought you said women like when men listen."

"You're my employer."

Not exactly the direction I hoped this conversation would go. "Hmm, and that word ranks up there with the other word guys don't want to hear."

"And what's that?"

"Let's just be *friends*."

Sophie moved back toward the pantry and Sebastian thought the conversation had ended, but she surprised him by continuing. "I saw you talking to the pretty blonde woman at your dinner and I assumed you went to her house for the riding party. Besides, it's your business." It pained him that the miscommunication between them happened because of a conniving woman.

"Miss Scott means nothing to me." Her back still faced away from him. *Why won't she look at me?* After an eternity of waiting, she slowly swiveled around but avoided his eyes. Seconds later, he gently lifted her chin with his finger. He gazed at her intently, desperately wanting to express his true feelings to her. When he finally summoned the courage to speak, Anastasia skipped into the room.

"Papa, I can't find your phone anywhere."

For a moment longer, he kept eye contact with Sophie. Gently squeezing her hand, he hoped his half-admission assured her. He looked at his daughter. "Don't worry, honey." Even as he said those words, mild guilt assailed him for sending Anastasia out on a fool's errand.

Sophie took a deep breath and he felt the slightest trembling in her hand. "Let's get started on those cookies."

"Sure." As Sebastian followed her lead, he tried hard to focus on the baking instructions. Keeping busy with locating all the necessary ingredients, his mind swirled with activity, scheming another opportunity to continue their conversation.

* * *

The next day Sophie sat at the dining room table with Sebastian and his family, celebrating Thanksgiving Day. Hilde had outdone herself with creating a festive atmosphere for the family to feast, fellowship and give thanks. Glad that Sebastian had decided to honor this holiday, she glanced around the table and smiled as bittersweet memories of similar gatherings with her own family assailed her. As expected, the delectable Thanksgiving feast left them all satisfied and content. Hilde came in to serve dessert. A few minutes later, David stood up. "Would anyone care to join me in watching a movie?"

Anastasia jumped out of her chair and grabbed his hand. "I will."

He grinned down at her. "I thought you would. Anyone else interested?"

Alexander followed. "I'll join you." At this point, Sophie started getting suspicious and wanted to also excuse herself.

David scooped his niece into his arms and she pointed back at the table. "Uncle David, wait, I didn't finish my cake yet."

Alexander walked back to retrieve the chocolate dessert. "I'll get it." Then he followed them out of the room.

Left alone with Sebastian, Sophie tilted her head. "That was smooth."

"What?" He held up his hands with an innocent expression on his face.

"You mean to tell me it wasn't your plan for us to be alone again so you can continue with our conversation?"

"No, it wasn't, but now that you suggest it, this is an opportune time."

Doesn't he play the innocent act well? She placed both hands on the table and started lifting up from her chair. "Then I guess I'll be joining them for the movie."

Sebastian blocked the doorway. She'd never seen him move so quickly. "Would you mind playing for me?"

"Excuse me?"

"The piano, I mean."

A moment of hesitation followed. Then resignation took over. *What would it hurt?* "Lead the way." Trailing behind him, she wondered again about the blonde woman and if he truly didn't have feelings for her. Entering the parlour, trepidation took over and her hands grew clammy at the thought of being alone with Sebastian. He had the power to send her emotions into a tailspin at any given moment. She longed to spend time with him yet feared the feelings he evoked inside her. He pulled the bench out. "Thank you." The scent of his cologne and his nearness brought the butterflies in her stomach into a frenzy. She stiffened and quickly moved away. Sitting down, she began to play, hoping he moved to the divan across the room—but he stayed right there next to her on the bench. Nodding in the other direction, she continued playing. "You can sit over there, you know."

"The sound is better over here."

Stiffening, she rolled her eyes. "You're making me nervous."

"I am?"

"Yes."

"What if I move to the other end of the bench?"

She shook her head, but couldn't help grinning at him. "You're very persistent."

"Yes, so I've been told."

Focusing again on the piano, she sighed and closed her eyes—very much in her element. The melody of a song she'd learned in her childhood flowed smoothly from the keys. Soon enough she began quietly humming the tune.

After several minutes, Sebastian interrupted her focus. "I enjoy listening to you play."

"Did you just move closer?"

"No."

"You're not a good liar."

"Hmm, I guess not." He gently touched her arm and his skin on her skin gave her shivers. "Please keep playing." She obliged as best she could. *How does he expect me to play normally when he touches me and sits so close by?* "Ana seems to be doing very well. Thank you for all of your hard work with her."

"You're welcome. I love teaching. It doesn't even seem like work to me."

"That definitely shows."

She stopped playing and turned toward him. *Should I even bring up this subject?* "Anastasia is ready for school, you know."

His momentary silence made her doubt her statement. "Yes. We'll cross that bridge when we get there."

Sophie wished he hadn't closed the subject so abruptly, but then she realized how often she'd clammed up the vault to her own heart—and cut him some slack. When Anastasia rushed into the room, her entrance halted any further contemplation on the subject. "Papa, Miss Sophie, will you come to watch the movie? Please…"

Sebastian got up from the bench. "Sure, honey."

Sophie waited for a moment as they left. She sighed in relief as he'd put some distance between them. The realization that no future existed for her and this wonderful man made his nearness feel like pure torture. All she wanted was for his arms to embrace her and keep her safe—unlocking the doors to her heart.

Chapter Nineteen

"What time is it, Miss Sophie?"

"It's two o'clock."

"Papa, where are we going to next?" They had just completed the tour of *Victoria & Albert Museum* and earlier that morning, they'd visited *Kensington Palace* and *Royal Albert Hall*. The trio had attended a special morning event of *"Christmas Carols with the Stars." If only I could harness her exuberant energy.* Thankful for a break, Sophie sat inside a café across from Sebastian and Anastasia eating lunch.

Sebastian teased his daughter. "My, goodness, Ana, I didn't know my day off was going to be so busy."

Her gleeful expression gave Sophie great joy. The young girl had burrowed a hole deep in her heart and took up residence. "Papa, you have to keep up with Miss Sophie and me. We're very active."

Both adults laughed and Sophie agreed. "Yes, you are very active, my little Miss." She checked the brochure in her hand. "It says here that in the winter months, the zoo closes an hour and thirty minutes earlier than during the summer months."

"That means we only have until four, so let's hurry." He urged Anastasia to finish her sandwich.

"Sebastian, have you ever been to the zoo at Regent's Park? I heard it was one of the main attractions in England."

"Yes, once." Briefly, Sophie wondered when that time had been. Had he gone with his wife and daughter?

"Finished, Papa." Anastasia responded proudly and pushed the chair back from the table. "Let's go."

He left money for the bill and tip, and took his daughter's hand. They started walking across the street toward the zoo. Concerned for Anastasia's stamina, Sophie glanced down at her. "Are you tired, little Miss?"

"No, I'm okay."

"I'm only making sure since we did a lot of walking today." As if proving her wrong, Anastasia skipped ahead.

They reached the zoo entrance and Sebastian purchased three tickets. Anastasia touched the map as they made their way through the entrance. "May I be in charge of the directions?"

Sophie deferred to Sebastian. He leaned close to Sophie's ear. "This is going to be an adventure to be led by the mind of a child."

His soft breath against her neck sent chills up her spine. She focused her attention back on Anastasia. "So where are we going?"

With the most serious expression on her face, she pointed to the map. "I was thinking we should see the penguin exhibit."

"What's so special about Penguins?"

She replied to her father. "I've never seen one in person before."

Her young student's cute, take-charge attitude brightened the day. "Lead the way."

Perusing the map once more, she grabbed onto both adult's hands and led them toward the penguins. Sophie enjoyed the few moments of silence as they strolled along. Anastasia dropped their hands to consult the map again. "Do you want to go riding with me some time?" Sebastian's question abruptly invaded her thoughts and sent her heart to racing. Her inquisitive mind wondered if this would be classified as a date or a friendly outing. *Why am I even worrying about the details…answer the question before he changes his mind.*

"Remember, I'm not a very experienced rider."

"Not a problem. You can ride with me."

Images of riding on his horse with her arms wrapped around his firm body distracted her. "I don't know."

"I'll take that as a yes." He dismissed any

further arguments and jogged ahead to catch up with his daughter. Sophie followed his lead but her preoccupation with Sebastian's invitation caused her to pass by the penguins. His conversation with Anastasia drew her back to the moment. "So, my dear, was this exhibit all you thought it would be?"

Remarking in her little grown up voice, she smiled. "It was lovely."

"We're still stuck on that word, huh?" Sophie tried to get back into the conversation.

"Miss Sophie, it's a good word."

"That it is."

"At least I'm not saying bad things."

"You can say *lovely* all you want." Sophie leaned down to give her a hug.

Sebastian looked at the map. "Where are we off to now?"

Anastasia grinned at him. "You decide next. That's only fair."

"Ah, so you're lovely and fair…like one of the ladies from Shakespeare's sonnets." He raised his finger as if a light bulb had gone off in his head. "I've got it. Let's go see the monkeys and no monkey business from you."

Sophie shook her head at his sad attempt at humor, but Anastasia replied before she got a chance to. "Papa! I'm good. I could never be doing any monkey business because I'm not a monkey. Besides, I'm too smart for that." She winked at him and started stomping off in as lady-like a fashion as possible.

"Did she just wink at me?"

"I believe so." Sophie chuckled softly.

"Apparently, my daughter has more wit than I do!"

Sophie watched him chase after his daughter. "You're not so bad yourself, Mr. Shipley."

* * *

Later the next day, Sebastian sat with his brother in the study, sharing David's office space. He listened to David drone on about their current project and his mind wandered to something his father had said last night. "You're going through a few changes in your life and there's the possibility of a new love interest…things are looking hopeful. Who would want to concentrate on work! Not me." Sebastian recalled wanting to refute his statement, but deep inside, he knew he craved this chance with Sophie.

David shook his head. "Here we go again. I'm trying to work. If you don't want to listen, why not go take a walk and clear your head of her."

"Her? I'm not thinking about Sophie."

"Who said I was talking about Sophie?"

"Well, whom else would I be thinking about?" Chagrined and realizing he'd fallen into David's trap, he stood up. "Do you mind if I take a break?"

"I welcome it." With agitation, he focused

back on his business report. "Maybe now I'll accomplish something." Sebastian started to walk out of the room and David stopped him with his words. "I am happy for you brother." He glanced back toward David. "Even if it doesn't work out with Sophie, I'm glad to see you cheerful again. You deserve happiness."

"Thank you." *Maybe now's a good time to go for a ride.* He started walking to the coatroom near the foyer in search of one of his coats. *Guess it would help if I had my riding clothes on before I go anywhere!* He went to his room to change. A few moments later on the spur of the moment, he rushed down the hall in search of Sophie. By the time he located her relaxing in the library he stood panting from his search all over the ground floor. Taking a moment to catch his breath, he then knocked on the doorframe.

"Hi, are you ready for that horseback ride?"

"Are you all right? You sound out of breath."

He brushed back the hair from his forehead. "I was actually rushing to find you."

"You really want me to go riding with you?"

He tried to read her expression but wasn't sure if she wanted to go or shoo him away. "Yes, but if you don't want to—"

Placing her e-reader on the end table, she quickly stood up. "Sure, I'll go." *She wants to go with me? Don't get too excited now*, he chided himself.

Sebastian started to laugh. "What's so amusing?"

"You're going to wear that?"

Sophie glanced down at her long blue skirt and fluffy pink slippers. "Oh, yeah, I took Anastasia to the theater today and we just got home. I never changed clothes."

"I'll wait in the foyer for you."

She nodded and hurried out. Sebastian watched her walk away and then he went in the front hall. He paced back and forth and finally sat down on the wooden bench, trying to relax. Restlessness assailed him like he was a teenager on his first date.

A few moments later, Sophie met him by the front door. "I'm ready."

He smiled hesitantly. "Let's go."

She wagged her finger at him. "Remember, I'm not an equestrian like you."

"Don't worry. I'll go easy on you." *Hopefully, we'll have many more times like this.*

"I thought you said I could ride with you."

He noticed her worried expression and hurried to assure her. "You are."

She let out a relieved sigh. "Good, because for a second there I thought you were going to give me a horse to ride."

"I don't work that fast on a first date." Now her anxious countenance transformed into one of horror and he held up his hands. "I was only teasing you, Sophie. I know this isn't a *date*." Though, as he spoke those words, he desperately wanted to classify this outing as the first of many romantic rendezvous.

She nodded and he remained quiet as he led her to the stables.

"We can't push the horse to full power here, since we'll be riding in the park."

"I bet you really want to fly."

She gets me and the thought made him smile to the core of his being. "Yes, you understand the idea."

He noticed a softening of her features. "So that's why you went to the riding party."

"I guess you can say that." He decided not to dwell too long on the subject. They'd already cleared the air and he didn't want to step backward and pollute the situation again. He turned back to the horse and his preparations. "I've never ridden double before, except with Katherine."

"Oh."

I guess I shouldn't have said that. He hurried to continue. "I'll get on first and then pull you up." He swiveled around and pointed. "You can stand on that crate, okay?"

"Sure."

"Are you fine back there?" Sebastian asked after he hoisted Sophie up.

"Yes."

Turning his head to the side, he grinned. "You should probably put your arms around me." He sensed her hesitation and teased. "I don't bite, you know."

Her merry laughter sounded like music to his ears. She gently put her arms around him. Sebastian enjoyed the feel of her arms and he tried to focus on the ride ahead. With Sophie near him, he rode unaffected by the cold wind. His adrenaline pumping, he rode the horse out of the stable. He then maneuvered down the driveway toward the street amongst the vehicles and people. As he neared the park, Sophie leaned closer. "Have you ridden through here often?"

"Yes, but I especially enjoy the open range areas. When we get home, I'll take you riding around the property."

"I look forward to that."

"Hmm…you weren't too excited about joining me today."

"Well, maybe I've seen the light."

They rode in silence for a few moments. "Are you enjoying yourself in England? This is your first time here, right?"

"Yes and yes."

"Would you care to elaborate?"

Her excited chatter touched a chord in Sebastian and he smiled as she continued. "I am enjoying myself. I'm doing something I love— teaching and I get to see the wonderful sites of your homeland."

"Maybe one day I'll get to see your Emerald Isle."

The wind picked up and she leaned closer to his ear. "When you go, take me with you." Her warm breath against his neck did funny things to his already nervous stomach.

He wanted to say, *I plan to*, but instead he settled for, "Sure thing." He kept the horse at an easy trot as they rode through the park. "You're not getting too cold are you?"

"I'm fine."

"Just making sure. I'm used to riding in the brisk weather." *It's now or never.* "May I ask you a personal question?" *This could go very badly if she's annoyed by my prying.*

"Sure, you can ask anything you want, but I reserve the right not to answer."

"Touché. Have you made peace with God yet?"

"Didn't you ask me that before?"

"Yes, but has there been any progress?"

Sophie's silence worried him and he thought he'd overstepped his bounds. "I'm getting there. Thank you for your concern. Oh, and thank you again for the Bible. I've been reading it."

"That's good." As he decided to drop the subject, they soon neared the end of the park. "Maybe we should head back now." Sebastian felt Sophie shiver in the cold. He turned the horse around.

"Thank you for coming out with me. I hope you enjoyed it."

"Yes, thank you for the invitation. I had fun."

He smiled, already envisioning another adventurous equestrian outing back home on his estate. Although there they could fly like the wind and settle in for a romantic picnic near the lake.

* * *

Sebastian entered the study and David glanced up from his work. "It's about time you came back. I thought you'd gotten a flight home and were leaving me with all this paperwork."

"I apologize. Sophie and I just got back."

He noticed his statement caught David's attention. "Sophie? Where did you go?"

"I took her riding in the park."

"Ooh, that's a nice first date."

Sebastian sat down, ready to tackle his brother and his to do pile. "It wasn't a first date."

David smirked. "Then let's finish up here because I have a *real* date to get to."

* * *

Sophie stood quietly staring out the window in her bedroom. Her thoughts played havoc with her heart as she recalled every detail of her conversation with Sebastian this afternoon. No doubt about it, she'd enjoyed riding with him and wrapping her arms around his strong body. She could feel the heat rising to her cheeks as she remembered wanting to run her hands through his wavy brown hair. Leaning her head against his back, she had felt the rumbling through his body when he'd laughed. When she'd understood how passionate he was about riding, she thought she'd detected a glimmer in his eye. The scent of his musky cologne still clung to her.

Each interaction with this intense man only further cemented her growing feelings for him in her heart. *So much for maintaining my distance.* Sebastian's flirtatious behavior of late came to mind. She tried to keep from getting too excited over it— still believing a romance with him remained far out of reach. All her wishing and hoping would not change the fact that they belonged to two very different worlds.

Chapter Twenty

Sophie tried to draw Anastasia's attention back to the geography lesson, but she needed to admonish her student three times already to pay attention. She closed the textbook with a thud and decided to try a different tactic. "Okay, let's discuss traditions. They're beliefs or customs passed from generation to generation. My mum and I baked cookies together. I loved to help her. At Christmas time it was very special because we made sugar cookies and delivered them to the nursing home to visit the elderly patients who didn't have any family."

Anastasia gave her a puzzled look. "Why did you call your mom *mum*? I never heard you say that before."

"That's because my mum and da were from Ireland. Mom is *mum* and dad is *da*." Sophie had caught her student's attention with this approach of combining history and geography. She shared more details about Irish Christmas traditions and others of that culture.

Later that hour Anastasia completed her math worksheet and Sophie started the grading process. She asked her student to take out her journal and work on free writing exercises.

"Miss Sophie, I don't know what to write about."

She looked up from the papers in front of her. "Start jotting down any word which comes to mind and then see if you can develop those thoughts further into the beginning of a story." A few moments later, Sophie held up the math worksheet. "You scored a one hundred. I think these worksheets are too easy for you," she teased.

"You told me they're for the next grade level."

"Oh, that's right. I did, didn't I? So, you're actually as smart as you've been telling me."

"Yes." Anastasia answered in all seriousness and then burst out laughing.

She flipped through the lesson plans. "We're almost done, but you do have one more workbook page. I'm glad we brought your schoolwork along…otherwise, I'd be in trouble. We'd be taking field trips all day and I would teach you that way." She wiped the imaginary sweat from her brow and let out a sigh of relief.

"It would be lovely to take field trips every day." She giggled and dramatically buried her face in the journal.

"I'm sure you would enjoy that because it would be *lovely*."

"Okay, I know." She held up her pencil. "I'm thinking of a new favorite word."

"Sure, if you say so."

"Seriously, Miss Sophie, it is time to move on."

She laughed so hard her sides hurt. When she recovered, she smiled. "You certainly are my favorite student."

"You only have one."

Sophie winked. "Oh, right but if I had another one, I'd like you best."

Anastasia closed the journal, laid down the pencil, and walked over to give her teacher a big hug. "Can I ask you a question?"

"Sure."

"Does my Papa like you?"

Not surprised to hear this observation voiced from the young girl, Sophie stalled. "Um…what made you ask?"

"A lot of things made me."

"Can you share them?"

"Papa is smiling more now. He talks to you all the time."

"I honestly don't know how to answer your question, my little Miss."

Much to her relief, Anastasia quickly changed

the subject. "What time is it?"

"Why, do you have a date?"

"I told Ginny I'd call her before three so we can discuss what we're wearing tonight for Papa's party."

"You're going to the party?"

"Papa said we can stay downstairs as long as we don't bother the guests before dinner. He said the dinner is for grown-ups, so Hilde is making a special feast only for us."

"How nice." Sophie wondered why Sebastian had neglected to share this information with her. "Well, it is two-fifty-five now, so you can skedaddle and go call your friend. Tell Ginny I said hello."

"Thanks, Miss Sophie." She blew her a kiss and raced out of the room.

Sophie headed in the opposite direction to speak with Sebastian.

* * *

As Sophie knocked on the cherry wood door of the study, she attempted to control her fluttering nerves. She hated to disturb the men, but she needed to discuss an important issue with Sebastian. She heard David answer. "Come in."

Taking a deep breath, she opened the door and stepped over the threshold into David's office. For a moment, seeing both brothers hard at work, she almost forgot why she came in the first place. Timidly stepping forward, she forced herself to speak. "Sebastian, may I talk to you?"

He stopped mid-stroke of signing some papers. "Can it wait? We're in the middle of finalizing this contract for Lord Scott to sign tonight."

"I don't think it should wait. I'll only take a second. It's about Anastasia."

He sat at attention and dropped his pen on the desk. "Is she all right?"

Great, now I alarmed him. "Can we speak privately?"

Sebastian nodded toward David. "I'll be right back."

Sophie thought she caught a glimpse of David smirking at his brother, but she turned to follow Sebastian out of the room. The short walk to the parlour felt like being shoved off the plank of a pirate ship. *Why am I even bothering him with this?* Emotions bubbled up inside her and erupted like hot lava in this statement. "She asked if you liked me." Horribly embarrassed for even bringing the subject up, she stopped speaking. *Why am I always so impulsive? I need a filter on my mouth!* His cheeky grin amazed her. *He's not the least bit concerned.*

"Isn't she an observant young lady."

"Maybe you should speak to her about this."

"She's right, you know."

Pressure filled her chest. Sophie stepped back

and wanted to flee out of the room.

Sebastian's brown eyes pierced to the core of her being. "Sophie, why are you always running from me?"

"I'm not." *What a bad idea to tell him.* "I should get back to Anastasia."

"Isn't she on the phone with Ginny?"

"Yes. Oh, she also mentioned she's coming to the party tonight with her."

"I forgot to tell you that and I wanted to formally invite you too, as my guest."

Did she hear right? She stared at him, not sure what to say. How could she go to the party as his guest?

He tilted his head and batted his eyes. "Please don't say no. You have to eat, don't you?"

His quirky antics amused her, but she couldn't comprehend the thought of being his *plus one* at his party. "Sebastian, I don't fit into your world."

The intensity in his eyes penetrated her defenses. Moving closer, he squeezed her hand reassuringly. "In my eyes, you fit in, Sophie. In case you decide to come, there's a present for you upstairs in your room." He brought her hand to his lips and kissed her skin. His electric touch buzzed through to her toes. As he walked out, she remained in the same position, not turning around. "I hope you come. I would love for you to be with me." She heard him leave the room. A tear started to fall, but it stemmed from hope filling her heart.

Slowly she swiveled on her feet and smiled. "He actually likes me."

* * *

Sebastian walked to his daughter's bedroom and saw her on the phone, but he knocked on the doorframe to get her attention. He heard her ask Ginny to hold on. "Can we talk for a moment?"

She spoke into the phone. "Ginny, Papa needs me. I'll call you later."

His daughter amazed him once again by her maturity and how she handled this situation. He felt helpless to guide her as she grew into her preteen years. At times like this, he sorely missed his wife and the impact of her godly, maternal influence.

"How's my little girl?" He sat on the edge of the bed.

"I'm good. I was talking to Ginny about what we're planning to wear tonight."

"I know you'll both be beautiful."

"I'm glad we can come to the party for a bit. Thank you."

"It is Christmas time and you are getting older." He tried to open this topic delicately, not wanting Sophie to appear like a tattletale. "I bought Miss Sophie a Christmas present."

"I saw the box in your closet. That's when I

slipped my present for her in there too."

"Excuse me, dear?" *Hmm, maybe I need to find a new hiding spot for gifts.*

"That's one of the reasons I forgot to tell Miss Sophie about."

Since she'd opened Pandora's Box, he forged ahead. "So, do you think I like her?"

She bounced on the bed in excitement. "Yes. I think it's wonderful."

"You do?" He spoke, with relief in his voice.

"I like her, too. I want her to stay with us. If I go back to school, she has no job and I want her to stay. That's why I'm glad you're going to marry her."

Out of the mouths of babes! "Whoa." He held up both hands. "I think you've been putting a little too much thought into this, my Princess. No one said anything about wedding bells." *At least not yet.*

"I thought—"

"Miss Sophie and I are only special friends right now." He peered in to her blue eyes, hoping she could grasp the delicate situation. His number one priority in life was his daughter and the last thing he wanted to do was cause her confusion.

"I'm glad." She responded by jumping across the bed and embracing him.

Well, that went easier than I thought it would. "I have to get back to work or Uncle David is going to have another lecture for me. What are your plans for the rest of the afternoon? Did your lessons go well?"

"Yes. I need to call Ginny back so we can finish deciding on our clothes for tonight. She's sleeping over."

"What about Lord and Lady Stiles?"

"Yes, that's what Ginny said. I think Grandpapa spoke to Lord Stiles this morning."

"All right, dear." He kissed the top of her curly blonde head. "I'll see you later. If you want me to, I'll come escort you downstairs."

"That would be wonderful."

"What happened to *lovely*?"

"Oh, I have a new word now. Didn't Miss Sophie tell you? Oh I forgot, I didn't tell her what it was yet. I have to go find her and tell her before I call Ginny. Excuse me." As she ran out of the room, she blew kisses at her father.

In the wake of her quick exit, he shook his head and smiled. "So mature, yet so cute and childish. She's my little girl."

* * *

Later on, Sebastian took the stairs to his daughter's bedroom, but this time on a different mission, as an escort. He stopped dead in his tracks when he came upon the scene inside. His heart welled with pride when he saw his beautiful young daughter all dressed up in lace and frills. He watched Sophie arranging the pink satin bow in Anastasia's hair and then she asked Ginny if she needed help. Like a thirsty nomad in the desert, Sebastian drank in the sight of Sophie in the elegant, cream-colored evening gown. Her auburn curls pinned and swept to the side drew attention to her one bare shoulder. He wanted to plant feather-light kisses all along her neck. Staring at her, he hoped his mouth wouldn't hang open like a hungry dog when she turned around. Somehow he managed to speak. "You decided to come."

The satin fabric shimmered and swayed as she strode gracefully across the room. His pulse quickened at her approach. "Thank you for the dress."

Relaxing a bit, he grinned devilishly. "You look stunning, you know."

Her shy response spoke volumes about her—compared to Miss Delilah Scott and her over active conceit. "Thank you. You don't look so bad yourself."

Anastasia came over with Ginny. "You look wonderful, Papa."

"Thank you. Both of you young ladies are beautiful. Like little Princesses." They beamed at him and held hands, walking out of the room.

Sebastian nodded his head toward Sophie. "Wait for me up here. I'll come back for you." He heard exclamations about the girls from his father, and Lord and Lady Stiles out in the main hall. A minute later, when he got back to Sophie he smiled.

"Thank you for helping the girls get ready."

"They did most of the work."

Reaching for both of her hands, he gave them a reassuring squeeze. "How do you feel?" He figured she must be experiencing some nerves and he didn't want her to change her mind and not come downstairs with him.

She raised her eyebrows. "A little nervous. I won't know anyone."

He stepped closer. "You're not backing out on me…"

"No."

"I won't leave you alone and if I have to step away, I'll make certain my father keeps you company." She still didn't appear completely convinced. *Do I have to kiss you Miss Sophie Baird?*

"If you're definitely sure you want me to come."

He brought her hand to his lips and gazed intently into her blue eyes. Kissing her hand, he locked eyes with her the entire time. "I'm absolutely positive." He hoped she'd felt the same intensity as he did in the special moment. She nodded and smiled hesitantly. He gallantly offered her his elbow and they made their way downstairs.

* * *

Relieved the evening progressed quite

successfully without any scenes from his stalker, Sebastian moved amongst the guests proudly—with Sophie by his side. Earlier, he and David had discussed the situation with Alexander and the possibility of confronting Miss Scott if she tried her flirtatious schemes again. Sebastian knew they needed to tread lightly so Lord Scott renewed his contract this year.

He turned and his gut tightened when he saw her behind them. He braced himself for a scene, especially since Sophie stood by his side as his obvious guest. Near the punch bowl, Miss Scott reached in front of him, not saying a word, and poured a drink. She brought the cup to her plump red lips and took a sip. Then she tilted her head to the side and tried for a seductive tone. "You lost and it looks like Lord Alimor won."

Sebastian raised his eyebrows, annoyed by her attempts to bait him. He hoped Sophie felt secure during this exchange. He poured a drink for himself and Sophie and raised his glass to her. Then he nodded and strolled off when Dudley Milton called his name and rescued him. Sebastian ushered Sophie away and surreptitiously glanced back and noticed Miss Scott appeared miffed again and she sulked in defeat. Her sour expression lasted only a moment. For when she saw Lord Alimor, an elderly and extremely wealthy gentleman—her latest conquest—she beamed at him and he soaked up her young attentions.

Sebastian and Sophie found Anastasia and Ginny giggling quietly near the far corner of the room. "Do you ladies need an escort to your dinner table?"

"Oh, Papa, it is time already?"

He leaned close and whispered conspiratorially. "Yes, I want to get this dinner party over with." The adults escorted the girls to the small informal dining room off the kitchen. Hilde waited for them with the small table set up for two, with candles and flowers and an array of food fit for two growing children. "We'll see you later. Pray for us, ladies." Winking and making a funny face, he escorted Sophie back toward the guests.

"How are you doing?" He whispered close to her ear, as he inhaled her fragrant perfume.

"I'm okay. Your friends are a bit intimidating, but I'm fine as long as I'm with you."

As long as I'm with you…those words made him smile and want to protect her even more. "They're mostly business associates and clients, but I'm happy about the last part." He hoped he'd be able to think straight during the remainder of the party. As he escorted Sophie into the dining room, his pride soared. Sophie may not completely believe him, but he truly considered her his *plus one* for this evening— and in the days to come, he wanted to explore their relationship further.

Chapter Twenty-One

After lunch, Sebastian had invited Sophie to join his family in setting up their Christmas tree. "If we were home in the States, we would follow our tradition of getting up early and choosing a tree from the grounds." Sophie recalled the vast concentration of coniferous trees surrounding the property. Picturing their branches covered with snow and icicles, she wondered if Nigel assisted with the tree cutting tradition. He appeared frail, but managed to accomplish many tasks in the big house. Sebastian continued explaining. "Ana has enjoyed this tradition since she was a toddler. I'm sure she'll miss it."

"Will you?"

He tilted his head. "Yes, but this year is different, though still as good and I'm enjoying every minute."

Daniel had left earlier to pick up the tree. He'd just returned and finished securing it in the stand. David had suggested keeping the tree in the front parlour where he'd set it up for the past few years.

Sophie watched Anastasia eagerly rummaging through a box of ornaments, while Alexander and David discussed the best way to untangle, test bulbs and string up the lights. Daniel and Hilde stood quietly waiting to see if the family required their help. *I still don't think I'm ever going to get used to having household staff around.*

Anastasia stopped suddenly and smiled at Sebastian. "Merry Christmas."

"Merry Christmas, sweetheart."

"This is my job, Miss Sophie, ever since I was a baby."

The excitement in her voice was contagious. "Sounds like a fun job." She knelt down on the floor near the box. "May I help?"

"Yes. Papa, will you help, too?"

"Sure, I'll be right over dear." Sophie smiled as Sebastian strolled toward his father and David to intervene in their animated discussion. "Now do I have to spread some holiday cheer over here?"

"Oh, you have enough cheer for all of us in this room." David retorted. "Any more cheer and the room will explode."

Alexander teasingly egged him on. "You're simply jealous."

"I don't think—"

Sebastian held up his hands as if calling for a ceasefire. "Gentlemen, please no more arguing. Let's relax and work together here, before Anastasia has to

come over and give her *peace on earth dissertation.*"
He winked at Sophie. "You know, this happens every
year."

David urged. "Don't listen to him, Sophie,
he's exaggerating."

Sebastian shook his head and Sophie smiled as
he walked back toward her and his daughter. When he
beckoned Hilde and Daniel to come into the room to
help, if they wanted to—the gesture made her respect
Sebastian even more.

"Begging your pardon, Sir, but I think I'll go
prepare some refreshments." Hilde declined his offer,
which did not surprise Sophie. Daniel nodded and left
as well to get back to his duties.

Anastasia picked out a small angel and looked
at her father. "I made this as a gift for Uncle David
last Christmas."

She stood up, straightening her denim skirt
and skipped over to show her uncle. "Yes, I
remember. That's my favorite one, Ana."

"Are you ready to put the lights on? We can't
do the ornaments until the lights are up."

David and Alexander answered at the same
time. "Yes."

Sophie watched Anastasia smile at them and
then she moved back to sorting through the box of
ornaments. After kneeling on the ground for a while,
Sophie needed to stand up to stretch her legs.
Sebastian followed suit. "She seems very serious

about her job."

"Her mother told her once that she had a very important task of hanging the ornaments. She said there was a lot of thought one needed to put into where the ornaments would hang and there was a special spot you must find for each one." Sophie nodded in understanding and Sebastian continued. "They would have a wonderful time of sorting and hanging the ornaments after I strung the lights." The love mother and daughter had shared brought joy to Sophie's heart.

"You both must miss Katherine very much, especially during this special time of year."

"As I'm sure you miss your parents, too."

"Yes." She sniffled and wiped away a tear running down her cheek. "I don't want to ruin the day for everyone. Let's talk about something else."

Her only escape was to kneel down again by the box. He stopped her by leaning close to whisper, "Special memories will never ruin the day. Don't ever forget the gift God gave you for a time." He quickly changed the subject. "Does anyone want some hot cocoa?" He received a chorus of assent. "I'll put your orders in with Hilde."

Back in her position as assistant ornament worker, Sophie allowed the twinge of sadness from the memories to wash over her. Running from her grief would not help her move forward. Stepping out of her comfort zone again, she decided to dig deeper with Anastasia. "Do you still miss your mother a lot?"

"Not as much as in the beginning, but it helps when I remember she's in Heaven with Jesus." She answered without looking up.

"Yes. She is."

Sebastian came back into the room, when David and Alexander had nearly completed hanging up the strands of lights. He inspected their work. "I love the white lights."

Sophie watched the exchange as Alexander patted him on the back and she enjoyed the sight of father and son together. "Your mother and I used the white lights since our first Christmas together. They reminded her of candlelight and how in the past her great-grandmother had used real candles on the tree branches."

Sophie agreed. "I like the white lights, too. I love Christmas time, especially Christmas Eve." Memories from past Christmases washed over her and she anticipated making more happy memories with the Shipley family this year.

Anastasia clapped her hands and exclaimed. "They're done, Papa. We can get started."

He took the two ornaments she handed him. "Okay."

David ambled over to the nearest recliner. "I'm too exhausted. I'll watch you finish."

Sebastian teased him. "So I guess Hilde and Daniel do a lot of work for you when we're not here."

Hilde entered with the refreshments at that moment. Sophie noticed her slight smile—and lack of obvious acknowledgement of the teasing—in deference to her employer. Sebastian let the subject drop and Sophie figured he wanted to keep the housekeeper out of an uncomfortable position. Sebastian thanked Hilde for the refreshments and they finished decorating the tree.

* * *

Sophie, Sebastian and Anastasia strolled around town and stopped at a little antique shop. "I need to find one last minute gift for my father." Drawn to the large display case filled with antique porcelain dolls, Anastasia let go of her father's hand and took off. Sophie watched her staring—small nose and hands pressed up against the glass, eyeing up those dolls—and nudged Sebastian.

He pulled her aside. "I already got one for her. One of Santa's elves gave me a hint."

"Your father, I presume?"

"Yes. He was out with Ana a few weeks ago and noticed her fascination with them." He excused himself to search for his last minute gift and Sophie joined Anastasia.

"They're very pretty. Which one do you like?"

She pointed. "The one in the middle with the red hair."

"I had one like that once."

After several minutes of Sophie chatting with Anastasia and watching her stare at the dolls, Sebastian came back and they left the shop.

"It's snowing!" Anastasia exclaimed. She started twirling in the snow with her arms wide open, palms held up and tongue stuck out to catch the snowflakes.

Sebastian exhaled. "It's a beautiful thing."

Sophie looked at him curiously. "What is?"

He opened his arms wide. "How much God loves us and keeps us in the circle of His grace, even when we can't see the beginning from the end." She listened intently and he continued. "Honestly, I never believed I'd see this day when my daughter would be so vibrant and twirling in the snow." He choked up and stared at Anastasia but directed his thanks to Sophie. "You believed for her healing. Thank you for showing me how to have faith."

"The funny thing is I didn't have much conviction for anything at the time, but something in me believed for my little Miss."

"God was working on all of us."

"I'm so dizzy, Papa, from all this twirling."

"Come, hold my hand." With his other hand, he reached for Sophie's hand. The trio strolled passed more shops and Sophie allowed herself the freedom to dream of life with Sebastian and Anastasia. A feeling of security with this man enveloped her, making her realize she wanted to fight for this dream—no matter what the cost. Timidly, she squeezed Sebastian's hand and he turned toward her. When she smiled, his face seemed to light up in return. He leaned forward and firmly planted a flirty kiss on her cheek. She surprised herself by not flinching or pulling away. They walked back the rest of the way in a comfortable silence, with Anastasia's childish chatter filling the stillness.

* * *

In her bedroom, Sophie plopped backward on to the bed and stared blankly up at the nine foot ceiling. She remembered her promise to herself that she'd planned to visit her parents' gravesites during Christmas—quite an impossible feat this holiday since she was in England. The ache of missing the graveside visit overwhelmed her heart. She visualized driving in silence to the cemetery along the scenic route, experiencing the beauty of God's creation.

In her mind, once she'd reached the cemetery and had driven down the long lane toward the gravesites, she'd visualized leaving her car running and staring out the windows for a few minutes. Thinking about all that had happened during the year, her rededication to Christ topped the list. Sophie pictured herself opening the door and walking across the snowy field to a site she knew well. When she'd reached her parents' tombstones buried a little under the snow, she wiped the snow away with her gloved hands.

Closing her eyes, she imagined taking her gloves off, needing to feel the cold stone. She'd trace the engraved lettering of their names, dates of birth and death. She would run her finger over the statement on the joint tombstone—*One in life and death. They lived for Jesus and loved each other*. That statement rang true to the life and character she'd witnessed in their lives. She remembered reading the verse about *a great cloud of witnesses*…and about *angels rejoicing in Heaven when one of God's children gets saved.*

Still lying on the bed, she whispered up at the ceiling. "I hope you're rejoicing mom and dad. Jesus found me again." Picturing herself placing flowers on the snow and saying a final good-bye, she would then turn to walk away. As she pondered that action, she realized she possessed a light heart even when thinking about her parents. *The peace which passes all understanding* began filling her being. She sighed and let the tears of mingled joy and sorrow flow down her face.

A knock sounded on the door and she quickly sat up and wiped her tears. "Who is it?"

"Miss Sophie, it's me. May I come in?"

"Sure."

Anastasia exuberantly pushed opened the door

and announced. "Papa's going to watch *Miracle on 34th Street* with me. Do you want to come down?"

The excitement in her voice was contagious, helping to pull her out from this fragile emotional state. "Okay."

"Were you crying?"

She shook her head and mustered a smile. "Um, I'm fine."

Anastasia came closer for a timid inspection and wiped away a tear. "Your face is wet, Miss Sophie. Those are tears."

She pulled the young girl into a hug. "Do you have to be so smart?" Moving back, she lightly poked her in the nose. "Honestly, I'm fine. I was only thinking about my parents."

"You miss them a lot."

"Yes, I do."

"Are they in Heaven?"

"Yes. They both loved Jesus very much."

Her smile grew bigger. "They're with my mom, now."

"That's right."

"Do you need another hug?"

"I think I do." Little arms embraced Sophie. Like a dry sponge, she soaked up the offered love and encouragement.

Another knock sounded on the door.

Sebastian peeked his head in. "Are you ladies coming? You went upstairs hours ago, Ana."

"No, Papa." She waved her hand dramatically. "It was more like five minutes. Miss Sophie needed to talk." With those words, she spun on her heels and left the room, blonde braids bouncing behind her. "I'll be downstairs."

Sebastian glanced at Sophie and she shrugged her shoulders.

"Is everything all right?"

"Yes. I forgot that I promised myself I'd visit my parents' grave sites during the holidays and now I can't. I simply got emotional."

"If you need to talk, I'm here." His comforting hand on her shoulder distracted her for a moment.

"Thanks for the offer, but I do feel better. For the first time in a while, I actually know a sense of peace."

"That's wonderful."

"Well, let's go." She stood up. "I hear I'm invited to the movies."

"Yes, you are." Linking arms, they made their way downstairs.

Chapter Twenty-Two

Sophie sat in the pew next to Sebastian—with Anastasia to his left, beside Alexander. Inching forward, she surreptitiously glanced over at David, glad he decided to attend the Christmas Eve service. The worship leader led the congregation in a few praise songs, but mostly Christmas choruses. The house lights dimmed as they ended the song time with *Silent Night*, and the drama presentation began. Sophie recalled her distraught, bitter state this year which had kept her away from church. In hindsight, she realized she'd desperately needed to run toward the fellowship of believers. Saddened at the commercialism surrounding this precious holiday, she watched the story of Christ's birth unfold before her eyes. The world had taken Jesus out of the reason for the season and had replaced him with a jolly old man in a red suit.

She enjoyed the final scene of the birth of the Christ child—Joseph holding him up for the entire world to see. In the background, the choir beautifully sang the words of *Joy to the World*. The Pastor came up on the platform when the music concluded and he gave a short devotional. He spoke of Jesus and pleaded with those in the audience to get right with God. Sophie closed her eyes as he started praying and then gave an altar call. Whenever she'd entered a church in the past, her mind always wandered during the altar call. However, now she made good use of her own efforts. She prayed silently along with the Pastor for all of the people wrestling with making decisions to accept salvation at that very moment. She also included David in her prayers and hoped he made a commitment to Christ.

A few people made decisions to commit to the Lord and strode bravely toward the front of the church to meet with the Pastor and the prayer teams. Sophie joined with the congregation in clapping. As the shared encouragement died down, the song leader stood up. He raised his hands, beckoning everyone to stand and join him in singing *Joy to the World* one last time.

Wishing a Merry Christmas to all, the Pastor gave a benediction and dismissed the service. Sophie spied David hightailing it out of the sanctuary and she wondered if the service touched any chord in his heart. She knew she must continue to pray for him. She turned back toward Sebastian and Anastasia. "Papa, can we open the presents now?"

He gently patted her cheek. "No, dear, we'll

be waiting until tomorrow morning."

Alexander chuckled. "I'm sure that will be bright and early."

Sophie scrunched up her nose. "Well, I know I'm sleeping in. I need my beauty sleep."

Anastasia tugged on her sleeve. "Miss Sophie, we have to get up early to open the presents. It's tradition."

She tilted her head. "Oh, I see."

Anastasia twirled around in excitement. "I'll have to wake you up then."

Sebastian looked down at his daughter. "I'm sure she will. We'd better get you home since it's past midnight and you need to go to bed."

"I'm too excited to sleep." She then challenged her father. "If it's past midnight, then it is Christmas morning already."

Sophie stifled her grin as she watched Sebastian playfully wag his finger at his daughter. "I think Miss Sophie is teaching you too well."

Alexander started to walk out of the sanctuary. "I don't know about anyone else, but I'm going to sleep. I can't keep up with all of you."

* * *

Sophie stood back, observing Anastasia race into Sebastian's room. She tried to reign in the exuberance in the child—yet surprisingly, the

Christmas spirit had infected Sophie too and she wanted to spread the joy. A few seconds later, Anastasia skipped out of the room, whizzing by Sophie. "I have to wake grandpapa and Uncle David."

Sophie started walking to her room, when Sebastian called out to her. Glancing back, she loved the big grin on his face "I told you she'd wake us all up."

She self-consciously pulled her pink fleece robe more tightly around her. "Yes, you did. I'm going to get ready. I'll be down shortly."

"Don't take too long. Ana's probably already sitting by the tree." She heeded his advice and hurried away.

About fifteen minutes later, Sophie came downstairs and the smell of bacon and eggs assaulted her senses. Her stomach grumbled and she couldn't wait to eat. She spied Alexander working proficiently in the kitchen making breakfast. She peeked into the room. "I thought you were still sleeping. Did you get Anastasia's wake up call, too?"

He chuckled. "Oh, I've learned, if you want to sleep in on Christmas morning, you can't, at least not with my granddaughter around. So I got up early to cook for everyone."

Sophie pulled back a chair and sat down at the breakfast nook. She winked at him. "How nice of you. I guess Hilde and Daniel are visiting their families?"

"Yes. Hilde left last night. Her family lives in London. Daniel left earlier yesterday afternoon. His family lives up north in the Lakes region, near Cumbria."

"I bet David won't be too happy with his wake up call."

Too late—she noticed Alexander's raised eyebrow and heard footsteps as someone entered the kitchen. "Yes, David was extremely disturbed by the wake-up call." Sophie sheepishly shrugged her shoulders and giggled nervously when she realized David had overheard her. With hand waving as he passed, he grumbled, "Merry Christmas to all." He wearily rubbed his eyes. "Father, have you started the coffee, yet?"

"Yes, I put the pot on."

Sophie rushed to stand up. "I can help."

"You're our guest. There's no need." David tried to dissuade her.

Waving away his protest, she persisted. "Honestly, it's not a bother. I enjoy helping."

Alexander glanced over his shoulder. "In that case, my dear, can you handle the toast?"

With a grin, she made her way toward the toaster. "Yes, I think I can."

Sebastian came into the kitchen. "Oh, why wasn't I invited to the party?"

"It's too early in the morning for your cheerfulness." David complained and got up. "I'll be in the study. Please call me when breakfast is ready."

With heaviness in her heart, Sophie watched David leave. "I'm praying for him. I hope he finds God's gift of salvation soon."

Sebastian gently squeezed her hand. "Thank you for praying."

"You're welcome." His warm touch distracted her for a moment and she hoped Alexander didn't notice when he turned toward them. "Where's Ana...in front of the tree?" Sebastian reached for the tablecloth from the drawer. "Surprisingly, she's still in her bedroom. I thought she was coming down, but she said she had one last card to work on."

"I hope she comes down soon. I'm almost done making breakfast."

Golden brown wheat toast popped up and Sophie pulled the slices from the toaster. She checked with Alexander. "Do you want me to butter them or are you leaving the toast on the table with butter and jellies and jams?"

"I was going to butter them, but your idea sounds better." He winked as she spun around.

Charming as ever—no mystery where his sons got their charm. She reached to open the refrigerator door the same time as Sebastian and they bumped into each other. His proximity, again, threw her for a loop. "I'm sorry."

He playfully poked her on the nose. "I'm not."

For a second, she thought he was going to kiss

her right there in front of his father. Thankfully, Anastasia chose that moment to rush into the kitchen. "I'm finally finished. Did I miss breakfast?"

The way Sebastian reassuringly wrapped his arm around his daughter resonated in Sophie's heart. "Of course not, dear. I would have come get you if we were ready."

She snapped her finger as she moved her arm. "That's too bad. I thought we were ready to open the presents."

Alexander laughed heartily. "My goodness, you are excited."

"Not for me, grandpapa. I can't wait to give out the cards I made for everyone."

"Oh, that's sweet, honey." Sebastian picked his daughter up and gave her a kiss. "You're getting so grown up, soon I won't be able to pick you up anymore."

"You can still pick me up when I'm a lady. I saw you pick up mama once."

Sophie took over the job of setting the table and smiled at the tender moment between father and daughter, which reminded her of her own father. However, this time she experienced complete joy, and not a twinge of sadness at the memory of him.

David trudged in. "Enough of this mushy stuff. Let's eat."

Anastasia put her hands on her hips. "Uncle David, why are you so grumpy? It's Christmas day."

Sophie overheard Alexander's whispered words. "Out of the mouths of babes."

With a general consensus of excitement—except of course, from David—the family quickly consumed breakfast. Afterward, Sophie offered to clean up. "You can all go ahead and open presents.

Sebastian stood. "I'm helping and we're waiting for you. You're part of the family."

"If you insist." Even as she spoke those words, she wished she hadn't. Now would be the perfect time for the onset of a headache and an excuse to escape to her room.

He carried the dirty plates toward the counter, then stopped behind her. His warm breath tickled her neck. "Yes, I do."

She trembled at his nearness. With great effort, she refocused her mind to the task at hand then started to load the dishwasher. She peered back, glad to see the others had left the room. "Did you get the information I forwarded to your email about enrollment in the school at church?"

He carried the rest of the dishes to the counter. "Yes. It seems like an option, but I do want Anastasia to be in on some of the decision making."

"Good idea." Loading the rest of the dishes, she feared she'd offended him. "I hope I'm not being too forward."

"No. I appreciate your help." With the cleaning finished, she allowed Sebastian to lead her out of the room. "I think we've kept my little princess waiting long enough."

* * *

Trailing behind Sebastian, Sophie took a deep breath, feeling like an intruder invading his much needed family time. She stopped short as they entered the parlour. Sebastian's obvious excitement in joining his family for their gift giving festivities, made Sophie smile—still, she thought she didn't belong here in this moment. "Finally, Papa, you're here!" Some might think the child quite petulant at times, but Sophie had come to overlook such behavior. Especially when she saw the joy reflected on Sebastian's face.

"Yes, my Princess. Thank you for being patient."

Anastasia gleefully patted the cushion beside her. "Miss Sophie, can you sit by me? Papa usually hands out the presents."

Great, there's no escaping now! Nodding, she moved to join her on the ottoman that someone had moved near the tree. *No big secret who that someone was.*

Sebastian deferred to Alexander. "I'll let you do the honors this year, Father."

Sophie paid attention as Alexander stood up. Rubbing his hands together, he practically skipped over to the tree. *This family certainly loves Christmas!* He reached out his hand to Anastasia. "I may need a helper. Are you ready?"

"Yes, Sir, I am!" She grew pensive then and fidgeted with her hands in her lap. "Oh, may I give out my cards first?"

Alexander patted her shoulder. "Go ahead, dear."

She got up and Sophie thought the young girl appeared ready to burst at the seams. *I guess the apple doesn't fall far from the tree when it comes to Christmas celebrations.* Kneeling down, she dug under the tree in search of her treasure. With a timid expression on her face, she handed the first one to Sophie. "Miss Sophie, this one is for you. I hope you like it."

For a moment, she stared at the child's holiday artwork on the front of the card. Five red stockings hung across the mantel of the fireplace. When she opened it and slowly read the words, the tender message struck a chord in her heart.

"Can you read it out loud?"

Sophie hesitated for a second then started to read the message. "*Miss Sophie, you are my favorite teacher. Thank you for helping me to learn so much. You are my friend and I love you. I hope you stay with us forever.*" The dam broke then. Her emotions got the best of her and Sophie started to cry.

"You don't like it?"

Sophie heard the tremor in her voice and hugged the child. "I like it very much. These are happy tears."

"Good." She moved back. "I made a bookmark, too. Did you see it?"

"Yes. You did a great job."

Proud as a peacock, Anastasia handed the next card to her father. He read it and thanked her. Then she moved on to her Uncle David and grandfather. Sophie was so engrossed in observing the displays of affection that Sebastian startled her as he snuck up behind the ottoman. "I can't wait any longer to give this to you." He unceremoniously handed her his gift. Presents…she hadn't been expecting to exchange any. Now what? "Well, are you going to open it or should I?"

Her hands trembled as she pulled on the red satin ribbon and it fell loosely onto her lap. Turning her attention to the silver wrapping, she couldn't help herself from tearing open the taped flaps. Briefly, she remembered the childlike anticipation she'd experienced before opening presents from her parents. Wrapping paper tossed aside, she opened the box. Amidst the packing straw, she discovered a snow globe with an English style house inside. The inscription on the brass plate read, *Jane Austen's House, Bath England*. Sophie blinked back the tears. She pulled out the other gift—a box set of the 1903 First Edition of five Jane Austen novels. Inside the card, Sebastian had written, "*I read Emma because you said it was so good. It was. I'm glad God brought you into our lives...Merry Christmas, Sebastian.*" The tears started flowing again. Instinctively, she caressed Sebastian's cheek, then quickly pulled her hand away.

"Thank you. This means a lot to me."

"You're very welcome. I wanted to get something extra special for you."

"You did." She hoped her eyes spoke more volumes than the few words she'd managed to say. Her practical nature figured he'd spent a small fortune on those books, but her heart melted at his thoughtful gesture.

David called out from across the room. "Hey, over there, are we missing something?"

Sebastian gracefully got to his feet. "No. So, who's ready to open some presents?" He tickled his daughter and hugged her, then glanced back at Sophie. She caught his subtle wink and cherished the warmth of their shared moment for a few seconds longer before rejoining the others. Holding his gifts close to her heart, hope began blooming in full force. She'd never expected to have a special Christmas this year. Maybe there was room in this family for her.

* * *

Later that same day Sophie found herself kidnapped and blindfolded by Sebastian. He'd interrupted her lazy afternoon of reading comfortably on the tufted settee in the parlour. "Can you get bundled up? I want to show you something outside." His soft-spoken words near the nape of her neck kept her guessing and nearly sent her senses over the edge.

She touched the blindfold covering her eyes. "I might need help with my jacket since I can't see anything."

He chuckled. "Hmm, I think I can assist you."

She gripped his hand as he led her out of the room. "Where are we going?"

He didn't answer right away and then after a few seconds, he halted their progress. "Here, let me put your jacket on you." As he guided her arms into the sleeves, her mind raced. What could he possibly have in store? She'd been surprised by him many times before. He reached for her hand again and locked fingers with her. "I have a surprise for you. Do you trust me?"

"Yes, at least I think I do." She giggled nervously.

His shoulder brushed up against hers as he moved closer to her. "I'm going to hold your hand and guide you down the driveway toward the sidewalk. Ready?"

"I guess so." Subconsciously, she gripped his hand even more tightly.

"Let me try a different tactic here." Sophie felt

the warmth of his body and his solid chest as he put his arm around her. "I think I can guide you better this way and maybe get back some of the circulation in my hand."

"Sorry. It's not every day I'm abducted and forced to walk blindfolded."

Though their measured steps took them longer to reach the destination point, she relished the security of being nestled in the crook of his arm. She never imagined strolling blindfolded outside on a cold winter's night—but if she had to pick anyone to share the moment with—Sebastian was the man.

"It's so beautiful out here. Do you feel the snow falling?" She held out her hand, about to remove her gloves. "I think it's better if you stick your tongue out."

"Aren't you fresh?" She teased but obeyed and cold snowflakes melted on her tongue. "Are we there yet?"

"You're as bad as my impatient daughter."

"Speaking of Anastasia, where is she?"

"I begged my father to keep her occupied for a few hours."

"A few hours? What are we going to do?"

"I can think of many things." She heard the devilish tone to his voice as heat warmed her cheeks. The anticipation of his surprise kicked her imagination into overdrive.

She lifted her head up close to his chin. "You

know, I'm beginning to think that deep down, men are adolescents at heart."

"I couldn't agree more!" He gently guided her to the left. "We're here, but he isn't."

"May I take this blindfold off?"

"Not yet. Oh, there he is. Can you cover your ears?"

"What?" Sebastian's gloved hands became instant ear muffs for her. Excitement made her heart beat faster. Who was coming and where were they going? It was enough to make a girl's head spin! Could this day get any better? It had completely exceeded her expectations by far.

Finally, he stepped in front of her to remove the blindfold. She blinked open her eyes and stared in surprise at a horse drawn carriage. Sebastian took hold of her elbow and led her forward. "After you, milady." The driver dressed in formal attire, including black hat and white gloves, stepped down and assisted Sophie up into the carriage. She shook her head. *Am I dreaming?* "So what do you think of part two of your Christmas present?"

His face showed satisfaction in accomplishing the surprise, but she hesitated in responding. "Maybe it's a bit inappropriate coming from my employer." She didn't need the light of the moonlit sky to see his excitement fading. How could it not, with her matter of fact statement. They weren't living in a fairy tale land and someone needed to remain grounded in reality in their relationship.

"That may be so, but I'm also your friend and—"

"Are you ready, Mr. Shipley?"

"Yes, we are."

"So you were saying"

"I'm your friend. I hope you might classify me as your *special* friend." He leaned forward to pull a red velvet blanket up onto their laps. Then he reached over to hold her gloved hand. "So, how do I measure up?"

Special friend…she liked the sound of those two words. "Oh, you classify." She figured he must think her a nut job for the continual hide and seek game she seemed to be playing. Yet it was not a game to her. Her emotions ran the gamut of calm and serene like a placid lake to tumultuous and ferocious as a raging sea. She needed clarification in their relationship. Maybe this was one step closer to finding that definition—maybe not. When he put his arm around her shoulder, she decided to break the barriers and snuggled close to him. Resting in his secure embrace during the entire carriage ride, she enjoyed the mutually agreed upon silence. Sebastian had opened the door to romance a crack and invited her to squeeze in. Sophie knew he only offered her an appetizer right now, but she believed he wanted her to stay for the main course. Up for the challenge, she looked forward to getting to know this intricate and delightful man on a deeper level.

* * *

Sebastian relaxed in the big overstuffed chair across from his daughter's bed in the guest room. He watched Anastasia sleeping peacefully in the big comfy bed with her new doll held tightly in her arms. *At least I bought the right present!* Her exhaustion satisfied him this time because it meant she'd experienced a day full of fun festivities with the family. What more could he ask for? Closing his eyes, he easily slipped into mentally revisiting his carriage ride with Sophie earlier that afternoon—and he'd surprised himself at his audacity in flirting with her. Taking a step back for a moment seemed necessary to evaluate his true intentions. He liked Sophie a great deal. She maintained a positive influence on his daughter and the home schooling had been progressing at an efficient pace. Her infectious smile and sweet personality made his heart melt and no one had affected him in such a way since Katherine had held her place in his heart.

Opening his eyes, he let out a deep breath. His dream about Katherine came to mind again. Part of him still carried guilt over his budding romantic feelings for Sophie. Loyalty to his wife had kept all hope of new love at bay. *Am I crazy for not letting go?* Agitated, he quickly stood and paced the room.

Anastasia's feelings for her teacher came to mind. His daughter wanted Sophie to stay with them indefinitely. His wired emotions ran wild and he moved toward the window, staring outside at the heavier snowfall. Why couldn't he have a new beginning like pure white snow covering all of creation? God's peace enveloped him and he recalled a verse in scripture, *Delight yourself in the Lord and He will give you the desires of your heart*. He sensed God urging him to seek His face and all would work out in the end for His glory.

Deciding to call it a night, he kissed his daughter lightly on the cheek, then quietly stepped into the hallway. On his way toward his bedroom, he heard the beautiful sounds of the piano floating up the stairs. Of course, he wanted to race down there to watch her play, but decided to refrain from appearing too eager for her attentions. After today, he hoped she understood his intentions better even if he didn't fully understand them himself. Gripping the handle on his bedroom door, he forced himself to go inside. He fully expected sleep to evade him for a while as he thought about Sophie downstairs running her delicate fingers along the piano keys and closing her eyes as she played.

Chapter Twenty-Three

Sebastian and David sat inside the palatial French estate of Louis Ricard Francois. They had arrived last night with Sophie and Anastasia in tow and planned to visit for a few days. Louis had invited the Shipley brothers to stay at his home to discuss their business plan and review the revised contracts—since he wanted to remain near his wife, as she lay restricted to bed rest during the last two weeks of her pregnancy. Seated around an ornate marble table in the study, the three men intently reviewed the paperwork. A few moments later, Sebastian surreptitiously observed their usually calm client as he continued to lose focus on the meeting. "How are you holding up, Louis?"

Shrugging his shoulders, he shook his head. "Not so good, mon ami. I'm nervous."

Sebastian reassuringly patted him on the back. "I'm sure Adeline will be fine."

"Merci, I know." He held up his hands. "I still

worry. She's had many complications." A knock on the solid oak doors interrupted their conversation. "I apologize. I have given my staff strict instructions not to disturb me unless it is Adeline's time." Sebastian glanced toward David and nodded in understanding then Louis went to answer the door. Sebastian heard whispered voices and Louis came back animatedly waving his hands. If the moment wasn't serious, Sebastian would be joking with him over the comical scene. Louis placed both palms on the table. "It's time! I must go."

Sebastian saw his expression imploring them to understand. "Of course, you must go."

Louis sighed audibly in relief. He started to rush out, but stopped and turned back. He laughed. "Hopefully, the baby will decide to come quickly. I don't want to keep you waiting."

David waved his hand. "Louis, no worries. This will be like a mini holiday for us."

In a flash, Louis raced out the door.

Sebastian glanced toward David. "Do you want to go riding?"

"I was thinking the exact same thing. Scary, huh?"

"Let's go get the girls." They stood up, tucked the paperwork away in their briefcases and headed upstairs to change first.

* * *

Sebastian breathed in the faint scent of lilacs as he stood near Sophie. They quietly watched David explaining the rules of equestrian safety to Anastasia, while the stable hands saddled the horses. However, with Sophie right beside him, he had a hard time concentrating on the training activity. "So, are you sure you want to ride alone?"

Sophie glanced up at him and grinned. "You don't think I'm ready?"

He took a step closer. "Actually, I was hoping you'd want to ride with me."

"Oh, but that might be a bit dangerous, especially with our PG audience."

He caught her teasing tone and nodded toward his daughter. "Yes, I guess, you're right." Sebastian hooked his arm with Sophie's and guided her to the other side of the stables near David and Anastasia. His own excitement mounted at the thought of riding on the expansive land—he knew it would prove much more delightful than riding through London's parks.

"Papa, look! This is the horse I'm going to ride with Uncle David."

"Yes, honey, I see." His daughter's outward excitement to ride mirrored his inner passion. He slowly ran his hand along the mare's shiny brown coat. "She's beautiful."

The stable hands led the horses outside into the brisk air and walked them around for a few minutes, then brought them in front of the guests. "This one likes to ride fast." One of the men handed the reins to Sebastian. *Perfect for me!*

David mounted his horse. "Oh, I don't think that will be a problem for him."

Sebastian handed the reins back to a stable hand for a moment and lifted Anastasia up to sit in front of her uncle. He directed his comment to David. "Now, please be careful."

David held up his hand, as if swatting Sebastian's concerns away like a fly. "Yes, yes, brother. We'll be fine. I'm spending quality time with my niece. Right, Ana?"

"Yes, Uncle David," she shouted gleefully. He turned the horse and rode off, while Sebastian's heart skipped a few beats in trepidation. *Please God, let David ride responsibly.*

Sophie touched his arm, bringing him back to the present. His mind had wandered off fearing the worst of tragedies. "They'll be fine and I changed my mind. I'd like to ride with you."

"Good, you'll be able to take over in case I faint from fear when I see my brother's reckless riding style."

"He knows he's holding precious cargo. He'll be responsible. Are we ready? We need to catch up to them."

Sebastian mounted the horse then Sophie put her foot into the stirrup and he helped pull her up.

When she wrapped her arms around him, the tension began slipping away. Snapping the reins, he started the horse out at a nice trot across the path. Most of the snow had melted, leaving only a few small piles left on the ground. The trot soon turned to a gallop and Sebastian slowly pushed the horse forward. "Hang on, Sophie." He welcomed the feel of the wind on his face and enjoyed the sense of abandon the equestrian sport enabled him to experience. Hopefully, Sophie could connect in the same way with this freedom, even if only a small portion.

Sebastian pressed the horse hard until they neared his brother and Anastasia. He slowed down and they rode in companionable silence for a few minutes. Sophie leaned closer. "I hope I'm not intruding on time you could be spending with your brother."

He gently squeezed her hand. "Not at all. I'm quite happy right where I'm at. Besides, David and I have been spending way too much time together with all of these business meetings. It's nice to spend time with my girls." He chuckled, then his tone turned serious. "I am thankful God brought me back to England, though, because it has given me a chance to get reacquainted with my brother."

"Good to hear. I'm glad."

The riders approached an old stone cathedral and David slowed down first, reining in his horse. Sebastian caught his backward glance and nodded assent to take a closer look—he knew his brother's fascination with architecture, especially old churches and manors. Sebastian had always regarded that interest as a subconscious factor in keeping David firmly planted in his beloved England. Wanting to indulge his brother's wishes, he leaned his head back to Sophie. "Shall we stop?"

"I don't see why not."

He urged the horse forward near a rock wall and assisted Sophie as she moved off the horse. He then dismounted and hitched the horse's reins to a protruding tree branch. They followed his brother and Anastasia inside the ruins. Sebastian stated the obvious. "It appears this building withstood a fire." Admiring the stone structure, he came to stand behind his brother. "How could someone burn a church? Where's the respect for God's house."

David turned sharply. "Why do you always assume the worst from people? Did you ever think that it could have been an accident or the result of a natural disaster?"

The accusation gave Sebastian pause and he lamely shook his head. "I guess I do that. I don't know why."

Sophie defended him. "We all have our moments of assumptions." Her rush to defend him, pleased Sebastian, but he kept thinking about David's words as they walked. In a moment of clarity, he realized there was some truth to his brother's claim.

The need to catch up to David and Anastasia negated contemplation on this subject. He moved it to the backburner for consideration later.

They explored further regions of the cathedral and Sebastian glanced at Sophie and pointed upward. "Look, the ceiling's destroyed, but isn't that blue sky brilliant."

Anastasia called out. "Papa, Miss Sophie, come here."

David rushed over and grabbed his arm. "You have to see this!" Sebastian shrugged his shoulders at Sophie and they hurried obediently after him. David explained on the way. "All of the wood that was used in the construction of this structure has been consumed by the fire, but one piece remains intact. Look!" He pointed up to the altar in the chancel area. They walked through the nave and Sebastian and Sophie glanced where David's outstretched arm directed them. With eyes wide in astonishment, he nearly shouted. "See, isn't that something? It survived the fire. Maybe there is something to this God of yours."

Sophie stood staring in amazement, seemingly at a loss for words.

"That's incredible, Papa."

Sebastian beheld the large wooden cross hanging behind the altar. He spoke the words inscribed there. "It is finished." He agreed. "Yes, there is definitely something to our God." It was one of those special times when Heaven and Earth intersected in a holy moment. Everyone, including David, stood reverently in the chancel and remained there in silence for about fifteen minutes.

As they walked back to the horse, Sophie lightly touched Sebastian's arm. "God is faithful even when we're not. I wonder why we take so long to see that He's there all the time waiting to love us."

"We're human and life gets in the way, I guess."

"Your father said something to me the other day that I'm still thinking about."

"What's that?"

"He said God loves me so much that He has handcrafted every single moment of my life…and doesn't let anything pass into it that He won't give me the strength to handle."

"Hmm, I guess my father is wise, after all."

"If that's true, then why was it so hard to let go of my parents? Why didn't God give me the strength I needed?"

They reached the horse and Sebastian swiveled to face her. "I believe He's there for us all the time." Taking a chance that she wouldn't bolt like a wild filly, he gently caressed her cheek. "He's simply waiting for us to reach out and get our strength from Him."

David cleared his throat, announcing their arrival. Sebastian quickly stepped away from Sophie and mounted the horse. He reached down to help her up. She leaned her head against his back. "I guess I wasted needless energy holding onto my grief and anger."

Snapping the reins, he turned the horse around to follow David back to the estate. "Did you learn something?"

"Yes."

Urging the horse into a gallop to keep up with his brother, he continued. "Then, in God's eyes, it was all worth it." When her silence met his statement, guilt assailed him. "I'm sorry for sounding so trite. I didn't mean to imply—"

She hugged him tighter. "You're right and I know you understand loss."

They rode back in companionable silence for the first half of the ride. Even if he had wanted to talk, he might not be able to. His mind remained distracted by how tightly she hugged him. Not too tight that she squeezed him, but the simple fact she seemed to want to hug him—that left him speechless. Nearing the half-way mark, he chuckled.

"What's so funny?"

"I was thinking about Louis and how excited and worried he looked at the same time. It was almost comical. I hope everything is going well with his wife and their new arrival."

Sophie switched topics back to the church. "Do you think the cross we saw is going to make an impact on your brother or maybe he'll rationalize its survival?"

"We can only hope and pray."

* * *

Later on in the evening, Sophie and Anastasia relaxed in the east wing parlour while a fire crackled in the fireplace. Sophie welcomed the warmth and comfort of snuggling up on the divan with a thick fleece blanket wrapped around her. Anastasia snuggled with her under the blanket. "Miss Sophie, I was trying to figure out when we're leaving, but I'm not sure. I thought I heard Papa say something about February second."

Sophie brushed back the young girls' wayward curls. She gently chided the child. "That's correct, my little Miss. You must have been eavesdropping because your father and I were discussing that last week, and we thought we were alone." Anastasia kept silent, obviously chagrined. "I'm not upset. You need to realize that you must make your presence known if two people are talking, you're listening and they don't know you're there." Exactly when she finished speaking, she recalled her own few eavesdropping adventures and felt guilty for criticizing her young student.

"What if they're bad guys?" Anastasia tilted her head upward with a serious expression on her face.

Sophie smiled and tried to think of the appropriate answer. She hadn't yet grown tired of listening to the child's interesting thought process and even sometimes audacious responses. "Well, if bad guys are there, then you should stay hidden. Though, I don't think your father and I are bad guys."

"No." She giggled then quickly changed the subject. "How many days are left until we fly home?"

Closing her eyes in thought for a moment, she figured out the days. "There are thirty-one days in January and we're on the fifth day."

Anastasia tapped her chin. "That's twenty-six days left this month."

"It's nice to see you're paying attention in math class. So, twenty-six plus one day in February—"

Anastasia clapped her hands. "Oh, an easy one, Miss Sophie. Twenty-seven days. Now, I can start counting down. I'm going to call Ginny about this." The young girl released herself from the blanket and skipped excitedly out of the room. Sophie readjusted the fleece and relaxed back into the cushions. She picked up her e-reader and opened to her copy of *Emma*—delighted for a chance to read.

* * *

Sebastian crossed his arms and leaned against

the arched doorframe, amused that Sophie continued reading—oblivious to his intrusion. He watched as she scrunched up her face in consternation, seemingly engrossed in the eBook. "So, who do you like better, me or Mr. Knightley?" He heard her sharp intake of breath and she nearly dropped the e-reader as she turned to discover her intruder.

"Definitely, that would be Mr. Knightley. He doesn't have the bad habit of sneaking up on me all the time."

Sebastian spanned the room in several strides and sat in the chair opposite her. "Yes, he's so charming. I hope to someday be like him."

"Hey, don't make fun." She closed the leopard-print tablet cover with a thud. "He is the epitome of the perfect gentleman."

"Actually, I'm serious."

"What do you mean?"

"I'm reading the same book as you. It must be a coincidence."

Sophie's expression softened. "You're only trying to get on my good side."

He leaned forward in mock surprise. "Whatever do you mean, my dear? I thought I was on your good side."

"That depends on my mood."

"I see. You're all about a woman's prerogative."

"Yes, I live by that rule."

He played along and enjoyed the teasing. "Oh, so you're one of those."

"You'd better believe it. It's my prerogative to change my mind whenever I want."

He fluidly maneuvered to the ottoman where her feet rested and he sat down. "I hope you don't change your mind about me."

"Well, that all depends on you."

"I'd better be on my best behavior then."

Sophie got up quickly and before he realized it, she walked across the room to the bookshelf. "So, you actually read *Emma*, too. That's still surprising and sweet."

He followed after her. "You're avoiding any serious conversation, young lady."

She moved away, running her delicate fingers along the spines of the old leather-bound books. He kept following like a lion stalking his prey, backing her into a corner. Leaning her hands against the windowsill, she backed up as far as possible and laughed nervously. He smiled inside as she avoided his steady gaze. He had her exactly where he wanted her. She glanced up shyly. "So, tell me again why you interrupted me."

"I did because I've wanted to do this for a long time now." His hands trembled slightly as he cupped her soft cheeks. With his thumbs, he gently traced the outline of her rosy lips. Staring at her for an eternity, he slowly lowered his mouth to hers. Kissing her gently at first, soon his fervor took over. Even though his brain operated in a fog, he realized she must be enjoying the kiss, since she wrapped her arms around his neck and moved in closer to his chest. Nearly breathless, Sebastian pulled away. "I…I'm sorry."

She caressed his cheek and for a moment he closed his eyes, relishing her touch. "Don't be. I've wanted you to do that for a long time, too."

Oh the sweet bliss of making the right-move at the right-time. He brought her hand to his lips for a kiss. "I should get back to work. David's going to wonder what happened to me."

Sophie giggled and batted her eyes. "Oh, I'm sure he knows."

"Now try not to compare me too much to Mr. Knightley because there's no contest." As he left the parlour, the warmth of her lips and the softness of her body in his arms still lingered—making it doubly hard for him to switch gears back into work mode. Taking a deep breath, he hurried down the hall in search of his brother and another inevitable lecture that awaited him for his tardiness. He couldn't wait for his brother to find the right woman to love. Maybe then, David would realize why Sebastian had one foot on earth and the other in heaven like a love sick puppy.

Chapter Twenty-Four

Sebastian and David leisurely strolled into the elegant lobby of an upscale London hotel and seated themselves near the main elevator. They had scheduled another business meeting with one of their clients, Mathilda Fayes. Sebastian had dreaded yet anticipated this meeting all year long. An interesting woman in her late eighties and still sharp as a tack, Ms. Fayes had once told the Shipley brothers—in a nasal matronly voice—that the secret to keeping her mind young revolved around her own involvement with her finances. "You have to use your mind or you're bound to lose it!"

As they waited, Sebastian recalled hearing how at a young age, Mathilda had married a multi-millionaire, by her father's matchmaking. "Mind you, now, the match was not made in Heaven, at least not at first!" Despite this business deal of a marriage, they'd fallen in love, remaining happy together for seven years until he had died of cancer at the age of thirty-eight—thus her career as a bride began. Sebastian smiled as he remembered the tale, told from Mathilda's perspective, of course. She had walked down the aisle for four more husbands, stubbornly wearing white each time. Her final and late husband, the Earl John Whetstone, left her with a tidy sum of money, an expansive country estate and an opulent London Townhome. Needless to say, the brothers had continually reminded each other of Mathilda's importance as a client of theirs.

The Shipley brothers treated every client with the same respect. However, some of their wealthier ones expected, even demanded coddling treatment. In recent years, Sebastian had deliberated about signing over his half of the company to David and moving to a tropical island somewhere to retire. Now that Sophie fit into the picture, the idea started growing on him with increasing appeal.

Glancing up, he noticed Mathilda exit regally out of the elevator. Carrying her poodle, Don Juan, in her arms, she gracefully strode toward them as she adjusted her purple feather hat. Sebastian quietly spoke through the pasted on smile on his face. "This is going to be an interesting lunch, although I much preferred our meeting with Louis." Momentarily, he pictured Louis with his wife and the new baby, Antoine Julius Francois.

David stood up next to him and grinned. "Keep on smiling. Once we survive this, you can go home and take your two ladies out to dinner." He teased his brother. "I've noticed you've been neglecting them lately."

Sebastian maintained a professional demeanor, but glared at his brother. "You haven't helped matters." He bantered back. "I have a workhorse for a brother."

With no time to reply, David reached out a hand. "Hello, Mathilda, dear, so nice to see you...and Don Juan."

"I never travel anywhere without my baby."

Sebastian watched as David offered Mathilda his arm and he felt relieved that his brother maneuvered in the social circles so expertly. He motivated himself. *Think about dinner tonight and everything will be fine.*

* * *

Back home in the library of the Shipley's London townhome, Anastasia worked on a puzzle while Sophie relaxed and scrolled through the news headlines on her tablet. Earlier in the morning, Sebastian had surprised both of them with a special invitation to a dinner date with him. He'd given his daughter a furry, white teddy bear with a big red bow and Sophie a box of nonpareil chocolates, her favorite. Any work Sophie had hoped to accomplish with her student today flew out the window when

Sebastian had left. Like a silly school girl, she kept thinking about Sebastian's lips on hers and now this invitation to dinner rattled her—she wondered about his intentions. "Did he actually call it a *dinner date*?" One of her fatal flaws—an over-analytical thought process—nearly drove her crazy on many occasions, especially where it concerned her relationship with Sebastian.

Anastasia complained. "Miss Sophie, why do they make puzzles so hard?"

In that moment, she desperately missed her mother who had never failed to listen to her analyzing so many issues. She could use her mother's advice right then to save her from slipping over the edge. "You like puzzles. Isn't that part of the intrigue, trying to put the pieces together?" *Hmm, maybe I should take my own advice!*

She leaned on the table with her chin in her hand. "Do you want to help me?"

Sophie continued hiding her face behind her tablet. "You never want my help with puzzles, and now you do? Something smells fishy here."

With a swish of her curly blonde ponytail, the young girl intently focused again on her task. "I only wanted to spend time with you."

Sophie crept up behind, reaching out to tickle Anastasia's sides. "You always spend time with me."

Anastasia screamed and nearly jumped out of her seat. "You scared me. I didn't even hear you sneak up on me."

Sophie chuckled and joined her student at the table. "You win. I'll help." She settled into the chair with a warning. "Now you're in for it. I'm extremely particular about putting my puzzle together and I might have a lesson or two for you."

Anastasia rolled her eyes, and then dramatically laid her head down on folded arms on the table.

"Uh-huh. Now it's coming back to you." With a satisfied grin, Sophie patted the child's head. "You remember why you never want me to help you, don't you?" She raised her head, scrunching up her nose. Sophie chuckled and teased her. "You only want help so the puzzle can get finished before our dinner with your father."

Anastasia feigned innocence and gave her a big toothy grin. "How do you like to do the puzzles again? I forget?"

Sophie reached out to separate the pieces. "I put the border together first."

She nodded her head, speaking in all seriousness. "Now that is a good idea."

"Oh, I'm glad you think so. I'm sure you like my help, too."

"Miss Sophie, we still have to decide what we're going to wear tonight."

"Hmm, I hadn't thought about that."

"Exactly the reason why I asked you to come

over."

"Oh, so now the truth comes out! I guess we'd better hurry up then."

* * *

Sebastian's heart swelled with pride as his little girl, all dressed up, stepped daintily down the stairwell. When she reached the landing, he held her fur-lined coat open as she put her arms in the sleeves. Kneeling down, he bundled her up with her favorite blue and white scarf and polka-dot hat. She frowned. "Ana, it's cold outside and you need to stay warm. Is Miss Sophie coming?"

"I'm right here."

He lifted his head and hoped he didn't lose his balance as he stared at her. She wore a stunning, form-fitting black dress with a demure slit up to her knee. "I didn't hear you come down." Her auburn curls swept up in an elegant bun, drew his attention to her graceful neck.

"Papa, that's too tight."

He faced Anastasia again and loosened the belt on her coat. "Oh, I'm sorry dear." Standing up from his kneeling position, Sebastian reached for Sophie's grey woolen dress coat and helped her put it on. From his position close behind her, he breathed in her fragrant perfume. No lilacs today…he thought he smelled the scent of jasmine. Then he handed over her dark grey cashmere draping scarf. The way she looked tonight had taken his breath away. He hoped some semblance of intelligent thought would return and he could survive dinner without making a fool of himself.

"Thank you." She turned to wrap the scarf around her. He wanted to gaze into her blue eyes, but she demurely glanced away.

Alexander broke the spell of the moment by entering the front hall. "Have a good time."

Sebastian nodded toward his father. "Are you sure you can't come along?" Even as he said those words, he felt a stab of guilt for hoping he stayed home.

He waved them on. "No, I'm a bit tired tonight."

Bidding his father good night, Sebastian breathed a sigh of relief and led the ladies outside. He leaned in to whisper to Sophie. "I only invited him because he looked sad that he wasn't included in the plans."

"It's fine by me. He can come."

"No, this is a dinner date with my two favorite ladies." He opened the car door and ushered them inside. Then he leaned forward to give Daniel instructions.

"This is going to be so much fun, Papa!"

About ten minutes later, they arrived. Sebastian asked Daniel to pick them up in two and a half hours, and then they entered the restaurant. He lovingly observed his daughter. Her wide-eyed expression spoke volumes. She held onto Sophie's hand and stared at the bright chandelier. The entire room sparkled and he knew Anastasia enjoyed every minute of strolling through the gilded lobby. A sense of remorse overwhelmed him—for allowing work to consume so much of his precious time with his daughter. *Not anymore…things will be different.*

"May I help you, Sir?"

"I have reservations under Shipley."

"Ah, yes. Please follow me." The maître d' promptly ushered them to a table near the large front window, as Sebastian had requested when he'd made the reservation earlier.

Sebastian directed his comment to Sophie. "I hope you don't mind sitting by the window. I thought Ana would enjoy the view outside…and take her attention off us." He winked conspiratorially.

She responded playfully. "Oh, I see and what shouldn't your daughter be witnessing?"

"I don't know. I might get the urge to kiss you again." Sebastian grinned and pulled out the chairs for Sophie and his daughter.

They sat down and the maître d' brought out a pitcher of water and filled their glasses. "Your server will be out shortly."

Sebastian nodded then turned his attention back to Sophie and Anastasia. He smiled. "See, she is enjoying the view outside." He reached across the table and lightly caressed Sophie's hand. Immediately, he noticed her warning look, but held out as long as possible before he withdrew his touch. "I can't wait to take you both to Italy."

"That's right, Papa. I forgot. When do we leave?"

Sebastian gently nudged her chin. "Now that's the excitement I want to see. We leave the day after tomorrow."

"You don't have to bring us along. We understand it's a business trip and we don't want to be in the way."

"Nonsense, you weren't in the way when I brought you both to France. Besides, Antonio and his family will enjoy your company." He caught the nervous expression on Sophie's face. For a moment, he wondered why she continued to doubt how much he wanted her around. Actions speak louder than words…*I have to show her*.

Sophie placed her napkin on her lap. "He knows we're coming along, right?"

"Yes." The waiter came by, halting further response. After the waiter left with their orders, Sebastian continued. "Antonio is an old friend and he said he'd be delighted to meet you both."

Thankfully, Anastasia started chatting and changed the subject. He listened as she eagerly spoke about their day. Sebastian did not want to spend the entire night defending his wishes to bring them to Italy. "Miss Sophie and I worked on a puzzle today. It was really hard, right?"

"Yes, but you did a great job."

Anastasia took a sip of water. "I needed your help to finish."

Sebastian commended their efforts. "Teamwork, that's good."

The waiter came back with the first course of salads. When he left the table, Anastasia leaned forward. "Papa, is the soup coming out soon? Grandpapa told me he loves the French onion soup here."

Sebastian found himself gazing across the table as Sophie's smile lit up the room. Desperately he tried to focus his attention back on his daughter. "I agree it is very good. After you finish your salad, the soup will be served."

"Goodie." She clapped her hands. "Do you like onion soup, Miss Sophie?"

"Yes, I do."

"Did you order it?"

"Not this time. I ordered the tomato soup and the salmon."

Sebastian wanted to discuss the subject of his daughter's studies when a heated argument broke out at the table to their left. The frustrated woman threw her drink in the man's face, said some choice words and exited in a huff. Anastasia watched the entire scene with eyes like saucers. Sebastian gently touched her arm. "Let's mind our own business dear."

"But Papa—"

"No, it's not polite to stare. We don't know their story and it's not our business."

Anastasia persisted in her questioning. "What if someone was getting hurt?"

Seeking an ally, Sebastian glanced at Sophie, but found no assistance as she tried to stifle her giggling. He paused for a moment. "In such an instance, it would be our business. However, it is important to keep your wits about you so you don't get hurt yourself while helping the other person." He quickly ended the discussion. "Let's pray for the food."

Relieved that his daughter now focused her attention on the plate in front of her, Sebastian observed the self-conscious man from the lover's quarrel—he left money for his bill on the table and made a hasty exit. The trio ate their salads and then the waiter served their soups. "So, Ana, how have you been feeling?"

"Fine, Papa. God healed me, remember. Right, Miss Sophie?"

She nodded affirmatively. "He certainly did."

"Yes, Ana. I know." He lovingly touched her cheek. "Could you allow me to be the concerned parent at some point in my life?"

She giggled and pretended to think about it for

a minute. "Of course."

"Good, well we'd better finish our soup before it gets cold." They ate and chatted and Sebastian inquired about her studies. "So, is Miss Sophie a good teacher?"

"Yes, she's the best teacher."

Sophie patted her shoulder. "Why, thank you."

The waiter brought their entrees to the table.

"Are you going to be able to eat all that?" Sebastian teased, holding his fork over her plate. "Your food looks tasty."

Anastasia joked back, making a funny face. "It's all mine!"

"Don't worry, my little Miss, I'll protect your food."

He started to get up. "Taking sides are we…don't make me come over there." He caught Sophie's smile, but decided to lay off the teasing in case his daughter took him seriously. So far, the rest of the meal progressed uneventfully with no further lovers' spats. Sebastian enjoyed the lighthearted conversation and delectable food.

"How do you like the salmon, Miss Sophie?"

"It's delicious. How's your chicken?"

"Great."

Sophie laid down her fork and sipped some water. "I am excited to go to Italy."

Sebastian hoped she truly was looking forward to the trip. He figured her hesitation earlier was due to her not wanting to get in his way. "Have you ever been there?"

"No."

"I hope you're ready to expand your horizons."

"Do you mean sight-seeing?"

"Yes, I love Italy. It's a beautiful country and I can't wait to show you the sights. You're going to love Antonio's villa." He pictured taking Sophie on a moonlit stroll along Antonio's property which bordered the sea. Memories of their first kiss came unbidden to his mind. The urge to kiss her again came over him in full force.

"Can we have some chocolate cake, Papa?"

With great effort, Sebastian tore his eyes off Sophie and indulged his daughter. "Sure, but I can't eat a whole piece myself."

"We can all share, right, Miss Sophie?"

"Fine by me."

The waiter came by to collect the plates. "Would you like to see a dessert menu?"

"No need. We know what we'd like to order. We'll take a large piece of the triple chocolate layer cake, one cup of tepid tea, a cappuccino and mint tea." As the waiter left with their dessert order, Sebastian quietly observed the genuine camaraderie between Sophie and his daughter. He thanked God for the millionth time that He had brought this special woman into their lives. If not for Sophie, he imagined their lives would still be stuck in the dark ages of emotional repression and illness.

"I can't wait to tell Grandpapa how good the onion soup was."

Sebastian continued watching as Sophie paid attention to his daughter. "I'm certain he'll be happy you enjoyed it."

"Miss Sophie, I need to use the restroom."

"Do you want me to go with you? We passed by it on our way in."

"I'm fine."

Sebastian nodded permission for her to go and Anastasia excused herself. *Time to make my move.* Reaching across the table, he gently caressed Sophie's hand with his index finger. He traced small circles across her soft skin.

"Oh, I see you don't waste any time."

"You said no affection in front of my daughter and she's not here right now. Of course, I have to take advantage of every opportunity I get."

"You are charming, I have to admit that."

"Am I as charming as Mr. Knightley?"

"Not yet, but there's hope." Sophie laughed— and hearing the musical sound, Sebastian couldn't help but grin like a smitten teenage boy. He decided to lean in for a kiss, but the waiter came back with their dessert and beverages. Perfect timing, of course! Anastasia neared the table and Sophie pulled her hand away. "Time's up."

He leaned back and grinned. "To be continued later." *I will find another opportunity!*

"I can't wait."

Anastasia settled back into her chair and picked up her fork, ready to dig into the chocolate cake. "Can't wait for what, Miss Sophie?"

"Oh, uh, I can't wait to try the chocolate cake."

"I can't wait either." With childlike excitement, Anastasia took the first bite. "Yummy and so delicious."

Sebastian shared a secret wink with Sophie, then gently pushed the plate toward her. "Ladies, first." He could tell she enjoyed his flirting and it had the desired effect upon her.

* * *

Sophie enjoyed her last bite of chocolate cake and pushed back from the table with a contented sigh. Sebastian playfully poked his daughter on the nose as he listened to one of her jokes. Sophie knew she'd never tire of such a sight—father and daughter sharing a cherished moment together. She mentally thanked God for all the special times she'd shared with her own father. Her mother used to say, there's nothing sweeter than spending time with those you love. As the years flew by, Sophie agreed more every day with her mother's sage words.

Anastasia tapped Sophie's elbow bringing her back to the present. "Do you want any more cake, Miss Sophie?"

She patted her belly and held up her other hand in protest. "No, I'm fine, thank you."

Sebastian took care of signing for the bill and handed the leather bill folder back to the waiter. Sophie helped Anastasia get into her coat and all bundled up then Sebastian assisted with her own coat. A cold blast of snowy air met them when the lobby concierge opened the glass doors. Sophie latched on to Sebastian's arm and Anastasia held his other hand as he guided them toward the waiting town car. Daniel appeared in a flash and opened the car door as the trio piled inside, all welcoming the warmth of the interior.

During the drive back, Sophie settled into the comfy leather seat quietly listening to Sebastian chat with his daughter. Her mind raced with images of a few intense glances—she'd pretended not to notice— which Sebastian had given her at dinner. His smoldering brown eyes had shown hints of his feelings. She'd be a dead woman walking if she hadn't noticed them. Sebastian's attention flattered and excited yet frightened her all at the same time. True to her form, she still entertained slight doubts about Sebastian's intentions for her. However, if actions speak louder than words, she'd soon need to squash those uncertainties entirely. How much more evidence did she need from this man before she completely allowed herself to take a leap of faith with him!

When they arrived home, Alexander met them at the door like an eager puppy awaiting his master's arrival. He stole Anastasia away as quickly as a jackrabbit swiping a carrot. "Tell me all the details."

Sophie glanced at Sebastian as he beamed and shook his head at his daughter's first excited comment. "There was a man and a woman who had a fight and she threw her drink at him. They sat right near us."

Alexander covered his mouth and gasped in feigned astonishment. Sophie knew he'd meant that gesture more for Sebastian's benefit than Anastasia's. She peeked at Anastasia and the young girl seemed oblivious to her grandfather's teasing of her father. "My, my, I'm so sorry you had to deal with that dear."

Sophie stifled her own giggles when Sebastian rolled his eyes at his father as Alexander traipsed down the hall with Anastasia in tow. Sebastian spun around. "What's so funny?"

Her giggling burst out then. "You and your father are hilarious."

"I'm glad you find us so amusing."

"It definitely beats going to the movies."

"No, this does." He stepped closer and took hold of her waist. Lowering his mouth to hers, he kissed her passionately. Sophie reached her arms around his neck and returned the kiss. She ran her fingers through his wavy hair. Was this actually happening again? When he pulled away, they both stared at each other in breathless anticipation. Sebastian gently caressed her cheek and kissed her forehead. They both froze in place when Anastasia's voice announced her near approach.

She called from the hallway. "Miss Sophie, can you read me a bedtime story?" Quickly trying to compose herself, Sophie took two steps backward and nervously smoothed out her dress.

Sebastian stared at her intently and she saw the fire burning in his eyes. "Maybe that's a good idea." Slowly turning on his heels, he started walking away then glanced back once more. "Goodnight, Sophie."

Helplessly, she watched him disappear from view and hoped her heart started beating normally before Anastasia rounded the corner. Closing her eyes and taking a deep breath, she started moving and met her young student by the stairwell. "Let's go, my little Miss. What are we reading tonight?"

She ran up the stairs in front of her. "I don't know yet."

Sophie took the stairs more slowly and ran her hand aimlessly along the glossy wooden banister. The kiss once again left her powerless to rational thought—placing her completely out of her normal comfort zone of assumed complete control. Like a sleepwalker, she touched her lips, still feeling the sensation of Sebastian's warm lips on hers. "Hurry, Miss Sophie. I'm in my room. Where are you?" Following the sound of Anastasia's sing-song voice, she desperately tried to rid her mind of thoughts of Sebastian, but knew that task would be impossible.

Chapter Twenty-Five

Sebastian waited with David in the conservatory for their client, Antonio Savati. As Sebastian wandered along the stone pathway, he vaguely noticed the wide array of tropical flowers and plants lining the sides of the path. Instead, he recalled his client's story. Savati, a recent transplant from Southern Italy had relocated to England for business reasons. However, he had told the Shipley brothers his body failed to tolerate the *cold, dreary climate—* so he'd kept a residence in Italy, located in Rome and a villa on the island of Sicily. Antonio had invited them to his villa in Sicily since the planning for his daughter's surprise sixteenth birthday party had occupied his time, allowing him no opportunity to travel to London.

Sebastian rounded the path and stopped near David. He held up his hands and whispered to his brother, as he counted on his fingers. "A mansion in London, a villa in Rome and a villa in Sicily...hmm, not too shabby, you think?"

David shushed his brother. "Antonio will be coming back any minute."

Sebastian apologized and shook his head, wondering why he'd continually acted like the old David and his brother had started behaving more seriously like he used to. Could it have anything to do with a certain blue eyed brunette? He certainly thought so! He watched as Antonio's staff milled about in activity, preparing the round marble table for the food tasting.

Antonio's deep voice and boisterous laughter echoed down the hall, announcing his arrival. He made his grand entrance. "Thank you gentlemen for coming to my humble abode." Then he laughed uproariously again and patted David on the back. "But it's not so humble, I don't think." Sebastian observed in admiration how his brother smiled politely and tried smoothly to maneuver the conversation away from Antonio's bumbling attempt at wit. Oblivious to his faux pas, Antonio led his guests over to the marble table. He invited them to partake with him of the delectable repast that the caterers had set out. "As my fellow Italians are known for, I, too, enjoy fine food." He patted his bulging belly. Sebastian found his host's sincerity extremely refreshing and after he recovered from his initial disinterest in the meeting, he realized that Antonio truly understood how to relish life. *I could definitely learn from him.*

David turned to Antonio. "This food is delicious. The tomato sauce is excellent."

He winked conspiratorially. "This is nothing compared to my wife's homemade sauce."

Sebastian glanced at Antonio. "I believe it."

He extended his arms wide. "Stay for a few days and taste the best food in all Italia."

Sebastian deferred to David and then smiled. "If you insist."

Antonio good-naturedly gripped David's shoulder. "And you?"

"You don't have to twist my arm. I'd love to. It's so beautiful here."

They sampled more of the food and listened with respect as Antonio mentioned his move to England, his big family—evident by the many little ones running around—and finally the grand event. "My bella Tatiana is turning sixteen."

Sebastian pondered the countless preparations and felt as if Antonio had planned for a trip down the aisle and not a birthday. The expression *when in Rome, do as the Romans do* came to mind. He sensed the deep love this man held for his family and wished them well. After their exorbitant dining, Sebastian sat back—stuffed with food and good fellowship—he excitedly anticipated Sophie getting to meet this eccentric man as well.

A short discussion followed their feasting and still the conversation had not taken a turn to business.

Extending his hand, Antonio offered, "Please, I can teach you how to play Italian cards." From the excited gleam in his brown eyes, Sebastian knew the man refused to take no as an answer.

Sebastian started to protest. "I'm not much of a card man, myself."

David drowned out his brother's objections. "I am. Teach away."

The Englishmen made a commendable effort, but Sebastian gladly welcomed the break when they finally began to discuss business. The sooner the meeting ended, the sooner he could escape to see Sophie. How this woman had gotten under his skin and into his every waking thought!

Their host stood up, as David took the documents out. "Let's walk and talk at the same time. We need exercise after all that eating!"

Sebastian acquiesced with their host's request and David stuffed the papers into the briefcase. The brothers followed Antonio down the back stone steps to the Italian garden. Sebastian welcomed the refreshing breeze after sitting in the humid air of the conservatory—and eating the great food and drinking the wine from their host's own vineyard. He observed how deftly David tried to get the conversation back on track of business. "We can leave the actual copies of the contract for your review."

Sebastian suggested. "You can sign it and send it back to us at your convenience."

Antonio waved his hand nonchalantly. "I trust you both. We've already discussed everything before and I'll sign the documentation as soon as we return from our walk."

Sebastian peered at David and shrugged his shoulders. "That's fine with me."

David agreed.

Antonio led them through the exquisitely manicured gardens. "You will join me and my family for the festivities tomorrow night, si?"

Sebastian patted Antonio on the back. "That seems more like a strong suggestion, my friend then a question."

He agreed by roaring with laughter. "Si, i miei amici, it would be an honor to have you celebrate with us."

"We'll stay."

"Ah, benissimo! Be sure to bring your daughter and your Sophie…e' molto bella."

The stone pathway led them back to the conservatory steps and Antonio turned to David. "Please show me the documentation. I'm ready to sign." Sebastian started to follow them inside, but Antonio waved him off with a wink. "Go to your family now."

* * *

Antonio's words, *your family*, kept swirling

around in Sebastian's mind as he followed the winding cobblestone path to the piccola villas on the estate. The sound of those two words tasted sweet to the tongue like specially wrapped dark chocolate. Stopping at the arched doorway to Sophie's rooms, he knocked and waited—his excitement building with each passing second.

Sophie opened the door. "Is something wrong? I thought you were in your meeting."

"Oh, it went well. David is finalizing the contract. Antonio sent me here." He'd barely caught himself before he'd repeated the exact words. She might run for cover if she knew exactly what Antonio had said.

She leaned against the stucco doorframe. "Thanks for checking on us. We're fine. Anastasia's taking her semester exams."

Here goes nothing, he dove right in. "Antonio invited us to stay for a few days. He even extended an invitation to attend his daughter's sixteenth birthday celebration. You should see all the arrangements. It's like they're preparing for a wedding."

Sophie hesitated before responding and he could almost see the wheels turning in her head—trying to drum up an excuse to leave. "I don't want to intrude."

He gently touched her forearm. "We're definitely invited. Antonio assured me he'd be honored to have us join his family in the festivities."

She crossed her arms, never a good sign as far as he was concerned. "Fine, but I don't have any elegant dresses suitable for a fancy party."

He ran his index finger down her cheek, trailing her chin line. "You'll look beautiful in whatever you wear. Even Antonio said you were *molto bella*." Her rigid stance loosened up and she uncrossed her arms.

"What does that mean anyway?"

"Literally translated, it means much beautiful one." He hoped she caught the signals he kept shooting from his eyes.

"It sounds better in Italian."

Leaning closer, he kissed her forehead. "Yes, it's more romantic. Can we go for a stroll after dinner tonight? I found a great place—"

"—to what?"

"Hmm, if you'd let me finish, I was simply going to say we can talk."

"Fine, as long as that's all you had in mind." She defiantly crossed her arms again.

"I can think of other things to do. That's no problem."

"I'm sure you can."

Anastasia called from inside the room. "Miss Sophie, I don't understand this question." She peered back. "I'll be right there."

Sebastian seized the opportunity to step forward a few inches. When Sophie turned her head, he surprised her with a playful kiss on the lips. "I'll see you later." He winked and waved goodbye.

"I can't wait."

As he walked down the path toward the main villa, inside his inner child skipped and danced like Gene Kelly from *Singing in the Rain*.

* * *

The festive chaos of a normal dinner with the Savati famiglia had ended and Sophie gave herself over to the excitement of spending more alone time with Sebastian. "So where are you taking me?"

"It's a secret."

"Not another surprise."

"I thought you liked them."

She shared her love hate relationship with surprises. "I do, but only if I'm the one making the plans."

"Where's the fun in that!"

She shrugged her shoulders. "What can I say, I'm very predictable."

"We're out of view of the villa. May I hold your hand now?"

"Do I sense a little sarcasm in your voice?"

"Frustration, that's all."

His serious tone made Sophie pause. She stopped walking and reached for his hand to pull him back. "Are you upset with me?"

He returned her steady gaze. "No." She observed the warring emotions evident on his face. "I simply wish you wouldn't mind when I want to hold your hand or kiss you in public."

Without wavering, she continued to search his face. "I've never been one for PDA's."

"Then it's not solely because of Ana?"

"Her too, but I need time to get used to this." Would he accept her reasoning and show her patience? She realized she needed to compromise— another lesson learned from observing her parent's godly marriage.

"I see."

An avid reader of romance novels—Sophie, the pragmatist—never completely understood the expression *time stood still* until that moment. When she saw relief wash over his features, the same emotion flooded her soul. He understood. He would be patient with her. Kissing her cheek, he grasped her hand again and pulled her further down the path. "Oh, let's hurry up. I don't want you to miss the surprise." Not often had this giddy child-like side come to the surface of Sebastian's personality—but she quite liked it! As they strolled in comfortable silence, Sophie realized she relished the feel of her hand held in his. Stopping short of rounding the bend, he quickly covered Sophie's eyes with his hands. "Perfect timing! I know you don't like surprises, but please humor me on this one." She nodded her head and he gently guided her slowly along the cobblestones. "I'm going to remove my hands, but don't open your eyes yet, okay?"

She nodded again. "This better be worth it."

"It is. I think Mr. Knightley would be proud." In addition to the animation in his voice, she heard the sound of metal scraping on the stones. Then Sebastian steered her again. "Please sit, milady."

Slightly disoriented from walking blindly, she reached out her free hand. Grabbing onto the lifeline of the metal chair, she gingerly sat down. "May I open my eyes yet?"

"You are impatient. I don't know if I can live with that." Sophie forced herself to remain in the moment and not to over-analyze his last statement. "You can open your eyes now."

She started to say something about waiting forever to open her eyes, but the view captivated her and halted further speech. She peered over the rock wall surrounding the stone patio. Staring out at the glorious setting sun meeting the dark waters of the calm sea, nearly took her breath away. *Yes, another expression from all those romance novels. I never thought I'd be living in one with the dashing hero!*

"So, what do you think?" He sounded like a young child who'd won first place at the school fair—completely proud with his accomplishment.

"I think I can learn to live with your surprises." Her serious words hung in the air, and even in the dying light, she saw Sebastian's face appear to register the underlying meaning. As if on cue, he swept Sophie to her feet in a tender embrace. Her right hand rested on his chest. While he drew her close for a kiss, the trembling of his heart vibrated on her palm. Another sign she needed to add to the list of his actions speaking louder than words. She pulled away. "I guess it certainly does get romantic in Italy."

His lips curved into the devilish grin she'd grown to love. "I'll try to control myself." He made a dramatic bow as if curtsying to his lady—then he beckoned her to join him near the rock ledge. She easily fit into the crook of his arm as they gazed out at the panoramic view. Without him even uttering the words, she knew in her heart that he cherished their time together as much as she did.

* * *

The next day, Sophie and Anastasia strolled leisurely around the villa grounds. Her evening excursion with Sebastian the night before still occupied her mind and kept her spirits light. Anastasia invaded her thoughts. "Are we invited to Tatiana's birthday party tonight?"

"Yes."

"I love parties. Do you like them, Miss Sophie?"

She thought for a minute. "I prefer a quiet

evening at home reading a book, but I guess a party every now and then isn't too bad."

"Papa goes to a lot of parties with Uncle David."

"It's good for business. They need to socialize with their clients."

"I don't think Papa likes parties, but Uncle David does."

The young child never ceased to amaze her—wise beyond her years. "I think you're right, my little Miss. You're very observant."

Anastasia surprised Sophie by grabbing her hand. "We'll have fun at the party. I'll stay with you and we can leave when you want to."

"That's sweet of you. Thank you."

"Are you having fun, Miss Sophie?"

"Like right now?"

"I mean, are you having fun being my teacher?"

Sophie spotted a stone bench up the path and pointed. "Let's sit down." How should she answer this question so that the young child would understand? When she had originally accepted this job as Anastasia's tutor, she'd never fathomed how God had planned a life detour for her. "I love being your teacher. You're a smart young lady and you enjoy learning."

"Do you think I'll like going to school?"

"You'll do great and have fun there." Sophie

hoped Anastasia didn't ask for a timeline on when she'd actually start attending school. That subject still remained unsettled and a decision for Sebastian to make.

Anastasia patted Sophie's arm. "Thank you for always making me feel better."

Sophie scrunched up her face and leaned closer—nose to nose. "You're welcome and you make me feel better too. How about we finish our walk?"

"Sure."

Anastasia skipped off ahead as Sophie called out. "Don't go too far where I can't see you." She pondered her young student's questions from earlier and hoped her responses calmed her anxiety. Anastasia slowed down to check out the flowers lining the pathway and Sophie heard her humming a tune. Her mind raced with apprehension over attending Tatiana's party and she lost her footing on the incline then twisted her ankle. Crying out in pain, she crashed to the ground with a thud. *I'm such a klutz!* Biting her lip, she tried to stand, but her ankle gave out.

"Miss Sophie!"

She grimaced. "Don't worry, honey, I'm fine."

"No, you're not."

She heard Sebastian's voice as he came upon the scene. Great, what is *he* doing here? Of all the times to fall, now would not have topped her list. The heat of embarrassment warmed her cheeks. "Where did you come from?"

"I was coming to find you ladies. David is getting hungry and he asked me to find you and Ana." Reaching down, he assisted Sophie to her feet. "Thank God I came looking for you."

Sophie noticed him searching the area and Anastasia quickly reacted. "Papa, there's a bench back around the path, that way." She pointed behind them.

"Thank you, dear. Can you walk on the other side of Miss Sophie and hold her hand? I'll support her on this side."

Sophie wanted to fight off the attention, but she knew she needed the help. When the hobbling trio arrived at the bench, Sebastian helped her sit down. He crouched in front of her. "May I?" She nodded as he moved to lift her pant leg. "It doesn't look broken, but I'm not a doctor. We'd better get you inside and call for professional medical attention."

Her protests began in earnest. "My ankle's not broken. I think I only sprained it."

He held up his hands. "Please don't argue with me, Sophie. I'm calling the doctor and that's final."

Begrudgingly, she agreed with his judgment call and kept quiet. She allowed Sebastian to assist her to her feet, but after a few staggering steps, she saw his growing frustration with their limited progress. "This is taking far too long." In one swift movement, he swept her into his arms as if she weighed nothing and they made their way to the main villa in silence.

* * *

"Right, Miss Sophie?" Anastasia rubbed Sophie's arm, trying to get her attention.

"I'm sorry. I didn't hear what you said."

"It was nice that Tatiana's mom gave you a long skirt to wear." The child moved in for a closer inspection. "You can't even see the bandage."

"Good, exactly what I wanted."

"Is your bone broken?" She held her finger out as if tempted to touch the bandaged ankle.

"No, it's only a very bad sprain. The doctor instructed me to ice it earlier. Now I need to keep it wrapped, elevated and rest it."

"Amen to that."

Sophie peered over her shoulder and teased. "Hello Sebastian, are you reporting for duty?"

"You bet I am." He tapped his daughter on the nose. "Has she been behaving?"

Anastasia covered her mouth and giggled. "Yes, Papa. She's been sitting here with me while you were gone."

"May I join you?"

Sophie inched over on the divan. "Sure."

Antonio's youngest daughter, Arianna, approached their hideaway. "Signior Sebastian, may Anastasia come and play?"

Sophie watched him melt like butter under the spell of the sweet child with big brown eyes and long black hair. "Certainly, have fun girls." Anastasia hugged her father and dashed off after her new friend with her own blonde pigtails flying.

"It's going to be good for her to go to school."

"You're right." He agreed without hesitation, which somewhat surprised Sophie. "I hope I didn't stifle her intellectual and emotional growth by having her home-schooled."

She squeezed his hand. "You are such a loving father and you did what you thought was best for your daughter. I'm beginning to see how God has His hands on our lives even when we don't see them in action."

"I'm glad He had His angels watching over you today and your injury wasn't worse."

"I'm thankful, too." Sophie perused the festive crowd. "The party is a success. Everyone seems to be having a nice time." She tilted her head. "Look at Tatiana. She's so beautiful and happy."

"Like someone else I know."

She dramatically rolled her eyes and sighed. "I knew it wouldn't take long for you to get all mushy again."

"Let's see if we've made any progress on the

PDA's." He slid closer and gently caressed Sophie's cheek, sending shivers down her spine. Ever so slowly, he moved his face toward hers, lips not quite yet touching. The physical tension of the moment sent her senses into a tailspin. When she thought she could bear it no longer, his lips touched hers with a feather-light kiss. In a matter of seconds, he kissed her more urgently. Completely lost in the moment, her eyes remained closed when he pulled away. "You're still sitting next to me, so I must not be in the dog house yet."

Opening her eyes, she managed to respond. "I'm getting used to this affection thing and I kind of like it." Sophie shuffled over on the seat, comfortably leaning against his chest.

"I can see that and I like it, too."

She peered upward and grinned. "Or it could be that we're half-hidden in this alcove so I'm not as shy." Without over-analyzing her own words, she swiftly changed topics. "I am going to miss being in Italy. It's so beautiful here."

"I'll bring you back someday, don't you worry about that."

Sophie tucked those words into the recesses of her mind—for pondering later. She would not allow anything to disrupt the special moment, not even her own inability to become vulnerable. As she snuggled with Sebastian, she enjoyed listening as he shared amusing stories about their time with Antonio. One of the most significant takeaways from the evening—her realization that she'd crossed over the barrier and reached the point of no return. Now the only thing distracting her was whether or not God agreed and thought Sebastian was the man for her!

Chapter Twenty-Six

Sophie held a red pen in her hand and focused on grading Anastasia's exams. She sensed Anastasia's eyes boring holes into her back, waiting for the results. Without lifting her eyes from the exams, Sophie waved her young student off. "Would you please back up a little bit, dear?" No movement from the peanut gallery. Sighing audibly, Sophie spun around in the chair to face her audience. "Why don't you find your shoes and coat? We'll be going to see the movie soon."

With a puff of fairy dust, the little sprite vanished! *If only she truly was such an angel.* Sophie shook her head and continued her review. *I guess my lessons have been working.* Satisfying for any teacher, she enjoyed not marking up the paper in red ink. Tap. Tap. She glanced up when a knock sounded at the door and seconds later it creaked open. His musky cologne gave him away immediately. "Hello, Sebastian." If she had to be interrupted by anyone, she welcomed his entrance.

"I saw Ana fly by. She seems excited about her outing with you."

"Good, I'm glad."

"Are you positive your ankle is better?"

Maybe his interruption isn't so welcome now. "Seriously, I'm fine. Besides, it has been three weeks since I sprained it. You know I've been taking it easy." She wagged her index finger at him. "You've definitely seen to that! Trust me…my ankle has healed well."

"Message received, but you should still take it easy."

"It's not like I'm hiking for miles in the Andes Mountains."

He waved away her protests. "I've asked Daniel to drive you."

Secretly she enjoyed his overbearing concern but smirked outwardly. "Of course you did, although that's not necessary."

He knelt down beside her. Grabbing the cushion of her chair, he twisted the seat to face him. With his most serious expression he decreed. "It's either Daniel drives or I crash your party and drive you ladies myself." Leaning closer, he reached for her hand. "You know which idea I prefer."

Anastasia skipped back into the room with her own fierce expression of a woman-in-control. "Papa, you cannot come." Sophie stifled her giggles as Anastasia rocked the hands-on-the-hips stance. *You go girl!* "This is a girl's date."

Sophie released her hand from his grasp and grinned coyly. "She's right. It's for girls only...no exceptions."

Rising to his feet, he held up his hands in surrender as if accepting defeat. "You win." When he planted a kiss on Sophie's cheek, she noticed his own satisfaction in kissing her in public—even if only, in front of his daughter. He then blew Anastasia a kiss, waved and made his exit. "Have fun, ladies, and I guess I'll see you both later."

* * *

Sophie ushered Anastasia into the foyer. The young girl shook off her coat, handed it to Sophie and rushed down the hall. *So much for acing the responsibility test.* Sophie made a mental note to review—*cleaning-up-after-oneself*—in one of her next class lessons. Animated voices caught Sophie's attention and she headed in that direction. She stopped dead in her tracks when she came upon Sebastian and David in the kitchen, preparing lunch. *Never thought I'd see that sight.* "This is nice."

"David and I decided to give Hilde the day off."

David glanced up from his task at the bamboo cutting board. His usually stylish blonde hair now in disarray and the crooked grin on his face warmed

Sophie's heart. She continued to pray for him and knew that God had special blessings in store for his life. "We were inspired by the caterers and wonderful food we ate in Italy."

Sebastian interjected. "How was the movie?"

Sophie began to speak, but Anastasia interrupted her. "It was good. Are we going home any time soon?"

Sebastian gently scolded his daughter. "Ana, apologize to Miss Sophie for interrupting her. You're being impolite."

"I'm sorry. I'm excited to go home."

Sophie nodded. "Apology accepted."

David wiped his hands on a towel and approached his niece. "Hey! Haven't you enjoyed yourself in my home?" He wiggled his fingers, threatening to tickle her. "You've loved my England, I know it."

A fair match for her uncle, she tilted her head and rolled her eyes. "*Your*, England, Uncle David?"

Sebastian explained to Anastasia. "He's zealously patriotic."

Sophie enjoyed watching the loving interaction between Anastasia and her uncle. She knew once they arrived home in the States, the young girl would sincerely miss him. As David hugged and kissed Anastasia's cheek and promised her extra dessert later, Sophie saw through to the less jaded portion of his heart. *There's hope for him...even though he doesn't know it yet.*

In the playful commotion, Sophie hadn't noticed that Sebastian now stood beside her until he whispered in her ear. "My daughter has all three of the men in her life wrapped around her finger."

"You said it, I didn't."

"It's true."

Anastasia tugged at his sleeve. "Excuse me, Papa." Inwardly, Sophie wanted to high-five her young student for opting for the polite route this time.

"Yes, dear—"

"Where's grandpapa?"

"He's in the library. Please leave him alone right now."

David lifted the tomato he held in his hand and brushed away Sebastian's words as of no consequence. "Oh, let her disturb him. He needs some attention these days."

Anastasia ran off in search of Alexander before her father could stop her. Strike three for disobedience. *Good thing I hadn't high-fived her before!* Sophie moved to the sink to wash her hands. "So, what can I help with?"

The phone rang and David left the kitchen to answer the call. "I'll be back."

Sebastian shook his head and Sophie knew he was strategizing a plan for speaking to his daughter about disobedience. *Maybe he might even bring David in on the discussion and tell him a thing or two about interfering.* "The chicken is in the oven with the vegetables so you can take over David's job if you want. He was working on the salad. I'll get started on cleaning up our mess."

"I'm still amazed that you and your brother can cook."

She heard him start running the water in the sink. "My father believed in his children being self-sufficient. He did not want us to become dependent on household staff. We had our lessons in cooking and cleaning and all that jazz."

"Good for him. It's nice to see you weren't spoiled."

"He kept us grounded in reality and made certain we knew the meaning of hard work. Look how I turned out." He flashed his debonair smile. "I'm not sure about David, though."

"Sebastian, that's not nice."

"I'm kidding. He's a good brother. I've seen him grow so much even in the short time since I've been back here." He shut off the faucet and began scrubbing the utensils. "The one I'm worried about is Anastasia. I think I've spoiled her."

Sophie decided to leave that subject alone for now. She finished cutting the lettuce leaves and put them in the salad spinner. "Do you want tomatoes, onions and celery in the salad?"

"Sounds good."

She walked to the refrigerator. "You know,

you never answered your daughter's question."

"About our departure plans, you mean?"

"Yes." She wanted an answer as much as Anastasia did.

"The business on this trip has taken longer than I thought it would. Honestly, I don't mind because you and Ana are here with me." She started slicing tomatoes and he continued explaining his thoughts. "I was thinking about extending our trip for a few weeks."

Hmm, not exactly the answer she'd expected. "Oh, but shouldn't Anastasia be enrolled in school soon?"

"Three more weeks won't hurt."

"I guess that will be fine. I could continue her lessons here." Her overactive imagination threatened to rev up again. Why would he want to extend the trip? He didn't technically say the reason was pertaining to his business dealings.

"Actually, I was thinking more along the lines of a three week holiday."

"You're going on vacation?" *Alone*, she wanted to add.

"Yes. I'm taking you and Ana to Ireland."

She stared at him for a minute as the outrageous statement sank in. "Ireland?"

"I can see that you agree, but I think you should put the knife down. You look kind of dangerous right now."

The shock of his plan wore off and she realized she had been holding the knife up in the air. She regained her composure. "Wait a minute. We can't actually travel alone together."

"We won't be alone. Ana will be with us at all times and we'll have separate rooms. Ana will stay with you."

"I don't know." Wow. His suggestion definitely came out of left field and caught her off guard. Just when she was starting to get used to the status quo of their blossoming romance, he threw a monkey wrench into her predictable routine.

He dropped the dishcloth in the sink and swiveled to lean against the countertop. "You know you'd love to go." Not again with those deep brown eyes and melt-worthy grin. How could she say no to him? Should she say no? The wall of her resistance started crumbling, but not enough for her to completely break through. He comically batted his eyes. "At least think about the possibility, okay?"

"Fine, I will."

"I'd really like to go. I hope you reconsider and I promise I'll be on my best behavior."

With nothing more to say, she focused her attention on preparing the salad. Much to her relief, David entered the room again and distracted Sebastian. She heard none of what they discussed because her own conversation took precedence in her head. For ages she'd dreamed of traveling to Ireland.

Now the opportunity presented itself, but also created a dilemma. It's not like she lived in the old days where she'd need a chaperone to be alone with a man. "I only want to do things the right way," she whispered. *When I'm near Sebastian, I can't think straight.* His argument of not being completely alone—since Anastasia would be with them—kept playing devil's advocate in her mind. The walls crumbled some more. "Maybe it's not such a bad idea..."

* * *

Later on that same afternoon, Sophie had acquiesced to Sebastian's wishes. She'd decided to lay her reservations aside and take a leap of faith. In her opinion, Sebastian's actions had spoken louder than mere words thus far, so this seemed the best option. What could be better than spending more time with Sebastian and his daughter? He had suggested they eat a quick snack before leaving to hold their hunger at bay. The plan—hurry to London's Euston station to catch a train at five p.m. to Liverpool. From there, they needed to take a cab from Liverpool Lime Street Station to the ferry terminal to catch the ten-thirty p.m. overnight ferry. Sebastian whispered in Sophie's ear. "I hope you don't mind these travel arrangements."

"I don't mind." His detailed planning only

made her adore him more. It showed how much he cared for her and Anastasia.

He raised his eyebrows. "Before you sign your life away, let me remind you that it's an eight hour ferry ride."

She patted his arm. "I know. I heard you before, but I agree with you that it should be fun for Anastasia."

"I thought she might enjoy taking the train and the ferry rather than a plane." His expression brightened at his plan to make his daughter's time more enjoyable. Another reason to admire this man! "So, are you excited yet, to be going to your homeland?"

"Yes, I am."

"You don't appear too excited."

"I'm not a very expressive person. I assumed you'd figured that out by now."

"I guess you're right. Ah, our train is ready to board. Let's go." They stood in line with the other passengers. "Your parents were both from Enniskillen, right?"

She nodded. "That's what I've been told, yes." The line started moving faster now and soon Sophie stepped up into the train. Excitement began bubbling inside her. Part of her still couldn't believe she'd agreed to take this trip with Sebastian.

"Where are our seats, Papa?"

"A little further. Follow Miss Sophie. I'm

right behind you." Sophie found their seats and Sebastian quickly stowed the carry-on luggage in the baggage compartment. "We'll be taking the ferry to Belfast, but then spending most of our time in the low country."

"I can't say I know the geography of the country well, so I'm glad you're our tour guide."

He leaned closer toward her ear. "Hmm, I thought you wanted me tagging along for more romantic reasons."

She shook her head and playfully rolled her eyes as she moved passed him to sit down. She let Anastasia take the window seat next to her. Sebastian sat down across from them and Sophie glanced over. "I hope you don't mind sitting with your back to the front of the train. I get motion sickness when I sit backward."

"No problem. I guess that means you might get sick on the ferry. I didn't know that. I'm sorry for choosing this mode of travel."

She noticed his concerned expression and held up her hand. "Don't worry. I get sick on planes, too. I'm fine as long as I take motion sickness medication. Well, it's not actually medicine, because that makes me drowsy. I started taking herbal ginger pills and they work like a charm." Sophie worried that her rambling might make him disinterested, but quite the contrary. He seemed to enjoy when she spoke. Still, she made a mental note not to ramble on in the future.

Within a few minutes of boarding, the train rolled into motion. Soon after, Anastasia dozed off on Sophie's shoulder. "That was fast."

"She had a busy day today."

Sophie replied teasingly. "We all did! One minute we're at home and the next minute we're traveling to Ireland. I'd say you move pretty fast."

"Certainly true when I know what I want."

"To clarify, what do you want?" She bantered back, enjoying their innocent teasing.

"Spending time with you is one thing I want."

His remark brought heat to her cheeks and she was grateful for the dim lighting. She shifted in her seat. "We could've spent time together in England. You didn't have to take us on this trip."

"I wanted to do something special to show how much I care about you." *Something special*…those two words made war in her soul. What did he mean? She placed her hands on her slacks and distractedly smoothed them out. *Remember, enjoy the moment and don't over analyze!*

An attendant came by their seats. "Would you care for something to drink?"

Sophie nodded toward the young woman. "Hot tea, please."

Sebastian continued staring at Sophie, but responded with his beverage order. "I'll have a coffee, please."

"Would you like anything for the little one

when she wakes up?"

"Oh, she'll be out for a while."

"I'll be back in a few minutes with your beverages."

As the attendant spoke, Sophie took the time to grab her e-reader from her purse.

Sebastian leaned forward, elbows on his knees. "I guess that means the discussion is over." His piercing gaze followed her movements.

Was that disappointment she read on his face? "I hope you don't mind. I thought this would be a good time to catch up on reading."

"I figured you might." He held up the newspaper. "I grabbed this to read since I knew you'd probably bring your library with you."

With feigned disinterest, she flicked away his words. "Anyway, you know you're going to find many more opportunities to bring up conversations on romance and your fuzzy feelings."

He obviously found her statement humorous and she loved the sound of his laughter. "Oh, my *fuzzy feelings*." He opened the paper with an exaggerated motion and held it in front of his face. Seconds later, he peered to the side and flashed his devilish grin. "You know where to find me if you get lonely."

Now that she'd gotten underneath his stoic front to know his charming side, she couldn't stop smiling around him—no matter how hard she tried.

Glancing up furtively, she observed him reading the newspaper and some warm, fuzzy feelings of her own settled in her heart. Focusing back on her e-reader, she tried to concentrate on the words, while resisting the urge to peek at Sebastian again.

* * *

Sebastian ushered Sophie and his daughter off the train. "Now the real fun begins!" They had arrived at Liverpool Lime Street Station and rumbling stomachs dictated the need to locate a place to eat dinner. Then Sebastian needed to find a location to hang out until ten p.m. when they'd take a cab to the ferry terminal for their ten-thirty p.m. departure. He hoped the words of the famous 18th century poet, Robert Burns did not come to fruition in his case. *The best laid plans of mice and men often go awry.* Sebastian had invested a significant amount of planning into this trip and he counted on everything falling into place.

"I've never been on an evening ferry before. This should be interesting."

"I know that's because I'm here." Sebastian caught Sophie rolling her eyes again. Teasing her came naturally for him and he loved every minute of it. He hoped she enjoyed it as well and didn't find his behavior annoying. When he glanced at her again, she winked, bringing a smile to his face. *Good, I'm in the clear!*

Anastasia rubbed sleepy eyes and interrupted their flirting. "How long is the ferry ride?"

"Eight hours."

She sighed irritably and stomped her foot. "That's a long time!" Sebastian knew her cranky response stemmed from tiredness and he immediately began second guessing his travel plans. *So much for the mice and the men!*

Sophie pulled her into a hug. "No worries, honey, you can sleep on the ferry."

Sebastian watched in amazement how she came to the rescue again. Her actions continually confirmed his growing belief that he'd met his perfect match in this gracious woman. He interrupted their tender moment. "First, we need to store our luggage for a few hours and go eat. I know the ideal place."

Sophie touched his arm. "Where would that be?"

"Do you mean the left-luggage facility or the restaurant?"

"The restaurant you had in mind."

"I hope you like Chinese food."

His suggestion caught Anastasia's attention and her energy level momentarily soared as she jumped up and down. "I do...I do!"

He checked with Sophie. "Fine by me."

Consulting the GPS on his phone, he pointed down the street. "It's across from the train station on

Elliot Street."

"Great, we don't have to walk far." Again, another dramatic response from his daughter. *Hopefully, she'll return to her usual chipper self after some much needed rest.*

He tried to comfort Anastasia. "I know, dear. You'll be able to sleep in a few hours."

Sophie asked, "What time does the ferry leave?"

"At ten-thirty and we should be at the terminal about thirty minutes early."

She checked her watch. "It's seven-forty-five. We have a little more than two hours."

Sebastian spied a bench not far away. "Why don't you ladies wait for me and I'll find a porter to take our bags to the luggage facility."

A short while later he returned. "We're down to two hours. Let's get something to eat."

Anastasia jumped up. "Good I'm starving!"

He grinned at her excitement. "I see someone's hungry."

At the crosswalk, Sophie commented. "Did you know England has the safest roads in the world?"

"No, I didn't know that."

They crossed to Elliot Street and walked toward the restaurant. "We perused the travel guides while you were taking care of the luggage."

"Oh, I see. Sounds like an interesting read." He joked and raised his eyebrows.

"Is this the place, Papa?"

"Yes, it is." He held the door open and followed them inside. "It's a buffet. I hope that's acceptable?"

"I've eaten at many."

"This is the first time for Ana."

"Oh, she's going to love it."

He tried to peek at his daughter's face. "I bet her eyes are as big as saucers right now."

The hostess approached. "Table for three?"

"Yes."

As the hostess led them through the restaurant, Sebastian managed to get a glimpse of Anastasia's face. She appeared mesmerized by the wide variety of food at the buffet.

"Here's your table. Please help yourself to the buffet and salad bar. Your server will come by to take your beverage orders."

"Thank you." Sebastian urged his girls. "Let's get our food." He held Anastasia's hand as they walked back to the buffet and motioned for Sophie to go first. Then he took two plates. "So my little Ana, what looks good?"

"Everything does!"

Sophie laughed. "Are you sure? You might not like everything at the buffet."

"I like most foods."

"Yes, you do. I don't enjoy eating every kind food either, but it's good to try new things."

Sebastian agreed quietly and grinned. "Trying new things is good."

They made their way to the salad bar and then walked back to the table. The server came over. "Can I get you anything to drink?"

Anastasia piped up. "May I have lemonade?"

Sophie asked for water with lemon, as did Sebastian.

He barely finished praying for the meal, when his daughter chimed in. "Papa, what are we going to do on this trip?"

"We're going to have fun, that's what!"

"But, what kind of day trips will we take?"

"Day trips, huh?"

"Miss Sophie and I take day trips sometimes."

"Yes, and they've been mostly educational."

Hmm, I guess I've got my work cut out for me. "On this trip, the main goal is to relax and have fun. I've made plans to go on the Belfast Safaris."

"Seriously, there's a safaris in Ireland?"

Point number one! He'd actually planned an outing which seemed like a possible hit for his girls. He addressed Sophie's question. "These safaris are tours to discover the local culture and such."

"That sounds good. Because I was curious about seeing wild animals roaming the hills!"

"The food is delicious, Papa."

"I'm glad you're enjoying it."

"So where else are we going?"

"Since you like zoos, my little Ana, I thought we could visit the Belfast Zoo and then explore the Aquarium."

Anastasia patted his hand. "Papa, you're coming up with great ideas for day trips."

He took a sip of water. *Now for the most exciting surprise!* "And for Miss Sophie, I thought we could take the C.S. Lewis Trail to visit places in Belfast. Then when we go to Downpatrick, we'll visit his childhood home."

"Isn't that the inspiration for the world of Narnia?"

Sebastian loved that he'd caught her interest. Point number two—looks like his planning was going to pay off with great dividends. "Yes. I knew you'd be pleased with this excursion."

"What else, Papa?"

He warmed up even more to their excitement. "We can check out the Down County Museum and the Saint Patrick Centre." He grasped Sophie's hand. "You're going to appreciate the Down Cathedral. It's where St. Patrick is buried and the grounds are beautiful."

"Everything sounds wonderful. Thank you, Sebastian, for this trip. I was beginning to think I'd never make it to Ireland."

He saw the faintest hint of watery eyes. In that moment he experienced a genuine glimpse of exactly how much visiting Ireland meant to her. "You should never, say never. Isn't that what they say?"

She responded with the beautiful smile he loved. "Yes, they do."

"We'd better finish our food before it gets cold."

"And we have to make sure to catch the ferry."

He agreed. "Yes, we don't want to miss our ride." As they focused on finishing the meal, his thoughts ran wild with all of the special plans he'd made—and his anticipation grew with each passing moment.

* * *

Sophie helped Anastasia unpack and get situated in the cabin. She then quickly red a bedtime story to her, said prayers and the child went to bed. Seconds later, she texted Sebastian—*She's in bed. Come say goodnight*. After a few minutes, they left the cabin and locked the door. Sophie welcomed Sebastian's hand as he led her back upstairs.

"Would you like to get a snack?"

She thought about his suggestion for a moment. "Sure, but I'm warning you I need my beauty sleep or else I'll turn into a grouch in the morning." *Definitely not something she wanted Sebastian to witness yet.*

"And we have to get up early tomorrow." He

chuckled.

"I know." She teased. "I think I'm going to speak to my travel agent about these trip arrangements. I may even need to get a new agent!"

Sophie enjoyed strolling together hand-in-hand like a genuine couple. When they reached the dessert table, Sebastian pointed. "Ever had marshmallow meringue cake?"

"I can't say that I have."

"Do you want to share a piece? I'm certain you'll love it."

"Okay, if you say so."

He kissed her cheek. "Why don't you find us a seat and I'll take care of this. What kind of tea do you want?"

"Any kind is fine, but if they have herbal lemon tea, that would be nice."

"And if they don't, I'll demand they stop the ferry immediately to get some."

Sophie shook her head and started walking away, scanning the dining room for an empty table. She located the perfect secluded spot near a window and sat down to wait for Sebastian. Her mind still marveled at the fact that she sat in a ferry on her way to Ireland. *I'm finally on my way, mom.*

"Snack is served madam."

"Thank you, Sir."

Sebastian placed the tray on the table and joined her. He surprised Sophie by feeding her a piece of the cake. "What do you think?" *I think I'm at a loss for words.* She started to wipe away a bit of cream from her lips, but he rushed to her aide. "Oh, let me."

The tip of his finger touched her lip and sent shivers down her spine. Not again. She relished the feeling, but tried hard to ignore it. "I guess you didn't have to stop the ferry."

He raised his hand, pointing to the sky. "No, but I was prepared to do anything to get you lemon tea." His thumb tracing circles on her palm nearly made her pull her hand away. "How are you feeling? Any motion sickness yet?"

"I'm fine. The ginger pills definitely help."

"Wonderful news! Because we're going skydiving too."

She took a sip of tea. "Yeah, right…I'm terrified of heights."

"Only kidding. I'm not keen on jumping out of planes either."

"Thank you again for this trip." She meant every word of her statement.

"You don't have to continue thanking me."

Her eyes brimmed with tears. "My parents would be ecstatic right now."

"I'm sure they're watching you from Heaven."

The tears threatened to spill out. "I'm thankful I now have a certainty that I'll join them there someday."

"Glad to hear it because I want to see you

there, too. Accepting Jesus is the most important decision a person can make. It breaks my heart so many are lost."

"I've been reading through the gospels during my morning devotions. It's been awesome to read about Jesus, His teachings and miracles."

"Faith comes from hearing the Word of God."

They finished the cake. "Delicious! Good idea to come here for a snack."

He stood up with a flourish and held out his hand. "My next wonderful idea is to go up to the deck and gaze at the stars."

"Haven't you noticed it is cold out there?"

"I'll keep you warm. Please, for a few minutes."

Imagining his arms around her, Sophie caved. "Fine, but only a few and I need to get my coat or I'll freeze."

"Great, let's go."

About five minutes later, Sebastian and Sophie climbed the stairs toward the main deck and he opened the glass doors, ushering her outside. The gusty wind assaulted her and she hoped they stayed out for only a short while. Huddling close to her companion she followed his lead to the railing. Glancing up, the clear sky and sparkling lights took her breath away. "Look at the stars!"

He kissed her cheek. "See, I told you coming outside would be worth it."

"Yes, another great idea of yours."

"You look cold. Come here." He pulled her closer into his embrace.

Perfectly at home in his arms, she desired to stay near him forever. She sensed his eyes on her. Leaning her head back against his chest and peering into his eyes, she observed a new intensity. The passion in his gaze unnerved her—yet aroused her curiosity to search his heart. He gently stroked her cheek and leaned down to kiss her lips. She closed her eyes, falling captive to his spell. She finally pulled away. "I'm not so cold anymore." Sebastian chuckled and Sophie enjoyed the rich sound.

"I'm glad I could be of service."

She took a step back. "I should probably head to bed." His passionate gaze continued to hold her prisoner. Barely able to speak, she stared into his eyes. "What's on your mind?"

He moved closer and his lips lightly brushed her cheek. "You've stolen my heart, milady." With those whispered words, he silently escorted her back down to her cabin. Sophie kept quiet too, but inside her heart began singing. With excitement, she anticipated enjoying the rest of this trip with her Prince Charming and little Princess.

Chapter Twenty-Seven

"Miss Sophie, it's time to wake up." Anastasia gently shook Sophie's shoulders. "We have to eat breakfast, remember?"

Sophie wearily leaned up on her elbows. "You know, you're better than an alarm clock. What time is it anyway?"

"It's five o'clock."

Pushing herself to a sitting position, she rubbed tired eyes. "How long have you been up my little Miss?"

"I think maybe thirty minutes."

"Oh, to be young again."

"I'm excited to try the breakfast. Papa says the English breakfast is the best."

Still half asleep, Sophie forced herself out of bed. "Haven't we been eating the traditional *English* breakfast every day at your Uncle David's house?"

"Papa says it's not the same. That when you go out to eat breakfast it's even better."

Sophie slipped into a pair of jeans and pulled

on a warm blue cashmere sweater. Quickly brushing her hair, she stepped into her black ballerina flats and then lightly poked the young girl's nose. *Hopefully Sebastian likes the fall-out-of-bed look.* "Well then, let's go get your father and see if he's right."

Anastasia skipped along in front of Sophie as they headed toward the stairs. Last night, Sebastian had told Sophie to meet him in the dining room for breakfast.

"Is Papa upstairs already?"

"Yes. He wanted to make certain we had a table next to the food." Her words brought giggles from her young companion.

Sophie opened the dining room door and spotted Sebastian waving at them. She self-consciously brushed back her hair. Anastasia raced ahead. "Miss Sophie was right. You picked a table near the food." Like a dog sniffing a bone, the young girl hurried over to check out the buffet.

Sebastian gave Sophie a quizzical look and she explained with a hesitant smile. "That was me. I told Anastasia that you'd probably get a table near the food."

"Oh, really—"

"She seemed fascinated with your statement about the English breakfast and even got up early eager to eat. I was exhausted and wasn't in my right mind…" She let her words trail off.

He reached for her hand and she saw him lock

eyes on his daughter. "I love Hilde's cooking, but she hasn't yet made one of my all-time favorite English breakfast foods since I've been back. When I saw that it was on the menu here, I got excited."

Hmm, another new food to try—he definitely kept endeavoring to expand her horizons. Sophie searched the crowd and saw Anastasia hovering near the Danish pastries. "And what would this delicacy be?"

"It's called kedgeree."

"Sounds Greek to me…I've never heard of it."

"It's flaked fish, usually smoked haddock, boiled rice and eggs and butter."

"Is that a common dish?"

"Not anymore. It was introduced to England in the days of the British colonies in India."

They neared the buffet table. "That dish traveled through time. Has it changed at all?"

"They used to add parsley for flavor, but now they add curry powder or turmeric."

She scrunched up her nose. "Sounds spicy."

"Well, you have to at least try some."

"If you insist, but only a little bite or maybe two is all I want. Actually, I'm more of a tea and Danish kind of girl."

He wagged his finger at her. "You know, young lady, breakfast is the most important meal of the day."

"Yes, so I've been told."

Anastasia marched over. "Papa, we need to eat. You said the ferry docks at six-thirty."

He picked up two plates. "You are correct, my dear. Now, what would you like to eat?"

Sophie stepped into line behind them. Observing Sebastian's display of tenderness with his daughter brought back her own childhood memories. She recalled her dad reading to her from her children's Bible. The stories of the Old Testament filled her mind and she nearly bumped into Sebastian where he had stopped at the beverage station. He seemed unaware of their near collision. "Are you having tea or orange juice?"

"Um, I think I'll have both." He put the cup under the spigot for hot water. She searched through the tea bags and located the one she wanted. Sensing him peering over her shoulder, she glanced back. "If you must know, I'm having raspberry tea today."

He winked at her. "Yes, I must. It's part of my master plan to learn everything about you." He left her staring after his retreating form.

She got moving again and followed them as they picked the rest of their food and walked back to the table. "Can I pray, Papa?"

"Sure, honey."

"Lord, thank you for another day. Bless this breakfast and please let us have a wonderful trip. Amen."

After Anastasia prayed, she focused intently

on eating her food—as if she ate her last meal before winter hibernation. Sophie leaned toward Sebastian. "She definitely was eager for breakfast."

"Now if only she was this hungry at home." He scooped a small portion of his food onto her plate. "As promised, you have to try some of the kedgeree."

"Gee, thanks, for remembering."

"You didn't think I would forget now, did you."

She brought a forkful to her mouth and took a bite. Savoring the food—and the fact that she'd made him wait a moment for her opinion—she finally responded. "It tastes pretty good. I might even like to learn how to make it."

"Ah, you'd make it for me, how sweet."

"No, actually, I'd make it for me."

He winked. "Well, then, we'd better hurry up and eat before our little commander in chief reminds us again of our time deadline."

* * *

Anastasia jumped up and down. "Miss Sophie, listen…did you hear it?"

She wished she had the same youthful energy. "Yes, I heard the captain's announcement. We're almost there."

"Papa, can we go out on the deck now?"

Sebastian placed his hand on Sophie's

shoulder. "Do you mind taking Ana out there?"

"Sure."

"Thank you. Did you bring a carry-on bag?"

"We have two in our cabin."

"You ladies can go and I'll get the bags."

He started to leave, but Sophie stopped him. "Oh, wait, we need to get our coats."

"I'll grab those, too, and be back in a few minutes."

"Are you happy to go on this trip, Miss Sophie?" Like night and day, the young girl's expression became serious. From the first moment she'd met Anastasia, she'd known the child possessed an old soul—from difficult life experiences no child should have to deal with.

"I'm thrilled. I've always wanted to travel to Ireland. Remember, I told you my parents were born there? What about you, my little Miss?"

She grinned and tilted her head. "I'm so excited."

Sophie tickled Anastasia's sides. "Oh, like when you couldn't wait for breakfast."

"Sort of like that." She giggled. "I can't wait to go to the zoo and take all the day trips."

"I can't believe how much energy you have for so early in the morning."

"It's not early."

She checked her watch. "When you're not a morning person and it's six-twenty, that's early.

Believe me!"

"Okay, maybe you're right."

"Oh, I know I am."

"What are you so right about?"

Sophie turned around when she heard Sebastian's voice. "That it's too early to be up. I'd rather be back in bed sleeping."

He patted her shoulder in mock sympathy. "Sorry, too bad. But you'll have lots of fun today...I promise."

She raised her eyebrows. "I'll have to take your word on it."

Anastasia tugged on Sophie's hand. "Let's go outside."

"Don't forget your coat."

"I already put it on." Anastasia twirled around, with her arms wide. "See."

"I guess I didn't notice."

Sebastian gently massaged Sophie's shoulders. "You must be tired, my dear."

She leaned her head back against his chest. "I hope our travel plans for tomorrow include sleeping in." With a deep breath, Sophie reached for Sebastian's hand and they followed Anastasia outside to the deck.

"May I walk to the railing, Papa?"

"Yes, but be careful."

"You and Miss Sophie will be right here with me."

Sophie put one arm around Anastasia and Sebastian braced his daughter from the other side. Peering over the railing, Sophie watched the ferry enter the port. "It's such a beautiful view."

Sebastian nodded in agreement and she caught him staring at her over his daughter's head. His attention warmed her to the core and took away some of the chill from the air. Anastasia vied for their attention and pointed out over the railing. "Look at all the ships over there. This is great!"

"So, what's the itinerary for the day?"

"Well, my dear ladies, we'll be visiting the Belfast Zoo and the Exploris Aquarium during the day and then going out to dinner at night."

Sophie held up her hands. "I don't know about you two, but sometime before dinner, I'm taking a siesta."

"What's a *si-es-ta*, Miss Sophie?"

"It's Spanish for an afternoon nap."

The little girl thought for a moment and agreed. "Sounds like a good idea."

Sophie bent low at eye level with Anastasia. "I thought you had so much energy."

"I do, but by the end of the day, I'll be tired."

Sebastian made an imaginary checkmark in the air. "Oh, I see, you're both going to desert me. I guess I'll have to incorporate the siesta into the schedule."

Sophie smiled in appreciation. "Thank you."

He gave her hand a small reassuring squeeze. "No problem."

"Papa, Miss Sophie. Look, we made it!"

"I think you're right, dear. Let's gather our things and try to find a seat near the exit."

* * *

Sebastian slipped his cell phone back into his jacket pocket. "It looks like you're going to get that nap sooner than we thought. The zoo doesn't open until ten o'clock."

"I thought that might be the case and was wondering what we were going to do until then." He noticed the satisfied expression on Sophie's face and smiled.

"Are we going to the zoo, now Papa?" Anastasia asked as Sophie opened the door of the taxi for her.

Sebastian climbed in after his girls. "Not yet. We're going to the rental car office and then I'll drive us to the hotel."

"So Miss Sophie can take a nap?"

He tried to keep a straight face and winked at Sophie. "She can take a nap if she wants to." He wanted to tease Sophie, but one glance in her direction and he thought better of it. *She definitely is tired.*

"I think I will. I'll need lots of energy to chase

after you all day, my little Miss."

Anastasia giggled and Sebastian focused his attention on the brochure for the Culloden Hotel where he'd made reservations for their stay in Belfast. He anticipated Sophie and his daughter would enjoy the palatial structure.

He whispered in Sophie's ear. "I hear there's an excellent spa at the hotel. We might have to check out the hot tub later." She ignored his flirting and tuned in to his daughter chatting about the zoo and aquarium. *She's a tough customer.* Lightly kissing her neck, he playfully tried again. "I can be your tour guide and show you around the hotel and gardens."

"You've stayed at this hotel?"

"Um, no, I haven't."

She teased back. "Then maybe I should check into a new tour guide."

"Wait, this hotel used to be," he hesitated and peeked at the brochure again, "the official palace of the Bishops of Down."

She snatched the brochure from his hands. "I think I can manage the tour myself."

"I can't win…deserting me again. Though, the date at the hot tub still stands." He hoped he'd persuaded her to join him.

She squeezed his hand and spoke quietly. "I'll think about it." *I will take that as a yes.*

A few minutes later, they arrived at the rental car office. "I'll be right back." When Sebastian went inside, he arranged to rent an SUV and picked up a travel magazine featuring the local attractions and shops. He came back to the taxi, paid the fare and loaded the luggage into the rental vehicle. "Ladies, let's go see this beautiful hotel!"

* * *

The drive to the Culloden Hotel took approximately fifteen minutes—and the butterflies in Sophie's stomach had taken to flight as soon as Sebastian had turned the key and the engine cranked to life. *This is truly happening. I'm staying in a hotel in Ireland with a man I adore.* What could be better than this? The exact moment Sophie laid eyes on the elegant structure, she fell in love. For a second, she imagined herself a princess returning home to her castle. Sebastian had barely pulled to a stop at the grand entrance, when she burst the door open and stood in awe. Her eyes soaked in the stately architecture and crisp attention to detail. Sebastian came up behind her and placed his hands on her shoulders. "I knew you'd love this place."

As if under a spell, she followed him and Anastasia inside while the valet attendant parked the vehicle. Her wide-eyed wonder continued as they traversed the ornate foyer toward the front desk. When she peeked at Anastasia, the young girl's face mirrored her own awe. Gorgeous marble flooring, rich dark woods, high vaulted ceiling, sparkling chandeliers—everywhere she focused, something amazing caught her eye.

A flash of light caused her to blink. Sebastian snapped a photograph of her. "Now there's the expression I want to see."

"What expression?"

"The one that says I surprised and dazzled you. I hope it stays on your beautiful face during this entire trip."

Back to reality for a moment, she rolled her eyes. "You didn't have to take a picture. I'm not too fond of being photographed." He pretended to write something down. "What are you doing?"

"Simply adding to the checklist in my mind…don't take too many pictures." He snuck a quick kiss onto her cheek. "The camera loves you." She stood staring at him in response. "I'll go check us in."

Sophie wondered where Anastasia had wandered off to. Scanning the vast room, she located her where she stood staring into the fireplace. Joining her in front of the crackling fire, Sophie crouched down. "What do you think of this place?"

"It's so nice and even bigger than our house."

She chuckled. "Yes, I think so."

With wide eyes and serious expression, Anastasia tapped Sophie. "Was this a castle?"

"I think they called it a palace."

"What's the difference?"

This one constantly keeps me on my toes. Hopefully I remember my history lessons correctly. "During medieval times, a castle was large with high walls and towers for defense. A prince or nobleman lived there. A palace, on the other hand, was the place where a king or queen, or bishop might have lived. In this case, the palace was the home for the Bishops of the area."

She held her finger to her lips as if deep in thought. "Oh, I see."

As Sophie observed the young child chewing it over, she hoped she'd explained the difference well enough. Sebastian came back. "Here you go." He handed her a room key. "The rooms are ready. If you want to rest for a while, I can stay with Ana."

What blessed words! Taking a short power nap sounded heavenly right then. "You don't mind?"

"Don't mind at all." He kissed her lightly on the lips. "Your bags should be upstairs. We'll come get you when we're ready to head over to the zoo."

"Thank you." She smiled sweetly and started to walk away then turned back—realizing she had no idea how to find her room. "Can you point me in the right direction?"

"I guess that would be helpful, huh." Gently turning her by her shoulders, he pointed straight ahead to the main elevators. "By the way, I haven't forgotten about our date with the hot tub later." His whispered words brought the butterflies back in full force.

"Hmm, I am warming up to the idea."

"Oh, aren't you witty."

She shook her head. "No, only sleepy. I'll see you in a little while."

* * *

Anastasia skipped down the path as Sebastian and Sophie followed closely behind. "I'm still amazed at how well she's doing. Thank you for fighting for her and being such an inspiration."

"Me?" She blinked in surprise. "We both know it was all God."

"He brought you into our lives to save us."

"Save you from what?"

"Save me from myself. I was locked up in my work. I needed a push to see my precious daughter required my attention."

This conversation began making her uncomfortable. She shrugged. "I did what any decent person would've done in the same situation."

He gently nudged her chin. "Can you simply take a compliment, my dear? Please let me thank you." She opened her mouth to speak, but he shushed her by holding his finger to her lips. "I know you're not good at that." He kissed her cheek. "You'd better get used to it because many more are coming your way."

Anastasia quickly stopped and swiveled to face them. "Where are we going next?" Her interruption halted further response from Sophie to Sebastian's words.

Sophie tousled Anastasia's curls. "Wherever you want to go is fine." They had just finished walking through the free-flight aviary.

"What about the penguins and sea-lions?" Sebastian suggested. "I hear they have an underwater viewing area."

Anastasia started skipping backward "Great idea, Papa."

"Then I think we should go to the Ark Café I saw back there."

"Why, is someone getting hungry?" He teased.

Sophie linked arms with his. "A little hungry. I need my three meals a day, you know."

"Do you want to stop now since it's right here?"

She checked her watch. "It is almost lunch time and it would be good not to have to backtrack."

He squeezed her hand. "Excuse me for a minute, while I go chase down our little Princess."

As Sebastian raced after his daughter, she realized he'd used the word *our*—one simple word which rang of sweet sounding music to her ears. With a flourish, he scooped up Anastasia and tickled her as he carried her back.

"Ana gave her okay."

"Oh, why thank you." Sophie lightly poked her on the nose, bringing forth more giggles from the young girl.

As the trio strolled the short distance to the café, Sophie enjoyed their genuine feeling of camaraderie. Sophie found an empty table in the midst of the crowded room. Sebastian took their orders. "If they don't have what you ladies want, I'll be back."

"Isn't Papa so nice?"

"Yes, he is." Before Anastasia dove in to ask probing questions about her relationship with him, Sophie quickly changed the subject. "Are you having fun yet?"

"Yes, lots of fun." She couldn't sit still in her chair and Sophie took that as a sign the young girl meant what she said.

"That's good."

"Are you having fun?"

"I am."

"You're Irish, right, Miss Sophie?"

"Yes."

"Were you born in Ireland?"

"No, my mom and dad were."

"Did they like it here?"

"They did and I heard many stories about it." Refreshingly, thinking about her parents didn't cause a torrent of tears any more. Now she sensed peace and gratefulness at the many memories they'd made together.

"Can you tell me the stories some time?"

"Sure."

Sebastian returned to the table with a tray of food. He handed a plate to Sophie. "Turkey and avocado wrap for you, my dear. For you, my Princess, a grilled chicken sandwich."

"What did you get Papa?"

"I have a corned beef sandwich."

"Can I pray?"

"Of course, you can, Ana."

"Thank you, for this wonderful food and my family and all the fun we're having. Amen."

Sophie opened her eyes and quickly wiped away a tear. She felt honored that in Anastasia's mind, she included her in *her* family. Glancing at Sebastian, they both echoed their *Amens* and all three dove hungrily into their food.

* * *

Later in the evening, Sophie had acquiesced to Sebastian's urging and they had indulged in a couples' massage at the hotel spa. Sebastian wanted the complete spa experience for Sophie so he had suggested they also sit in the steam room for fifteen minutes. The best part of the spa awaited and he led her to the unoccupied Jacuzzi. *We have it all to ourselves!* He stepped in first and held out his hand, helping her down the stairs. He exhaled as the hot water enveloped him and he leaned back against the wall. After a few seconds of closing his eyes, he sensed something amiss and glanced at Sophie. "All right, out with it. What's wrong?"

"Nothing."

"You seem worried."

"Are you sure Anastasia will be okay by herself in the room?"

"She's sleeping and we told her where we'd be. We gave her your cell phone to call me if she needs help."

She shook her head. "You're right. I worry too much."

"Think of it as if we're home, she's asleep in her room and we're downstairs watching television."

The way she raised her eyebrows made him smile. He loved her feisty attitude. "No offense, Sebastian, but this hotel is a lot bigger than your home. She could wake up disoriented and walk out of the room and wander around."

He wanted to say her concern reminded him of his wife, but decided against that response. "Thank you for caring so deeply for my daughter. I appreciate it more than you know."

They sat close enough that he saw her eyes begin to water. He held out his hand welcoming her closer. "Come over here and I'll take your mind off your worries." Immediately, he noticed her hesitation. "I don't bite."

Biting her bottom lip, she slowly inched closer to him. When she bumped his shoulder, he carefully put his arm around her. "Don't take this the wrong way, but I feel weird sitting here in a hot tub with you."

He ran his fingers along her forearm. "Hmm, maybe you should elaborate."

"We're in our bathing suits and you're my employer."

Closing his eyes, he prayed silently for wisdom. He feared pushing her away again. "I thought we were passed this already."

"Yes and no." She wore a terrified expression.

Had he misread all of their interactions? He pulled his arm back. "Have I misunderstood your feelings for me?"

"No." She moved sideways to face him and gently caressed his cheek. Her touch gave him hope he hadn't been wrong. "I do have feelings for you. It's because of those feelings I think I should move out when we get back home."

"Move out?" Those two words knocked the wind out of his sails. He couldn't imagine life without her living each day in his home.

"Since Anastasia will be starting school, she won't need me anymore."

"But, I do…" His whispered words trailed off.

He noticed a tear start to fall down her cheek. Gingerly, he held her face in his hands, wiping the tear away. Closing the distance between them, he kissed her fervently. When they came up for air, she managed to disengage from his embrace. "Now that's a perfect example. I want to be true to God and not let our passion tempt us too far."

Now he understood her concerns. He reclined against the wall with a sigh and ran his hand through his hair. A deafening moment of silence ensued. He reached over and grasped her hands in his. "Please forgive me for not taking the lead. I should have been the one to bring up this subject. Thank you for sharing your heart."

"You're welcome and there's nothing to forgive. Besides, it's not like I want to move out. I desperately want to stay with you." She modestly turned away. "If we're moving forward in our relationship, this is what I need to do."

He beckoned her to his arms again. "I heard everything you've said. You're right and we'll work out the details when we get home. But for now, let's enjoy the rest of this trip…and I promise to be on my best behavior."

Her audible sigh seemed to flow through her entire body, lessening her tension. "I accept your terms and look forward to discussing this further." She giggled and the sound warmed his heart. She settled back comfortably into the crook of his arm. As he listened contentedly to her relaxed tone while she chatted, a strong sense of peace settled upon him. Freely he surrendered the weight of his anxiety over to God, knowing He directed his path.

Chapter Twenty-Eight

"Wow, C.S. Lewis married when he was fifty-eight years old. Did you know that?"

"No. I knew his wife died of cancer, but I didn't know that he got married so late in life." Sebastian stepped closer and the scent of her lilac perfume assailed his senses. He found it hard to concentrate around her. "What are you reading anyway?"

"I was skimming through his biography." She glanced back and flashed him her beautiful smile. "Thank you for suggesting that we come here. I'm sure a library is not top on your list of exciting places to spend your vacation."

"Nonsense, I love libraries, especially when you're in them." He gently massaged her shoulders.

She leaned slightly into his hands. "I could get used to this treatment."

He grinned, but held back his true intentions that he hoped to keep her in his life. "Back to the not so exciting world of libraries…this is the Linen Hall Library. It's home to a great collection of C.S. Lewis' books." He extended his hand. "I would've been remiss to neglect this spot on my tour."

"And it's the oldest library in Belfast."

He agreed. "Yes, that, too."

Sophie peeked around the bookcase.

Sebastian guessed why she looked. *I love this woman.* "She's still there…reading."

"Just checking. So where are we off to now?"

"I can't take you to the home where Lewis was born because it was demolished in 1952. Their family home after that, Little Lea, is now a private residence. The home of his paternal grandfather is also a private residence now."

She snapped her finger. "Three strikes and we're out."

"Not exactly. I wanted to go to Downpatrick in the afternoon to show you ladies the sites there, but I can take you to Belmont Tower now."

Sophie took the guidebook from her handbag. "But it says here that the C.S. Lewis Exhibition is under development and won't be open to the public until early summer."

"They have a café, right?"

"Oh, yes, the Belmont Tower Coffee Shop."

"Good, we'll go there and get some pastries. I

have to run out to do a quick errand, if you don't mind."

"Sure."

"Ready to go?"

"Yes."

He waved Anastasia to come over. "It's time to leave already, Papa? This is the best library. Can we come back again?"

Handing his daughter her coat, he led the ladies outside to the SUV. "I'm not sure. If you want the book you were reading, I'll buy a copy for you."

She shook her head. "No, that's okay."

On the short drive to the coffee shop, Sophie got Sebastian's attention. "Do you have any relatives in Ireland?"

"No, only in England, Wales and back home in the States." He nodded in her direction. "You have an aunt here, right?"

"Yes, Aunt Grace and my cousins Erin and Aidan."

"I'd love to meet them." They arrived at their destination and he parked the SUV. He rushed around to open the doors for both his girls and ushered them inside.

"Do you want me to order something for you?"

He peered at the menu board. "Can you get me a caramel apple cake and a cappuccino?"

"Yes."

"I'll be back in ten minutes." He started to rush away and then came back to hand Sophie some money.

She waved his offer away. "I got it Sebastian."

"No, really, I insist. Everything on this trip is my treat."

She chuckled. "Okay. I won't argue. I'll ask them to wait ten minutes before making your cappuccino."

"Thank you." He blew Anastasia a kiss and left the café.

* * *

Anastasia twirled around like a little wood sprite. "Where did Papa go, Miss Sophie?"

Her curiosity aroused, she wondered the same thing. "He had to run an errand. He'll be back in a few minutes."

"It's not lunch time yet. Why did we stop here?"

"Your father thought it would be a good idea for a snack."

"I'm not allowed to have snacks before lunch."

Exactly what I thought, but I'm not asking any questions. "Hmm, well, I guess we can make an exception this time, especially since your father brought us here, right?"

She spun in circles again. "Right!"

Sophie gently pulled the little twirler back into line with her. "Let's check out the menu. Oh, that sounds good."

"What sounds good?"

"I think I'm going to try the glazed Irish tea cake."

"Can I have one, too?"

"If you want to try one, sure."

They moved further up in line to the counter. "May I take your order?"

"I'll take two glazed Irish tea cakes, one caramel apple cake and one hot lemon tea." She touched Anastasia's shoulder to get her attention. "What would you like to drink?"

"I'd like lemonade."

Sophie asked the clerk. "Do you have lemonade?"

"Yes."

"Okay. I also need one cappuccino, but could you hold off on making that one for about ten minutes. I'm waiting for someone and I don't want it to get cold before he gets back."

"Of course, not a problem." Sophie paid for the order. She reached for Anastasia's hand before her little Miss started another twirling session. "Can you save us that table by the window?"

"Uh-huh." Then she hopped over to sit down.

Before Sophie moved out of the line to wait

for their order, she inquired about the exhibition. "Excuse me. Do you know if the C.S. Lewis Exhibition is open to the public?"

"Not until summer."

"I thought so."

The clerk smiled and nodded toward the tables. "You can sit down. We'll bring your order over when it's ready."

"Thank you."

She joined Anastasia at the table. "It's nice in here."

"Is Papa coming back soon?"

Sophie folded her hands and leaned them on the table. "I'm sure he will. He said he wouldn't be gone long."

"I wonder where he went."

Wondering the same thing, Sophie kept her true thoughts to herself. "I don't know."

"Maybe he forgot something at the hotel. I'm going to ask him when he gets back."

A young man timidly interrupted their conversation. "Excuse me, ma'am, here's your order." He set the tray on the table.

"Thank you."

"The cappuccino will be out in a few minutes."

"Should we wait for Papa or can we start? The cake looks yummy."

She winked. "I don't think he'll mind." Sophie

leaned close, as if sharing a big secret. "If we eat slowly maybe he'll be back before we finish and then he can eat with us."

"Can you pray for us Miss Sophie?"

"Of course." She closed her eyes. "Lord, thank you for this time we have together. Please bless this food and watch over us. Amen."

A few minutes later, Sebastian pulled back a chair and sat down. "I apologize for taking so long."

Anastasia innocently piped up. "Where did you go, Papa?"

He poked her nose. "What, no hello? Aren't you glad I'm back?"

"Yes. I was only wondering."

Sophie worked at keeping an expressionless face. She didn't want Sebastian getting any idea she also wondered where his errands had taken him.

"I was working on the rest of the travel arrangements for today."

The young man came back to the table. "Your cappuccino, Sir."

Anastasia focused her attention back to her cake and took a mouthful. "This is very good, Miss Sophie. Did you try some yet?"

"No." She tasted a bite of cake. "Mmm, yes, you're right. It's delicious."

"Papa, you have to try yours."

"Yours must have been good."

Anastasia licked some frosting from her lips.

"It was yummy."

Sebastian took a bite of the caramel apple cake and Sophie watched him close his eyes. "Ana, you really need to try this. It is tasty." He pushed his plate across the table and urged his daughter to eat.

"Sophie, you have to taste it too."

She held up her hands in protest. "That's okay, my cake filled me up."

"I can feed you a piece." She gave him the no-way look and nodded toward Anastasia, who seemed oblivious to his flirtations. "Okay, got it."

"You seem to be in a very good mood right now. You must really like that cake."

His grin spoke volumes yet told Sophie nothing at the same time. "I'm simply happy to be on holiday with my two special ladies, that's all." She stared at him, pondering why he appeared so excited. No use speculating—she decided to accept his answer and focus on enjoying the moment. Sebastian pushed the chair back and stood. "Are we ready? We have much more to see today."

* * *

Sophie groggily opened her eyes and realized she'd napped longer than she'd originally planned. After their afternoon excursions to Down County Museum and the Saint Patrick Centre in Downpatrick, Sebastian had taken Anastasia out to get ice cream—

giving Sophie a short reprieve to take a nap. Before dinner, he wanted to take them to one more tourist stop, the Down Cathedral. She hurried to freshen up and slipped into black slacks and a lavender open cowlneck sweater. Running a brush through her unruly curls, she pinched her pale cheeks and raced out the door. She gave a hesitant smile and waved when she saw Sebastian and Anastasia in the hotel lobby. "Sorry, I'm late."

"No problem." He kissed her on the cheek. "You look beautiful."

"Thank you. You don't look so bad yourself." Sophie followed Sebastian and Anastasia outside. After the valet brought the SUV to the front entrance, they climbed inside and Sebastian drove ten minutes into Downpatrick. "Thanks for letting me rest for a while. How was your ice cream?"

"It was de-li-cious." Anastasia piped up in a sing-song voice from the back seat.

Sophie glanced her way and smiled. "I'm glad you enjoyed it. We'll have to go back and get some more before our trip is over."

She nodded enthusiastically. "That's a great idea."

Sophie turned to Sebastian. "Did you know the Down Cathedral is considered to be one of the holiest sites for Christians in Ireland?"

He took his eyes off the road for a moment and pointed his finger at her. "Now were you napping or reading that guide book again?"

"Checking up on my tour guide. I want to make sure I'm getting the facts straight."

They neared English Street and the awe-inspiring cathedral came into view. "Wow, I've never seen a church like that before." Anastasia exclaimed and leaned forward as far as her seatbelt allowed. "When I'm older, I want to get married there, okay, Papa?"

Sophie caught Sebastian grinning and looking at his daughter from the rearview mirror. "Hmm, maybe you can pick a church a little closer to home."

"No, it has to be this one. It's so beautiful."

Sophie's awestruck meter soared when she rolled down her window and took a closer look at the structure. "It definitely is a sight to see."

"That's why I brought you here. I knew you'd appreciate its beauty."

She touched Sebastian's arm. "David would be so jealous if he knew all of this beautiful architecture we've been visiting."

"Oh, he knows. He's been to Ireland before and loves it—almost as much as his beloved England."

Sebastian parked the vehicle and they piled out in silence, each in a momentary individual universe—taking in the massive structure. Sophie noticed the protruding facade with two taller spires and a larger arched stained glass window. The left and right facing facades had one spire each and smaller arched stained glass windows. In her enraptured state, she barely heard Sebastian instructing Anastasia not to run around and to be respectful. Sophie followed Sebastian and Anastasia through the front archway and he pointed for his daughter to sit in one of the pews. Shaking herself out of her reverie, Sophie was shocked to see a completely obedient, quiet child walking to the front of the church to sit down. He came back toward Sophie and she wondered what he'd said to his daughter. "Is she all right?"

"She's fine." He spoke softly. "She wanted to go up front to talk to God."

"I hope she always keeps that childlike faith. It's awesome. She taught me so much in my own journey back to God."

"I've learned from her faith as well." He motioned toward one of the pews nearby, which still maintained a clear vantage point of Anastasia. "Let's sit for a few minutes."

Sophie scanned the sanctuary. "You know, this church looks strangely familiar and I don't understand why. I've never been here before. Have you come here?" She titled her head. "Maybe I've been to a similar church in the past."

Sebastian put his arm around her as they sat in the pew. "Or maybe you've seen photographs of this church."

She shrugged her shoulders. "That's possible. I could be thinking of all the photographs and information in the guidebook."

Sebastian squeezed her hand. "Could it be that you've seen photographs of this church from your parents' wedding album?"

Parents' wedding album? What was he talking about? Wouldn't she have remembered the name of this church if her parents had gotten married here? She searched her memories for any mention of the Down Cathedral. Nothing came to mind and she turned to face him as the reality of his words dawned on her. "Are you saying—" She dared not finish for fear of crying.

"Yes, my love, your parents got married in this church."

"But, how did you know?"

"I did some digging and I really wanted to make this trip to Ireland special for you."

In disbelief, she sat forward in the pew, soaking in the serene surroundings. "Wow. That's all I can say right now."

He shifted in his seat. "I hope you can say more because, I have something important to ask you." When she turned back, he knelt down on one knee.

Her mind raced and she barely took her next breath. Fear and happiness threatened to overtake her at the same time. She watched in amazement as

Sebastian began to speak. "Sophie, I love you." He reached for her hands and held them as he continued. "You are such a beautiful woman inside and out and I need you in my life. I can't imagine living my life without you in it, by my side. You are my special treasure and I am asking you to be my wife." Pulling back one of her hands, she wiped away the tears on her cheeks. "Will you marry me, Sophie?" He reached into his coat pocket, withdrew a small red velvet box, and opened it. She stared at the sparkling diamond ring inside.

Was this actually happening? Had the man of her dreams just proposed to her? Sophie exhaled and moved away slightly. Did the heroines in the romance novels feel woozy like this too? *Man, I think I'm going to faint.*

"Are you okay?"

With a clammy hand, she brushed her hair back. "A bit overwhelmed, but fine." He moved to sit next to her again and kissed her lightly on the lips. When he leaned back, she cupped his face with both hands. "With no reservations, you want me to be your wife?"

"I do. Is that so hard to believe?"

Her hands trailed down to his chest. "I feel like I'm in a fairy tale, but I'm afraid to dream of a life with you."

He covered her left hand with his and brought it to his lips. "The dream is real and with God at the center, we can make it possible."

As if a movie reel started playing, she saw flashes of her life from this last year—how God had his hand on her every step of the way. Throwing any lingering fears to the wind, she started smiling through her tears. "Yes, Sebastian, I'll marry you."

She heard him sigh as he placed the ring on her finger. They hugged and kissed, and tried to be respectful of the holiness of their surroundings. Anastasia walked back toward them. "Why are you crying, Miss Sophie?"

"These are happy tears."

Sebastian pulled his daughter up onto his lap. "Ana, we have something to tell you."

Like a satisfied cat lapping up milk, she grinned. "You're getting married?"

"How did you know?"

She clapped her hands. "I was wishing and praying you would."

Sebastian hugged Anastasia and then she stepped down to hug Sophie. "Does this mean I can call you mama?"

Mama—one word which caused a myriad of emotions to rumble through her heart. Sophie glanced over Anastasia's head, seeking Sebastian's eyes. She would follow his lead on this issue. Without hesitation he responded. "If it's okay with Miss Sophie, it is fine with me."

Those words nearly were her undoing. She

barely controlled the tears. "Yes, my little Miss, you can call me mama." The word *mama* sounded foreign on her tongue, yet strangely welcome and right.

"Papa, can we walk around outside?"

"Sure, Ana, let's go." She started to skip along the aisle, and then stopped herself, walking the rest of the way. Sophie's new fiancé turned in her direction. "I'm so glad she will have you in her life."

"I will love her as my own, but I'll never try to take Katherine's place."

"I know." She searched his eyes and knew that he understood her heart and intentions where it concerned his daughter. Sophie welcomed his hand and they followed Anastasia outside. He kissed her cheek and expressed more vibrancy then she'd ever seen from him. "I'm so excited. You've made me the happiest man alive." They hugged and he twirled her around. She never wanted this moment to end.

Chapter Twenty-Nine

Sophie woke up with a start and glanced at the clock. She'd forgotten to set the alarm last night. When she'd gone to bed, her mind wasn't exactly functioning clearly. All she could think about was a tall, dark and handsome man, soon to be her husband. Peering over at Anastasia's sleeping form, she smiled and remembered the young girl's excitement at the news of the engagement. "I'd better wake her up or we're never going to make it on time." *Sebastian is going to think I'm always late!* Wrapping her mint green terry cloth robe around her, she stepped over to Anastasia's bed and gently touched her shoulder. "Honey, it's time to get up. We have to meet your father for breakfast soon."

Anastasia rolled over and yawned. "I'm so tired. Do I have to get up?"

"I know you're tired. You had a late night."

She sat up in bed and stretched. "I wanted to celebrate with you and Papa. I'm so happy."

Sophie tousled the young girls' unruly blonde

curls. "I'm happy too but we really need to get ready now."

With a sigh, Anastasia grudgingly climbed out of bed. "What are we doing after breakfast?"

Sophie called out from the bathroom as she put toothpaste on her toothbrush. "I'm not sure. Your father didn't say, but I'm certain he has something planned for us."

"I know, he always does." Anastasia giggled and Sophie heard her rummaging through the closet for clothes. "What should I wear? We don't know where we're going today?"

Sophie thought for a second. Smart girl...she's got a point there. "Wear whatever you'd like and if you need to change, we can come back to the room after we eat."

"Okay."

Thirty minutes later after they both showered and dressed, Sophie led Anastasia downstairs to the dining area. Anastasia tugged on Sophie's hand. "Are we late?"

She checked her watch. "No. Amazingly, we're five minutes early."

"Wow, we did get ready fast."

"Yes, we did." Sophie spotted Sebastian speaking to the maître d' and she led Anastasia over to her father. He welcomed them with a big smile and kissed Sophie, then Anastasia.

"Are you ladies ready to eat?"

Anastasia patted her belly. "Yes, Papa, I am."

He took her hand. "Follow me."

Sophie noticed Sebastian walked by his favorite type of table near the windows and headed to one of the private rooms. She sensed something amiss immediately. Sophie stopped him. "Don't you usually enjoy eating near the windows?"

He shrugged his shoulders and acted above suspicion. "Thought I'd be unpredictable today, I know how much you love that."

Hmm, he's still up to something. With her analytical mind in high gear, she followed him. Sophie halted in the entryway at the sight before her eyes. It took a second for her mind to register the situation. Anastasia voiced the words that failed to leave Sophie's own mouth. "Papa, why are Grandpapa and Uncle David here?"

Am I dreaming? How could this be possible? Sophie finally found her voice. "Aunt Grace? Erin? Aidan? What are you doing here? How in the world—?"

Her head began spinning as dizziness assailed her. Thankfully, Sebastian rushed over to stand near her, offering his arm for support. *Let's not add fainting to the list of things I do on this vacation!* She gripped Sebastian's hand like a lifeline to solidity. Her Aunt Grace came forward and broke the silence. "Sebastian contacted us and shared the good news. He brought us all here to celebrate with you."

Sophie turned from her Aunt to Sebastian. "How did you contact them?" In her muddled state, reality dawned on her. "Now all of your mysterious trips into town are starting to make sense."

The room erupted into laughter and the shock overwhelming Sophie began to wear off. She accepted hugs, kisses and congratulations from her loved ones. Sebastian stayed close by. *He probably fears I might be the runaway bride or faint on the spot*. He raised his hand to get everyone's attention. "Thank you all for coming on such short notice. Now it's time to eat." He turned toward his father. "Can you pray for us?"

Sebastian pulled out the chair for Sophie and his daughter and everyone else joined them at the elaborately set brunch table. Alexander remained standing as he prayed. "Lord, thank you for Your blessing upon us and for bringing Sophie and Sebastian together. We pray for favor upon their new life as a couple and for Your blessing upon this food for which we are about to eat. Amen."

Sophie sat with Sebastian on her left and her Aunt Grace on the right. She reached for her Aunt's hand. "It's so good to see you."

The older woman smiled in response. "I'm overjoyed for you, dear." Tears filled her eyes. "I apologize for not being able to attend your parents' funeral."

"I understand."

Aidan grinned. "Congratulations, cousin. It feels like ages since we saw each other."

Erin interjected. "I think the last time we were in the States was ten years ago."

"I'm thrilled you're here now. I still can't believe it. I hope you'll be able to come to Pennsylvania for the wedding." She noticed her cousins' quick glances at each other. *Hmm, am I missing something? Everyone seems to be in on a big secret except for me.*

Sebastian pushed back his chair and stood up. A *ding, ding* sounded as he tapped a fork on his glass. When the conversation stopped, he gazed directly at Sophie. His dark brown eyes pierced her soul. The butterflies started fluttering in her stomach. What else could he want to say? She tried hard to quiet her mind to listen to her fiancé speak. "I hope you enjoyed this surprise, but I have another one." He paused as if allowing her time to process that new information. *He knows me well. Another surprise?* "I invited everyone here today, not only to congratulate us on our engagement, but to attend our wedding."

She blinked several times with no intelligent words immediately coming to her lips. "Today? Are you crazy?"

He laughed and sat back down, reaching for her hand. "Yes, I am crazy!" His hesitant smile touched her heart. *To think of all he's done to show how much he loves me.* The thought was more than enough to bring more tears to her eyes. "I made special plans for us to use the hall at Castle Coole for our reception. We'll get married at Down Cathedral."

"Where my parents got married?" *This man continues to amaze me. I think I am living in a fairy tale.* She closed her eyes and remained silent for a moment. When she opened them, she touched his cheek. "Am I dreaming or did you actually plan all this?"

"You're not dreaming, my love. I wanted this day to be special for you."

They hugged and shared a light kiss on the lips. Then she remembered they weren't alone. She felt the heat of embarrassment color her cheeks, but this PDA did not bother her as much as usual. *I'm about to become Mrs. Sebastian Shipley! How amazing is that? I never thought this day would come.*

David grinned. "And it's Valentine's Day, too. How sweet is that?" She glanced at her future brother-in-law and couldn't quite tell if he was being sarcastic or not. *Enough with the over-analysis already.*

Sophie smiled at David and turned to Sebastian. "Was that part of the plan, too?"

"Actually, that's the one thing I didn't plan, but we'll always have a special Valentine's Day from now on."

Alexander cleared his throat and interrupted the joyous conversation. "We really should eat now.

We have a big day ahead of us."

* * *

Back in her hotel suite, Sophie embraced her Aunt and cousin again. "I still can't believe this is happening. It seems like a dream."

Erin beamed and squeezed Sophie's shoulders in support. "It's a fairy tale that you deserve. No more tears. We need to get you ready."

Sophie watched Grace reverently trace the embroidered flower pattern on the edges of the white silk wedding gown. Seeing her Aunt lovingly inspect the dress brought a tinge of sadness to Sophie's heart—in that moment, she desperately missed her mother. Yet, having her Aunt and cousin with her, eased the pain. "I respect this young man you're marrying, Sophie. To think of all the planning and effort he put into this special surprise for you."

Erin clasped her hands together near her heart. "And choosing this exquisite gown, especially for you. He's a regular Mr. Knightley. Don't ever let him go."

"I don't plan on it." Her cousin's reference to Sophie's favorite male literary character brought back memories of the times they'd spent together as giggling school girls, dreaming of their respective wedding days. She hoped to someday be part of Erin's special day as well.

Anastasia ambled out of the dressing room with white tulle hanging off her curly blonde head and carrying her flower basket in her hands. "Miss Sophie. Oh, wait, now I can call you *Mama*, right? Or do I have to wait until after the wedding?"

With tears in her eyes—mingled with laughter in her heart over the adorable picture the young girl portrayed—Sophie knelt down in front of her "You can call me *mama* from now until forever. I am honored."

Anastasia smiled. Cupping her hand near Sophie's ear, she whispered. "Please call me Ana, okay…*mama*?"

She enveloped her new daughter in her arms. "Of course, Ana, but you will forever be my little Miss."

Anastasia loosened herself from Sophie's embrace and kissed her new mother's cheek. "Perfect! I like that nickname."

With a deep breath, Sophie stood up. "Ladies, let's do this. I need to look beautiful for my Prince Charming." The love in the room was evident as they laughed, chatted and readied the bride for her Valentine's Day wedding.

* * *

David straightened Sebastian's bow tie. "I hope Sophie can fix your ties as well as I can, because you'll need help in that area."

Sebastian chuckled. He loved his brother, no doubt about that fact. "Thank you again, for being my best man. I wasn't sure how you were going to react with the sudden engagement and wedding." He carefully watched the expressions flitting across David's face.

David stepped back, inspecting his handiwork. "Everyone can see how much you two love each other. It's plain as day, at least it was to me from the beginning." Sebastian got a kick out of his brother's sarcasm. "I'm happy for you."

"Thank you." Sebastian faced the floor length mirror to check his appearance.

Alexander strolled into Sebastian's suite with his arms open wide. "My two sons, what a glorious day this is."

"Thank you, Father, for your support. I appreciate it."

Alexander placed both hands on Sebastian's shoulders and peered in his eyes. "Sophie is perfect for you. A gift from God. You'll have an incredible life together."

David glanced up from his cell phone. "Are you almost ready? Aidan sent me a text. He has his vehicle outside waiting for the ladies. Where are the keys for the SUV? I'll drive."

Alexander held back the drapes and looked outside. "How far is the church?"

"Only about ten minutes from here. Castle Coole is about fifty minutes from the church." Sebastian adjusted his cuff links. "We could have gotten married at the castle, but I thought the church would be more special."

David sent a text message and slipped his phone into his pants pocket. "So, that's really the church her parents got married in?"

"Yes."

David shook his head. "Amazing. I have a good role model when it comes to love and romance."

Alexander joked. "Don't tell your girlfriend, or she'll expect as much from you."

David waved away his father's comment. "Oh, I'm already in trouble. I've spilled the beans about every romantic thing Sebastian's done. Besides, Susan and I are far from a wedding date. I'm not even sure she's the one."

Sebastian patted him on the back. "When the right one comes along, you'll know."

* * *

Sophie stood in the grand foyer of the church—poised on the outside, but shaking like a leaf on the inside. Ever since she'd met Sebastian and the idea of marriage came to her mind, she'd wondered how she'd react on her wedding day without her father to walk her down the aisle. Here in the moment, a sense of sadness threatened to overwhelm her, but she thought about Sebastian waiting on the other side of those sanctuary doors. She wanted to walk down the aisle with joy on her face and not mourning. Timidly, she glanced up to smile at Alexander standing next to her. "This is it."

"Are you nervous?" She heard the fatherly expression of tenderness in his voice.

She motioned with her hand. "Just a hint of butterflies."

"Nerves on your wedding day are natural."

"Were you nervous?"

"Definitely, but I knew marrying my sweetheart was God's will for my life. If we kept Him in the center of our lives, He would see us through anything that came our way."

Sophie nodded. "I believe that, too. Right now, though, I can barely think."

He gave her hand an encouraging squeeze. "Look straight ahead at God and Sebastian…who's waiting for you on the other side of those doors."

"Thank you for your support and for welcoming me into the family."

"Soon you'll truly be my daughter and will always have my support and love."

Tears misted in her eyes. "I'm honored to be your daughter." *Get it together…remember to smile for Sebastian.*

The music began playing. "That's our cue, my

dear."

Sophie inhaled deeply and accepted
Alexander's arm as ushers opened the arched wooden
doors. Taking the first step across the threshold to the
aisle made her heart skip a beat. No turning back
now, she jumped in with both feet. Her first glance
into the decorated sanctuary astounded her because
the room had taken on a fairy tale atmosphere. Pure
amazement overwhelmed her that Sebastian had
planned their wedding to happen in the same church
where her parents had spoken their vows. Holding
back tears, she realized all the effort Sebastian
underwent to plan this day without her knowledge. He
truly knew her heart and had become such an intrinsic
part of her life. She loved him beyond words.
Sebastian smiled at her and she reciprocated,
mouthing the words *I love you*. She imagined her
parents smiling down from Heaven, watching this
special day. Missing them immensely, she truly
sensed their presence as she made her way down the
rest of the aisle.   Alexander gave her away and
Sophie moved toward Sebastian. He gallantly offered
his arm and leaned over to kiss her cheek. "Hello,
beautiful."

Sophie listened to the Reverend's words. He
spoke about the union between a man and a woman—
and the need for God to exist in the center for a
marriage to flourish. She agreed wholeheartedly with
those words. Sophie had witnessed firsthand a true

model of a God-centered marriage, as she'd watched her parents live, love and teach her how to consistently trust God.

They finished repeating their vows and held hands as two vocalists sang *The Prayer*. Tears ran down Sophie's cheeks as she listened to the lyrics. She gazed into Sebastian's eyes. "That's my prayer. God will be our guide."

After the ring exchange, they faced the Reverend again and he invited them to partake of communion. Then they lighted the unity candle as a worship song played in the background. When the song ended, they came back around to stand in front of him. "I now pronounce you husband and wife. You may kiss the bride."

Sebastian smiled and Sophie's heart soared. He leaned close. "I'll keep this PG rated for now." His lips met hers and he kissed her tenderly, sealing their union.

She tried to keep a straight face, but welcomed his elated mood and turned to face their family as the Reverend spoke. "May I present to you for the first time as husband and wife, Mr. and Mrs. Sebastian Shipley." Cheers and applause erupted in the once serene sanctuary as the newlywed couple stepped off the platform to greet everyone. Sophie slowly digested the sound of those words, *Mr. and Mrs. Sebastian Shipley*.

Sophie glanced lovingly at her new husband.

"This really isn't a dream."

"No, it isn't. You are my wife, and I'll cherish you forever."

* * *

Sebastian surprised Sophie by grabbing her hand and leading her out into the grand hall. "Mrs. Shipley, take a walk with me, please."

"Certainly. Where are we going?"

"For a stroll near the lake."

"We can't be gone for too long. Our family is waiting for us." Saying the words *our family* still sounded foreign on her tongue, but she knew she'd get used to it rather quickly.

"Oh, we just got married. They'll understand." He smiled and coaxed her outside for a short excursion along the recently restored Lake Walk.

"The views are beautiful." From the vantage point near the Castle, Sophie could see across the lake to the distant hills. "How did you manage to get the reception here on short notice?" In her mind, especially after such feats of accomplishment, it seemed there wasn't anything her new husband couldn't conquer.

"Actually, I called in a favor from someone I know. Castle Coole isn't open to the public until April."

She shook her head and smiled. "I had a

feeling that was the case. I'm going to start calling you *My Mr. Knightley*, just like *Emma*. You truly are a romantic at heart."

He tipped an imaginary hat. "I do my best."

She tilted her head, shyly glancing up at him. "So, are there any more surprises I should know about?"

He feigned a pose of deep thought. "Hmm, no. Oh, wait. There is our honeymoon in Italy which I forgot to mention."

"We're going to Italy? Will you never cease to amaze me?"

"I hope not." He stopped walking and pulled her close to him, then gently cupped her face. "I want to continue surprising you every day for the rest of your life. I want to make you happy. I want to protect you, love you and cherish you. I love you so much, Sophie." He kissed her slowly at first then more passionately.

With a newfound confidence as Sebastian's wife—and the fact that they were alone outside— Sophie eagerly returned the passion of his embrace. She sighed audibly and stepped back. "I know what you mean. I want to make you happy and love you forever. Sometimes loving this much is risky. I'm so afraid to lose you. Yet, if I never took a leap of faith to love you, I would be alone…not ever finding this special treasure of love in my life. What about Ana? Will she stay with your father?"

He reached for her hand and brought it to his lips for a kiss. "Yes, my father and David will keep Ana with them while we're in Italy for three weeks. We'll fly home directly from there and have one more week by ourselves. My father will bring Ana back to the States and stay with us for a few weeks afterward."

"I like your plan." She grinned in gleeful satisfaction. "Four weeks alone with you…are you sure you won't get tired of me?"

He gathered her back into his embrace. "I will never, ever tire of you, my dear, Mrs. Shipley." She received proof of his declaration when he proceeded to lovingly kiss her again.

Epilogue

Sebastian leaned back on his arm and gazed at his new bride sleeping on the plaid blanket. The setting sun had provided a beautiful backdrop to help end their afternoon picnic. He'd planned to wake Sophie so she could experience it with him. However, mesmerized into inaction, he continued to watch her sleep. Even as she rested, his wife touched a chord deep in his heart.

She stirred and half sat up, resting on her elbows. "I caught you red-handed. Were you staring at me again?"

"No, no…I was enjoying the beautiful sunset."

"Without me, how could you?" She teased.

"I didn't want to wake you up. You made such a pretty picture, lying there with the sunlight glinting off your hair."

She sat up completely and kissed him soundly on the lips. "So you were staring at me again while I was sleeping."

He held up his hands. "Guilty as charged. What's my punishment?"

"A million kisses." Snuggling close to his chest, she shifted to admire the sunset with him. He enjoyed embracing her close to his heart.

"Oh, what a cruel punishment, I don't think I'll survive." He kissed the top of her auburn curls. Enfolding her in his arms, he reclined against the tree they sat under, and drew her back with him.

"I'm glad Ana will be home tomorrow. I've missed her."

"Me, too." Hearing Sophie's ease of use of his daughter's nickname brought a sense of comfort to Sebastian's heart. Ana had a mother figure in her life again and he couldn't have chosen a better mom than his gracious wife. "Didn't she sound so excited on the phone earlier?"

"Yes, she did." He loved the feel of Sophie's fingers tracing circles along his forearm as she chatted. "I can't believe she'll be attending school now. She's so happy for this new adventure. I don't know how I'll fill my time now that I won't be tutoring her."

"You can tutor me anytime."

"Seriously, Sebastian, have you thought about it?"

"I have and I'll support you in whatever you want to do." Silence met his words. "You know, you don't have to go back to work. You've talked about writing a children's book. Maybe you should think about that."

She tilted her head back to look at him. "Sounds like a great idea, but we should definitely pray for direction."

"I couldn't agree more."

They sat together until the sun nearly set completely. "We'd better ride back to the house or soon we won't be able to see anything." He mounted his horse and helped her onto the saddle to ride behind him. Sophie wrapped her arms around his waist. Her embrace settled on his body like a favorite blanket providing warmth on a cold winter's night. He urged the horse forward at an easy trot, but soon pushed the animal faster. He thanked God again for bringing this fascinating woman into his life— especially, during a time when both he and his daughter most needed a touch of grace. He planned to love unconditionally, forgive freely and be the best man he could be for his new wife.   When they arrived back at the stables, Sebastian helped Sophie dismount. He immediately noticed her damp cheeks. "Honey, are you okay?"

She sniffled and wiped away her tears. "Just remembering how far I've come since the day I first walked into your life. How God had His hand on me the entire time, patiently waiting for me to lean on Him."

Sebastian wrapped his arms around her

slender waist. "When you came into our lives, I had no idea that we would fall in love, but God knew. The work He begins, He finishes." He rested his forehead against hers as their noses touched. "He's not done with us yet." Closing his eyes, he slowly ran his hands up her back and to the nape of her neck. Tangling his fingers in her brown curls, he tilted her head and kissed her. As he shared this passionate embrace with his wife, God deposited a strong sense of peace in his spirit. He knew their lives together held many more seasons and he eagerly leapt forward by faith to experience all that God had planned for them.

Foot Notes:

1. Chp. 20; info on Bath: *The Official Roman Baths Museum Web Site in the City of Bath,* http://www.romanbaths.co.uk

2. All scripture taken from the New King James version.

About the Author

Joanne Troppello is an author of inspirational and romantic suspense novels. She and her husband are Network Marketing Coaches and owners of Mustard Seed Marketing Group, LLC. They have several active blogs and readers are encouraged to visit their Author's Corner Blog, a place for authors and readers to connect. They host various blog parties throughout the year and many guest authors stop by to meet with readers.

Mustard Seed Marketing Group, LLC

It Only Takes a Mustard Seed to Make a Dream Grow

www.mustardseedmarketinggroup.com

.